Exit Strategy

a novel by
Douglas Rushkoff

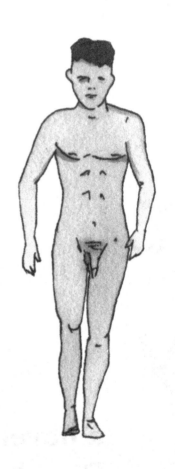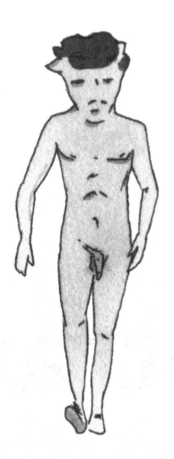

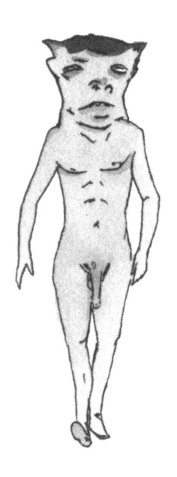
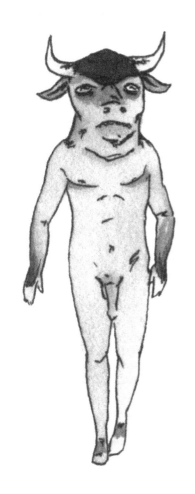

exit strategy
douglas rushkoff
soft skull press
new york, new york
2002

exit strategy
isbn: 978-1-887128-90-2
©2002 by Douglas Rushkoff

Drawings: Marcel Dzama
Book Design: David Janik
Editorial: Nick Mamatas, Abby Weintraub

Douglas Rushkoff will donate his
profits from the sale of this book to
the Electronic Frontier Foundation
and Free Software Foundation

Soft Skull Press, Inc
New York, NY

www.softskull.com
Printed in the United States of America

For my most devoted reader and mother, Sheila.

Acknowledgments

This wouldn't have been possible without the incisive and unrelenting guidance of my UK editor, Nicholas Blincoe. I'm also deeply indebted to David Bennahum, Mark Frauenfelder, and Matthew Bialer, whose honest feedback in times of crisis pushed me to say here what it is I really meant to.

Thanks to the Markle Foundation, Zoe Baird, and Julia Moffett, for creating a space and time for me to get this done.

I must salute Jay Mandel and Lisa Shotland at William Morris, who, on being told I wanted to give this book away online, still worked tirelessly on making that vision a reality.

Larry Smith, Scott Alexander, and the staff of Yahoo Internet Life remain this work's true unsung heroes. They conceived, created, and maintained an Internet home for the "open source" novel project—the heart and soul of this whole endeavor.

We all owe a debt of gratitude to Brooke Belisle, who tirelessly compiled this open source edition from its many sources, and then refined all of our writing to fit together into one book.

I am inspired by everyone at Soft Skull Press for their relentless dedication to publishing as it should be done. I am honored you consider this project vital enough for inclusion in your canon. Thanks also to Zach Schisgal at iPublish, for believing in the future of interactive media, even if his bosses didn't.

A heartfelt thanks is owed to Rabbi Seth Frisch, whose uniquely clear-headed and unencumbered analysis of Torah led me to find something at its core that I now believe to be an indispensable compass for our disorienting times. Also to Rabbis Irwin Kula, Brad Hirschfield, and Dr. Shari Cohen, great partners and co-conspirators in the effort re-infect the Jewish community with what are essentially their own ideas.

This book is also informed, enriched, and inspired by the members of the Media-Squatters mailing list, whose devotion to parsing the real from the illusory has been of immeasurable value to me—as well as quite humbling.

Thanks, most of all, to those of you who have already or are right now participating in the "Synapticom game" online. You are the reason I began this book, and the reason it is now alive.

And, of course, to you, the reader, whose indulgence and generosity keep us all writing.

I began writing Exit Strategy before the bull market of the late nineties had even really begun. I was concerned, even frightened, by how many of my friends were leaving their vocations to jump into the dot.com madness, and how faith in the eternal expansion of the market economy had become our nation's new religion. To express any doubt in the market was to be an enemy of the state.

So I wrote this little allegory of the Bible's Joseph, in which a modern-day dreamer builds pyramids in the service of his own, greed-driven Pharaoh. Just to make sure readers were able to distance themselves enough from the story to experience the satire (rather than just the critique of their values) I decided to engage in a bit of Talmudic-style commentary on my own work.

I'd reframe the whole book as a document that was written now, but only unearthed 200 years in the future. I knew I wanted to show that we all get past our obsession with money, but I didn't want to presume exactly what this new world might look like. Instead, I created the footnotes that readers of the 23rd Century would need in order to understand the people and institutions of today. Today's readers can then infer a lot about the fictional 23rd Century by looking at what future readers—and anthropologists—do and don't know.

I had such a good time creating these footnotes, and re-experiencing the present from the perspective of the future, that I decided to let the readers in on the game. Why should I be the only one getting to participate in this experiment? So I put the whole book online—it's still up at Yahoo Internet Life's site, http://www.yil.com—for readers to become writers and add their own commentary to the text, in the voices of their own 23rd Century annotators.

The core text of the novel remains the same, providing a bit of continuity and structure to the work, but each new commentary has the ability to recontextualize the entire story. The resulting body of collaborative work is a hypertext labyrinth of references and cross-references. Ultimately, the commentaries themselves become their own book—an open-source-inspired, community riff on our bizarre age.

One hundred of the collaboratively developed commentaries appear in this, the first open source edition of the book, and the first print publication of the book in the United States. (As you might imagine, most mainstream publishers—clueless about how the Internet works—were not too keen on publishing a book that already existed online, for free!) With any luck, we'll be coming out with other editions that include even more notes, or different sets of notes. Or, perhaps, only notes.

My own notes appear under the pseudonym of the Chief Annotator, Sabina Samuels. But, as you'll shortly see, the commentaries contributed by the community of several thousand who participated in this experiment surpass my own in humor and insight. And this, of course, is the whole premise of the experiment, and one of the great and still largely unrecognized strengths of the open source movement, to which I am in great debt.

To those who have contributed to the project, I thank you deeply. I have learned a tremendous amount from you all, and am a better author for having relinquished my authority over this book to you. This is not a profit-making venture. If, by chance, I do see any profits from this book at some point in the future, I'll share them in the form of donations to other open source projects.

—Douglas Rushkoff
New York, 2002

Exit Strategy

the open
source
edition

The 'DeltaWave' manuscript, popularly known as 'Exit Strategy,' has continued to stir controversy in academic, religious, and, of course, anthrotechnology circles. Although forensic evidence strongly indicates that the file was created over two hundred years ago in about 2008, experts have not ruled out the possibility that it was generated much more recently by historical pranksters or even revisionist activists.

Whatever its origin, this text presents us with a unique outlook on the rise of marketphilia in the 21st Century, as well as the proliferation of reactive architecture in the early Internet Era. It also serves as a rare case study in the Great Capitalist Experiment.

This new, annotated edition includes explanatory footnotes and primary source data culled from the archival resources of over thirty universities and research institutes. Each commentary has been appended with the Network ID of its author.

It is hoped that we have made the two-century-old text more accessible to the modern casual reader, while providing the scholarly community with references for additional study. Unfortunately, a dearth of accurate information about the period—and the rise of radical revisionist thinking about the capitalist experiment—has led to conflicting accounts and interpretations of the events depicted herein. Please understand that our inclusion of these alternative viewpoints does not imply an endorsement of their credibility.

—Sabina Samuels
Editorial Director and Chief Annotator
Chair, Institute for Post-Capitalist Studies

1. Ante Up

1. Statements such as these must be understood from within the mindset of the narrator's own contemporaries. Two centuries ago, market fascism was just reaching its zenith. All values were still measured in dollars, and the 'bottom line' for this society literally meant the bottom line of a balance sheet. Money, as the narrator suggests in his opening quip, was a hard currency to resist for victims of this era's pan-cultural psychosis, especially when the most-watched medium of that period—more than radio, television, or even the internet—was capital.

This may seem odd to modern readers, given the ease with which funds could be obtained at the turn of the century. Indeed, detailed analysis of the financial metrics of the era leads most historians to conclude that money was virtually everywhere. Although the stock market had suffered extended downturns—most notably the "correction" of

I wasn't in it for the money. Honest. I was in it for the game.[1]

Maybe it was the setting—that fresh Hamptons[2] air. Or the Merlot. But when Alec's father offered me a position as a technology researcher at M&L[3], somehow my job writing the back-stories for video games no longer felt like a high leverage point from which to alter the very the current of American culture. No, it seemed like the sidelines. Mr. Morehouse was giving me the chance to play for real, in the big leagues. A game with genuine stakes: money[4]. And I knew as long as I remembered it was just a game, I'd be okay. Hell[5], it was 2008. We'd made it through the Great Correction. Now, everybody knew what was really going on.

I[6] tried to tell myself this a month later as my limo made its way over the

notes continue on page 5

2001—such wild fluctuations merely served to reinforce what could only be called a societal obsession with market speculation.

Bear markets were recontextualized by major media outlets as concerted efforts in price manipulation by institutional investors—a time-tested tactic to "shake out" nervous day-traders and over-margined retail investors before pumping up the very same sectors all over again. Everyone, at least everyone who mattered to the elite-sponsored media, was getting involved in the stock market. And even those who weren't wealthy themselves invested what they had into the system with every unit of currency they could borrow. Yet the more money people invested, the more desperately they sought what were called 'vehicles' through which they could invest still more. Cash was cheap; bankable ideas were harder to come by. People and institutions with money competed to prove they were 'qualified' to invest it.   —Sabina Samuels

1b. In the 1900's and 2000's the collective soul of humanity became obsessed with evaluating life on a cost/benefit analysis system. All decisions were made with this guiding principle in mind from the day a child commenced to reason or from the day it grasped its first offering of pocket money, whichever was the sooner.   —FUTURPHILE

2. A shore of Long Island's 'south fork' which was fully submerged by 2240. The district, by group consensus, was considered more valuable than any other. Its beaches were no cleaner or more convenient than the Island's many other shores. Careful price manipulation and media representation are thought to

have accounted for the disproportionate property valuations, compounded by the preponderance of famous film, publishing, and cosmetics industry personalities who purchased estates there in order to publicize their own success. The area was also associated with a tradition of literature about toxic wealth and self-destructive financial ambition—a fact that detractors use as evidence to question this manuscript's authenticity as non-fiction.   —Sabina Samuels

3. At this time, the sum knowledge (such as it was) of our race was still stored in so haphazard and clumsy a fashion that research was a notable skill, and hence a career in itself. This situation continued until 2046, when the Greek shipping magnate and philanthropist, Jeff Minos, founded the Daedalus Project, which now employs over 70,000 people. Popular legend suggests that Minos began this first attempt at Universal Information Management after spending several months in a fruitless attempt to discover the difference in meanings between the words 'labyrinth' and 'maze'. The truth was eventually revealed to him in the form of a factoid printed on the back of a cereal box.   —ROB_R

4. A system of exchange where notes (rectangular pieces of paper) and coins (discs of metal) were used to acquire items.   —DUSTYONE11

5. Used here as a linguistic pausing device. The speaker, unclear on what to say next, fills the silent space with a slang word. Other such words include "Uh" and "Fuckin'."

The literal meaning was known for many centuries as the destination of condemned souls after their mortal death.

The word was reappropriated in 2057 when an entertainment program titled Hell broadcasted the extreme torture of convicted criminals from national prisons. The prisoners were given meta-narcotics that enhanced their natural regeneration ability and allowed them to live through deep lacerations, electrical shocks and severe beatings. Capital punishment was modified as this program gained popularity, so that inmates facing a death sentence were instead doused with napalm and burned alive. As a result of their daily injections, these prisoners never died from the burns, as every day their wounds healed and their flesh burned anew.

As human culture resisted theological doctrine and became largely atheist, the definition of Hell changed again. When the program went out of distribution in 2212, the word had become synonymous with any form of reality-based entertainment.   —CASE_MAKER

6. It is important to realize that the meaning of "I" has evolved over time; it is difficult to remember constantly that the "I" of this text refers to a singlet, rather than a group-personality. Without anything other than the most primitive forms of communication, an "individual" was left almost completely alone to develop meaning from experience.

This led, of course, to delusional, inconsistent and rapidly changing reality models, over-concern with the physical experience of a single organic form, and near total disregard for the physical and relational environment. These characteristics are now recognized as symptoms of Singlet Disorder. This was not aberrant for the period, but was the norm. Imagine—a world of such impoverished creatures!   —GMCNISH

7. The Triborough Bridge opened to traffic on July 11, 1936 as the first bridge in New York City to be designed and built exclusively for automotive traffic. Composed of three spans, it got its name from its interconnection with the boroughs of Queens, Manhattan and the Bronx. It was destroyed in the Palestinian Liberation Terror attack of 2004, which poisoned the East River for several years. It is believed that Palestinian Mullah Yasser Arafat ordered the attack shortly before his own assassination in late 2004.
—JACOBYACOV

8. The use of animal parts for food, clothing and utility objects was widespread in the period.   —RAYGIRVAN

9. A phrase in archaic English meaning "to risk too much." The phrase is derived from the twentieth-century criminal practice of fabricating one's own paper money (see note 4) with a machine called a "press." This was highly illegal, as the making of one's own money undermined the authority of the capitalist governing body. Also, as the midpoint of the twentieth century was reached, the term "luck" became synonymous with "money," because of the common perception that only the wealthy (those with more money than average) seemed to experience any good fortune, or "luck." So, to "press one's luck" was to engage in risky activity in the pursuit of bettering one's station in life.   —KINGCATFISH

10. It is not clear from the context whether the author is referring to the purchase of (A) an early portable self-contained computer, or (B) the experience of a full-contact seductive dance provided by a "stripper" or sex worker. Both were favorite status symbols of the

notes continue on page 7

Triborough Bridge[7] into Manhattan. There were fresh newspapers—a New York Times and a Wall Street Journal—neatly tucked into the chair backs, and a little gooseneck lamp[8] with which to read them. A cellular videophone was mounted in the center armrest, its green flashing light indicating readiness. No credit card slot. Just credit, courtesy of M&L. But I figured I was still too new to press my luck[9]. I'd just expensed a laptop[10] and the latest wrist communicator, and didn't yet know how these things actually got paid for.

The Knicks[11] game was on the radio. A rookie center from Bosnia[12] scored an aggressive slam-dunk[13], and I figured it was a good moment to break the ice with my driver. I couldn't get used to having anyone play the servant to my master.

'They finally have a center who can take it to the basket,' I said, hoping that a few exchanges about what the Times in the seat pocket was calling 'the new international flavor of basketball' might help me bond with my driver, man to man rather than class to class.

'Yes, sir,' the driver politely agreed in an accent I assumed was Jamaican[14].

'Like Ewing in his prime.' No response. 'You from the islands?' I asked, feeling my own speech involuntarily sliding into a more Third World[15], almost Caribbean lilt.

'No sir,' he replied. 'I am from Zambia.'

'Oh, really? What'd you do there?'

'I worked for the government.'

'As what?'

'I was a computer scientist, actually.'

'Oh.' I tried to hide my surprise—as if driving and physics were equivalent professions. 'Do you plan to pursue computer science here, as well?'

time, prized gifts sought by the morally weak executive class.

—JEREMYISAAC

11. Short for Knickerbockers, the New York Knicks in the 20th century was a basketball organization that played in the NBA (National Basketball Association). In the latter 21st century, the New York Knicks became a subsidiary of GMHS (Global Military Hardware & Software). With the banning of all sports, including basketball, in the GeoSummit Pact of 2087, the New York Knicks ceased to be a basketball organization, and eventually became Knicks All Defense System, a missile defense system fused with artificial intelligence. Their motto, "All-Court Defense," resonated from the traditions of basketball. By 2111, the Knicks All Defense System was discarded when a missile from an unknown sea ship fired from the Indian Ocean penetrated the interior defenses of the U.S.A, and destroyed a farm outside Virginia. It seemed that that the missile defense system was as uncoordinated as the defense of the Knicks basketball team.

—FILMMUSO

12. Now the Croatian Region.
—Sabina Samuels

12b. Now one of the most frequented places in the United Europe, due to the fact that there are people there who claim to have seen Tesla, who was born in the region in 1874. The number of people to whom Tesla allegedly appeared has been increasing over the 23rd century; he has been celebrated as a messiah, although known for saying things like 'soul is only a bodily function.' The place already hosted another pilgrimage, the one to the Virgin Mary's shrine, since

there were people who claimed to have seen her there. Perhaps the potential of the natives to attract paranormal contact was the reason for the first official UFO landing precisely in this area.—JELENA13

13. It seems that in the aggressive and individualistic climate of the era, the "slam-dunk" was the most prized of all scoring techniques in the game of Basketball. Strangely, players were more revered for their ability to violently throw down a ball into a hoop from close range than they were for their ability to do so from far away. Different sources disagree on whether or not there was a ritualistic dance that immediately followed a "slam-dunk."

—SINGINGDEER

14. A person from the island of Jamaica. Jamaica was a member state of the Monrovian Policy Federation under the protection of the United States. The member states pledged their vast raw material resources in exchange for small amounts of money. How this was beneficial for the Federation members is not known. Citizens of Jamaica traveled north to the United States to compete in sports.

—ZAC6HAND

15. A term used to categorize the majority of the human species who, at the time, still suffered in abject poverty.
—Sabina Samuels

15b. A number of designated "banana" countries where there was permanent political instability due to permanent economic crisis. This was in fact a clever maneuver by the designated "developed countries" to obtain cheap labor and cheap natural material resources. This

system is seen in our century as slavery and has been discontinued.   —SILELF

16. This item of social collateral was well on its way to becoming extinct at this point. It consisted of a small piece of heavy paper mechanically imprinted with a series of identification codes for communicating with the presenter.

As personal and professional space began to collide, the number of unique communication channels that business professionals had at their disposal began to rise exponentially although the cards remained a fixed size.

It is useful to note that the very act of physical exchange was of primary importance (hence "social" collateral despite the business usage). Often, a fashion accessory to contain and dispense these cards would be utilized. An individual's status could be assessed by the ease, dexterity, grace, and speed with which they could retrieve the container, remove a card, and proffer it.

The irony was that after the initial exchange, the recipient of a card would often not maintain possession of it, for the management of that amount of information wasn't conducive to their already paper-intensive professional lives.
—PORTIGAL

17. A Doctor of Philosophy. A highly educated person. Someone who had studied long and hard in his or her chosen field of interest. Often they were addressed as Doctor although they had no medical training.   —DUSTYONE11

18. Obsolete notions of competition between former feudal empires prohibited employment across nation-state boundaries without special written approval from federal authorities. The H1-G visa was created to allow for the employment of what amounted to slave labor in data and programming mills.
—Sabina Samuels

'I have been here twelve years,' he said, looking back at me through the rear-view mirror.

'But you must miss it, don't you?'

'I miss the trees. Only the trees. I make more money here driving this limousine, and my children live in a free country.'

'But isn't Zambia a free country?'

'Not free like America,' he smiled knowingly. 'I'm free to earn a living here, any way I choose.'

'I work in the industry, myself,' I offered. 'Do you have a business card[16]? I know lots of firms looking for people.'

'I was a university professor. My credentials, my PhDs[17] are not accepted here.'

PhDs? Did this guy have more than one? And here I was making a quarter million in salary alone with a single undergraduate degree. I could help this guy. M&L had a whole floor of programmers from Bangalore on H1-G[18] visas, making 60 bucks an hour. It had to be more than he pulled in driving a black car.

'Really, maybe I can help...' But we were already at my destination, a converted warehouse on Twelfth Avenue. The driver handed me a small clipboard with a receipt to sign. I slid one of my new Morehouse & Linney cards under the metal clamp before returning it.

'Thank you, sir,' the man said gently.

'I mean it,' I said, closing the door. 'Feel free to call.'

Mine was just one of many black cars pulled up in front of the derelict building. It was the only vehicle with a big number in the rear windshield, though—evidence of an inferior, generic car service. The rest appeared to be private limos. Didn't anyone take taxis, anymore? I changed the trajectory of my approach in an effort to distance myself from the low-status ride.

I got to the velvet rope[19]—the only sign of a working economy on the block—where two young women in tight black sheath dresses were checking names against a list. A trio of over-fifty businessmen argued their case for entry to one of the young judges, who no doubt was working off years of parental issues each time she looked up blankly from her digital clipboard and said, 'I'm sorry, but I don't see your name on the list. Who is it you say invited you, again?'

I kept one hand in my trousers pocket, fingering a business card, but as I approached the checkpoint one of the girls gracefully unclasped the velvet rope for me to pass. I didn't recognize her, and I know she didn't recognize me. I was simply of the right age, the right style, and the right demeanor to gain admission, no questions asked. I guess I could have been anyone, which is why I had to be treated as if I were someone[20].

I considered spending my unearned cache on behalf of the elderly businessmen, but it was about to drizzle and I didn't want to break the flow of my unexpectedly smooth entrance. Besides, they were just suits[21]. Fuck 'em.

Inside was a zoo. A giant concrete room booming with nineties electronica that rattled the huge mylar sheets hanging from the rafters above. Men in European suits that should have had expiration dates stamped in the collars and women in dresses that either hid or showed off their figures[22] all held plastic cups and shouted at one another. Too much noise and too many people to distinguish anything or anyone of value. And it was hot. I made a mental list of my priorities: 1- Check coat[23]. 2—Get drink. 3—Find Alec, my best friend in New York and a walking Rolodex[24] of Silicon Alley.

I saw a long line, composed mostly of women holding coats over their arms, snaking down a staircase to the building's basement. Just as I took my place at its end, someone grabbed me by the elbow.

'Forget that. Come with me.' Rescue! It was Alec. His straight blond hair

19. Apparently, ropes of this kind conveyed the status of such an establishment. It is thought they may have been given out as awards for excellence by some kind of central industry body, and hung around the entrance to a club to attract potential customers. —DRZARDOZ

20. This reference to 'being someone' on its surface would confuse modern readers. As the artificial atmospherics of the period (referred to as media by people of that era) were confined to the purposes of market fascist priorities, only certain types of appearance and personality were allowed to participate in the scarce 'media space' of the early 'information age.' This scarcity of space in the artificial atmospherics created rivalries and social hunger for 'fame' by appearing in that space. Thus, to 'be somebody,' one must appear similar in appearance, style and personality to those that appear in the artificial atmospheric marketplace. —MIAHKING

21. Derogatory name given to corporate-minded drones, usually middle-aged white men. Name comes from their archaic type of clothing, which consisted of a matching set of jacket and pants, dress shirt, and swath of decorative fabric tied around their neck. —MANDOMANIA76

22..At the time corporeal concerns—

9

notes continue on page 10

especially one's weight, and the size and form of various surface organs—were widely prevalent, but involved at most physical exertion, changes in diet, surgery, and drugs. The advent of later technologies such as genetic engineering and portable holographic imaging afforded much better results.

At this more primitive time in history the altering of one's body was socially motivated. Images presented by spontaneous broadcast dissemination and the then-infantile Net (part of the reason why this particular neurosis was symptomatic of wealthier nations) was spreading the belief that acceptance and completeness depended upon physical beauty. Many otherwise normal people subjected themselves to bodily modification and worry in order to fit in.

It is interesting to note that luxuries that could, when abused, damage one's physical state were promoted alongside images and messages that promoted a good outer appearance. It is this dissonance, most believe, that led to the infamous "Frito-Lay" riots of 2018.
—RSDIO

23. This phrase has two possible explanations, both of which relate to the fashion for "dress codes" at places of entertainment. (A "dress code" refers to the obsolete practice of judging people by the clothes they happened to be wearing.)

We can assume from promotional literature of the same era that "jeans and trainers" deemed a person unfit to partake in prolonged human interaction and that "soiled clothes" were probably the mark of a criminal or emotionally disturbed individual. Bearing this in mind, it is easy to see why our protagonist feels the need to "check his coat." It may have been that he needed to inspect it for stains or marks. Alternatively he may have needed to consult a list of "house

rules" to confirm that his coat matches the requirements set by the management.

The alternative explanation is that the establishment required customers to wear "checked" coats (a pattern formed by a repeated square motif). To avoid embarrassment, the proprietors may have offered a "checking service" much like restaurants of the day provided 'jackets and ties' to patrons. —NITRICBOY

24. Obscure. A paper-based directory on a wheel. Here, it most likely refers to Alec's knowledge of names and the businesses with which they are to be associated. The ability to recall names and numbers had diminished precipitously in 2004, a side-effect of dependence on electronic devices. —Sabina Samuels

was center-parted and slicked back so tight that I almost didn't recognize him. Not that I had the chance. My slender young escort in the herringbone suit[25] whisked me around the disgruntled line and all the way down the stairs with nary a 'pardon me,' past the coat counter to an open door around the back. In one fluid motion, he helped me off with my coat, handed it to the goateed attendant, and slipped a claim check into my breast pocket.

'Never wait in those lines, Jamie,' Alec advised as he took me back up the stairs. 'They're not meant for you.'

'Who's here?' I asked as we penetrated the pandemonium once again.

'Who's not?' Alec grinned. 'What are you having?'

The crowd pressed against the bar was an even denser mass of unsatisfied humanity than the one on the stairs. They were all desperately trying to hail one of two bartenders, all the while attempting to hide this desperation from one another.

'It's okay, Alec. I'm not really thirsty.'

'What are you having?' Alec insisted.

'Just a beer[26] is fine. Any beer.'

Alec handed a fifty-dollar bill to a lanky young model with a silver tray of sushi. 'Two gin and tonics, please.'

She glanced to the bar and rolled her eyes. I reached out to take back the bill and let her off the hook, but Alec intervened.

'Thanks, gorgeous, really,' he told her, sending her off into the fray. 'She can go behind the bar and make them herself. It's what she's paid for, Jamie. Chill[27].'

'I just—'

'I'll give her a big tip, okay?' My new partner put his hands on my shoulders. 'This is an important party. Try to have fun.'

In my head I was busy reconciling 'important' with 'fun' while Alec

28. The last phase of basic education in the 21st century was undertaken at institutions at which young adults paid for instruction from experts in fields relating to their interests. Students selected "universities" based on their perceived name value for subsequent employment and for social standing. "Princeton" in this case signifies an institution noted for retaining excellent experts, though the basic four-year course of instruction undertaken by the protagonist is unlikely to have included much actual interaction with such persons. Instead, his education was dispensed by older students paying for closer interaction with those experts, the theory being that the older students learned through such information transference and that younger students would be content with proximity and the subsequent appreciation of that proximity by the community. This system, known (ironically?) as "higher education," withstood the advent of Internet-based learning well into the 21st century. However, rising costs and increased general awareness of the essentially commodified nature of such information-acquisition caused serious devaluation of name value for institutions such as Princeton, and hastened the demise of the "university" system in the closing decades of the century.
—MISS_AG

29. The SAT, or Scholastic Aptitude Test, was a college entrance exam originally employed to combat the extreme wealth advantage of America's upper classes in securing places for their children at elite universities. By the late 1990's, however, wealthy parents had more than compensated for this admission gateway by investing in expensive preparatory courses and private tutors.   —Sabina Samuels

30. Even those accommodations had seen much better days. In the 1800's, every Princeton student was entitled to his own three-room suite—a bedroom, living

notes continue on page 13

dragged my body towards an arrangement of sofas.

'Wait. How will she find us?' I asked.

Alec threw me an exasperated sigh that said 'get a grip,' and instinctively surveyed the terrain for a prestigious spot from which to hold court.

Unlike me, Alec knew how to work a party—that much was certain. My entire Princeton[28] experience could well be summarized as having two main phases: Before Alec, and After Alec. Entering college as a scholarship student in the computer program, I socialized mostly with fellow hackers. My undeserved infamy as the writer of the DeltaWave Virus made me something of a legend amongst the other nerds, who were mostly public school graduates with outstanding SAT[29] scores. But by my sophomore year, I realized that I was merely in the upper echelon of what amounted to an underclass at Princeton. In an almost unconscious but well-practiced form of self-segregation, we relegated ourselves, along with most of the college's African-American students, to a small cluster of modern but low-prestige dormitories on the far south side of the campus. Princeton's ghetto.

The institution's famous fake-gothic structures on the campus's north end were inhabited by an entirely different social set. The sons and daughters of successful alumni, southern gentlemen, New York investment brokers, and America's surviving idle rich somehow found one another before freshman week, and scored places in four-person suites overlooking the slate courtyards and stone archways that were photographed each semester for the cover of the course catalogue.[30] They may have gone to competing prep schools but they were all in the same club now, and accepted one another as brothers.

Determined to rise above my station, I canceled my eating plan at the school's kosher[31] facility. Utterly dependent on a functioning meritocracy for my entrée to collegiate high society, I tried out for lightweight crew and earned a place in the second boat. We rowed together as a single unit, but that's where any pretense of solidarity ended. Win or lose, after each match, the inner circle of Choate, Andover, and Exeter alums would hop into their cars and drive off to a conveniently undisclosed location, shouting rebel yells through the sunroof.

Still, I held on to the notion that if I could become an indispensable member of the first boat, I might be able to earn my way into their good graces. I went to the boathouse three nights a week and worked out on the rowing machine[32] until the calluses on my palms bled through. While I eventually got a better seat, I never did place out of the second boat. But my efforts put me in the right place at the right time.

Late one night as I labored against the machine's counterweights, about a half a dozen preppies were throwing a private kegger[33] by the dock. They jabbered on about the various girls they hoped to bed, as well as which ones had herpes and which ones had rich daddies. They got drunker and rowdier, until one of them had the bright idea of dragging the beer keg into one of the shells and rowing out to the center of Lake Carnegie.

When the boat finally capsized, the boys were so disoriented that they barely made it back to shore. The Neanderthals just laughed as they pulled their wet bodies onto the dock, and I wondered why I ever aspired to be accepted by such a moronic tribe.

Then I saw something bobbing up and down in the darkness of the lake that wasn't an oar, the shell, or the keg. It was a person.

I shouted and pointed. But the soaked and groggy boys only squinted feebly towards the lake, unable or unwilling to consider that there might be a tragedy in progress. So I yanked off my sweatshirt and dove off the end of the pier. Out in the darkness I found a small, panicking blond boy. It was Alec, the sophomore coxswain of the first boat—not a rower at all, but the

room, and smaller chamber for the valet. By the late 20th Century, these quarters each held three or four of their descendants, who commemorated their gallant lineages with confederate flags, prep school sports trophies, or, in the case of young women, historical décor from their parents' homes, local antique shops, and mail-order catalogues.
—Sabina Samuels

31. A reference to Jewish dietary laws, already several thousand years old at the point that this manuscript was written. These laws underwent a startling change in the 21st century as Judaism became increasingly concerned with the contemporary world and proponents of an eco-kashrut made their voices heard. Instead of focusing on Biblical proscriptions against certain sea and land creatures, Jews shifted their focus to eating in ways that sustained the health of the planet.
—212SRA

32. A term that describes a stationary device used for personal fitness by people in the late twentieth century. The equipment's purpose was to replicate the act, as well as the physical results, of rowing a boat. The act of rowing made its move from the water to domestic status during the early 1980's. This was caused by the advent of more precise information linking personal fitness with longevity and quality of life. All this coupled with the increase in average hours worked per week by individuals made home fitness the only practical fitness. Other popular domestic fitness machines included the "ab-roller," "stairmaster," and "treadmill," all created to imitate physical acts that could not reasonably be completed in their natural capacity due to lack of time or access.   —BOURNETOO

33. A social gathering organized around a large metal beer dispenser.
—Sabina Samuels

one who sat in front with a megaphone and kept the pace. He was drowning.

As I approached, Alec panicked, grabbing me by the head and pushing me under the surface. I never believed the instructor in my summer camp's water safety class when he said this would happen. But now that it was, I used the technique he taught me: submerge the drowning victim's head whenever he fights you. A crude behavioral modification through instantaneous feedback that, under the circumstances, worked surprisingly well. Once Alec was sufficiently subdued, I locked an elbow around his chin and towed him into shore.

By the time he was back on the dock with his friends, Alec was acting as if the whole thing were a joke—that he had lured me out into the water as a prank. I allowed Alec the face-saving ruse. I was done with crew, anyway. But both of us knew what had really happened, and Alec Morehouse wasn't going to let the guy who saved his life, and, more importantly, his reputation, go unrewarded.

He began inviting me to parties and campus functions I previously never even knew took place. There were banquets for visiting lecturers, cocktail receptions at the Dean's home for big donors, and alumni events at the Princeton Club in Manhattan. Alec had a gentle grace about him in these situations that made him stand apart from the posers and climbers. He'd listen with interest to businessmen as they boasted about their latest investments, and give them such heartfelt approval that they seemed to feed off his every nod. It wasn't just that his dad was so important—though that might be part of what made Alec so relaxed—it was that Alec genuinely enjoyed other people's successes. He got off on making people feel good about whatever it was they were doing. He cheered them on.

Me, well, I got off on everyone else's ignorance—especially about technology. I just loved finding out how all these important men knew so very little about their own industries. And I was still young enough to have nothing to lose by spouting off. On being introduced to the CEO of a retail[34] office supply chain who had lost millions in his migration online, I sketched out a web-phone architecture on a paper napkin that would take four steps out of his company's archaic electronic ordering process. At a fundraiser for a political candidate, I threw the would-be senator a sound bite about how 'new media literacy means teaching kids computers, not software,' which became a constant refrain in his education platform.

Alec gave me access to a new world, and I gave Alec some intellectual credibility there, precocious as I was. We trained one another in the process, and became best friends and roommates—up-campus, of course. I didn't even have to apply for membership at the 300-year-old Eaves House. When the time for 'bickering' arrived—I had been dreading the grueling audition process for months—Alec got me waved in.

I knew that Alec's dad was an investment banker, but hadn't put the whole picture together until I was invited that first time to the family's compound in the Hamptons for spring break. These were the Morehouses of Morehouse & Linney—one of the top twenty financial firms in the country. Alec had told his parents about the boating accident, and even embellished it a bit so that the Cohens of Whitestone's absence from the social register would never be an issue. Not that the Morehouses were prejudiced, but a week is a long time at the beach, and balancing an entire guest list is a delicate art. I charmed them in spite of myself, and within a few days they were almost proud that they owed the life of their sole heir to a rabbi's son from Queens like me.

It was not the only reason Alec's dad, Tobias, asked me to join the firm—but it was the one still foremost in my mind as I tried to determine just what role I was supposed to play at the Silicon Alley Reader's monthly soiree. I was

34. Distinctions were made between merchants who sold to 'consumers' and those who sold to other merchants. Retail businesses purchased their goods from wholesale distributors, then sold them to their own customers at a mark-up. This was the basis of consumer capitalism, and was not considered unethical.
—Sabina Samuels

35. Predictably, those who maintain that this text is a work of fiction have seized upon this line as proof. Those who see the work as nonfiction dismiss the suggestion as ludicrous—pointing out that similar statements, i.e. "I bake pies" or "I design supertrains," do not at all imply that the sayer is a pie or supertrain. —YLIFEJOSH

36. An early, inefficient hypertext protocol on which a passive form of networking called "browsing" was based.
—Sabina Samuels

37. Banal and overused expressions that attempted to explain a segment of the sales, marketing or technology uses of the day. Often these phrases came to represent categories in which people invested heavily and often created massive amounts of wealth.   —JACKPOT321

38. Many debates continue upon the meaning of this passage. Period scholars are largely in agreement upon the meaning of the words when examined individually. "Counterfeit" meant an imitation or duplication without authorization of a standards organization while a "chandelier" was most likely was a period device used to provide a source of light energy. Since all indoor light of the time period was generated by a means other than the storage and regeneration of natural sunlight, the debate centers on why anyone would produce an imitation of an artificial light source. Some scholars argue that this portion of the text was produced in error and is the result of sloppy proof reading. Others contend that one or both of the currently accepted definitions for these archaic terms are incorrect. A minority of scholars are gaining acceptance for a theory that the chandelier held a position of much greater importance in the lives of the people the era, possibly used in some form of worship.
—JEFFRINE1

notes continue on page 17

only a game designer, after all. And not really a game designer, but a conceptualizer. I dreamed up fictions[35] while other people, real programmers, actually implemented them.

This was no time to lose heart. Most of these people hadn't even heard of html[36] a decade ago, and here they were prancing around as if they had invented the thing. They didn't know a search engine from a portal, even if they had made more money in a year investing in those buzzwords[37] than my Uncle Morris did in a whole lifetime importing counterfeit chandeliers[38] for the prefab homes of Levittown.

No, I had nothing to fear from the wealthy. Their money didn't make them confident; it made them scared. Every seven years they lost it all. Seven years of feasting followed by seven years of famine. And these people had mortgages and lifestyles to protect. Personal burn rates that would make a dot.com[39] CEO shudder. Net worths tied up in NASDAQ[40] portfolios that were worth no more than what people were willing to pay at any given moment for the highly speculative securities in them. The super-rich were only as wealthy as other people perceived them to be. But that was pretty damn rich, all the same, and I wanted to win some of that perceived worth for myself and then cash in my chips before the game was over again—which I figured would be pretty soon.

'Have you met Jamie Cohen? He's just joined us at Morehouse,' Alec told the tall young man in an Armani suit and turtleneck who was shaking my hand.

'Didn't I see you at Comdex earlier this year? Weren't we on a panel together?' he asked. I didn't know him, and he didn't know me. But you could never be sure. 'Ty Stanton. IDPP Partners.'

'Pleased to meet you,' I said, slipping into the shmooze groove. 'IDPP's an incubator[41], right?'

Ty snorted as if this were an insult. Alec laughed nervously.

'The age of incubators is over, Jamie.' Ty fanned out a deck of colored business cards.

I felt my intimidation flip into aggression. 'Is this a magic trick?'

Ty was unfazed.

'It's meant to demonstrate our one-to-one philosophy, Jamie.' He used my name at the end of every sentence—a technique straight out of the NLP[42] business books. 'Each person gets the kind of card they choose—just like each of our clients, if you can call them that, gets the company they choose. It symbolizes and even actualizes our corporate philosophy: multidimensional, improvisational, and environment-specific.'

'Clever,' Alec said, taking a card. 'Hmph. I got pink.'

'You *chose* pink, Alec,' Ty corrected him in the manner of a new age guru.

'I'll just take a white one.' I put it in my pocket, and handed one of my own freshly embossed M&L cards to Ty.

'No thanks, Jamie,' Ty said, waving it away. 'I never take them. They just make clutter. And I'm good with names, Jamie. Besides—anytime we need to contact someone, well, we're in a lucky position. They usually find us, first.'

I didn't know whether to take this guy seriously or not. Alec resolved the issue.

'How many of IDPP's companies have reached IPO,' he asked. '50?'

'Closer to a hundred, actually, Alec,' he replied. 'But our function goes well beyond incubation. Each company we launch serves a different and synergistic role in the IDPP family. We have firms that make everything from chips to routers, others that do branding and strategy, some shared-satellite plays, a couple of wireless portals, and of course a full spectrum of e-commerce and shopping aggregators.'

The shotgun approach.

39 Due to an artificial scarcity perpetuated by a former government agency called Network Solutions, all online businesses took names that ended in the letters 'com,' sometimes paying upwards of a million dollars for the words preceding the suffix.   —Sabina Samuels

40. The National Association of Securities Dealers Automated Quotation system opened in 1971. The short-lived stock exchange promoted mostly technological issues, as well as transaction schemes that depended on computers for their execution. The exchange introduced the notion of 'over-the-counter' stock trading, in which the margin between 'bid' and 'ask' prices could be collected as profit by the market maker, much in the manner of a sports betting bookie. Devotees of the NASDAQ erected a temple in honor of the exchange in Times Square, New York. Its exterior walls were made of liquid crystal display video screens.
—Sabina Samuels

41. Basically, a protective hatchery for new companies. Use of nurturing and biological base metaphors for capitalism was commonplace.   —Sabina Samuels

42. Neurolinguistic Programming—A branch of hypnotherapy that was adapted for use in negotiations, the courtroom and sales, NLP used visual, tactile, and linguistic cues to trigger cognitive responses in its subjects. Certain applications of NLP were outlawed in 2011, when it was used in television commercials for children's toys, leading to hundreds of cases of epilepsy and several class-action lawsuits.   —Sabina Samuels

'I guess you've got the bases covered.' I tried to be polite.

'That's just the point,' Ty continued. 'We had the same bases covered as everyone else. Our business plan used to be unique. Now it serves as the template for incubators around the world. They're all getting the same ROI.'

'ROI?' I was expecting a ploy that had become popular in hacker circles, where programmers use fake acronyms to test one another's BS quotient. If you pretend to understand an acronym that has no real meaning, you expose yourself as uninitiated.

'Return on investment, Jamie.' Ty smiled. 'And you're the one who's supposed to bring Morehouse into, what was it, the 1980's?' Ty's barb was delivered perfectly—dangling between insult and humor.

'So you've been unsatisfied with your returns?' I offered.

'They're great, of course, but everyone else is catching up. Besides, once you're looking at ROI, it means you're done for. That's the great lesson of 2001."

"Is that what we learned?" I asked.

"You have to keep your eyes on the prize. It's our competitive advantage that keeps us in a leadership position. That's why our CEO conceived the next phase.' For drama as much as sustenance, Ty grabbed a baby quiche[43] off an hors d'oeuvres tray that was floating by him.

'Which is?' Alec took the bait.

'Well, the press release isn't going out until tomorrow,' Ty said as he picked a tiny bacon bit from between his teeth. 'I'm not sure it's kosher.'

'That's okay,' I called his bluff. 'You better not reveal privileged information.' Companies like IDPP announced earth-shattering paradigm shifts at least twice a week, especially when they had no real news of mergers or acquisitions to report.

'I suppose it'll be all right...' Ty pretended to relent.

43. Amongst the affluent, it was fashionable to eat flesh from only the youngest animals, which was said to have a lower fat content and be less likely to contribute to heart disease—a common problem for people who lived on hors d'oeuvres.   —FERGLE

'No, really,' I needled him. I was having a good time, now. 'I don't want you to break any rules on my account.'

'Look.' Ty tried to retain some intrigue for his revelation. 'As long as you promise not to act on anything until the market opens tomorrow.'

'I don't know, Ty,' I said hesitatingly, as if it pained me. 'It's hard for me to make a commitment like that. At a party and all. I have been drinking, and there's other people in my firm to think about.'

Alec shot me a harsh glance, like I was pushing this too far. No one spoke for a moment.

'Not bad, Jamie.' Ty took a step back, regarding me as a pecking-order[44] competitor for the first time. 'Not bad at all.'

'Thanks.' I was actually grateful to him for helping me get my sea legs. 'Now tell me what the hell your CEO decided, okay?'

'Well, since it's too late to make any real advances in the incubator game, we decided to take it one step further. Basically go 'meta' on the whole proposition.' He looked deep into my eyes. 'We're going to be incubating incubators.'

'What?' Alec was confused. 'You just said incubators were over.'

'Which is why we took it to the next level,' Ty finished the syllogism.

'I get it,' I said. And, much as it pains me to admit it now, I did. 'The struggle is against commodification. The bright idea you have today is the repeatable, mass-produced commodity of tomorrow. Microchips used to be cutting edge—now they're designed by computers and churned out in Singapore. Then it was computers, then networks, then e-commerce sites, and so on.'

'Right,' Ty chimed in. 'Look what e-commerce did to everyone who tried it. Once there was more than one company selling the same thing online, those aggregator sites could create side-by-side comparisons. Prices went

44. Before the advent of advanced mood normalizing supplements, the emotional and cognitive processes of most people were dominated by patterns that had evolved thousands of years earlier on the Serengeti. —Sabina Samuels

down, taking margins with them.'

I felt propelled by something outside myself—like I was on speed. 'The whole trick is to get yourself situated in an area with endless novelty,' I raced ahead. 'Unique ideas. That's why incubators became all the rage. Firms dedicated to hatching ideas and spawning them off into new companies. Keeps you 'in the new.'[45]

'Until everyone starts doing incubators, that is,' Ty steered the conversation back towards his paradigm shift. 'So we realized we could be the next big thing by generating idea generators, systematically. We're going to churn out three new incubators every month.'

'And what if someone else starts making incubators?' Alec asked.

Ty seemed stumped by the possibility of infinite regression.

'Well,' I rescued him. 'I guess that's when you go 'shift paradigms' again, Ty.'

All three of us laughed. For different reasons.

'So what do you at IDPP?' I asked. 'Strategy?'

'Heavens no,' Ty snorted again. I couldn't help but notice how huge his nostrils got when he did. 'I'm like Alec, here. I do PR.' Then he was off.

That explains it, I thought, as Ty sidled off to glad-hand the marketing director of a banner ad company. He's just a PR guy. But what made 'strategy' any better? This industry wasn't even running on fumes, anymore, but perception. Strategy had more to do with predicting and tweaking image than it did with technology. And the technology that did exist was dedicated mostly to creating images, anyway. Another infinite regression. Did anyone really think this would work, or were they only trying to find an easy exit before the next burst of the bubble?

Alec didn't waste time pondering all this. While I mulled, he snared another executive.

45. A person 'in the new' was one who had knowledge of the most current trends and information. The idiom became popular in the early 21st Century—to be 'in the new' was even better than being 'in the know.'
—Sabina Samuels

'Was that Ty Stanton?' asked Alec's next catch— a bald, stocky man in a crisp ventless suit. 'He's with an incubator, now, right?'

'If that includes pretending you're not an incubator,' I said, holding out my hand.

'Jamie Cohen is our new Technology Strategist, Karl,' Alec said, elevating my title in the process. 'Karl is CFO at Consumer Solutions International.'

'Jamie Cohen, the hacker?' Karl inquired suspiciously.

'In a former life,' I answered as we exchanged cards. The back of his was in Japanese. 'You guys have done some great work,' I said, hoping to compensate for my dark-side reputation. 'You've really made e-commerce sites a joy to use. Put some fun back into the whole genre.'

'Well, thanks,' Karl grumbled, 'but who said 'fun' ever fed the colonel's cat, eh? The more fun they have the less transactions they're making. There's only so many eyeball hours[46] in a day, if you can get my drift. No room for growth. The consumer sector is saturated.'

'Better not say that too loudly,' Alec joked.

'So where do you go, then?' I wanted to know.

'B to B. Business to business[47]. Exploit margins, create efficiencies, disintermediate all along the supply chain.'

'B to B peaked in '99,' Alec said. 'And again in 2004. Then B to G, then C to C, P to P...the cycle is almost over.'

'But there's a twist,' Karl said. 'We call it 'B to C as B to B.' Hell, everybody's in this business, anyway. Look around you. Even people are businesses, so why not treat them as such? It shows them more respect than if they were consumers, lets them participate in the profits, and stimulates brand loyalty that goes off the charts. This way we can focus entirely on reducing risk, enhancing deal-flow, and networking externalities.'

46. Human attention was measured in quantities known as eyeball-hours.
—Sabina Samuels

47. Wholesale.   —Sabina Samuels

48. After the near collapse of the airline industry in the late 20th Century, the surviving carriers engaged in a desperate and, in hindsight, ill-advised promotional scheme designed to encourage people to fly more. In a nutshell, customers were rewarded for frequent flying by earning "miles," which could be cashed in for service upgrades on future flights. Originally, frequent flier miles were to be granted only to those people who actually flew. But airlines eventually began licensing frequent flier miles to secondary vendors, such as credit card companies and durable goods retailers. Toward the end, customers could earn frequent flier miles for engaging in almost any economic activity, from purchasing a home to buying a stick of bubble gum. And since most people did not travel much, these mile credits simply piled up in cold accounts. This led to a silent hyperinflation, as more and more miles were issued to make up for those that had effectively dropped out of the economy.

And then the dam burst. With billions of dollars worth of untapped credit simply lying around, it was only a matter of time before a cadre of enterprising travel agents began buying up these miles at pennies on the dollar and using them to provide cheap fares to their regular customers. The airlines simply could not handle the increased demand for first class treatment and the quality of service plummeted, culminating in the infamous American Airlines Flight 201 incident in 2011, which was at that time the worst example of mass air rage in US history.

For years after this, the term "frequent flier" was used to describe someone who has succumbed to a violent fit of rage, as in "oh, he's a frequent flier" or "he went all frequent flier on my ass" (see "postal," circa 1995). —SHANKEL

49. This phrase has baffled scholars for some time. At first glance, given the argot

notes continue on page 23

'How?' I asked. 'I mean are you making business transactions more like consumer experiences, or the other way around?'

'There's no difference! That's the point! In the new model, every consumer earns a fraction of a share in the network each time they make a purchase. Buying from a CSI-affiliated web site—and we've got companies selling everything from airline tickets to automobiles—earns you shares in the CSI network. You can keep the shares in your CSI e-trading account, or use them towards other CSI purchases.'

'Like a frequent flier[48] program,' Alec said.

'Except it's not just miles you're earning, Alec. It's shares. The consumers are the shareholders. It's their own company they're buying from. And they can track their own share value as they make purchases, right on their browser or web-phone. They can even earn shares by including our advertising in their personal email. Then it gets viral. You should see the user tests we've done. They're through the roof.'

I was appalled and intrigued—a cognitive dissonance I would learn to get used to. On one level I hated this guy. He wasn't in the technology business at all, but the business of business. At the same time, this hack of business networking fascinated me. I couldn't help but wrap my own brain matter around the concept. In the spirit of play, of course. Then, out of nowhere, I got a tremendous urge to fuck with this guy[49].

'Have you considered creating more than one network?' I asked.

Alec shifted uncomfortably, afraid of where I was going.

'Why would we want more than one network?' Karl asked.

'Well, let's say you've got the lead players in each category—American Airlines, McDonalds, Coke, Hertz.'

'We do.'

'Right, well what if someone is already brand loyal to some number two brand, like Continental, Burger King, Pepsi, or Avis?'

'Then they'll switch to the CSI affiliate. The program is magnetic.'

'Yeah,' I was in full gear now, 'until Burger King and the others create their own network.'

His eyes began to wiggle. I was freaking him out.

'We'll beat them. That's why we've chosen number one brands exclusively.' Karl laughed proudly, repeatedly scuffing one of his Bruno Magli loafers against the parquet dance floor as he did.

'But why don't you just bring them in?' I asked.

'We can't have competing brands in the same network.'

'That's why you create a *second* network,' I said, slapping his shoulder. 'If the first has Kelloggs, the second has Post, and so on. Create another network with all the second brands. If the prime network has AOL/TimeWarner, Crest, Microsoft, Coke, GM, AT&T, Nike and WalMart, then your secondary network can have Disney, Colgate, Macintosh, Pepsi, Ford, MCI, Reebok and Kmart. Then you can have an alternative, 'Peoples' network for people who don't like to think of themselves as brand-conscious. Say, Miramax, Tom's of Maryland, Linux, Dr. Pepper, Volkswagen, Working Assets, Airwalk and, gosh, I dunno, Price Club. And maybe some portion of their kickback shares go to some charity so they feel good about the whole thing. You could do another with deluxe brands, like Sundance Channel, Mentadent, SGI, Mercedes, Lucent, Donna Karan and Neiman Marcus.'[50]

Karl had pulled a tiny leather-covered palm device out of his jacket pocket and was scrawling notes—entering one character at a time with a tiny plastic stick, desperate to keep up.

'What were the brands for the alternative network, again?' he asked. I couldn't believe he was taking me seriously.

of the time, it would seem Jamie is interested in making amorous advances on this individual, and their ensuing conversation can be seen in the context of an elaborate mating ritual (also, Alec's anger can be interpreted as thinly veiled jealousy). Yet, while the person he is talking to is male, we are shown Jamie fantasizing about having sex with a woman later in the text. At this time, there was still considerable societal baggage associated with freely maintaining intimate relations with both sexes. When these ambivalent situations are encountered in literature of the time, it is often fodder enough for entire volumes, and it seems odd that the issue doesn't surface again, even in Jamie's internal monologue. It has been speculated that Jamie's blasé air around these matters marks him as a harbinger of future common-sense attitudes toward sexual choice, hence his adoption by some groups as a "prophet of pan-sexuality."
—DRZARDOZ

50. These were mostly consumer corporations, whose brand recognition was used to fuel stock purchases. Most of the corporations mentioned in this conversation are no longer in existence.
—Sabina Samuels

'That's not the point,' I said. I was lost, myself. I had spent most of my energy trying to keep the lists of brands in the same order. I knew I could wrap it up by throwing some of the guy's own terms back at him—chances are he didn't understand them, anyway. 'It's about enhancing your ROI by networking externalities. Look, does Morehouse & Linney do your mergers and acquisitions? You can just come down to the office and we'll go over the whole thing.'

'No,' Karl smiled weakly. 'We're with S and S.'

'Well,' Alec sidled in opportunistically, 'maybe you should consider...'

'That's okay,' Karl said, putting his palm device back in his pocket. 'I think I got most of it. Thanks. Please give my regards to your father.' And then he was off.

Alec was fuming.

'What the fuck was that, Jamie?'

'Huh?'

'Whose side are you on, anyway? They're going to go do what you said, man. And make a ton of money at it."

'We're not in that business, Alec.'

'We're *supposed* to be. That's what you were hired to do. This isn't some shareware convention.'

'Gimme a break. It was a fantasy biz plan. No one could execute it.'

'Who said anything about executing it? Nobody executes anything around here. It's just ideas, Jamie. *Ideas.* You get people to invest in an idea, take it to IPO, and then get out before anyone tries to do it for real. Your ideas belong to *us.*'

Alec's eyes had turned red with something approaching rage. He was breathing hard, like a miniature beast of burden.

'I'm sorry, okay?' But before I could gauge Alec's response, I heard a voice so familiar I couldn't even place it at first.

'Assembly of the corporate machine's incarnate manifestation is proceeding on schedule, eh?'

I swung around and saw him. It was Jude. Three years older than the last time we'd met—at a computer game developers' convention in Atlanta—but pretty much the same. His bushy red hair was a bit thinner and his wiry red beard a bit thicker, but this was the same angry, inspired, and manic Jude. I felt an urge to cover myself up. My suit made me feel nude.

'Well that's what's going on here, right?' Jude gave one of his Jack Nicholson glints. 'The conversion of the communications infrastructure into a physical home for the corporate life form? So it can have eyes and ears?'

'I'm Alec Morehouse.' My current best friend shook hands with my former best friend.

'Pleased to meet you, Alec,' said Jude. But he never took his eyes away from mine. It felt like that staring contest between boxers while the ref gives final instructions.

'It's good to see you, Jude.' I didn't mean it, but I really wanted to. 'I've been intending to call, but things were so busy and then, well...'

'It had gotten to be such a long time that you got scared to think of how I'd react,' Jude said, breaking through the small talk.

'Yeah. I guess.'

Alec ever discreet, pretended that a Morehouse associate across the room had summoned him over, and left us alone.

'Expanding ROI?' Jude made sure I knew he had heard it all. Every last bit of my sold-out, profit-driven rhetoric.

'I just learned that acronym tonight, Jude. I was blowing smoke up his ass to get a reaction, that's all.'

'Yeah, well, where there's smoke there's buyers, eh? Blow enough of it in that guy's butt and he'll float on air like everything else around here.' He paused a second, and looked in both directions as if to make sure the coast was clear. 'Those CSI guys are Nazis, you know. It's all online. Look at where their money was in 1939.'

'If you looked at where everyone's money was in 1939, Jude, you wouldn't be able to do business with anyone.'

'Q-E-D,' Jude smirked, in the language of a geometric proof. 'Q.E. fucking D.'

'You haven't changed a bit.'

'That makes one of us,' Jude started in. 'How far into the service of the machine do you plan to get, Jamie?'

'Like you should talk? What the hell are you doing here, anyway?'

'Hey, I always liked the circus,' he said. 'Besides, I figured I'd find you here.'

'Yeah, right,' I goaded him. 'You got into the Silicon Stars list this month, didn't you?' The Silicon Alley Reader put out a monthly chart of the 500 most influential Internet players.

'For the 'zine, yeah,' he said defensively of his online hacker's magazine. 'But for the opposite reason as most of these people. We don't even take advertising.'

'That hack that brought down six trading sites for four hours—' I pretended to be putting two and two together. 'Wasn't there some mention of your web site in the news reports? Something about being a node for anonymous distribution of denial-of-service programs?'

'They never proved anything.'

'But it got you on the Reader's list. Now you'll be famous.'

'Just following in DeltaWave's footsteps.'

That was a low blow. Too low, considering his role in my capture.

'I'm sorry, man,' Jude said. 'Really. That's all old history, right?'

'Yeah, I guess so. You fuckers got me into college, after all. Even got me this job.'

'That's what I'm apologizing for, Jamie.'

My fellow Jamaican Kings, as we called ourselves, may not have had it in mind at the time, but they were responsible for everything. We had been tight as brothers. I remember fantasizing how I would submit to torture or even death, if the opportunity presented itself, rather than reveal my comrades' identities to the Secret Service. Such was the loyalty our posse of hackers felt for one another. Most of the time.

We all took the same train from Queens to Stuyvesant High— a smart kids' public school that served as New York City's last ditch attempt to keep a few upper-middle-class white kids in the system. On the long #7 ride into Manhattan, we'd gather in the last subway car and dig through one another's boxes of disks, exchanging the 'warez' we'd garnered during our previous night's exploits on the Net. Most of it was the software for new arcade games—the ROMs which could then be played on a computer through an emulator. No more quarters wasted on Streetfighter[51] at Star Pizza. Just mount the game's ROM on a PC and play for free. Whatever one kid found or stole he shared with the rest of the Kings. It was the rule: no personal ownership, and no personal fame. All hacks and spoils belonged to the posse.

I was the only member with a real conflict of interest. Each year, one senior student was selected to maintain the school's computer lab—and to manage access privileges for everyone else. I appeared trustworthy enough to win this coveted honor when I was still just a junior. Mr. Unsworth, the computer instructor and lab supervisor, had even given me a digital pager so that I could be alerted in the event of a system failure. My quasi-girlfriend at the time painted it in day-glo colors to balance the inherent authoritarian dork-

51. A violent video arcade game. *See note 39.*
—Sabina Samuels

27

iness with some skateboarder's edge. I was good—really good—but certainly not the very best programmer among us. I was simply the best at hacking the faculty—and maybe the least likely to crash the system just for the fun of it.

It's how my double-life began, really. By day, I was the shining young do-gooder, entrusted with master keys to the building, full access to the school's computers, command over all other student users, and encryption of the Board of Education's security codes. By night, I was 'DeltaWave,' youngest member of the Jamaican Kings.

Our posse took this name even though we were mostly from Flushing because both Queens neighborhoods used the same telephone routing station. If someday a hack were traced, the posse's name might lead the authorities off-track to Jamaica. Plus, it made us sound like Rastafarians with dreadlocks, when we were actually Jewish kids from the boroughs. All except for El Greco, a chubby Armenian boy who earned his name not for anything to do with his bloodline but the extensive graffiti landscapes he'd paint on the walls of underpasses. It didn't stop everyone's parents from asking him questions like 'who sells the most authentic baklava in Astoria?' when he came to dinner.

If I hadn't felt so conflicted, I probably would have been able to maintain a divided allegiance and double-identity. I could have kept my exploits as a King completely secret, and my teachers unaware. Everything the Kings did was anonymous, anyway. No one had to know. But I felt like a traitor whenever I'd sit by Mr. Unsworth's side after school working on security codes, knowing I would be turning them over to the Kings the next morning. Meanwhile, my responsibilities at school made me feel like a fake among my fellow hackers. As far as the Kings were concerned, my day-gig as Stuyvesant's Über-Programmer was just a cover. But, deep down, I cherished the authority I'd earned.

52. In the early part of the 20th Century in the United States, having artifacts from other cultures indicated that one had traveled to those cultures, and consequently had the significant amount of money required to do so. The status conferred by these artifacts remained in the culture, even after travel became cheaper, and inevitably led to their commodification. They were brought into the country en masse by "importers" who worked with "distributors" to disseminate them across the U.S. Ironically, natives of the countries being imported from could sell their wares to importers at far higher prices than they could to their countrymen for whom the artifacts had been originally designed. This led to the mass production of "native artifacts" by these artisans, all of which were specifically designed for export to Americans, thereby reducing their authenticity, but not

notes continue on page 29

As if to reveal myself, I made constant, almost counter-phobic blunders. I once bragged to Mr. Unsworth about how I could sabotage the Board of Education's mainframe with a single keystroke. And I gloated to the Kings about how 'Someday you'll all be coming to me for jobs.' No one seemed to care but me.

By spring of my junior year, a new fearlessness took hold of the Jamaican Kings. All of them except me were seniors, and had already gotten into college if they were going to go. They were bored with classes, oblivious to grades, and ready to work on what they thought might be our final act together. It was the project that would make us famous: the Ultimate Hack.

It all happened in less than a week. The original plan was masterminded by Jude, our default leader. Some said he earned this position because his was the first stop along the 7 on the way to school, making it appear as though he owned the rear car while the rest of us simply arrived there. Others chalked it up to the fact that he lived alone most of the time—his parents had a business importing Sri Lankan[52] hats and were out of the country more often than not, leaving Jude with 24-hour access to the phone line and the only reliable server.

But, in the end, Jude probably earned his place atop the pecking order because he knew how to intimidate people. Wherever my sweet-talking wouldn't work, Jude's scare tactics would. A curly red-haired boy and the first among us to sport a passable beard[53], Jude had a sinister way of talking through his teeth and rolling his eyes up in his head—mannerisms he copied from *The Shining*[54], and that worked to dissuade bigger kids from messing with him. The rest of us, sadly, remained Stuyvesant's most-probable targets for wedgies[55] and whale-hooks.[56]

While Jude would have stood only as good a chance as any other King of physically defending himself (meaning none), he alone understood that per-

(happily for the artisans and importers) their selling price significantly.
—DRZARDOZ

53. Pseudo-estrogens were common industrial byproducts in this period. By the early 21st Century, the buildup of these chemicals in the environment was having a noticeable impact on adolescent development. It was not uncommon for girls to express secondary sex characteristics as early as eight or even six years of age. Conversely, many boys had their development delayed into their late teens and even early twenties.

The cultural impact of this biological shift could be seen in the teen-targeted media of the time: eroticized, midriff-baring pop-divas and their bland, sexless "boy band" counterparts. —SHANKEL

54. A classic horror film based on a story by a period fiction hack named Stephen King. —Sabina Samuels

55. Wedgie: an attack meant to cause pain and embarrassment simultaneously, in which the rear waistband of the underwear is pulled upward so that the rest of the garment lodges snugly and somewhat visibly between the buttocks.
—Sabina Samuels

56. Whale-hook: a similar maneuver to the 'wedgie' (above), performed by reaching through the victim's legs from behind, grasping the front waistband of his undershorts, and pulling them over and around the belt-line as hard as possible for considerably more infliction of discomfort. For additional descriptions of these rituals, as well as their psychological impact, see George Thomas Duncan, 'Initiation Rites among the Pubescent,' Oakland: EC Press, 2005. —Sabina Samuels

57. Ritalin was an amphetamine, pre-scribed during this period to young men who resisted coercive electronic pro-gramming. It appears that once corporations redefined the social and public stra-ta as 'attention economies,' all restraints on commercial messaging were removed. As a result, children growing up in an American city were exposed to market-ing and brand messaging literally every-where they set their eyes.

As an adaptive strategy, many of these children evolved a primitive version of what we now call 'skim-sight.' At the time, however, it was considered a mental ill-ness, because it rendered children imper-vious to media 'stickiness,' and thus resist-ant to advertising messages. It also pro-duced serious side-effects, such as the inability to follow linear arguments. Many children who were prescribed the drug sold the pills to their peers as 'speed.'
—Sabina Samuels

58. An inefficient suite of programs that modeled office tasks such as typing and spreadsheets, but which was used mostly by Microsoft as a way of leveraging its operating system and perpetuating mar-ket share before the company's eventual downfall. It is also thought that the pro-gram's outlandishly cumbersome code was designed to necessitate the purchase of faster computer chips, and new ver-sions of the Microsoft operating system, in a tiered scheme of planned obsoles-cence. —Sabina Samuels

ception is nine-tenths of the law, and made this altered axiom his life credo. He wore torn-up heavy metal t-shirts under a black leather jacket and pre-tended to act crazy whenever he got in a tight situation. After a few years, it was as if Jude bought his own act and became a delinquent—in relative terms, at least. Halfway through his senior year, he stopped going to any classes except computer science and philosophy, and decided to forgo the college application process altogether. This gave him the time to hack while we were all in class, studying for the SAT's, or begging for recommendations. It also gave him the ability to act as though he were above such petty, mun-dane, and sold-out pursuits. Which, in effect, he was.

After dipping into one of his infamous stay-awake-for-a-whole-month-on-other-kids'-Ritalin[57] binges, Jude emerged having successfully hacked a feature in Microsoft Office[58] that was originally intended to allow the com-pany to conduct market research on consumers through the Internet. Then, he and Reuben— our Alpha-Nerd—exploited this security breach to create a tiny email virus that could alter the functioning of Office in any way we wanted.

We spent longer trying to figure out what to do with the hack than actu-ally writing it. Our arguments took place on an almost Talmudic level: 'If an innocent person is delayed by our hack, then do we get bad karma?' 'If a per-son uses a Microsoft product, have they implicitly put themselves in the line of fire?' 'What if a person is depending on the services of someone who uses Microsoft Office? Are they to be inconvenienced or even damaged just for their unwitting patronage of a Microsoft user?' And so on.

Jude finally convinced us that Microsoft posed such a noxious threat to free flow of information and technology that an absolutely indiscriminate, scattershot launch of the virus qualified as a morally sound strategy. More importantly, the less targeted the attack, the less likely it was to be traced back to us.

But given that the virus was to be spread to all Microsoft users, regardless of their level of complicity with Bill Gates' plan for global domination, we would keep the damage on a semiotic level. Whenever a user created a new Microsoft Word file, the document would open with one sentence already written on the top: 'Microsoft sucks.' Crude, but to the point.

The plan was for us to launch the virus from eight different public access facilities simultaneously, using eight different carrier messages. One claimed that the attached file was a free teen porn picture, another promised a stock tip, and another was a certificate 'to claim your jackpot prize.' When users attempted to open the attachment, they would be informed that the file was incomplete. Meanwhile, the virus would nest itself deep within Microsoft Office, and then launch itself three days later.

As fate would have it, on the Saturday of the planned attack my parents forced me to go to shul for the bar mitzvah of an influential temple board member's son. In truth, I was relieved to be forcibly yanked from battle. I had more at stake than the others; my permanent record still meant something to me. In any case, by Saturday afternoon, when the rest of the Jamaican Kings were spamming[59] the known Internet universe, I was dancing the hora in the back room of Goldstein's Restaurant.

Later that night, I was so racked with guilt that I couldn't even bring myself to attend the Kings' midnight debriefing. I had missed the call to action, and I knew they would blame it on my do-gooder tendencies—my innate inability to live as a daring prankster. It was in my effort to deflect this charge that I made my tragic error.

I decided to play a part in the attack, after all. Better late than never. And in order to prove my loyalty to the Kings, I inserted my own hacker handle deep into the code of the virus. If the authorities were to take apart the virus

59. In this period, electronic mail was used mostly for the transmission of primitive marketing pitches called 'spam,' in which the very same advertisement was sent to millions of people at once. This technique was still employed long after computer-generated 'one-to-one' electronic target-marketing had became economical. "Spam" was also the brand name of a canned food made from a variety of animal flesh products. The two terms may have been related.   —Sabina Samuels

itself, and analyze the code line by line, they would find the word 'DeltaWave' nested in the commands. Although no one except the Kings knew the handle belonged to me, it showed I was willing to take an even bigger risk than them.

Of course the Kings didn't see it that way. By the time the story hit the headlines, the 'DeltaWave Virus' had become synonymous with hacker subversion. I had effectively taken credit for everyone else's hard work. It was a sin that could not go unpunished.

Several days before launch, we had sent a warning message about the virus to a producer at 'Inside Edition'[60] through an alias email account. Although she didn't believe us at first, the success of the virus—three days of havoc before Microsoft developed a patch—made her wet for an interview with any of the offenders. Jude picked a chat room on a public web site through which we could converse with her, and appointed me to be the Kings' spokesperson.

I should have guessed something was up. I logged into the chat room from home through the account Jude had set up for me—unaware that he had purposely neglected to use an anonymous channel. Before I had finished my treatise on the open source[61] movement, three Secret Service agents were knocking at the door. At least they didn't break it down.

I was a first-time offender, a minor, and awfully cute—to adults, anyway. Microsoft had no intention of being known as the company that imprisoned a sweet-looking kid with braces[62], blue eyes, and dark, wavy hair. (I wore my retainer for my court[63] appearance.) They encouraged the judge to sentence me to a year of counseling and a bit of public humiliation. I lost my computer privileges at school and was forced to go on television talk shows and bemoan the dangers of hacking.

In my first few interviews, I personified penitence. I apologized for all the

---

60. Inside Edition: news had devolved into a form of entertainment. "Magazines" such as Inside Edition mostly featured stories about the actors in "reality television" programs—social experiments based on ritualized survival sagas. The program also sensationalized the mundane, such as the sex partner choices of politicians and corporate celebrities.
—Sabina Samuels

61. Until 2020, most computer software was still produced with encrypted code. This meant that only the company that published and owned the software could modify it! It was an anti-evolutionary posture adopted by most of the software industry that stunted technological development. Current analysis indicates that by 2009, computer software was thirty years behind where it would have been had open source been the dominant development model. —Sabina Samuels

62. An archaic and presumably painful system of wires to distort young people's teeth to fit social norms of appearance. The author suggests that these "braces" evoked attraction, but we don't know what such tooth-wires symbolized. Was it admiration for the wearer's stoicism; sympathy for their social disability, or even some fetishistic interest? —RAYGIRVAN

63. An inefficient law system by which a logic defying person was hired to argue that a criminal was either justified in committing the crime or was being falsely accused because of ugliness or misfortune. Often laws themselves were changed rather than justice achieved.
—BARGAMER

trouble I caused, and reflected with appropriate contrition on the addictive quality of the Internet. Soon, however, I found myself speaking more about the power one feels at the keyboard than any of the vices to which that power might lead. Before long, I had become a strident Internet proselytizer, spinning intricate visions of the connected society that lay ahead for America's wired youth.

A Princeton admissions officer happened to see one of my impassioned diatribes on Rivera's World,[64] and subsequently offered me a full scholarship to enroll in the school's new Computer Studies program. I got a free pass to the Ivy league by taking the fall for a hack I didn't even write! After all, if I admitted it wasn't my own work, I'd have to reveal the true perpetrators.

After graduation, I won a string of jobs developing networked gaming concepts for Internet start-ups in Boston, Los Angeles, and Toronto. Every one of these companies peaked then failed before my options could be vested. That's when it occurred to me that I wasn't in the computer game, at all. The real networked game was being played by brokers, angel investors, and CEO's. This was the real game. Instead of writing the back-stories for Playstation disks, I'd write them for business plans.

Most amazingly, tonight it looked like Jude—far from condemning me— was hoping to play, too.

'There's something I have to show you,' he said, leaning in confidentially. I could tell he was uncomfortable in his role as the solicitor.

'What? Where?'

'No, no, not here. It's a new technology me and the guys put together. I think it could interest you.'

'You've got a business proposition? Is that what you're saying?' I wanted to force him to admit his intentions. That he wanted to get in the new.

'Yeah, but it's the business proposition to end all business propositions,'

64. Rivera's World: a television show created, apparently, to explore the social ramifications of the murder trial of former football hero OJ Simpson.
—Sabina Samuels

33

Jude said a bit mysteriously. 'You have to see it to know what I'm talking about.'

'See it? You mean you actually developed something?' I joked. 'From what I can tell, that's the last thing we're supposed to do around here.'

'Well, that's what makes us different.'

'Us?'

'Me and Reuben, mostly. El Greco helped at the beginning, but then he got a job somewhere.'

'El Greco's in New York? What's he doing? Is he still fat?'

'Come see,' he baited me. I got the feeling Jude really wanted me to be part of what he was doing. That he really missed me as much as I, begrudgingly, missed him. 'Greco's got a day job over at a place in Jersey, doing commerce as entertainment software, or entertainment as commerce software. I forget which.'

I felt myself smiling at the memory of sweet El Greco, waddling around the old neighborhood as his spray paint cans clanked against each other in his sweatshirt. 'He was the best.'

'*We* were the best.'

For a minute I had half a mind to just walk out on that whole world of shiny suits and plastic cups and go back to my posse, where I belonged. Where the rent was low and the walk-ups were only one flight.

That's when I saw her, and the mental escape hatch suddenly slammed shut.

'Uh, Jude,' I said, trying to cut our exchange short. 'I better deal with stuff.'

'That's cool. I'll watch.'

I noticed his clothes for the first time. Torn jeans, a ratty black T-shirt. I didn't know whether associating with him would give me street cred with

Carla, or peg me once and for all as an impostor in her shop.

'No, I mean, I better do the business thing. They are paying me.' I shook his hand, and patted his shoulder.

'It's okay, you do the business thing.' He wasn't moving, and Carla had already spotted me. She was working her way over. My worlds were about to collide.

'Who is she?' Jude asked.

'She's kind of my boss, I guess.'

I hadn't fully considered this before, but Carla Santangelo, Chief of Internet Strategy, was my direct superior at M&L, at least for now. She was a spirited, selfish, and thus successful thirty-something fund manager who worked her way up through the tech-related commodity pits before landing a job at the center of the firm's cyber-intelligence vacuum. She had the brains, beauty and bullishness to achieve a high profile in Silicon Alley, if not on the Street, but she had no instinct for the way networks had changed the securities landscape, and still used obsolete statistics like earnings estimates to determine share valuations. She had become famously frazzled in the fall-out after IPO-mania, and her need for a mind like mine was outweighed only by the threat someone like me posed to her position.

At least that's how I justified what I could only interpret as her romantic overtures since I arrived at M&L. Although Alec had been introducing me as a strategist, I was still just a lowly researcher—one of hundreds at M&L, and over a dozen in Carla's Internet division. I figured her brushing up against me at the conference table and those frequent glances down to my crotch were a kind of hazing. A power game. Keep the boys in line through sexual intimidation. On the other hand, I knew what landing a girlfriend like Carla could do for my career and sex life in the same stroke. But I resisted these thoughts on principle. I would not be used.

Besides, she was a little too high-strung for me. During the day, she wore silk blouses with extra thick underarm shields that betrayed her perpetual anxiety, and square horn-rim glasses that served to accentuate her desperate, panicked gazes. She pulled back her frizzy black hair into a tight bun that, by four or five o'clock, released enough random wiry strands to give her the appearance of a recently electrocuted witch. Or so I reminded myself whenever I caught my imagination wandering to the various parts of my body I could place between her ample breasts. No. She was an ornery, demanding, hysterical bitch.

But tonight, her glasses were off, the contacts were in, and her hair was riding her shoulders. Her architectural, Italian features now seemed to absorb some of the impact of her otherwise driving intensity, and her long, dark, wavy mane had liberated itself into an homage to spontaneity. She wore a flowing dress with a pastel floral pattern that softened her kinetic movements into rounded sashays.

Of course I wanted her, at least until she tired of me. Or maybe the gin had finally kicked in.

'Tell you what I'll do, Cohen,' Jude said, drawing me out of my trance. 'I'll spare you the embarrassment of having to introduce me if you promise to get me a demo at M&L next week.'

'I'm not embarrassed of...' I began, but Carla was upon us and this was the most expedient solution. 'Okay, Jude. Deal.'

'Call me,' Jude said as he disappeared into the crowd.

'Howdy, Cohen,' Carla pushed her shoulder nonchalantly against mine, as if she were simply trying to gain the same vantage-point of the room. 'Who was that you were talking to?'

'Just an old friend from the neighborhood.' I tried to read her expression in profile. She was inscrutable.

'Who'd you meet?' she asked. 'What'd you learn?'

God, I really did admire her, sometimes.

'Ty something from IDPP,' I answered. 'Karl somebody from Consumer Solutions.' I thought it best to keep my cards close to the chest for the time being.

'Well, *that's* pretty specific.'

'Nothing new,' I confessed.

'We have ways of making you talk...' Carla turned towards me, narrowing her eyes. 'I hear you've been introducing yourself as a strategist, Cohen.'

'That was Alec, not me. You know how he gets.'

'Yeah, but I don't know how *you* get, yet, Jamie.'

Her face inches from mine, and she was breathing hard. If I were the woman in this scenario I could've won a harassment suit, hands down. I endured her advances, though, because they gave me an excuse to act provoked by her presence—which I suppose I still was. Then again I may have simply been horny and misinterpreting everything. Maybe I was the one taking her every gesture as a come-on because I didn't feel comfortable reporting to a woman. A beautiful woman, at that, who didn't know as much about technology as I did.

I wanted her body, but I also wanted her job.

'You make any progress puffing up that IPO for the home security company?' I asked. I shouldn't have demeaned her efforts so, but all the other tension I was under made it come out that way.

Carla, and everyone else at M&L, knew full well that I thought her latest underwriting effort was short-sighted and doomed to failure. The company, mydoorman.com, had patented a process through which people would be able to program their home security systems over the World Wide Web. If a subscriber happened to be at work when someone rang his doorbell at home, a window would pop up on his computer desktop with a picture of the guest. This way, he could automatically open the door for a friend, family member or deliveryperson. It even allowed him to generate a "virtual signature." The technology required a special camera that needed to be plugged into the person's home computer through the serial port and then mounted on the doorframe. The business plan called for mailing the devices to subscribers free of charge, if they agreed to let their guests and decisions be recorded by the company's servers for market research. This brought the total cost of acquiring a user to over $470, while the revenue remained zero.

'It's not puff,' Carla defended the idea. 'It's called permission marketing. Networking externalities. Once everyone is programming their home security systems on our standard, we can exploit it in any number of ways. Advertising, special promotions, broadband.' She put her hands on her hips. 'It's a good play, Cohen, and I wish you'd stop undermining it.'

'I'm sorry. I just have trouble imagining my mom ever using it.'

'Well, I'm sorry too if your Internet strategy is based on the consumption demands of a 50-something rabbi's wife.'

That stung. Especially the part about my mom being the wife of a rabbi. It came out of an assumption that was gaining steam on the op-ed pages in recent months: that people with religious or left-leaning sentiments—not necessarily Jews in particular, but activists, environmentalists, policy wonks, public school administrators, and consumer advocates—were impediments to the necessary expansion of the GNP. They had been blamed, along with an increased focus on real revenues, for the correction of 2001: the great collapse of blind faith.

Now, unemployment was again down to below two percent, and the minimum wage had soared to above the poverty level. Inflation. This stoked fears that Ezra Birnbaum, Chairman of the Federal Reserve and also, incidentally, a Jew, might increase interest rates at the expense of the needs of capital.

At moments like this, I saw myself as an enemy to both camps.

'God, Cohen, lighten up.' She must have read my expression. 'I was joking, okay? Take a chill pill[65]. It's just business.'

It's just business. I kept forgetting. Carla didn't appear to have any misgivings about her role at M&L, and she was a practicing Catholic by all accounts—a registered Democrat with strong ties to the Secretary of Education's 'new media literacy' program. Plus, she was a woman, which in my admittedly prejudicial schema meant she was hardwired to nourish people. How did she reconcile all this with her dedication to feeding the corporate beast? How did she keep it all in perspective?

It was in the hope of answering these questions, as well as avoiding another night at my parent's house (where I was staying until my M&L-sponsored apartment was ready), that I decided to sleep with Carla.

65. This is not, as some scholars wrongly believe, a reference to thermanix, the hyperthermia and frostbite suppressant developed for early Mars exploration. First of all, this would be an extremely obscure and cryptic reference to drop into casual conversation. Secondly, whether genuine or fictional, this text predates the development of thermanix by some four decades. Most likely this is slang for "calm down". Cross references to other works of the period associate it loosely with the terms "been there, done that, got the t-shirt" and "talk to the hand, cuz the face don't wanna hear it."
—SHANKEL

65b. Chill was a term used to tell someone to relax, or not to mind the goings on around them. Most probably from the term chili, a hot vegetable, which caused endorphins to flow in the brain, increasing relaxation. Chilies were extinct by 2022 after it was found that they were a cure for what was called "the common cold."
—DUSTYONE11

2. The Beast

The machine had me trapped between its sharp, aluminum alloy jaws and was about to go in for the kill.

How had it come to this? I had only joined the Prime Network because it was the first to go online. I had planned to change once another one more suited to my tastes and character was established. But from the moment I clicked the 'agree' button on the web site I knew I had probably made a mistake.

I chose to take my dividends in electronic cash, usable only on the network. Each time I made a phone call, I'd get a dime of credit for every dollar I spent in long distance. By agreeing never to use a carrier other than AT&T, the dividend went up to 25 cents. The same with frequent flier miles. As long as I never used another airline on a route serviced by American, I'd earn two miles for each mile flown. The same with E-Trade, Nike, and Coke. It was easy enough, at first, because my Visa card[66] was programmed not to pay for Pepsi or Reebok. I couldn't make a mistake if I wanted to.

When the second and third networks were launched, the incentives program got a bit stickier. Most of my Queens friends had joined the People's Network while Alec and my M&L associates chose the Deluxe Group, and my family had elected not to join a network at all. As the networks all grew in size and struggled for competitive advantage, they began to dis-incentivize mingling.

It was easy enough to order Coke while my friends ordered Snapple, or to fly to a funeral on American and then meet up with my family flying United[67]. But when they tied in institutions like HMO's[68], private schools, and political parties, the consumer space became a war zone. It got so you weren't allowed to watch a movie distributed by an enemy studio, or, worse, apply for a job in a non-affiliated company. Phone calls to people in competing networks cost triple.

When I finally decided to change networks, it was too late. My agreement stated that the only way to opt out within in the first ten years was to pay back all the dividends I had received—in cash. Since I'd already earned and spent over $50,000 in dividends, this was not an option.

Luckily, a black market arose to provide people with aliases they could use to make unauthorized transactions. It gave me the ability to spend time with my family at events that were not affiliated with the Prime Network, and to go out to unregistered clubs with my friends. Everybody was doing it, and the infraction was practically unenforceable.

When the networks caught wind of how much revenue was leaking out of the system through illegal transactions, they began a nationwide crackdown. Because the Commerce Department and other potential enforcement

66. Credit cards were ways of incurring debt.   —Sabina Samuels

64b. In the early 21st century, citizens had to carry around large amounts of information on small data encoded cards. Credit cards were used to make payment for goods and services, presumably after cash & precious metals became devalued. In addition to a card for purchases, they also needed to carry personal identification, and something called a "preferred customer" card that seems to have granted the user a small discount at stores in exchange for allowing the company to track their buying preferences. In addition, most people carried small metal objects that would allow them to gain access to their homes, offices & vehicles. All of this started to become obsolete in 2015, when mass data chip implanting made it possible to consolidate all of these functions onto a small chip implanted in the wrist. While people were initially resistant, they were convinced by the relatively small discounts on products they were given.
                    —FLYINGEAR

67. An airline that went out of business after losing a class action suit in which it was sued by its customers and flight attendants for reducing the amount of breathable oxygen onboard below legal limits.   —Sabina Samuels

68. A profit-driven medical insurance scheme where computers were used to deny necessary health services to paying subscribers. Amazingly, widespread dissatisfaction with Health Management Organizations was used to dissuade Americans from endorsing a state-administrated national health plan.
                    —Sabina Samuels

agencies had been scaled down to a token role, the networks initiated their own compliance policies. Violators, once discovered and captured, were stripped of all benefits and forced to work off their penalties in forced labor at an affiliate company.

Although the resistance movement had grown in strength and numbers, so, too, did an incentivized force of network vigilantes. Anyone who successfully exposed a neighbor using an illegal alias was rewarded with $10,000 in credits. It made violations tricky, but not impossible, as many smaller shops still welcomed non-network business because it could be kept off the books. Not that taxation was a problem anymore, but many local merchants were being driven out of business for their inability to keep up with mandatory network commissions on sales of their products.

I had learned not to use any of my aliases except in emergencies, but this, I figured, was an exception. Carla said she was allergic to latex condoms[69], so I needed to buy the organic rubbers, made by a People's Network affiliate. Besides, I had bought small items at this corner bodega before, uneventfully. I could have more easily shoplifted the three-pack than initiate an aliased transaction, but I didn't want to steal. That was a real law, listed in the Bible right next to murder.

I checked around the store before taking action. An old lady was reading magazines, and Jude was choosing a diet cola. The coast was clear, so I pulled out my cash and counterfeit network alias. Who'd have thought my best friend would turn me in?

Jude must have surreptitiously flipped the panic button on his digital pager, sending an alarm to the nearest Prime Network enforcement vehicle. The metal grill on the store entrance began to descend and a strobe light flashed over the door. As I dove under the falling spiked grate, I looked back and saw Jude's face. He was gritting his teeth and pointing at me in an angry,

69. A form of birth control—basically a rubber glove for the penis—that also prevented the transmission of disease. Although originally made of lamb intestine, by the mid-20th century most condoms were composed of rubber, which was in turn replaced by latex and synthetic polymers. As one might guess, condoms greatly reduced sensitivity, and many wearers were reduced to ingesting prescription medications to maintain erections sufficient for coitus.
—Sabina Samuels

accusatory gesture, as if to say *how could you?*

How could *I*? I thought as I dashed down the cold, narrow streets. How could *he*! But there was no time to feel betrayed. The enforcement vehicle was in pursuit and closing. I reached into my pants to discard my wallet, along with its Visa Card transponder, but it was too late. The EV had already shot out one of its grappling cables, hitting the transponder dead-on and snaring my groin in the process.

The cable wrapped itself around my thigh like a snake, slowly raising me towards the machine's open jaws and the hundreds of tongue-like plastic tentacles within them. Each finger was stamped with a different corporate logo that attached itself to a different section of my pelvis and began to suck. They were sucking the life out of me. I knew if the EV completed its attack, I would no longer be human at all. I screamed in pain but no sound came out. As the tentacles sucked, they replaced my blood with a thick, white fluid. I felt an immense pressure in my groin, expanding me against my will until a fearsome hard-on burst through my pants.

That's when I realized I was dreaming—and whose head it really was bobbing up and down between my legs. Carla. I must have dozed off just minutes after I came. Now she was sucking on my cock in the hopes of one more ride before dawn.

The pot[70]. We smoked some pot, right? That must be it.

'Mmm,' she moaned, in the manner one learns from a porn film. 'Mmmm,' she repeated, deeper this time, as she lifted her head, looked into my eyes and licked her lips.

I rolled my head back, both to hide my horror and to simulate passion. Before I knew it, she was straddling me again, her eyes closed, in her own world.

That's okay. I was in mine. Trying to piece together the evening that led

70. A nickname for cannibis, which was illegal at the time. Inconsistencies in drug laws of the period—both alcohol and tobacco[a] were legal—have yet to be fully explained.   —Sabina Samuels

a. tobacco. Also known as "soft-weed," the farming of this dried leaf transformed the economy and the society of the American continent. Addiction to smoking its dried leaves contributed to millions of deaths, which curiously seemed to add to its appeal. (See Robert Klein, "Cigarettes Are Sublime," circa 1990s.) After the legalization of marijuana in the early 2000s, tobacco farming was phased out within a decade.

Scientists today have re-created this long-extinct plant from genetic samples retrieved from an unopened pack of "Newports" (a brand of cigarette laced with chemicals meant to offset the generally toxic flavor and odor), cured it in the fashion of the times, and tested its effects on medical-simulator bots. The bots and the control group were separated socially from each other, and while the control group, acting on its self-defense system, began to erect physical barriers between them and the offensive tobacco-bots, the tobacco-bots continued drenching their circuitry in smoke from the leaf, which apparently overrides any of the programmed urges toward social acceptance, defense from poison, or aversion to bad odors. You can still see a tobacco plant today at the Universal Museum of Mortal Mistakes, Station B6.   —ADAVEEN

to this. Counting the drinks that went down between seeing Carla the first time and then again at the coat check, when her hand was in my pocket, brushing her fingers against my erection[71]. How did it get there, again? Something about counting the business cards I'd collected?

We had talked for a while, flirted a bit, and then split up to cover more ground. I met up with Jude again, downed what must have been two more gin and tonics, and got introduced to another succession of tech salesmen. Everyone had some new way to maximize future ROI, minimize risk, extend market share, or narrow the competitive landscape.

Then Alec was trying to tell me something. We were off in a corner while the shmooze-fest reached a crescendo. He was saying something about school, about how he almost drowned, but he was slurring his words. And the room had started to spin a little bit. Then a little bit more.

I could only make out isolated words in people's conversations. Network externalities. Stickiness. Server farms. Vested options. Options vesting. That's when it started to happen. I saw Ty across the room, his mouth moving a mile a minute, 'confidentially' disclosing his company's meta-incubator scheme, no doubt. And Karl, off to another side, excitedly reading the notes he had scrawled in his palm device to some of his associates. Their mouths were watering, and they were slapping one another on the back.

The frenetic, well-dressed crowd had become a single, multi-headed organism. I could see it reflected overhead in the mylar sheets. We were a herd of some kind, stampeding in place. Each giant mouth shouting something different, between the heavy thumping bass of the disco music that pounded all around us. It sounded like the women were screaming, and the men were chanting a tribal war cry.

Alec looked up at me. Was he concerned, or still relating part of his college story? I couldn't tell. I didn't care. I just wanted out, and Carla's return

71. Despite the implication to the contrary, penises were not yet at this time detachable. The narrator's erection is not in his pocket, but rather locked in standard position next to his pocket. Today, of course, it would be considered the height of bad form to attend a professional gathering with one's penis attached.
—SHANKEL

was the best excuse I could find. She nestled against me in that non-commital, interpret-it-how-you-will way of hers, and I decided to do just that. Interpret it how I will.

I leaned into her and planted an unnecessarily sloppy kiss on her mouth. (I could always pass it off later as drunkenness, which was the best thing about being drunk.) And just as I took that bold step, I sensed the room getting stiller around me. The cacophony of voices left my head, and returned to the confines of their own conversations. I had either silenced the game, or jumped too far inside to hear it, anymore.

We went to get our coats, saying a polite 'goodbye' to Alec, who just stood there, looking forlorn. I tried to throw him a glance—that we would talk tomorrow. But Alec just made a half-hearted thumbs-up sign—that 'go for it, dude' college party gesture that we'd give each other at the Eaves House when one of us managed to lure a drunken frosh-girl up the stairs.

I tried to pull off the cut-in-line strategy that Alec had used earlier, but succeeded only in getting myself shoved against a wall by a pair of angry Dutch cell phone designers. 'Who do you think you are, eh?' they practically spit in my face.

Carla rescued me, more thrilled by my attempt to impress her than dismayed by my ineptitude. She smiled at me as if she were a little girl, and stood very close, nuzzling her cheek against my neck.

I was in over my head. Hoping to make the whole situation go away, I began to talk about business. Maybe my subservience would be a turn-off. I respectfully reported how well I talked up the company and how many people I'd met. That's when she started digging through my pocket for the business cards, and once my dick got hard there was no turning back.

Nevertheless, my strategic descent into an employee-boss power differential set the tone for the rest of the evening. Not that Carla would have had it any other way. Even as she mounted me, I felt more like a hired gun than a future boyfriend. She seemed to take what she wanted from me in the way Alec took cocktails off a waitress's tray—as if the human waitress were merely an extension of the tray itself, providing locomotion, like wheels. That's how she treated the parts of me that weren't directly in contact with her erogenous zones. The vulnerable side of Carla that I had seen earlier was gone. She was all business, now, which, on the plus side, meant she knew exactly what she wanted.

And she was beautiful, in her way. A little heavier with her clothes off than I had imagined, and her breasts hung down low over her abdomen. But this is what a real woman looked like. Not some pert child, but a woman in her mid-thirties who made up for anything that sagged with an unashamed determination to do whatever was necessary to get herself off.[72]

I was thankful for that much, because maintaining my erection now was about all I could manage. I knew I wasn't going to come again—not with my mind wandering every which way—but if I could stay up long enough for her to finish, we'd go to sleep and I could wait until morning to figure out how this night was going to impact the rest of my life.

Morning did break. I lay on my stomach as the sun woke me, streaming through the plate glass windows on the other side of Carla's long, loft-like apartment. I turned my head away from the light and closed my eyes. The pillowcase was soft against my face. The sheets were made of a thick, dense fabric. Like those napkins from the restaurant in the Plaza Hotel. I stretched out to soak in their sturdy softness against my naked skin. It was a sensation I'd never experienced before, except maybe that week at the Morehouse compound. Where did these people get such sheets? I felt like I was being swaddled in a Brooks Brothers shirt.

That's right. I was naked in Carla's fluffy soft bed. Somehow the night-

72. At the time, it was believed that women were more difficult to arouse to the level of orgasm than men. As a result of this self-perpetuating fallacy, a female's satisfaction threshold was put at a premium.   —Sabina Samuels

mare of the previous evening had faded. Now I felt oddly childlike and free. I turned my face back toward the light and cracked my eyes just wide enough to make out Carla sitting at her breakfast table, smoking a cigarette, drinking a coffee, and reading the sections of Sunday's paper that got delivered on Saturday. She looked so able and educated with her glasses on and her legs crossed as she turned the broadsheet page, careful not to get ink on her hands[73]. I just lay there in the bed—a boy-toy resting in my mistress's chambers, ready to do her bidding. It was refreshing. No decisions to make, no responsibility for steering anything. Just respond.

As I stared at my previous evening's sex partner, I wondered just what we were going to be to one another. Were we falling in love? Would we present ourselves as a couple from now on? How would my parents respond to the fact that she's not Jewish? What kind of mother would Carla be? Could I get out of my lease in order to move in with her? Or was this just a one-night stand with a woman who just happened to work in the same place as me— something we'd shrug off as a drunken coincidence, like two molecules in a beaker of water that just happened to collide when the heat was turned up?

Oddly, I found myself hoping not. This was my world, now, and pairing up with a woman like Carla made sense. I'd be good for her, too, mellowing her more frazzled edges, and backing up her instincts for business with some real vision of the techno-future. We'd be unstoppable. Winners. I had a job and girlfriend, now, all thanks to Alec. Then why was I having such awful dreams?

I rolled out of bed and stood there a moment, regarding my naked image in Carla's antique full-length mirror. My arms looked strong from their work-out the night before, especially with Carla's nail scratches streaked across them, and my cock was still at nearly half-mast from residual morning hard-on. I decided to approach Carla in confident nudity. I walked through

73. Newspapers of the period were printed on large sheets (a legacy from an earlier era when periodicals were taxed by the page) and with toxic ink that transferred easily onto the reader's hands.
—Sabina Samuels

47

the open archway into the large main room and stood before her at the table. She was engrossed in the Arts section. I picked up her coffee mug and took a sip.

'Hey,' she said, taking back the mug and wiping its lip with her sleeve. 'Get your own.'

Fine. I accepted her little challenge, went behind her and put my hands on her shoulders. A morning blow-job was still within the realm of possibility. I gently massaged her neck.

'What're you doing?' she asked, shrugging her shoulders up.

'You're tense.'

'I like it that way,' she said. 'Tense.'

I gave up, and went to the coffeemaker to pour a cup.

'Where do you keep those mugs?'

She finally looked up to see me standing there, nude in her kitchen.

'Look, Jamie.' She used a measured cadence. 'I can't play today, I have a lot to do.'

'That's cool.' I was surprised at how much this hurt. 'I have to meet with the contractor at my new place before noon.'

'Good, then. We won't have time for an uncomfortable brunch.'

'Don't say that.' I was sure she had assumed the worst. That I didn't really care about her, that she was too old for me, that we'd made a drunken mistake, or that I was only trying to sleep my way to the top. I wanted to counter that impression. 'I think I could really fall for you, you know?'

'That's why it would be uncomfortable, Cohen,' she said, picking up her coffee, paper, and ashtray, and heading out towards the terrace. 'The mugs are over the sink. Towel's on a rack in the shower. Wipe up the floor with it when you're done, and leave it in the hamper.'

I passed on both coffee and shower, got dressed, and then stood in the

74. No one was ready to admit that global warming had reached a critical stage, even though the polar ice caps had melted into lakes. Many journalists off-handedly referred to their personal, sneaking suspicions that the run of record temperatures, floods, and environmental disasters may have indicated a pattern worth addressing. But OPEC—a cartel of Arab-speaking nations with no actual genetic or racial commonality, who allied for economic leverage—was keeping oil prices artificially steady, and the numbers at the gas pump were this society's only means of gauging climactic crisis.
—Sabina Samuels

75. A chain of apparel stores, originally known for their inexpensive blue jeans, which became the supplier of inoffensive clothes for working technology professionals. Their children's line was quite popular with the upper middle class, who tended to use their children as exhibits for their own lifestyle commitments. Such children were called "designer babies." See Daryl Pritchard's "The Joys of Autonomous Consumption." New York: Signifier Press, 2011. —Sabina Samuels

notes continue on page 49

middle of the well-appointed space, unsure of what to do next. I went back to the terrace to say good-bye, but Carla must have heard me coming. She waved 'toodle-loo' without looking up from her paper.

'See you Monday,' I said casually, in spite of the anger I felt welling up. I turned away from her and left what now seemed like the scene of a crime in which I had been the unwitting victim.

Fine with me. I strode out through the lobby, winking at the doorman as if we were comrades allied against the ruling class. I threw him my best 'I fucked a wealthy tenant' smirk before stepping out into the sunny street.

It was a mild, if windy, March morning. Winters weren't what the used to be,[74] and kids were still playing outside in their shorts. I made my way around the perimeter of Gramercy Park. A couple with two small Baby GAP[75] children were letting themselves in through the iron gate and locking it behind them. Carla probably had a key to the private garden, too. The bitch.

And I had actually fantasized about moving in with her! What did I need with this snooty bullshit neighborhood? I was moving to the newest, most authentic, and genuinely coolest section of town: Awbry, a recently renamed corner of the Lower East Side just above the Williamsburg Bridge.

Artists, Puerto Ricans, punks and ravers, all living in the same tenements that my Jewish ancestors inhabited a hundred years before. Now the *New York Times* Real Estate section, in deference to the agents who advertised on its pages, was supporting their claim that Awbry was the 'next hot district.' In the process, they made it so. I had scored a two-bedroom in a painstakingly restored landmark building, a structure that was once the second-oldest synagogue in Manhattan.

The Sanctuary, as the new condominium[76] was called, was developed with the swelling population of second-wave hi-tech millionaires in mind.

75b. Pedisartorialist Barbra Blaquechippe offers this comment in her study, Mini-Mes: Toddlers As Jewelry (2015): "Ostentatious childless women of ten or fifteen years ago would signify the attention to absurd aesthetic detail that is the hallmark of privilege by decorating a dog, genetically engineered to be small and defenseless and to shake uncontrollably, with expensive sweaters and other parodies of human clothing, in which the dapper dog could then urinate happily upon full-grown human beings who had neither indigenous fur nor well-constructed wardrobes, let alone secure and permanent habitat. Young couples with children traditionally transferred this role to their offspring. The windows of a popular toddler clothing store in the United States, Baby GAP, are an ominous example. The name derives from the image the average passer-by confronted: brightly colored, sturdily-constructed, toddler-sized clothes, complete with caps and shoes, jumping, playing, all in the shapes of children, so that at first glance they appeared in fact to be children, although where there ought to have been a baby, there was in fact a gap. Clothing was given the appearance of containing invisible children through the clever use of wires, thereby representing a fantasy of parenthood that is all wardrobe and no actual messy, excreting, jumping, bleeding, wailing baby." —ADAVEEN

76. Nickname for an apartment building, referring to the level of indiscriminate sexual activity that took place therein, requiring the use of condoms. —RAYGIRVAN

The entire building was outfitted with state-of-the-art multiplex networking capability, Dolby surround speaker enclosures in the walls and ceiling of every room, saunas, Jacuzzis, and a choice of five standard decorating schemes: Colonial, Cosmopolitan, '50s Retro, Tokyo Modern, and Ralph Lauren[77].

The appliances, communications, and ambient preferences of each unit were controlled from a central console attached to a mini-super-computer housed in one of the walk-in closets. The console was responsible for coordinating everything from the web-accessible security monitors and house-plant irrigation system to the revolving collection of liquid crystal display art works—high definition video reproductions of original master paintings, rented on a time-share basis through the Microsoft Louvre. Face recognition software and a biometric fingerprint system eliminated the need for clumsy key rings, while at least a half-dozen armed guards patrolled the lobby and corridors for that added sense of safety while going to and from the gym, spa, or heated rooftop pool. The architects were at pains to invent new ways for the rich to spend their money, and consulted psychologists specializing in what was called RWS, or 'recent wealth syndrome,' to develop The Sanctuary's many conveniences. All this, starting at just $2.5 million for a studio.

As I strolled through what would in two days be my new 'hood, I wondered how long it would take for the rest of these dilapidated streets to take part in the urban revival. Amazingly, the residents didn't seem to want things to get better. Over a thousand protestors showed up the day that the developers broke ground on The Sanctuary. Why were these people resisting what could only be seen as a cash cow for their neighborhood? A building like this only improved everyone's property values. *Time* magazine said the activists were mostly artists and squatters, people living off their parents

77. aka: Ralph Lipshitz, a fashion and housewares designer originally from New York City, best known for popularizing the 'River Runs Through It' aesthetic. The underlying mythological promise of Lauren's aesthetic was that transplanted Eastern Europeans could use clothing and plastic surgery to experience themselves as if they were late nineteenth century cowboys of Anglican origins.
—Sabina Samuels

money or on the dole, protesting for a myriad of diverse and poorly articulated rationales having to do with cultural diversity and the threat of global capitalism. In the end, they were probably just looking to keep their own sweet deals in force through the few remaining rent control laws.

And if they were just families afraid of getting priced out of their own neighborhoods, well, that would be a shame. But who could reasonably object to the urban renewal that had been sweeping New York City off and on since the 1990's? This was a safer and more convenient city for almost everyone who lived here, I assured myself. People who don't like it can move to the outer boroughs. Maybe I was suffering from the early symptoms of RWS, myself.

Just two blocks from The Sanctuary, I saw a long line of street people pushing old shopping carts and dollies filled with junk. It reminded me of the old days, when the homeless would collect cans and bottles for recycling and line up outside grocery stores for the redemption money.

I followed the line to where it led: the garage of a Sanitation Department sub-station. Five uniformed city workers sat at computer terminals, as homeless people described the goods in their carts.

'What are they doing?' I asked an old woman holding two large bags of clothes.

'E-Swap,'[78] she explained. 'You list your stuff and come back on Monday to find out who bought it.'

See? Everyone was on the bandwagon. They were all in on the game. The bigger I could make this thing, the better everyone would do. There was no downside.

'So this is an improvement for you, then?' I asked, hopefully. 'You can make a living this way?'

'It beats giving head[79]!' she cackled, exposing a mouth devoid of teeth.

78. A subsidiary of a popular online auction site called Ebay. The parent company catered to the obsessive collector, while this off-shoot popularized the concept of second-tier consumption. Although the recycling of used merchandise actually decreased GNP, it was seen as a way of rehabilitating those who had proved resistant to market ethos.
—Sabina Samuels

79. Because organ sales and auctions were not yet legal in most parts of the world, they were largely confined to black markets, with parts supplied primarily by homeless persons. Scholars speculate that "giving head" may have been a slang term for the sale of eyes, ears, noses, or, as in this case, teeth. —MRNORMATIVE

Several young men and one woman, all wearing orange caps, walked up and down the line of homeless, handing out fliers and speaking enthusiastically about a new employment opportunity working for a 'last mile' networked delivery service. They were met with indifferent shrugs. The leafleters remained unfazed, and hawked their job offers to the last unemployed people left in town.

Even the 'have-nots' had options, or so I told myself. No matter how many people the Networking Revolution left behind, it was creating new opportunities for them at the same time. But one of the homeless, a large black man wearing a pink comforter, was unconvinced.

'What's the problem?' he asked the leafleters in a voice somewhere between sarcasm and outright hostility. 'Ran out of slaves to bring the rich people their stuff?'

'By joining Last Mile,' the young woman countered with a broad grin, 'you'll get to *be* one of the rich! We're giving options in the company to every employee, whatever their role in the fulfillment cycle[80].'

'Yeah, well, fulfill *this*,' the man said, raising his middle finger. He began to shout for his fellow homeless to take notice. 'You hear this, people?'

I inconspicuously edged away from the awakening mob. Apparently not everyone wanted a stake in the Internet's future.

'They don't want us selling stuff no more,' another man joined the first. 'They want us *carrying* it!'

'No no,' the young woman pleaded with them. 'This is your opportunity. Don't you see? I came up as a messenger, myself.'

'And look at you now, missy,' the old lady shouted. 'Pitching scams to the likes of *us*!'

'You're not getting us off this line,' another homeless man entered the fray. 'I've been waiting here since eight o'clock.'

80. This term derives from a 1990's dialect developed by corporate public relations people. It constantly changed, as one term became popular another fell into obscurity. The entire premise revolved around finding new ways to make unpleasant circumstances seem more favorable by describing ideas with more flattering terminology. —JEFFRINE1

'I'm only trying to help you get somewhere better,' the exasperated girl explained through tears. She and the other leafleters backed into one another as the crowd gradually closed in around them.

'We've heard that before,' the black man said, spitting with every syllable. 'We've got our stake, lady. We're organized. We've got angel investors interested. We're e-commerce merchants, got that? Commerce, not pack animals.' He began to chant the awkward phrase as if it were a protest slogan, and the others soon joined in.

'Commerce, not pack animals! Commerce, not pack animals!' Sanitation employees spilled out of the building to pull down the giant galvanized steel garage door against the tumult.

These people weren't fighting against e-commerce at all. They were afraid of losing their stake! But if not them, who *would* serve as the delivery people for all this stuff? Then I became concerned with my own safety. I was still in my Hugo Boss suit from the night before, and didn't want to be mistaken for, well, for who I was, so I made a hasty retreat around the corner towards the structure I would soon be calling home.

Sanctuary. The shouts of the angry crowd faded as the automatic doors whooshed closed behind me. Two young valets who could have passed for models greeted me with nods. One escorted me to the elevator and pressed the button. The young man stood patiently beside me in his brown, collarless tunic as I waited for a car.

'They're still a bit slow, sir,' he said, gently brushing a wisp of his long black hair up behind one of his ears. 'We're working on the program.' He probably went to clubs in Brooklyn I'd never even heard of.

'Thanks,' I said. 'I'll be fine. You don't have to wait here with me.'

'No problem at all, sir.'

Did this guy want a tip, or what? It was so strange to have an entire human being at my service like this. And one so much cooler and better-looking than me. I wondered how he felt about behaving so subserviently to someone his own age.

'Your architect is in your unit, now, Mr. Cohen.'

'Thanks,' I said, entering the elevator. 'But how did you know my name?'

'It came up on the console when you were scanned. But everyone will recognize you after a few days.'

I put my hand on a glass scanning tray, which told the elevator where to take me. Six. It wasn't in the exclusive tower addition, which held only one unit per floor, but down in the original building. This gave my unit a certain historical cachet that the modern, twenty-two-story rooftop extension lacked. I got out and went to the right—the West unit, slightly more expensive than the East because it had sunset views.

The door was open. I liked the sound of my shoes against the lacquered, hardwood floors[81]. My apartment was done in the Tokyo Modern theme, chosen by the original owner. Apparently, he abandoned his mortgage before he even moved in, because his IPO had been canceled. It's what allowed M&L to take possession of the apartment and give it to me for only $12,000 a month, debited directly from my salary for tax purposes. This was more than a third of my gross income, but many people these days were spending over half of what they made on rent, and I was already anticipating ample bonuses.

The architect stood in the kitchen area, a large blueprint unfurled before her on the slate countertop. She was a tall Asian woman, about forty, wearing a pastel, 1970's-style printed pant-suit.

'Looks like everything is in order,' she said, shaking my hand through the large galley window.

'Sure does.' I raised my arms wide, so she'd know I wasn't taking this lux-

81. Despite what some scholars have asserted, this casual, almost boastful reference to the use of natural tree fiber in his home is not evidence that the narrator is a sociopath. Horrifying as it may sound, natural hardwood floors were quite commonplace at the time.

The practice of using lumber in building construction continued well into the 22nd century. At the time this was being written, trees were still relatively plentiful and durable synthetic substitutes were expensive.

As natural wood became more scarce in subsequent years, it became a status symbol, a luxury that only the ultra-rich could afford. It was only when the true impact of deforestation became apparent that the use of natural wood fell out of favor.

Today, of course, bragging that one's floors are made of wood would be like bragging that they are made of human bone (see "Ivory," "Bear Skin Rug"), but we must not judge the narrator's attitude by our modern standards of decency.
—SHANKEL

ury for granted. 'It's absolutely gorgeous.' I didn't even presume to think I'd be able to afford a place like this once my days at M&L were over. But it was fun for the moment.

'The windows are self-tinting,' she explained as she made her way out of the kitchen and into the sunken living room. Two huge glass walls formed the room's corner, which looked out over Nolita—one of the *New York Times*' previously 'new' neighborhoods. The effect was of being on a precipice. 'But you can bypass them from here if you want full sun, without sacrificing any privacy.'

She flicked a small switch next to the windows, changing them from gray tint to clear.

'Wow.' I stroked one of the low cushions embedded into the living room's steps. 'And the couches are just great.'

'Yes,' she said. 'I think you were right about the fabric. It's very success-ful.' She was referring to my solitary disagreement with her last week—a diversion from the standard white upholstery to an easier-to-keep-clean avo-cado. 'It's not strictly authentic to the aesthetic, of course, but it does add a bit of warmth. It's less severe, if a little less striking.'

'This place is plenty striking.' I fell into an involuntary 'aw-shucks' dialect. 'Just beautiful. They've really got their act together here. I'm sure glad my company was able to get me in the back door.' I wanted to make sure she knew I was foreign to this world. 'I mean, most of the people who live here must be pretty well off.'

'I'm glad it's to your liking,' she said, not giving an inch[82]. Clearly, she was more comfortable treating me as a client than a human being, but I was still compelled to convince her that I was from a working professional class, like herself.

'I mean, those people in the tower,' I went on. 'God knows what kinds of

82. one inch = approx. 2.54 cm
—SHANKEL

zillionaires are up in there.'

'My husband and I are on seventeen,' she said plainly. So much for smoothing class differentials. This broad was far richer than me. Now I had to tack back the other way.

'I bet you've done a beautiful job with it. I'd love to see it, sometime.' We were neighbors, after all.

'Yes,' she said formally. 'I'll have to check our calendar.'

'Cool.' Cool?

'I left the manual on the dining room table,' she said, rolling up her plans and slipping them into an aluminum tube. 'It should explain all the security features, how to program the irrigation, lights, entertainment, and sauna.'

'Thanks. I'll read a chapter a night.'

No response. Hadn't I learned not to joke with this woman?

'You can always call downstairs for help,' she said. 'If any of it is too confusing for you.'

'I'm in the industry,' I defended my intelligence. 'Technology.'

'Well then,' she said, leaving through the open door. 'I don't see why you'd have any trouble. Good-bye.'

I waited until she had passed out of sight before turning back into the apartment. I wanted to enter fresh, without the taint of that encounter.

It was marvelous. What would my parents think of it? Too expensive, that's what they'd think. A waste. But Uncle Morris might get a kick out of it, especially the way it towered over the old neighborhood. A former study hall for Yeshiva students, now housing a third-generation American Jewish business hero.

Is that the role I was playing? A business hero? What was it I did for a living? What did I provide? Capital? Not my own, that's for sure. But I'd be helping worthy enterprises get the capital they needed to survive and grow.

I was a filter. A judge. Better, a spotlight shining on pursuits that deserved attention. I could direct the future by recommending where the energy of the present should be invested. Moreover, I was responsible for generating the kind of sustained enthusiasm for new technology that would prevent another market crash—I mean, "correction." Nobody was supposed to call it a crash. It wasn't. Just a temporary lapse of faith.

Thinking about work made it easier for me to justify the sickeningly luxurious accommodations society had seen fit to bestow upon me. I went to the second bedroom, for which I had elected the home-office package complete with an automatically calculated tax-deduction. Most people who had chosen the office were doing so just for the exemption, and would be secretly remodeling it as a second bedroom. But not me, I told myself proudly as I surveyed the built-in cherry wood bookcases. I would be working in it for real whenever I wasn't at the office. In fact, I deserved all this more than anyone else in the building.

Who was I kidding?

I leapt into the air and flopped down onto the bed.

'This is fucking great,' I said out loud. I had scored—big time. And I was gonna suck every last drop out of these people before they realized I had no idea what I was doing.

Then I heard a voice calling to me. 'Halloo? Anybody in there?'

'Hello?' Had I done something wrong, already?

In the doorway stood a small, balding, middle-aged man in a bright, multi-colored sweater.

'G'day,' he said, smiling broadly. 'The door was open. Wanted to make sure nothing was wrong.'

'Like anything could go wrong in this place?'

'You got a point there, mate,' he said, holding out his hand. 'Theo Miles.

57

I live next door. 6E.'

'Jamie Cohen. I'm moving in the day after tomorrow.'

'You went with the Tokyo Modern, eh?' Theo said. He had an Australian accent. 'Internet?'

'All the units have networking.'

He laughed. 'I mean *you*! You're in the industry, right? They all went with Tokyo Modern.'

'Yeah. But the style was set before I got it.'

'Never mind that. It's nothing to be ashamed of.'

'Want to come in and see it?'

'No, I've seen the one downstairs,' he said. 'And the one two below that.'

'You mean they're all…?'

'Yip. Tokyo Modern was a popular choice.'

'But did anyone else choose avocado cushions?' I raised my eyebrows in jest.

'Why, no, Jamie,' he smiled. 'You're a renegade, at that. Walking to the beat of a different drummer.'

We laughed together. He saw through it all, too. A fellow player.

'Come on and see Ralph Lauren,' he said, gesturing towards his apartment.

'You're sure now is a good time?'

'Come on!' He darted back down the hall.

I followed him into the apartment, a mirror image of mine, but with country tiles in place of the lacquered floor, white panes in the windows, and big fluffy couches in the sunken living room.

'Kinda scary, huh?' Theo nudged me in the ribs.

'I guess.' I spotted something of interest on the faux-antique[83] wood table. A loose-leaf notebook with the words 'MyDoor.com Strategy' printed

83. The practice of artificially aging something, usually deceitfully. This stopped in 2017 when the advent of personal age scanners allowed people to accurately determine age.   —JACOBACOV

on the cover. 'Is that yours?'

'You mean my company or my notebook?' Theo asked.

'Either. Both.' I wasn't used to riddling Aussie trolls.

'Both, then,' he said. 'The notebook is from Staples. Seven forty-nine. The company, MyDoor.com, just completed second-round financing of twenty million dollars.'

I was amazed by the coincidence. 'It's that thing where you open your door over the web, right?' It felt good to be so plugged in.

'No, no,' Theo corrected me. 'That's MyDoorman.com. We're MyDoor.com. Completely different technology.'

'Really?' I hid my disbelief in what I imagined was a cloned business plan. 'How?'

'Do I need to make you sign a non-disclosure?'

'We're neighbors, Theo. And I'm not in this business to fuck people around. Who knows? Maybe M&L will be interested.' I wasn't about to tell him that M&L was already backing the competition.

'Well, basically,' Theo said, taking a breath to explain what he had probably had to explain a thousand times before. 'Like you say, MyDoorman.com is entirely web based. You connect a camera to your computer, then access it remotely over the web. MyDoor.com is next generation. It's wireless. The camera and microphone we supply comes with a built-in wireless modem. No need for a home computer at all.'

'But you still need to be online at work…'

'Not at all. MyDoor will call your wristphone, palm video, anything at all, with sound, or picture, or both.'

'Damn.'

'And it's free.'

'Where does the revenue come from, if you don't mind me asking?'

84. Dynamic Market Psychology, or DMP, was a metric initiated by the Dow Jones after the correction of 2001. It was hoped that self-imposed restrictions on unsubstantiated cynicism, particularly in the media, would maintain a more bullish market sentiment. —Sabina Samuels

"ROI?"

"I know. It's a dirty word."

"Three dirty words, actually."

Questioning a technology businessman about cash flow was about as impolite as interrogating someone about the consistency of his bowel movements. And it went against the new principles of dynamic market psychology[84], a shared emotional metric of which we were all components.

'You're bold. I like that.' Theo approved. 'We'll be selling the logs back to electronic polling and compliance companies. It's a B to B model, really. They're paying a lot to learn how people make their security decisions. What factors lead humans to trust.'

'That's smart,' I said, while I mulled over whether it really was. 'Do you have the technology up and running?'

'Well now,' Theo hemmed. I'd stepped beyond the bounds of propriety. 'That's not really the point, is it?'

'No, I suppose not.'

The point was, Theo had come up with a story that would make Carla's obsolete. And I was just about pissed off enough to fuck her for real.

85. Streetfighter 2 was an early two-player fighting game. Many megabytes of RAM have been spent trying to explain why early computer entertainments were dedicated almost completely to combat scenarios.[a] Most analysts have concluded that it was a result of the technology's first implementation as a military training tool. Still, this does little to explain the popularity of violent play in this era. It

notes continue on page 61

3. Goyim Naches

may have its roots in the society's undiagnosed glucose addiction.

—Sabina Samuels

a. combat scenarios: For the class of people who could afford to buy the equipment necessary to play these games, daily life was generally absent of violent struggle. For the class of people whose living allotment was lower, gunplay, fistfights, and other relics of life on the savannah were more common.

The casual student of this era might assume that simulations of combat would be more useful as training for individuals likely to see physical combat in life, but the act of pushing a button on a keypad to make "superman" characters (impossibly muscled, attractive, and flamboyantly dressed) attack other similar characters bore little resemblance to the techniques and the skills required to survive in actual combat. (See also "Violent Films" esp. "Kung Fu Films," and "Painted Wrestling Man" in the Universal Museum Encyclopedia.)

Therefore, it was the perfect pastime for children, "office workers," and other powerless individuals to admire the aesthetics of combat as a sort of improvised dance, to simulate achievement by scoring high points and unlocking secret game modes, and to generally substitute for tangible achievement and status in life, which in reality were only allocated to an elite few. For a while, this substitute prevented any collective revolutionary effort by the disenfranchised by isolating players in their homes, their limbs and vision weakened, their social skills atrophied. But, as game hardware became more sophisticated and networked, "button mashers" met, exchanged ideas, and fomented the GameBoy Coup of 2010 that hijacked the communications systems of almost all the governments of the few technologically advanced countries.

—ADAVEEN

You'd think that living at home those first couple of weeks would have given me misgivings about my business schemes, but somehow it led me to even greater resolve. Spending my evenings in Queens made me feel essentially uncorrupted by the reality of what I was doing back in the city. As if the East River kept me a safe distance from the consequences of my actions in the game. Plus, my dad's constant stream of sanctimonious critique made the whole idea of keeping a moral compass seem silly. Didn't he know this was merely the way men with money entertained themselves?

Sitting in my old bedroom that Saturday night executing Streetfighter 2^{85} special moves against my 14-year-old cousin Benjamin, I felt more like a recent bar-mitzvah boy, myself, than the cunning technology analyst I played by day. We were huddled together in front of an ancient VGA monitor, the intimacy of our bodies and warmth of our laughter betraying the violence occurring between our on-screen avatars.

Benjamin manipulated Dhalism, the lithe Hindu martial artist, as if he had grown up playing this 1980's classic arcade game. He miraculously discovered the complex key combination to release his character's secret fireballs just moments into the second round, and I could do little more than freeze in a defensive crouch, waiting for a break in the onslaught to wage a counter-attack. By the time I found my opening, just a hairsbreadth of strength remained on my power gauge. I hurled Blanka—the monstrous green hulk who made up in brutality what he lacked in dexterity—against the skinny Asian. But I wasn't fast enough. A single, tiny, precision slap from Benji's bald guru wiped out Blanka's remaining strength, flinging his huge frame into the air. We watched as he fell to the ground in a primitive stop-frame slow-motion animation. The flat, antiquated graphics made my death all the more exhilarating.

I was still winning, four matches to two, but Benjamin was catching up. My mother was already calling us down for dinner, and I reached over to flick off the machine.

'Championship of the known universe?' Benjamin stopped me, hoping for a final match to wipe the win/loss record clean. Now that he had the moves down, he was dominating.

'Sure,' I relented. For once in my life, I didn't care about winning; I just wanted to play. And I was thrilled that a game from my own childhood could engage Benjamin, a 21st Century teenager. We weren't even using a Playstation 2[86] or broadband set-top box, but my old Mac, running an arcade emulator that the Kings and I compiled ourselves over a decade ago.

It's the only reason we discovered coding at all. We were sick of spending

86. The second in a series of a quickly obsolete video game consoles. The original PlayStation debuted in the mid-1990's, followed by "PS2" at the turn of the millennium. Due to fraudulent production shortages reported by its parent company, the now-defunct Sony Corporation, the demand for the PS2 was just short of fanatical. Consoles were sold on the World Wide Web at as much as 5 to 10 times the retail price. The popularity of the PlayStation consoles faded into oblivion by 2010, mainly due to the introduction of interactive holographic games. [Incidentally, Sony Corp. went bankrupt in 2014, when a corporate-sponsored concert reviving 1980's music turned violent. Numerous lawsuits followed.] —ISERCLE

our money buying game cartridges at ToysRUs or, worse, dropping streams of quarters into the arcade consoles at Star Pizza. Reuben, a math geek, taught us how to program, and together we struggled to develop our own game emulator—a simple piece of software that could serve as a platform for almost any video or arcade game. We each worked on a different section of code, one of us figuring out the graphics, another the sound, and so on, trading and compiling the pieces over the Internet until we had a complete and working version of a program we called 'Anygame.' Then, we'd download a bootleg version of the ROM code for any game, mount it on the emulator and play it on the PC for free. Or most of it, anyway.

For just as I managed to trap Dhalism in a headlock and gouge the Indian's forehead with Blanka's huge teeth, the entire image froze and then dissolved into a flurry of square pixels. Large blocks at first, then increasingly smaller ones until the screen filled with primary-colored snow. It had something to do with the way that the emulator bitmapped images to the monitor—a bug that El Greco could never quite fix. We watched in silence as the Sega-cum-Kandinsky swirled before us.

'Downstairs, now!' my dad's voice barked, spinning us both around. How long had his bearded face been at the door? He made a plaintive gesture with his upward hands before disappearing down the hall. Benjamin looked at me with wide eyes and giggled. I knew what he meant: had the rabbi magically crashed the game because it was violating Shabbat? The moratorium on electronic entertainment wasn't really over until dinner on Saturday night, after the Havdalah prayers had been recited.

I flipped off the switch and we raced one another out of the room, practically tumbling down the narrow carpeted stairs, adding a few more scuffs to the fifteen-year record of rough-housing chronicled on the faded walls.

'Walk like human beings!' my mother, Sophie, cried from the kitchen.

I trapped my little cousin in a real headlock and dragged him down the remaining steps. My mom was waiting for us at the bottom, her hands on her hips and her best scowl on her face.

'What?' I asked, as if I didn't know, while Benjamin struggled to free himself, kicking one foot against the war-torn wallpaper.

'Never mind, Yossi,' she said. My parents still used my Hebrew name instead of the one I gave myself in junior high. 'Go ahead and make the house a shambles. Let the Temple Sisterhood see for once how hard it is for a family to live on a Rabbi's salary.' That part was intended for my dad to hear.

Membership dues at the synagogue hadn't been raised in ten years. There was a time when a rabbi, or a rebbetzen for that matter, was held in high regard and compensated accordingly. Now people spurned anyone and anything that reminded them of a priority other than profit.[87]

But, my parents, Rabbi and Mrs. Cohen, were from the old school. To them, religion and, more specifically, Judaism were about a different bottom line altogether. While they weren't communists, exactly (my dad's parents did first meet at a socialist summer camp in the Catskills), they saw themselves as the last line of defense. Against what? They weren't quite sure. Still, they knew their commitment to the mitzvot, God's commandments, would keep them from succumbing to the madness of the crowd. Sophie and Samuel lived for the chance to hide an Anne Frank[88] in their attic—I remember overhearing them take perverse pleasure in imagining which area of our home could be turned into a secret hiding place, should the opportunity (God forbid) present itself.

As my mom retreated to the kitchen, I carried my squirming captive all the way to the dining room, where our fathers were engaged in their own form of fraternal combat[89].

87. Not that plenty of rabbis, reverends, and gurus hadn't been cashing in on the self-improvement craze with complex regimens for a brand of greed called 'self actualization.' Best-selling books all had numerical titles—Seven Habits, Six Programs, Nine Insights, Ten Truths. Most of their authors boasted ordination by one religious institution or another. Capitalizing on a fad that, according to historian Assaria Glib, 'would make even a Calvinist blush,' two such self-help gurus created spiritual e-commerce websites that earned listings in the S&P 500.
—Sabina Samuels

88. A famous victim of the Nazi genocide.
—Sabina Samuels

89. In this era, of course, people raised their own children. It is not clear whether the level of conflict in this scene represents individual variation or the norm for this, by our standards, grotesque and damaging form of relationship. The 20th and early 21st centuries saw a trend toward ever smaller social and reproductive units. Viewed as a sign of affluence and progress, compared to communal living, this 'nuclear family' limited the child's socialization and exposed it to the neuroses of a small number of people.
—RAYGIRVAN

'Now I should wear one?' my uncle Morris asked rhetorically, waving away the skullcap that his younger brother offered him. 'God knows I'm bald, there's no use trying to fool him, Sammy.'

I let a laugh escape. I couldn't help but admire his logic. I admired almost everything about the old guy. The 68-year-old had become a self-made millionaire back when a million dollars still meant something. And he'd kept his sense of humor through it all. I suspected we had a lot of genes in common.

'You're just afraid it'll fall off,' I teased him. 'Maybe we have some Scotch tape.'

'Or a thumbtack!' Benjamin chimed in, devilishly tormenting his old daddy.

'How 'bout a piece of chewing gum?' Morris asked, confident enough to make jokes at his own expense.

'Funny, funny,' Samuel nodded, reluctantly surrendering the moment to earn some reciprocal cooperation. He pushed the yarmulke towards his older brother one more time, and Morris relented, as always.

'We're all reform, here, Sam,' he said, placing the knitted blue circle on his shiny crown. 'We're supposed to do what we want.'

'You're in someone else's house, Morris,' Aunt Estelle scolded from beneath her flaming red wig. 'You do what *they* want, for a change.'

'I put it on, okay?' he said. 'Just having a little fun with my brother the rabbi, that's all.'

Morris acted as if this was his right. Maybe it was. Although no one talked about it anymore, we all knew the brothers' story well. Their father was a survivor—not of the Shoah, but of the Russian pogroms before it. Entire shtetls were burned to the ground overnight. When the Cossacks arrived at Kishnev, Grandpa Tzve was too young to fight, but too wily to give in. He climbed down a dry well and hid there for three days plugging his ears to the sounds of all hell breaking loose above ground. When he climbed out, his parents and sisters were gone.

He finally came through Ellis Island as a child in the 1930's, and managed to make a small business for himself on the Lower East Side, converting tenement gas fixtures into electric lamps. With no one to support but himself, he put away enough money to take a vacation smack in the middle of the depression—two whole weeks up in the Catskills at a Marxist camp called Kedem, where he fell in love.

Tzve and his wife worked hard, and dreamed their two young sons might someday even go to college. By the time Morris was in high school, however, it was clear that the Cohens were not going to share in America's post-War prosperity, and would need their first born son's help to make ends meet. Still just a teenager, Morris went to work with his father, and was soon running the business, building it into a full-fledged retail lighting store on Bowery.

After meeting a man who imported cut-glass beads manufactured in Hong Kong, Morris made the business decision that would get our family out of debt, forever. He contracted a printer to forge the tags of expensive French chandeliers, and began assembling and selling knock-offs at a fraction of the price. As the suburbs of Long Island filled in with Italians, Germans, and Jews, Morris Cohen filled their dining rooms with counterfeit crystal candelabras. (Many hang there to this day.) By the early 1970's, Morris had opened another store on the ground floor of a four-story walk-up in Crown Heights. The second floor held an inventory of fixtures and chandeliers, as well as a small workshop for them to be assembled, and the whole family lived on the upper two levels.

Meanwhile, my dad graduated from Brooklyn College with honors and then enrolled at the Seminary, both as a way to pursue his passion for

Talmud, and to avoid the draft. Morris paid for it all, proud that he had the ability to shield his younger brother from the perils of the Vietnam War, even though Samuel's chosen path made my uncle somewhat uneasy about the integrity of his own.

Morris wasn't fully conscious of his own misgivings until fate changed his life. He had been vigorously courting Estelle, a petite, red-haired schoolteacher who was the younger sister of his cut-glass supplier. The New York City teachers were on strike, and, with nothing else to do, Estelle had gotten herself involved in the Zionist struggle. As a way of demonstrating an interest in her pursuits, Morris escorted her to the YMHA one night to hear a speech by a controversial new activist named Meir Kahane.

Sitting on a folding chair in the basement of a run-down shul, Morris heard the words that would forever change his Jewish identity. Kahane began by evoking the pogrom at Kishnev. He condemned the Jews for their cowardice—for trembling in shadows while their wives were raped. He went on to blame the Holocaust victims for their own fates—for lining up like pathetic cows to their slaughter. He said that Israel's independence heralded a new era for the Jewish people—one in which they would protect themselves and their loved ones against all aggression, not just in Israel, but right here at home. Four elderly Jewish women from the neighborhood had been attacked during that month alone. He invited every man present to commit himself to a new spirit of resistance by joining what he called a Jewish Defense League.

Kahane's words inspired Morris. They made the uneducated, street-wise businessman feel more righteously Jewish than any of those effete intellectuals—people like his younger brother—who Kahane referred to as 'nice Irvings.' The future of the tribes of Judah lay not the endless analysis of Torah but in the resolve to defend their very right to exist. In the JDL, Morris found Jews with whom he could at last identify: not the bookish

Yeshiva boys of the Upper West Side, but his working class comrades from Canarsie, Rego Park, and the outer boroughs. They established night patrols and block watches, reclaiming their neighborhoods and their collective pride.

As they gained momentum, they took on every Jew's fight as their own. They funneled money to Israel and smuggled weapons to Soviet Jews. They felt they were restoring long lost manhood to the people of the Book. Morris's increasing wealth made him a key player. His lack of faith in God and the Bible no longer meant he was less of a Jew. No, in some ways it made him—much more than his brother—his people's greatest hope for survival. Uzi, Hebrew for 'my strength,' had always meant to imply the power of God within a man's soul. In Morris's eyes, that strength now took the form of an Israeli-made, handheld machine gun.

The family didn't discover the extent of Morris's JDL involvement until he was brought in for questioning by the police following a 'stink bomb' attack on members of the Russian Ballet who were performing in New York. Although Morris was never charged, his parents and wife were so trauma-tized by the ordeal that they made him swear, in shul and on the Torah, to end his association with the JDL forever. He agreed for his own sake as much as his wife's. The League had grown too violent for Morris—he felt more comfortable protecting local bubbes than heaving Molotov cocktails at Carnegie Hall—and, more to the point, he was afraid that an ongoing inves-tigation might expose his thriving chandelier-fraud business.

Samuel, for his part, tried to ignore the fact that his education was being paid for with such questionably earned profits, and with the same dollars that sent grenades to the Sinai. To him, this was not the Jewish way. We were a people of culture and intellect. With God's grace, we would lead the goyim towards a higher ethical standard, not descend to their level of violence and duplicity. Though he owed a lot to his older brother, he would never con-done his actions—especially not in front of the family.

Besides, Morris always, eventually, put on a yarmulke whenever he was told to.

'Come in, everybody,' Samuel announced. 'We're praying.'

'What's this game you were playing?' Morris asked, exploiting his con-cession to Samuel's conventions to make a little of his own conversation. 'Can we buy one for Benjamin?'

'It's not really a game, Uncle Morris.' I took a moment to calculate just how far back into computer history I'd need to go in order to communicate how an emulator works. It was a perennial problem for people like me. 'It's a platform that lets you play any game you want on a computer.'

'For free!' Benjamin added enthusiastically.

'That's better than wholesale!' Morris laughed. Samuel pretended to look for his place in the tiny prayer book.

'It's something we wrote in high school, actually.' I was trying to add a bit of technological integrity to something that amounted to a utility for the premeditated theft of services. 'It took a lot of work, but it became very pop-ular. It's still used today in a lot of places.'

'You'll give Benjamin a copy of this program?' Morris asked.

'Um, sure,' I said. 'If it's okay with you, I mean, because technically speaking...'

'It's stealing, am I right?' Samuel asked in a forced Yiddish syntax. To me, his ghetto-speak was an affectation as glaring as a white suburban kid feign-ing hip-hop. That he'd choose to echo a shtetl dialect made me sick to my stomach. He was nostalgic for Old World persecution.

'Come on, Dad. To you, all hacking is stealing.'

'If it's against the law, then it's against the law,' he countered contritely.

90. 21st century Americans were obsessed with property rights. In an age when poverty and starvation were common, private property was seen as essential for survival. As such, crimes against property were treated almost as harshly as crimes against humanity—sometimes more harshly, depending on the particular property or human in question.
—SHANKEL

'Trespassing, theft, vandalism[90]. You, of all people, should know.'

I didn't need this.

'I think Sony's stock price will survive.' Morris came to my defense, well aware that the game company made up the majority of Samuel's retirement portfolio. 'Jamie, you'll give us a copy before we leave.' Morris could order the Cohens around like this and, most of us anyway, were delighted to oblige our pear-shaped patriarch.

'I'll need the games, too,' Benjamin added, while the going was good.

'You can get them online,' I said, proving how widespread, if not quite legal, the bootlegging of games had become. 'Right off the Net. There's plenty of servers for that, now.'

'Just because everybody does it...' Samuel began.

'Sha. Not tonight,' Sophie interrupted, entering with the ceremonial braided candle, bottle of wine, and wooden spice box.

'We'll take care of it after dinner,' Morris whispered to me.

'It'll be a pleasure,' I agreed, every ounce of pleasure having been already drained from the experience by my father, the Talmudist.

'Come on in, everybody,' Samuel repeated, a little louder. He didn't use Miriam's name, even though hers was the only empty chair. 'Jamie, why don't you go get your sister?'

Morris pulled a toothpick out of his pocket and placed it in his mouth as I headed for the living room.

Miriam, my 33-year-old sister, was sitting on the couch, weaving a potholder on a small plastic loom. My attention was momentarily diverted by an image on the television set—aerial coverage of what appeared to be a bull, running up a Manhattan avenue. Cars and buses were pulling to the sides of the road, as police vehicles slowly moved against the traffic, following the frantic bull's path. The words 'live' and 'breaking news' were superimposed in the top left corner of the screen.

'Hey, Miriam,' I spoke gently, 'time for dinner.'

She looked up at me through her bottle-bottom glasses, and smiled with the broad, open-mouthed glee of a person who just doesn't know how hard life can be.

'I'm making this,' she said proudly. She held up the half-completed multi-colored masterpiece for me to approve.

'And it's beautiful, Miriam. Gosh, it really is.' I knelt down before her. 'I can't wait to see it when it's done.'

'You really mean that?' she asked. She wasn't fishing for a compliment. She really wanted to know.

'No, I can't wait. Not one bit.'

She laughed. 'I know you can't,' she glanced away shyly, blushing as if I had been flirting with her. She reached a hand to her head and twirled a lock of hair around her finger.

She never really looked like a person with Down Syndrome[91], I thought to myself as I gently took her hand away from her hair and began to help her up. Her eyes were a bit further apart than normal, perhaps, and she had a high, square forehead. But she was the first friend I ever had, the first face I really remembered. She used to bring me my bottle, for God's sake. She even taught me to count.

'You're visiting a long time,' she said as I escorted her into the dining room.

'Yeah, that's right,' I answered, half-amazed she was even aware I'd moved away and returned. She always acted as if she lived in an eternal present—oblivious to my comings and goings—like she had a different sense of time and space, altogether. 'I'm visiting.'

It was a profound insight on her part. For the first time in my life, I felt

91. A genetic variation that inhibited physical and mental development. At the time, it was still inconceivable that such conditions were treatable, and the debate over the ethics of corrective genetic displacement hadn't yet begun.
—Sabina Samuels

like a visitor in the house where I grew up. Miriam had pegged it.

'So this simulator or what you call it—' Morris asked as we came in.

'Emulator, Daddy,' Benjamin corrected the man who was old enough to be his grandpa.

'Emulator, yes,' Morris continued, rolling the toothpick across his teeth in a manner he usually reserved for business negotiations, 'you ever think about selling such a thing? Maybe creating a dot-com from it?'

'Well, it's not exactly the sort of program on which you'd base a business,' I said. I wasn't sure where to begin. I was thrilled that Morris was so enthusiastic about something I'd created. But the old man's understanding of its value was so misguided. Or misinformed. 'See, the emulator was a way of breaking business, not making one.'

My father handed Morris the braided candle, but the elder continued unabated.

'You make one business by breaking another, Jamie, am I right?' Morris leaned forward and gestured with his toothpick for emphasis. 'Maybe they'd pay you just to keep it off the market.'

'That's not really how it works,' I said. 'Besides, there's a ton of emulators out there. This is just one of them. Not even the best.'

'With the right marketing, Jamie,' Morris continued to talk business even though he had been handed the ceremonial candle, 'I bet you could still put the fear of God in some people.'

Samuel seized his opportunity. 'Maybe it's time for all God-fearing men to say their b'rukhas.' He knew Morris wouldn't get the reference. In the Torah 'God-fearing' people weren't Jews at all, but goyim who merely feared the power of the Hebrews' God. I could tell he got a perverse tingle of righteous pleasure in spite of himself.

'We'll talk about it later,' Morris said, lighting the candle and faking his way through the phonetic transliteration in his prayer book. When he was done, he passed the candle back to his brother, and inspected the tiny paperback book. He pointed to the Whitestone Temple sticker on the back. 'You stole this from the shul, Sammy?'

Benjamin giggled. My father looked over at his brother, sternly. It was hard for him to enforce too much discipline, under the circumstances. This wasn't Shabbat, after all, but Havdalah—the celebration of Shabbat's ending. Most Jews didn't do anything at all to commemorate sunset on Saturday, especially not reform ones.

He sighed, lifted the braided candle, and addressed his Lord—first in Hebrew, then in a language the rest of us could understand. 'Blessed are You, Lord, our God, King of the Universe, who distinguishes between the sacred and the secular.'

Samuel dipped his finger in the wine, and used the drops on the ends of his fingers to douse the flame with the precision of the professional he was. Shabbat was over; the line between the sacred and secular drawn, as only my father could.

Conversation resumed, but the prayer had changed the prevailing wind.

'So, Sammy,' Morris began. 'When's the vote?'

'Not for a couple of weeks, yet,' Sophie interjected. She knew my dad didn't like to talk about his professional crisis, least of all in front of us. 'We're not worried. It's just a formality.'

The all-congregation vote on my father's contract was anything but a formality. The new temple president and most of the existing board were beginning to think that their veteran rabbi's ways were too traditional for the modern world. He was a liberal from way back, and used his pulpit to remind the congregation of their obligation, as Jews, to serve as ethical watchdogs for the greater society, stand up for the oppressed and, most of all, remain mindful of the commandments they were gifted at Mount Sinai. 'Just as Moses had two mothers,' he'd sermonize, 'so, too, do we belong to two communities: that of the nation in which we live and that of each other as Jews.'

Such preaching went over well back in the nineties, when the working class community in Queens had to stand by and watch helplessly as their counterparts in Manhattan reaped the financial harvest of the first Internet boom. Now that these commoners were fully invested in the joys of the market themselves, they took their rabbi's words as criticism. The president and treasurer had met privately with Samuel to suggest he soften his rhetoric, and rumors had surfaced that several other board members were demanding a new rabbi for the 21st Century. Rather than approving his contract renewal, as they had every year before, the board members decided to put it to a vote by the congregation—a humiliation compounded by the fact that it would be held right on the temple's website.

'You're going to fight this, Sammy, right?' Morris asked.

'Why should I fight?' my father responded as Sophie placed his soup before him. 'I've known these people for twenty years. They know who I am.'

'Maybe that's the problem,' Morris said, couching the critique with a bad Groucho Marx[92] imitation.

'Shush,' Estelle nudged him. 'Sam knows his congregation.'

'Don't shush me, Estelle. He needs to hear this.'

'I'm right here, Morris. What do you have to say?' He put down his spoon and waited.

'Don't be like that, Sam,' Morris said with rare compassion. 'I'm just making sure you've considered your options.'

'What options? They'll vote. We'll see.'

'You could bend a little. Maybe soften around the edges. You speak to

92. An early 20th century comedian whose appearance inspired the 'Groucho masks' much sought-after by collectors of 20th century memorabilia.
—RAYGIRVAN

these people every week. Show them you understand their problems.'

'I understand their problems all too well,' Samuel said. 'That's their trouble.'

'See?' Morris said, pointing with his spoon. 'That's what they're talking about.'

'So you think they're right?' My dad was getting angry, now. Morris just shrugged.

'Maybe you can send out an email or something,' I offered.

'Great,' my dad said, returning to his soup. 'Now we're a re-election campaign.'

'I mean it,' I pressed. 'They're the ones who decided to do this on the web. Let's use it to our advantage. We've got the mailing list, and it wouldn't cost anything.'

'A rabbi doesn't sell himself to his own congregation, Yossi. This isn't retail. I'm not on the market.'

'But you are, Sammy,' Morris said. 'They pay their dues. They pay for this house. You've got to think of them as customers. Maybe I could make a donation.'

'It's not about money!' Samuel suddenly shouted. We sat in silence for a moment, as the soup in our bowls steamed before us.

'The broth is very good,' Estelle said, sipping delicately. 'You're using more pepper?'

'Fresh ground,' my mother said. 'It makes a difference.'

'Mmm,' Estelle agreed. 'Which testing kit[93] are you using, now?'

'Squibb. Series C.'

'Does that scan for subvariant r-12?'

'I imagine so,' my mom said defensively. 'It's the most expensive one.'

'Hmm.' Estelle said, stirring her soup, then slowly placing her spoon

93. Still carnivores, Americans were plagued by a number of meat-borne diseases. The most famous of these, called "Mad Cow," began in cattle, but variants quickly spread to poultry and fish. A number of pharmaceutical companies sold home-testing kids that allowed people to test meat for a range of diseases before consuming it.   —Sabina Samuels

down.

'Just eat the soup,' Morris said. 'For God's sake, Estelle.'

The ancillary conversation fell into another uncomfortable silence, so my mom tried to start another—this time with me.

'Jude called before. He said he wants to speak with you, urgently.'

'Jude?' Miriam asked. 'Will he come over?' She hadn't seen him in years. Not since the fall-out, when all the Kings except El Greco were banned from the house.

'I didn't know he was allowed on the property,' I said.

'Don't be silly,' my mom said. 'You're all adults, now.'

'What are you doing?' Benjamin asked, excited. 'Another hack?'

'No, Benji,' I said. 'Just a business idea. He wants to pitch something to us.'

'Us?' my father asked. 'You mean the firm you work for?'

'Morehouse & Linney. Yeah. He and the guys have been working on a new technology we might be able to exploit.'

'Exploit?'

I hated the way he picked apart my words as if they were grist for the 'drosh[94].

94. Slang for Midrash—an ongoing tradition of Biblical commentary.
—Sabina Samuels

'Christ, dad, I'm legitimizing what they're doing. You think they need protection from the big bad world? They're the ones who almost got me in jail.'

'If they're such hoodlums and you're so angry at them, then why do them these favors, Yossi?'

'Look,' I said, defending my path, 'this is important to me, okay? I've become an important person, however hard that is for you to believe. In New York City. You should see the kinds of people who are asking me for advice. They're trusting me with millions of dollars. You should be proud.'

'Your father's proud of you,' my mom played peacemaker. 'Aren't you Sammy?'

'Of course I'm proud,' he answered.

But my father didn't approve. He said so by the way he used the soup spoon to dissect his matzo ball into tiny pieces before taking a single slurp, as if to show he was in such great command of his animal instincts that he could postpone satiating his earthly desires indefinitely.

'What?!' I asked. 'Just say it, okay?'

'Nothing,' Samuel shrugged. 'You say you're proud, she says I'm proud, so we're proud.' He took another small sip before mumbling in Yiddish, half to himself, 'goyim naches.' He meant these are the sorts of things that gentiles, not Jews, should be proud of.[95]

'Goyim naches!' Miriam repeated, enjoying the sounds of the foreign syllables in her mouth. 'Goyim naches! Goyim naches!' she sang, conducting a symphony with her butter knife. Sophie reached across the table to still her daughter's hand, smiling into Miriam's innocent eyes as she did.

'It's not just about the money, dad,' I began, then stopped myself.

No one was coming to my defense, not even Morris and, thanks to Miriam's outburst of sing-song, the moment had well passed. I was fighting a losing battle, especially under the circumstances. At a dinner table, the rabbi is always right.

95. According to Isaac Schwartz in 'The Passions of the Hebrews,' goyim naches were traditional American achievements to which most Jewish people were still unaccustomed, such as growing award-winning roses, winning football trophies, or shooting a large buck.
—Sabina Samuels

4.Pump and Dump

96. Males in this absurdly status-obsessed society were endlessly comparing the size of their poultry. The fattened roosters, however, were mostly bragged about and rarely seen. Talk about the roosters dominated many male-to-male conversations, and when engaging in intimate relationships with others, males were known to let others see or handle the rooster. Threats to shove this rooster into some orifice or other were common. Many students of male culture posit that at this late point in human history, in technologically advanced, urban societies, it would be impossible to keep so many chickens around. Therefore, all this talk about cocks may be purely symbolic. These men may have no cocks at all.   —ADAVEEN

97. This presumably refers only to the prestige of Moorehouse's family origins. Genome readouts had not yet become the prime criterion for corporate hiring and promotion.   —MRNORMATIVE

Tobias Morehouse had the biggest cock[96] on Wall Street, and everybody who was anybody knew it. Only a few elder statesmen could attest to having actually seen the legendary capitalist's tool up close and in person, and even they didn't know its full extent.

Back in the 1960's, brokers used to joke that Tobias won more money betting on the length of his johnson than he ever earned on the commodities exchange—which was untrue, of course, but it gave his fellow club members some consolation.

He hadn't the same pedigree[97] as they did, the same education, nor the same connections. No, it was a few miraculously well-timed crude oil calls at the launch of the Vietnam War that had earned Tobias his place at the table.

Although most assumed Morehouse had bribed an old navy buddy for the information, there was very little about his machinations they could protest openly. Times had changed by then, and a tip from a navy purser to a former fighter pilot over a beer was no more scandalous than one gleaned over a brandy snifter at the Coachmen's Club. Morehouse, then a junior trader at a no-name firm without even a seat on the exchange, had to be let in before he got any bigger.

But they made him pay for entry.

It began as a dare late one night in the Red Lounge at the Coachmen's Club, or so the story goes. Tobias, just 23, had been telling stories about those two fags back on the aircraft carrier, USS Valley Forge. How they used to stare at his package. How each morning he'd stuff it down into a different section of his tight white sailor pants just to watch the way they'd scramble around the deck to find an optimum vantage point. How once he wrapped it all the way through his legs and around his thigh so they could marvel at the way it lodged itself so majestically into the tuck of his buttock.

That's when the gentlemen of the Coachmen's Club convinced their newest member to take the challenge. To wager ten thousand dollars that he'd outsize anyone else in the room. With bemused disdain, Tobias scanned the thirty-or-so well-groomed heads protruding from their starched wing-tip collared shirts. Soft to the core, the lot of them, he thought to himself of the assembled elite as he set down his umpteenth Scotch and lifted his burly frame up out of its leather armchair. He'd been through this before and against rivals much more imposing than any of these dandies. His only condition: that any challenger unfurl himself first. Tobias would only expose as much as necessary to win the bet.

The older men accepted his terms with gentle handshakes, while a small cadre of their younger associates gathered over near the bar, Tobias presumed, to decide who amongst them best represented the club's manhood. Or perhaps they were fluffing themselves up to make the most of their meager endowments.

When the penguins finally parted, it wasn't Louis, Spuds, or even Rhodes scholar Marshall Tellington who stood in their midst, but one of the help. A busboy, his trousers pulled down to his ankles and his long, black, uncircumcised penis[98] dangling freely beneath his white waistcoat.

'Anyone in the room,' Spuds wheezed between his sickly girlish giggles, the sad African youth in tow. 'The boy was in the room at the time, Toby!'

So what if Tobias won? As far as he was concerned, it cost those bastards just 300 bucks a piece to watch him measure his dick against a boy they called 'nigger.'

Forty years of stiff-dicked market making, underwriting, mergers and acquisitions later, Morehouse & Linney's sole surviving founder again felt like something of an outsider. Times had changed, and maintaining one's bullishness in a market so abstractly bloodless as this one wasn't easy. At 74, Tobias Morehouse might still have had the longest, widest, and most revered prick on the street, but he just didn't have enough spirit to fill it anymore.

At least that's what Alec told me as we waited for his father at one end of a thirty-foot black granite conference table in Morehouse's spacious conference room. A mahogany door on the far wall led directly to Morehouse's office, while a glass door in a tremendous windowed wall looked out over the maze of cubicles[99] where M&L's researchers, underwriters and their assistants toiled. On the perimeter of the space were offices and conference rooms just like Morehouse's, if a little smaller, each shielded from the din of the main room by thick plate glass and, sometimes, tasteful white vertical blinds. The remaining wall of the conference room overlooked the financial district, from a respectable height of 37 stories.

98. Circumcision, or male genital mutilation, was a common practice in the 20th century and continued well into the 21st before being outlawed by the United Nations. The practice was, and technically still is, a requirement of Jewish Law, though the modern version is much less damaging. In the past, the operation, performed by a specially-trained rabbi called a 'mohel,' consisted of complete removal of the penile foreskin. Nowadays, of course, the procedure is much more symbolic, consisting only of minor scarring of the foreskin[a] by a specially ordained automated surgical device (see Ronco's Bris-O-Matic 5000). —SHANKEL

a. scarring of the foreskin. Foreskins were, of course, not yet sentient[b]. —RAYGIRVAN

b. not yet sentient. There is still some debate on this issue. Most scientists agree that foreskins, along with other body parts, became sentient during the neurogenic epidemic that resulted from the widespread consumption of genetically modified food (see 'Smart Pop: The Corn That Pops Itself,' Monsanto, 2014). However, some people believe that 20th century science simply lacked the language necessary to communicate effectively with body parts other than the brain, if that. —SHANKEL

99. A tool used to maximize space and limit interpersonal contact within a work environment. Considered unethical by the United Nations in 2116. —RABBITROAR

Everyone thought the old man had simply gotten better at hiding his assets. But the truth was that there were less assets to hide. He just couldn't make a dime in this market, not when there was nothing real to invest in. Morehouse came up on the commodities exchange: oil, cotton, and copper. When values were tied to things, not stories. Materials, not hype. He bullied his way into this ring, but now he was getting sissied out of it.

The hi-tech industry (if one could even call it that given how little genuine industry was going on) was yet another leap into abstraction. There was no supply and demand, nor any real commodities. Just stories. There were still winners and losers, but no one in sight was playing a game—at least not a game that Tobias or most members of his generation could detect. Everyone was betting on a mirage. And those without faith in the new religion couldn't even see the illusion. Last time, the mirage vanished just five years after it appeared. By the time Tobias got onto the bandwagon in 1999, it was already heading off a cliff. This time, buoyed by a conspiracy of optimism, the illusion had become the new reality. Wealth wasn't earned, it was created. And to Tobias, this just didn't make any sense.

That's why everyone else from Tobias's generation had a kid or two around like me who could show him the ropes without making him feel too stupid. Guys smart enough to evaluate a new technology, but not smart enough to have launched a company of our own when the going was good and the window of opportunity was still open to the independent entrepreneur.

In the 1990's Tobias deferred to outside consultants. But he learned the hard way that no matter how much money you throw at them, you can't tell if they're really on your team or merely making you feel that way. 'They're like hookers,' Morehouse once told me. 'They give you better head than your wife, but they never swallow.' So this time he looked elsewhere, luring young 'new media' journalists away from business magazines at the same day rates he used to hire MBA's from Harvard. But they all had their own agendas—their careers, the popularity of their bylines with the counterculture, their integrity, even their own personal convictions.

And though consultants and journalists knew more about the technology business than most of the kids who would accept a full-time gig, they couldn't be held up as evidence that qualified Internet specialists were climbing aboard your ship. They came without fanfare or press releases. They didn't help the story (unless of course they chose to write about their exploits on your behalf, but even then, they only highlighted how they singlehandedly saved your dumb ass from doom).

'Carla Santangelo was the best my dad could do until you,' Alec confided.

'She's good,' I said. 'Smart, aggressive, well-spoken.'

'You should watch who you sleep with, Jamie. What were you thinking? She's utterly incompetent. You're her replacement, get it?'

'You're not serious, are you?'

'To her, just getting in the ring is victory enough. This is the world of Game*boys*, Walk*men*, and Wrist*dudes*[100]. Women are just another target market—prey, not players. They don't even respect one another's exploits—why should we?'

'You guys never said anything about.... I mean, I know a little technology, Alec, but—'

'It's not a matter of 'if,' but 'when.''

'But—' I stopped myself as Morehouse, the senior, came through the mahogany door. I rose. Alec didn't.

'Nice suit, Jamie.' Tobias sat at the far end of the table and leaned back, relaxed.

'Yeah, I kind of like it. Agnes B.'

100. Early 21st century Americans were almost pathologically unable to tolerate sensory deprivation of any kind. These portable devices would entertain them whenever they were separated from their beloved televisions and personal computers.

Some historians have concluded that this compulsive self-distraction was necessary to keep market slaves from confronting the negative consequences of their lifestyles. Others equate 21st century media consumers with lab animals whose pleasure centers had been wired to a remote control. —SHANKEL

'She's doing two-buttons, now?' His knowledge of the fashion industry surprised me.

'I guess so, yeah.' I traversed the room to Morehouse's side. Even the closest chair was a good six feet away from the man.

'Where's Carla?' he asked, withdrawing a Mont Blanc from his shirt.

'I don't know,' I answered defensively, as if it were my job to keep track. Morehouse pushed a button on the phone in front of him.

'Where's Carla?' He sounded as if he'd been through this too many times before.

'A doctor's appointment, Mr. Morehouse,' a chipper male voice responded through the speaker. 'She left a message yesterday.'

'Christ.' Morehouse pushed the button again to turn the speaker off. Then he sighed. 'So tell me something about that home security venture. What's it called?'

'MyDoorman.com,' I said.

'Yeah. It opens tomorrow, right?'

'Yes. Tomorrow.' I still hadn't decided whether to wait until after Carla's company had its IPO to introduce what I believed could be its successor.

'Well whaddya think, Jamie?' Morehouse asked me. 'Is it fully subscribed? Are all her ducks in a row?' He looked at me with trusting eyes.

'I guess so,' I hedged. I didn't want to undermine her efforts, but I didn't want to get blamed for approving her imminent failure, either.

'Just say it, Jamie.' Alec could read my ambivalence. I welcomed being cornered. It made me feel less guilty for what I was about to do.

'Well, I reviewed the business plan over the weekend,' I started. 'And it's certainly a convincing strategy.'

'But...' Alec coaxed me on.

'You don't like it?' Tobias asked, leaning forward onto the table, his huge arms testing the seams of his jacket sleeves.

'Well, it's a great idea, and well thought out,' I said. 'But I don't know that she's taken into account the breadth of the competitive landscape.'

'Pardon?' Tobias asked, his eyebrows hardening from rounded trust to angular rage. He was breathing heavily now, his nostrils flaring with each inhalation—even though he pretended to be absolutely calm. 'She said the field was clear.' Morehouse pushed the button on the speakerphone again. 'Get Santangelo, now.'

'You want me to try her at the doctor's office?' the voice asked.

'Just get her, Brad, okay?'

'I haven't seen Carla yet to brief her on this, sir,' I said, already afraid that I'd made a terrible mistake.

'Hasn't she even been in today?' he asked. I couldn't say anything.

'Jamie.' Tobias spoke softly and gently, for my benefit. 'We're all honest here. There's no time for BS, and no time for sparing anyone's feelings. We're all on the same team.'

The team, right. It's just a game, I told myself. We're playing here, but we're playing to win. Besides, Tobias was paying my salary, not Carla. My misgivings sufficiently addressed, I proceeded to stab her in the back.

'Well,' I began. 'I found out about an Australian company that just completed their second round. It's called MyDoor.com, and it's giving the same service as MyDoorman.com, except you don't need a home computer at all. The whole thing is wireless, and it'll even call you on your wristphone.'

'Is that possible?' Morehouse asked.

'Sure it is,' Alec said, thinking he was defending me. 'Right, Jamie?'

'Strictly speaking,' I explained, 'it's not possible right now. But neither is MyDoorman.com. That's not the point.'

'Well, then, Jamie.' Morehouse measured his breaths, clasped his hands, and brought his fat knuckles to just under his nose as if to hold down the smoke. The hairs on his fingers danced as he exhaled. 'Tell me the point.'

'They'll both be possible in the future. You might have to think of the development space in a slightly more Darwinian way. Ideas compete for dominance. The ones that sound the best at the time get funded, until a better idea comes along. Very few get past prototype before they're obsolete.'

'And what about earnings projections? Cash flow?' Morehouse asked. 'I hate momentum plays—they're too dependent on psychology and we can never get out fast enough.'

'It's a different market, Dad,' Alec explained. 'That's why PR is so important. Come up with a story that people will invest in. Get your angel money, then your VC funds. Do a second round and maybe a third, and then fill in the last layers with an IPO. Then, just keep the company's story alive long enough to execute your exit strategy and get out. It's a growth economy.'

'What are we, fucking Amway[101]?' Morehouse slammed his fat fist on the marble table. The surface was so hard, it barely made a thud. 'I want M&L to stand out from these schemes. Get known for bringing some common sense into the new economy. Carla promised this wouldn't just be another momentum play. Is she full of shit?'

Time seemed to stop while I reckoned with the proportions of Tobias's huge skull, filling with blood. A vein pulsated visibly on his forehead. For a moment, everything went fuzzy, and I thought I almost made out the shadows of two small bumps protruding from the man's scalp. Then I blinked myself back to reality and everything returned to normal.

Tobias took a deep breath. 'Jamie, it's your job to evaluate new ventures and determine whether they can be monetized. In this regard, is Carla's IPO in M&L's best interests?'

'Look, Mr. Morehouse,' I said, still uncertain if I would twist my dagger.

101. A popular multi-level marketing program in which members were encouraged to sell expensive memberships to their friends and family. Scores of psychology studies were done on the victims of such schemes before the practice was outlawed in 2023.   —Sabina Samuels

'I'm not a businessman. You know how you want to invest. Fundamentals, momentum, whatever you want.' Images of Carla reading the paper on the porch flashed through my head, energizing my impending treason. 'All I'm saying is that MyDoor.com is a better idea on paper than MyDoorman.com, and when it goes public I can't imagine anyone wanting to bet on a complex series of wire patches over an end-to-end solution.' There. I did it. She was as good as dead.

'I've got Carla for you,' Brad proclaimed proudly through the speaker. 'I kept ringing her cell phone until she picked up.'

'Jamie,' Morehouse whispered sternly. 'Let me handle this, okay? Just listen unless I ask for you.'

Alec gestured with his eyes for me to be cool.

'Thanks, Brad,' Morehouse said into the phone. 'Put her on.'

'Jesus Christ, Tobias!' Carla's sharp voice penetrated the plastic mechanism. 'I'm on the fucking gyno table with a speculum half-way up my twat.'

'That's funny, Santangelo, I was just thinking about you, too.' Morehouse joked in revitalized sarcasm.

'Ha! At least the doctor uses lube before he shoves his thing in me.'

'Still got that dryness problem, eh?' Morehouse teased her. 'It gets worse with age, or so I'm told.'

I was freaked out. How could they talk like this? Were they once lovers?

'Ow!' Carla shouted. We could hear the smack of her phone dropping onto the floor.

The two Morehouses laughed. 'She's probably getting fitted for a cock,' Alec joked in a whisper.

'Then take off your gloves and pick it up, okay? Hello?'

'Look, Santangelo, I hate to interrupt while you're remodeling, but I have some good news for you.'

'You're dying of prostate cancer?'

'Next best thing,' Morehouse said. 'I'm freeing up the rest of the IPO shares on your MyDoorman scam for the members of your fund.'

'Huh?' she asked, confused. 'Those are retail clients, Tobias. Less than a hundred grand a pop. Why give it to them?'

'We were just talking about the company image, Carla,' Morehouse explained. 'And we thought it might be a good idea to show that little people who invest through M&L get the same access to breaking deals as the high rollers.'

'What gives?' she asked, suspicious.

'You should thank me, Carla,' he said. 'You don't want 'em, don't take 'em.'

'No no,' she softened. 'Thanks, Tobias. It'll give the fund a real shot in the arm.'

'Good, then. It's settled,' he said.

'What do you want in return?' she asked.

'Just a promise, Carla.'

'What?'

'That whenever you're back from doing whatever it is you're doing at the gynecologist, you promise not to spot the furniture.'

Alec giggled through his nose.

'Very funny, you sick fuck,' she said.

'And I love you, too, Santangelo,' he said, pushing a button and disconnecting. 'She's so crass,' Morehouse shook his head in disgust. 'I could hardly keep up. She thinks we really talk like that?'

I was so confused and conflicted I couldn't speak. Alec, confused but not conflicted, was still coherent enough to formulate a question.

'What are you doing?'

'Making her pay for her own mistakes, for once,' Tobias said. 'That's what.'

'You're letting the IPO go through?' I asked.

'It's too late to pull it and save face,' Morehouse said. 'But it'll be her loser accounts that go down when you two announce that we're underwriting MyDoor.com.' He clicked a new button on his phone. 'Mort?'

'Yeah?' a scratchy voice responded.

'We're going short on MyDoorman.com—but only in the Platinum Fund, and maybe some of the Circle Investors. Just top tier, and keep it quiet.'

'Sure thing,' Mort said, clicking off.

'I still don't get it,' I said, even though I was beginning to understand what was going on all too well.

'We're going to let Carla pump this loser with her own pathetic fund. We're committed to holding six-hundred thousand shares for six months. Better limit the damage to her people. We'll wait a day or two then pull the rug out from under her. Her fund will tank, but we'll leverage with a ton of puts. It's the weasel's way out, but we'll still make a killing, overall, after commissions. And we'll end up with a great excuse to sack her and move you in.'

'We can use the whole saga to promote the new spirit of M&L, Dad,' Alec said, excitedly outlining his PR strategy. 'We'll give an exclusive to the *Journal*, positioning Jamie as the young renegade who went ahead and underwrote a company in direct competition with one of our other issues simply because it was the best technology. They'll eat it up.'

'I like it,' Morehouse said. 'It'll shield us against another class-action suit, too.'

'I've got your quote already,' Alec said, scrawling madly on his pad. 'Fire him? Hell, I'm promoting him! That's the kind of guts we reward here at

M&L.' We should probably bring Jamie to the retreat in Montana, too. Show him off.'

With friends like Alec in your corner, who needed to feel guilty about anything?

'Montana?' I asked innocently.

'It's not 'til next week,' Morehouse said, getting up. 'Alec will fill you in.'

As I went back to my office, I wasn't sure whether to celebrate my pending promotion and introduction to the power elite, or weep for my own lost soul. I kept my eyes on my shiny new shoes as they padded across the royal blue carpet, making a rhythmic leather squeak. They sounded like voices, musically scolding me for my sins.

'*Traitor*,' my shoes whined. But it was Morehouse who thought of the pump and dump, I defended myself against the Greek chorus on my feet.

'*Yes*,' my shoes sang, '*but you knew all along what would happen!*' I hadn't really thought the whole thing out, I insisted. '*Only because you knew what the outcome would be!*' But I was pissed, acting out a bit, driven by my emotions. '*It looked like a plot to us! A Machiavellian scheme!*' I think of schemes fast, I guess. Faster than I can control them. '*You had the chance to stop. You had the chance to stop!*' The chorus was gaining momentum.

'Fuck the Greeks,' I said out loud, the sound of my voice overpowering the squeak of my shoes and sending the chorus into remission. I wasn't a Greek, anyway. I was a descendant of the Maccabees. They drove the Hellenists out of the holy land. This chorus shit was probably why.

My switch-track to the Jewish rail provided only a temporary respite. My father's voice dolefully echoing last year's Yom Kippur sermon replaced the frantic Greeks. He was wailing on about how, according to Jewish lore, the first thing you get asked by God when you die is how you conducted yourself in your business dealings. That's okay, I decided. I'm not dying today.

All the way back then, the Jews realized that business was the easiest place to go astray—even easier than with sex. The system of laws was invented foremost to deal with the dark side of money. Somehow the pursuit of wealth led to self-interest, and self-interest led to corruption. I vowed I would be more upright in the future, even if it was all just a game. I'd let this one shady scheme go through, and play on the up and up from here on out.

Hell, I was still learning the ropes, and I certainly wasn't responsible for Carla not being around when it all went down. But once I was promoted from Researcher to Strategist, I'd be benevolent. I'd learn from my experience. I would evolve. Everyone in the Bible made mistakes before they got their act together. What I learned from this little lapse would make me a better boss than Carla was. If nothing else, I'd never put myself in the position to get screwed like I just screwed her. As for the sex, well, I'd just try not to think about it for the time being.

Waiting for me in the small, shared conference room next to my office, as I had scheduled but only half-expected to find, were Jude, Reuben, and young Benjamin. I called Jude back on Sunday morning, and agreed to let him come in and demo his idea for the 'ultimate killer meta-app.' Something he and Reuben were calling TeslaNet and promising would make cable modems and high-speed telephone access obsolete, overnight. Jude wanted me to see TeslaNet working on my own laptop, and asked me to bring it to them in Queens and maybe smoke a bowl, or let them come over to my new place and pick it up. I decided to let Benjamin deliver it to them, instead. I didn't want a reunion on their turf, but I wasn't ready to let them see the luxury in which I would soon be living. Besides, Benjamin was pleading to meet the remaining Jamaican Kings. By allowing my young cousin to visit, I was demonstrating my trust in them.

Apparently they took Benjamin under their wing, because now the boy was tapping away at the keys on my computer, making final adjustments for the demo.

'Hey, Jamie,' Reuben said, scratching his neck. Reuben was even taller than I had remembered, which made him look all the thinner. His acne was gone, but his straw-like hair still covered his forehead in unintentionally spiky bangs. Although Jude had always been the gang's leader, Reuben really was our Master Hacker. It made him something like a pope to Jude's king. Jude was in charge, and quite capable of writing a mutating virus or executing a daring break-in, but Reuben always had the final word about technological methodology. He knew facts that the others didn't, whether it was phone-switching protocols or machine language. And we all trusted him, because he answered to no authority other than the elegance of code.

This made him come off as something of a libertarian, but he claimed he was really more of a benevolent technocrat. He believed that markets, culture, and matter itself would reach maximum efficiency as humans perfected their social and technological programming. When Jude wrote the DeltaWave Virus, it was Reuben who minimized the code down to a minuscule 78k. And while the rest of us were drooling over the damage we would wreak on Microsoft's public image, it was Reuben who thought of the virus as a gift to Bill Gates that would allow the software magnate to correct the security flaws in his internet software. This was Reuben's main reason for spending so many hours paring down the virus to its essential lines of code. He wanted the virus to communicate as clearly and succinctly as possible.

Reuben wasn't dangerous, as long as you could keep track of whom he thought needed to be gifted with an important lesson at any given moment.

'Reuben!' I pinched his cheek. 'I think you've grown!'

'It's been a long time,' he said quietly. He was right. We hadn't seen one another since high school.

Jude put one arm around each of us, and pulled us close. 'And then there were three!'

'Four!' added Benjamin.

'Three and a half,' I joked, crossing over to him. 'So, did you trash my laptop?'

'Come on, Jamie,' Benjamin protested in all seriousness. 'I know what I'm doing, right, Jude?'

Jude winked at him, knowingly. The boy beamed.

I put my hands on Benjamin's shoulders. 'I know you do. I know you do.' It was a little strange how quickly Jude had usurped my role. I wasn't sure which bothered me more, the risk that Benjamin would be corrupted by my former friends, or that I'd lose the boy's respect in the process.

'The coffee and stuff is for you guys, you know,' I said, pointing to a small chrome cart near the door, with two severe, cylindrical black plastic urns and an octagonal plate of cookies. Everyone looked over at the cart. 'I mean, it's what they do here when someone from the real world comes to visit.'

'So that's what 'they' do,' Jude said, putting two cookies in a preposterously designed square teacup and then pouring coffee over them. 'Want some coffee, Reuben?'

'No, thanks,' he answered, examining one of the cup's corners. 'On principle.'

Alec scurried by, holding a stack of brightly colored folders against his chest. I waved at him through the glass wall[102], hoping this would suffice as a greeting. Alec took the hint, and continued on his way.

'Let's get on with this before we're interrupted,' I said.

'Sure thing,' Jude began. 'What we've got here is a prototype, mind you.'

'Don't worry,' I said. 'Most of the stuff they fund here never even gets that far.'

102. Businesses of this period often used glass constructions to limit the movement of employees. Some accounts describe glass ceilings, which in some unknown manner prevented promotion of female staff.　　　—RAYGIRVAN

Reuben was still inspecting the china. 'Not surprising.'

'Well,' Jude said. 'Let's see what 'they' think of this.'

He hit a few keystrokes on my laptop, which brought up a simple splash screen: TeslaNet.

'It's loading,' Reuben explained. 'That will happen faster.'

'Okay, Benjamin,' Jude ordered the boy. 'Launch it on that one, too.'

Benjamin opened a second laptop at the other end of the table, and started up the same program.

'Now,' Jude said in the voice of a carnie, 'you'd think these computers would need to be networked in order to communicate with one another.'

'If they were communicating, they would be networked by definition,' I responded in alpha-geek.

'Yeah. But you'd need them to be connected, right? Through a phone line, network line, infared, or some kind of network, right?'

'Sure.'

'Well watch this.' Jude held a simple piece of wire with an alligator clip on either end. 'Remember Tesla's experiments with static electricity and ground? How he thought he could light up the Eastern Seaboard with a big coil, and that no one would need any electric wires?'

'Yeah?'

'TeslaNet uses ground to establish network connections. One end attaches to your laptop.' He clasped one of the clips to a screw in the back of my laptop. 'And the other, to ground.' He attached the other end of the wire to the metal plate over a light switch. Benjamin worked simultaneously, attaching his wire on his computer to the metal window pane.

'Now watch,' Reuben said. I had forgotten that way he had of standing with his arms clasped over his chest, as if to demonstrate he was so confident in the technology that he wouldn't be called upon to touch the keyboard.

103. Sun Microsystems' proprietary precursor to the Linux computer operating system.   —Sabina Samuels

The screen changed to a simple Unix[103] prompt.

'And?' I asked.

'Go ahead, Benjamin,' Jude said.

Benjamin typed into his keyboard.

Magically, words appeared on my laptop:

Chat request, user 17014. Accept? (y/n)

I typed Y. The screen changed to a simple chat interface.

Hello, cousin. How's it hanging[104]?

104. A standard greeting of the era: one male would inquire as to whether the other's genitalia were comfortably situated. Roughly analogous to "are you well?"   —MRNORMATIVE

'That's incredible!' I said. It was. 'It goes both ways?'

'Indeed.' Reuben allowed himself a smile. 'It's using TCP/IP protocol. Just through ground, that's all.'

'You mean the computers are connected because they're basically touching each other through the metal in this room, right? They're communicating through the grounding wires?'

'Essentially,' Reuben agreed. 'But they're actually able to communicate through ground, itself. Over vast distances.'

'Right,' Jude said. 'You could as easily hook up to a drainpipe, or a stake planted directly into the soil.'

'Anyone grounded is in the network,' Reuben explained proudly. 'As long as they're using the software. It automatically finds you a unique address when you log on.'

'Jesus.' I was awed. 'But can you use it to get onto the Internet?'

'That's the beauty of it, Jamie,' Reuben said. 'As long as one node on TeslaNet is connected to the Internet, then the whole network is. The minute any major server like a University, search engine, or access provider installs TeslaNet, we'll have more than enough bandwidth to support millions of TeslaNet users.'

'But that's not the point,' Jude interrupted, almost angrily. 'The power here is that with TeslaNet, we don't need an Internet. It replaces the Internet. There are no centralized servers. Everyone is connected as soon as they touch their computers to the ground. Most of the time that just means plugging into the wall outlet, and most computers are plugged in already. If you're outside or using batteries, you just put a wire into the ground. Should even be able to work with a cell phone - we're working on a port. It'll work with anything. The earth itself is the network. The more people who use it, the stronger the network and vaster the distances we can traverse. And it's absolutely uncontrollable.'

I looked at my computer, the green wire connecting it to the light switch, and the flashing message on the screen. I didn't know what emotion to have. Greed? Joy? Jealousy? Excitement? Fear? This could be a billion-dollar technology. Unless it can't get patented. In that case, it would just kill a dozen other billion-dollar technologies, like Internet Access Providers, the phone companies, the satellite industry. That would make it revolutionary. Or catastrophic.

And did I really want to work with these old friends again? If what they were showing me really did what they said it did, I had no choice. Then again, it might not even work at all. That would be a relief, in some ways. I chose cynicism.

'So it works across a room,' I said. 'What makes you think it could work across an ocean?'

'It's all ground,' said Reuben. 'The earth is magnetic. It's charged from its rotation. There's more potential voltage in there than all the world's power plants put together.'

'It's okay if you don't believe us,' Jude said.

'I'm not saying that,' I backed off. 'What you've accomplished right here is terrific, really.'

'Let's go further, then,' Jude challenged. 'How about the lobby?'

'How 'bout the roof?' I upped him. 'And get me on the Internet, too.'

'You got it,' Jude agreed. 'Benjamin, get your laptop online so we can tap through when we connect.'

'Okay, Jude,' he answered in cheerful obedience. Just like I used to when I was a sophomore at Stuy and a disciple of Jude. 'Where can I plug in?'

I didn't relish the idea of letting these guys tap into the office network with my user ID and password, but it was the only way to make this work without calling in Tech Support and I didn't want to look like I needed professional help to make a simple IP connection. Or like I didn't trust my old posse. Besides, I figured they'd figure there was firewall or something. So I helped Benjamin configure a connection to the M&L system, and the Internet beyond it.

Then Jude and I headed up in the elevator. We ascended the M&L tower in silence, surrounded by men in gray suits and French blue shirts, just like mine. I had thought my blue shirt would make me stand out as an individualist, but it had just become another uniform. Blue was the new white. By the time we got to the 52nd floor, we were alone in the wood-paneled car.

'So you're really into this now,' Jude said.

'Not really.' I could feel my ears popping. 'It's just a good way to come back to New York, that's all. Learn about the industry, make connections, try to contribute something of value to this crazy hi-tech business before it bursts again, for good.'

'And make a few million dollars in the process, too.'

'It wouldn't hurt,' I admitted. 'But I'm not like these guys. I'm only in it for a year, max. Then I'm starting a game company. For sure.'

'He who sups with the devil should use a long spoon,' Jude quoted Shakespeare, loosely.

'I'm keeping the whole thing at arm's length. Don't worry. I know it's all just smoke and mirrors.'

'You're sure, right?'

'Yeah, I'm sure.'

'I mean, you really have the perspective to see it as a game?'

'Absolutely,' I said, feeling more confident in my stance as I put it into words. 'We're subverting the system from the inside.'

'Good to hear it, Jamie,' Jude said, putting a hand on my shoulder. 'Because I'd feel bad if it were otherwise.'

'What do you mean?' What *did* he mean?

'Nothing, Jamie. Just that I'm glad you aren't taking any of this too seriously. You had me worried there the other night.'

'I know I can get carried away,' I said as the doors opened onto the 68th and final floor. 'That's why it really means a lot to me that you brought this here. To me.' I felt oddly emotional at the thought. It was the first time I'd felt any kinship with my former partner in crime since the sabotage. 'I mean, it kinda lets me know you guys don't think I'm some evil person.'

'I never thought that, Jamie.' Jude held the door for me. 'It's just easy to get your head turned around in a place like this. You've got to remember that. Keep your perspective.'

I felt an urge to admit all I'd done that morning. How I had undermined Carla, a woman I'd slept with just last week. But I settled for an honest, if extremely condensed, confession:

'Tell me about it,' was all that came out. We laughed together and headed towards a stairwell leading up to the roof.

The wind gusted through our hair as we crossed towards a ledge where I could put my computer. My necktie flew up and whipped about behind me, symbolically reminding me of my bondage. Sixty-nine floors below us, Wall Street's minions went about their business. Tiny, pathetic creatures completely unaware of the technology that stood to change their world forever.

'How about here?' I motioned with the alligator clip to a large air conditioning unit.

'That should work,' Jude said. 'Go for it.'

I made the connection while Jude initiated the program.

Connection established.

'Damn!' I shouted over the din of rooftop machinery. 'I can't believe you really did this!'

'Reuben did most of the work,' Jude said modestly.

'Let me type something,' I said, giving in to the excitement of the moment.

'Make it something good,' Jude said. 'This is historic.'

I took him at his word and typed:

Watson, can you here me?

In a few seconds, the reply appeared.

This ain't no telephone, you geek. And learn to spell. It's *hear*!

'Show me how it connects to the Internet,' I said, with an enthusiasm for technology I hadn't felt since high school.

'You just open the browser,' he said.

I double-clicked on my Microsoft Explorer icon. I was a little embarrassed that I didn't have the more egalitarian-seeming Netscape[105] on my machine. But I was even more shamed by the personal 'start page' that filled the screen: a list of the company's stocks-to-watch.

'Let me try something with a little more bandwidth,' I said, typing in the URL for a streaming video company.

The browser connected to the site about as quickly as it would have with a standard modem. Not blazing, but fast enough to make the point.

'This is amazing, Jude,' I said, before dropping into business mode. 'Have you arranged for a patent?'

'We don't know about all that business stuff,' said Jude, reminding me of my own claim to Tobias that morning. 'That's why we came to you.'

'I'm honored, really.' My brain involuntarily schemed ways of stealing the rights to this technology. Even quitting M&L and joining Jude as CEO. I could probably convince them to let me run the company. But I managed to calm myself. 'I know I can get M&L to back this.'

'You can?'

'Absolutely. They don't know what the hell they're doing here. They'll listen to anything I say.'

'Hmph,' Jude said.

'I didn't mean it like that. I just meant—'

'It's cool. It's your world, man. Not mine.'

'It's your world, too, now. Just you watch.'

'Well then,' Jude said, pulling a fat joint out of his leather jacket pocket. 'Let's celebrate.'

I instinctively looked left and right, then laughed at my own fear.

105. The Internet was accessed through clumsy hypertext programs known as browsers. Netscape was the browser owned and distributed by America Online. Though originally developed as freeware at the University of Illinois at Champagne-Urbana, Netscape was the first Internet program to be sold commercially, and was often blamed for turning the online software development space into a market-driven phenomenon. Compared to Microsoft's 'Explorer' browser, however, Netscape seemed positively proletariat.   —Sabina Samuels

'Paranoia strikes deep,' Jude sang, torching the joint.

'Into your life it will creep,' I finished the Buffalo Springfield lyric as I took a hit.

We exhaled our smoke into the wind, then leaned far over the ledge to gaze down at the street below.

'Man,' Jude said.

'What?'

'Down there. How organized it is. Look how much cooperation goes into maintaining a functioning metropolis.'

Vehicles stopped at red lights, and pedestrians followed the instructions of flashing signs in the crosswalks.

'It's so precise,' Jude continued. 'So organized. Cars in their lanes, using flashing lights to signal their intentions, navigating the intersections through consensual hierarchies of right-of-way. And the people on the sidewalk. Making eye contact ten yards away from each other and then initiating infinitesimal adjustments to avoid collision. Communicating their vectors and velocities through subtle kinesthetic cues.'

As Jude spoke, I experienced the activity of the city beneath us as a symphony. Or schools of fish dancing around a coral reef, whose synchronous, collective motion defied cause-and-effect analysis. It was a delightful, dynamic system. The culmination of myriad agreements. A perfectly functioning organism[106].

'Then again,' he spoke while toking deeply, 'you could choose to see it all the other way.' He passed the joint back to me. I took another hit. 'A chaotic jungle of individual will. Look how that car just cut off the bus.'

The screech of a city bus's tires against the asphalt carried all the way up to the roof.

'People squeezing to get past one another,' Jude went on, his words find-

106. Ironically, it was common at the time to use biological analogies to explain markets and other complex systems, rather than the reverse. cf. Hayek, Friedrich August von (1945) "The Use of Knowledge in Society" [uniref HAY334a] and Open Source Document (2036) "Connectionist Manifesto 1.7" [ZZZ543g]
—MRNORMATIVE

ing a more desperate cadence. 'Women angrily pressing their cell phones into their skulls, unable to hear. Men gobbling down their processed bacteriostatic meat sandwiches as they step around the bodies of homeless derelicts.'

Jude was right. Several men in dirty gray coats lay sleeping on the sidewalk. Were they there before? A trader, in a bright green vest, spit near one of the quasi-corpses in disgust. Meanwhile, a stream of pedestrians were taking advantage of the bus's temporary paralysis to cross against the signal, sending a taxi swerving out of its lane.

'It's a nightmare,' Jude said. 'Private desperation against a background of constant panic. Each person following his own selfish goals, oblivious to the needs of the rest. Thinking of one another as marks, customers, or even products. Losers to be fucked or simply fucked over. Everybody in the others' way.'

The movements of the people in the street had become more angular. More aggressive. Furious. Two men unloading a truck dropped a huge box of machine parts. They spilled out on the sidewalk. Pedestrians scattered in all directions, waving their arms and cursing at the workers. Several tripped and fell. The taxis, already veering to avoid the stalled bus, now darted every which way, struggling to steer clear of the debris. One smacked loudly into a black car in the approaching lane. The drivers got out of their cars and began to argue. Traffic stopped in all directions. Horns blared. Pedestrians scrambled to take advantage of the impasse. It was pandemonium.

'What happened?' I asked. 'How did you see that coming? What did you do?'

'It's the same street, Jamie.' He turned from the ledge and leaned with his back against the wind to light a cigarette. 'It's all how you look at it.'

5. The Run-Up

107. Encryption was not only used for business purposes and for conducting secure transactions over the net, but had gained popularity as a backlash to world-wide governments and other institutions which infringed on individuals' rights to privacy.

In fact, some countries of the world had implemented acts whereby, if a person ever used encryption, they could be required, at a later date, when requested by government bodies, to reveal the encryption passphrases needed to decrypt documents and messages "in the interests of national security." Failure to disclose the correct passphrases resulted in a two year prison sentence. Therefore, many people were imprisoned merely due to their poor memories. —alumpot

The customer in Toronto types the order. '4000 at 74.' It is encrypted[107] by the secure browser, and assigned a secure key—a combination lock with as many digits as the Old Testament. The resulting numerical sequence is translated by his home computer into binary commands that are, in turn, converted into packets for TCP/IP transmission through the telephone wire. The strings of data—a succession of bits of numerical information—arrive one by one at servers in Detroit, Chicago, Toledo, and St. Louis. Each server identifies the packet it has received, and directs it further on its journey to New York.

There, the destination server waits until all the packets have arrived before stringing them back together into a single numerical sequence for its final transfer to M&L's server, on the 24th floor of the M&L tower on Wall Street. The final server receives the recombined numerical message, then uses its own key to unlock the sequence and reassemble it as a binary command. Recognizing it as a sell order, the server translates the code into the appropriate command string, and shunts the sequence through M&L's intranet to the correct dedicated line. It arrives at a server located on the second floor of the Commodities Exchange, which translates the binary command back into a numerical sequence that the commodities trading software can display.

On a small screen in the M&L booth next to the copper trading pit, the order from Toronto appears.

4000 at 74

A man in an orange and black checkered vest, M&L's signature design, writes the order on a small piece of paper, and brings it to a woman dressed in a similarly colored vest. She stands on the second of three levels descending into a carpeted crater—one of twenty such octagonal amphitheaters sunken into the huge room's floor. Other shouting people, almost all men, in brightly colored vests designed to attract the human eye, stand in concentric rings facing the center of the pit. Synapse.

The woman looks at the piece of paper that has been handed to her. The rods in her eyes distinguish the pencil marks from the white background, and send this information to the optic nerve, which transmits a signal to her superior colliculus. There, the impulses are converted to shapes that are immediately compared and contrasted with symbols previously processed and recorded by the parietal lobe. Almost immediately, the creature known as Carla Santangelo has successfully interpreted the data as an order to sell

4000 November copper options at an average price of no less than seventy-four dollars each.

She lifts her head and regards the rest of the activity around her. Men's mouths shout numbers. Their hands indicate quantities and prices. 200 for 78. Sold. 300 at 77 1/2. Sold. 100 at 78. Sold. Two young men in brown smocks, the only humans of African descent in the cell, sit in a crouched position at the very center, recording each successful transaction into handheld devices, which transmit their data directly to computer servers. Some of these servers transmit the data elsewhere. Another translates the data into a sequence capable of organizing a series of light emitting diodes into numerical formations that race across the wall of the commodities room.

Although 74 is cheap, 4000 is a big chunk to dump all at once. If she isn't careful, she can single-handedly bring the price down to 72. She waits for a lull in the selling, when buyers might get nervous about the quantity of available contracts. She relaxes the muscles in her face so as not to betray how many futures she must sell, or at what price. She starts high, hoping to catch some locals—independent traders who buy and sell with their own money, and not at the best prices. '400 at 79,' she says. No one bites. She repeats '400 at 79.'

A fat man across the pit counters, '400 for 78.'

'400 at 78 and 1/2.'

'Sold.' The transfer is made, the circuit complete.

'300 at 78 and 1/2,' she offers.

'78 and 1/8,' an available relay responds.

'Sold.' Another spark arcs across the potential voltage, establishing equilibrium.

And so on, and so on. Once the independents catch wind of Carla's volume, they pass on her offers for fear of not being able to unload them by the day's end. Institutional buyers move in and drag her price down to 76, 75, 73, and even a few at 71.

Each sale is physically recorded on a tiny transaction slip by its buyer, who hands it off to his assistant, who enters it into computers, which translate and transfer the data through a series of servers to a waiting client. Somewhere, at some point in a fictional future, some copper belongs to someone else. It will belong to hundreds, perhaps thousands of different people and institutions before November actually arrives.

The woman I replaced as M&L's Technology Strategist sold her 4000 commodities options at what turned out to be an average price of 75 1/8. Her brain had surrendered itself completely to the process of shifting ownership of copper futures for a customer she would never meet, or even attempt to imagine. She was a perfectly functioning neuron, testing potential differences and maximizing the value of each transaction. When she was done, she handed off the last of her transaction sheets to an assistant, and gave her place at the pit to another orange-and-black-vested trader.

'That was impressive,' I told her as she left the ring.

'It took me a few hours to get the hang of it, again,' she admitted.

'Well, I don't think I could ever get the hang of that.'

'Don't patronize me, Cohen,' she said, stepping up out of the pit and joining me a few meters from the fray.

'I'm not,' I said. 'I mean, well...'

'Yeah?'

'I'm just sorry for the way things turned out.'

'Don't be. I've still got my key to the executive washroom.' Carla spoke in the same deadpan she employed in the pit. 'Besides, you're the one in the hot seat, now.'

She sat down on a stool by a computer in the M&L station. It was more of a phone booth, really, filled with computers and separated from a multitude of others by temporary dividers decorated with sports photos and raunchy pin-ups—much in the fashion of an auto mechanic's shop. Political correctness[108] hadn't yet reached the pits. Or maybe this is how they reacted.

'Really, Carla, I had no idea they were going to use mydoor to crash mydoorman.com. It just looked like a good business plan to me. And you weren't available to talk to.'

'Don't even try.' She swung her stool around and pretended to check some prices on her monitor. 'You fucked me over. You took over my fund. It's yours now. And I'm back in the pits where Morehouse wanted me, all along. I knew it was coming. You had nothing to do with it.'

'But you two were...?'

'What?'

'You know...you and Morehouse had some history, right?'

'You think I *fucked* him?! Jesus Christ, Cohen. He hasn't been able to get a hard-on for decades. Especially not with that giant thing of his.'

'But the way you two were talking...'

'You've got a lot to learn, kid.' She looked at me with pity.

So she hadn't slept with him? If I'd only known that at the time.[109]

She opened a small plastic bottle of Evian[110]—the only evidence of high culture in this otherwise Godforsaken locker room—and took a swig. She wiped her mouth with her sleeve. 'I've got other options. Don't you worry about me. Worry about yourself.'

'What's that supposed to mean?' Was she planning her revenge?

'You think that this bullshit is going to last forever?' She rolled her eyes. 'The market is flat. 'Stealth rally' my ass. How long you think it's going to take the street to realize it's already over?'

'There's still plenty of money to be made. Beyond the hype. The Internet

108. A term first used by the Communist party in the Soviet Union, meaning that a statement or view conformed to the state ideology. As Jamie employ's the term, it refers to America's efforts to weed out racist or sexist language and actions through self-repression rather than insight.   —Sabina Samuels

109. From events as he depicted them in the preceding chapters, Jamie betrayed Carla before he incorrectly assumed she had slept with her superior. We do not know whether he is misrepresenting himself intentionally, here, or if has simply revised his own memory.
          —Sabina Samuels

110. Widespread water pollution and additives led to the use of bottled water. To make this less upsetting, many people chose to make their brand selection a fashion statement. Contamination of the polar ice caps eventually made brands such as Evian even less safe than highly chlorinated "tap" water. —Sabina Samuels

is just beginning to penetrate globally, and broadband and wireless are in their infancy. Sure, there'll be some casualties, but it's still a young market.'

'Yesterday's novelty is today's commodity, Jamie. It all ends up right here in the pits, sooner or later.' She blew a lock of hair off her forehead. She was positively sexy when she was sure of herself. Or maybe it was the fact she'd been defeated. All I knew was I wanted her on top of me again.

'Computers used to be the hot thing,' she said. 'Now they're giving them away to people who buy Internet access. And Internet access? Now, they're giving that away with online trading accounts. And those? They're giving people a thousand dollars just to open an account, just like they give old ladies fifty bucks and a bus ticket to go to Atlantic City. You have to make 50 transactions in the first month, though, just to make sure you're hooked before the free doses run out.'

'They're just incentives, Carla. To get people over the initial reluctance.'

'You don't get it, do you?' Carla seemed genuinely surprised. 'You know how baseball cards[111] started? They used to give one away in a pack of gum. An incentive. Then everyone started doing it. Then the cards became more valuable than the gum. Soon, they were giving away a stick of gum in a pack of cards. Now they don't even sell the gum, anymore, just the cards. That's what's going to happen to your dot.coms.'

'But the cards are still valuable. Content is king, right? You know how much people are paying for just a dot.com name these days?'

'That's called artificial scarcity, Cohen.'

'New ideas are still valuable,' I retreated. 'I'm reading twenty business plans a week.'

'Used to be closer to a hundred.'

'They're higher quality now, that's all,' I said. 'The market's more discerning. That's a good thing for everyone.'

111. Small cardboard rectangles with the photograph of a sports figure on one side, numbers rating the figure on the other side. Used by men and young boys for worship.   —RABBITROAR

'Keep telling yourself that.' She finished her Evian and spiraled the bottle into a basket at least ten feet away. 'There's no more new ideas. As soon as one is thought up, someone copies it or one-ups it. Your bright idea is just another commodity in a couple of weeks. It all comes down to this,' she waved her arm across the expanse of pits. 'Gravity.'

'Well, then,' I gave up on apologizing. 'I guess you're in the right place.'

'We both are, Jamie.'

'I'm glad you see it that way.'

That stung her the most, for some reason. I could tell by the way she averted her gaze for moment, then re-established eye contact with a squinty, guarded malevolence.

'So is that it?' she asked. 'Just apologizing for stealing my job?'

'Well...and the stuff that went on between us, I guess.'

'Nothing went on between us,' she said.

'But, Carla...' I couldn't believe I was getting to play it this way. As if I were the innocent in all this. 'We could still, you know...' And as I said it, I actually felt it. I would have slept with her again that very night. Not just out of sympathy, or even out of conquest.

'Don't worry your guilty little head,' she said. 'We both got laid.' Did she really mean this?

'So it was nothing?'

'I was drunk.'

'Yeah, I guess I was, too.'

'Quid pro quo,' she said. 'I better get back to work.'

'One more thing, Carla.' I didn't want to leave it like this. I had to make sure she knew what she was missing. Or maybe I really wanted her advice. 'Morehouse wants me to go with him to some meeting. In Montana.'

'He's taking you to the Bull Run?' She seemed genuinely impressed.

'Yeah, what is it?' I asked, not letting on I knew as much as I already did. 'You been?'

'No, Jamie. That's boys only. No girls allowed.'

'What do you mean? Is it a business thing, or what?'

'I guess it would count as an 'or what." And with that she went back to the pit.

I felt like a video game character after conquering a particularly powerful creature at the end of a level. I had absorbed her strength.

I decided to walk downtown to M&L. The reconciliation with Carla, if one could call it that, took less time than I had anticipated and I needed a little breather to recover, anyway. It was unseasonably mild outside. Global warming? Maybe, I thought as I unbuttoned my overcoat. The weather just wasn't what it used to be. Radicals blamed it on the market, and its dependence on massive consumption and disposable products. They had a point: the more we waste, the more we buy. But if the environment became a truly serious issue, wouldn't business arise to profit off it the way it rose to profit off everything else?

Yes, the game of commerce, properly played, was a good thing. My home security strategy had driven Carla's off the map because it was better. The mere announcement that M&L would be underwriting the Aussie venture sent her entire fund plummeting. The *Wall Street Journal* article announcing my promotion to her position was all M&L could do to stop the hemorrhaging. And who was I to refuse the company, no matter how much I stood to benefit personally? After all, I was on the team.

But what did Carla mean by warning me like that? *Worry about yourself.* She was just trying to harsh my mellow. I'd knocked her out of the game, that's all. Sore loser. But she'd be just fine. She still had her key to the washroom. And her options package. No harm, no foul.

The streets were filled with men who were playing by the same rules of the new economy as me. Surely they had all made one or two of the same questionable moves in their careers, especially at the beginning when they were just learning the ropes. We all strode about the newly refurbished downtown, pleased with ourselves for the effect we were having on the city around us. The sidewalks were clean, the office buildings had sparkling facades, and the clothing designers were making a mint. I had bought six new suits myself in the past month, doubling my wardrobe. My checking account had over ten thousand dollars in it for the first time, ever.

And tonight, I'd be flying on a private jet with the Chairman of M&L to attend a weekend retreat so exclusive that it could only be alluded to in *Forbes* and *Vanity Fair* as an 'annual NYSE-elite soiree' and a 'private vacation spot for New York's old money,' respectively. Just three weeks since I arrived, I was at the center of the game.

That's when I saw one for the first time. The man was turning the corner, but I saw it for a full second before he escaped from view: protruding from the top of a starched blue collar, the unmistakable profile of a bull[112]. I ran to catch up, nearly slipping as I reached the corner. I had a clear view all the way down Broad Street, but the bull had vanished. Or perhaps the man's head had returned to normal. It could have been anyone. Or nothing at all. No one else seemed to notice anything out of the ordinary. Weird.

When I got back I figured I should check in on Morehouse. I'd be doing a presentation at the retreat, and he might want to see it first. Besides, it made me feel important to stroll into his office unannounced. The cubicle people wouldn't dare do such a thing.

Morehouse's dashing young black assistant, Brad, was at his desk, struggling to synch Morehouse's Palm data with a new cell phone.

'Is Tobias in there?' I asked, loud enough for everyone to hear me using

112. One of the most problematic aspects of the manuscript. Morwenna Cool Granite Cohn suggests this to be factual, an early experience of the phenomenon of Mithraistic zoomorphic avatars as a precursor to the Cretan Revelation. But the more common critical view is that this is a fictional experience designed to reinforce a 'bull' metaphor consciously explored throughout the work.
—RAYGIRVAN

their founder's first name.

'I think he's free,' Brad said, the word 'think' being his only qualifier. No one knew quite what to make of me, yet. The kid who treats Morehouse like a colleague instead of a superior. The stakes felt low enough to pal around with Tobias the way a *Who Wants to be a Millionaire*[113] contestant does with Regis on those first few rounds, before there's thousands to lose and the life lines are spent. And I think Tobias appreciated whatever candor I could muster. It's what he was paying me for.

I found him in his office reading the *Post*. On the cover, a story about that runaway bull[114]. It had apparently trampled a little girl—still in critical condition—and the animal was scheduled to be sacrificed tomorrow. Maybe that's what accounted for my hallucination in the street. I must have seen the picture out of the corner of my eye.

'I guess you saw this,' Morehouse said, dolefully.

Did Tobias identify with that poor, imprisoned bull? A mighty beast, out of his natural environment, about to be executed?

'Yeah,' I answered. 'They're gonna kill it.'

'He can really be a self-righteous bastard, sometimes.'

'Who?'

'Birnbaum,' Tobias answered, turning the paper around for me to see. 'Who do you think?'

'Oh, yeah,' I recovered. 'Birnbaum.' He had been referring to a different story, entirely. Rather than simply admit I had no idea what Tobias was talking about, I tried to scan the article on the spot. It had something to do with Ezra Birnbaum, Chairman of the SEC, launching an investigation into online trading. The Fed's Consumer Protection Bureau. Fraud. Risk. Penalties.

'This doesn't really affect us, though, does it?'

113. Who Wants to be a Millionaire was still just a television game show and web site, and hadn't yet grown into a church.
—Sabina Samuels

114. It is important for readers to appreciate the layers of meaning within this passage. The bull was a symbol of economic prosperity for market capitalists. "Bullshit," or simply "bull," was also slang for misinformation. So, the phrase "runaway bull" can be taken to mean "runaway prosperity" or "runaway misinformation." Of course, given the highly speculative nature of the 21st century marketplace, prosperity and misinformation were closely tied. (Readers should not be shocked by the reference to sacrificing the bull. While religious sacrifice was uncommon in the day, many forms of animal murder were still perfectly legal.)
—SHANKEL

'Of course it does.'

'But we're not involved in any fraud,' I said. 'This will just weed out the illegal daytrading scams.' Over the past few months, many amateur online traders had been taken in by shady schemes. *60 Minutes*[115] had done a report.

115. A whistle-blowing news program. *60 Minutes* uncovered many instances corporate corruption until the parent network was purchased by an aerospace media conglomerate, after which its investigations focused solely on government.
—Sabina Samuels

'We depend on online trading for seventy percent of our commission revenues. Retail clients—not our investors. We don't care why they trade or how much they make, as long as they keep trading. Inquiries like this, Senate hearings, SEC investigations, they all change the public sentiment. They reduce the number of transactions.'

'I never really looked at it that way.'

'Well you better start,' Tobias said, grabbing the paper back. 'Ezra will be there this weekend, and we're going to have to work on him.' He could see I was still green when it came to the laws and psychology that governed trading. 'Shit. Go talk to Alec. We all have to be on the same page with this one.'

This was it. A crisis at the very heart of free enterprise. And my knowledge of computer networking gave me exposure to the kinds of decision-making that maybe only a few dozen people had around the world. I felt like a White House staffer in the war room. What I did and said now could end up affecting headlines in the *New York Times*.

Yet I had no idea what was really going on. Maybe Alec could get me up to speed before anyone found out.

'You don't think our market makers ever bid down the price of a stock just to take the stops out?' Alec asked from behind his desk—a slab of thick plate glass on chrome sawhorses.

'Look, Alec,' I began, hoping for a sympathetic reception. 'Trading isn't my thing. I can help with information architecture, networking strategy, e-commerce, content ideas, interface design…'

'But this *is* interface, Jamie,' Alec said, turning his monitor for me to see and typing a web address into his keyboard. 'Take a look here on the message boards.'

On the screen appeared a long list of postings about a tiny NASDAQ stock called XTXT. Alec clicked one of them open, written by a user calling himself 'DayTradingFool.'

'Look here,' he said. 'DayTradingFool says he's just sold short on XTXT.'

DAYTRADING FOOL (12:31PM)

Subject: Selling Short

I just got off a conference call with management, and these guys are screwed. The xtxt line of servers is meeting fierce competition from IBM and the other big players. They don't have the contracts or revenue to support their valuation. At $1.30 per share, I calculate their real P/E at over 3000! All I can say is TIMBER!!!!

'So?' I asked. 'The guy is selling short. Big deal.'

'Yeah,' Alec said, turning another monitor around for me to see. 'But look at the trades that followed immediately after his posting.'

The screen showed a list of transactions—white numbers in columns on a blue background. Each one had a little red or green arrow next to it.

'The arrows indicate whether it went at the bid or ask,' Alec explained.

At precisely 12:32, all the arrows changed to red. A hundred shares at $1.28, another hundred at $1.27, four hundred at $1.27 1/8, all the way down to fifty shares at $1.21 by 1:00 pm that afternoon.

'So? People sell on bad news.'

'Let's go back to the videotape,' Alec narrated in the voice of a sportscaster. 'Take a look at the next series of posts.'

XTXT MAN (12:40PM)

Subject: Timber My Ass

I don't know who you were talking to, FOOL, but as far as I'm concerned, XTXT has positioned itself into a unique category. Their servers do Digital Transfer Tracking, using a proprietary technology. No other company is even working on that. And the 30-day moving average on this stock, combined with analysis of the Brodinger Bands, indicate that the stock is about to pop. You sell short all you want. Can't wait until you have to cover.

DAYTRADING FOOL (12:55PM)

Subject: Digital Transfer Tracking

Since when did you become an expert on XTXT? I haven't seen you on these boards before. How much of this issue do you currently hold? DTT technology is just another acronym for Daytraders Talking Tripe. Why don't you come clean?

XTXT MAN (1:08PM)

Subject: re: Digital Transfer Tracking

I'm a technical analyst with over 1.2 million in small cap investments. If you check the boards on Lucent and PRPS, you'll see how accurate I've been over the past 18 months. I've been following XTXT since its IPO last April, and the recent downturn looks to me like market makers shaking out the stops before a run-up. My question to you, DAYTRADING FOOL, is how did you get a conference call with management? Insider information is illegal.

DAYTRADING FOOL (1:15PM)

Subject: Libel

I've forwarded your last posting to my attorneys. You should be hearing from them by the end of the week. These are public bulletin boards, and you are responsible for everything you write. If anyone else on this board is following the thread, take note of how when XTXT runs out of anything substantive to say, he immediately stoops to the kind of mud-slinging reserved for politicians. He's run out of reasonable arguments. Sell while you still can. I'm out of here.

PAMELA THE PICKER (1:21PM)
Subject: Outing the Daytraders
Thanks Fool, for sticking with this thread in spite of the insults. I, for one, appreciate your insights. I sold my stake half an hour ago, at a buck and a quarter.

XTXT MAN (1:30PM)
Subject: Attorneys
I'll be ready for their call. ;) And I'm very impressed by how charitable you are with the other members of this board. You're a regular Mother Theresa. By the way, I emailed the VP of investor relations, and he assured me that no such conference call occurred this morning. In fact, the entire management team is at a convention in Las Vegas, doing a demo at the NPP trade show. They've been there all day. Check out the press release at http://www.xtxt.com/release122A.html.

GOLDDIGGER (1:41PM)
Subject: NPP trade show
What gives Fool? Explain for us how you got to management. I just read the release. XT Man looks legit.

XTXT MAN (1:50PM)
Subject: Outing
So who has outed whom, eh Daytrading Fool? I've forwarded this thread to XTXT management. You should be hearing from them by the end of the week. ;)

'See,' Alec said, pointing to the other monitor. 'The selling stopped around then. Up to that point, over 100,000 shares in all, sold at the bid.'

'I see the trades, Alec, but I don't get what's the big deal. People read these boards and make their decisions. It's their own problem who they trust.'

'We're not there yet, Jamie.' He scrolled down the messages. 'Daytrading Fool is completely silent until the next morning. And look what he ends up posting.'

DAYTRADING FOOL (11:45AM)
Subject: Good-bye
I have been posting messages to this board over the past six months with the pseudonyms of Daytrading Fool, Mark24, and Yinvest. In an agreement with XTXT management, I am posting now to disclose the fact that I never engaged in the conference call I claimed to have engaged in yesterday. I have no knowledge of the company's competitive status or their XT servers. I am sorry for any inconvenience my postings may have caused, and I will no longer be participating on these bulletin boards. Good trading to all, and good day.

'You mean he was faking it all along?'

'It gets better,' Alec said. 'Look at how the price skyrocketed immediately after Daytrading Fool's confession.'

He scrolled down a long string of transactions, all with green arrows next to them. By 3pm, the stock had reached $2.10 per share.

'Amazing,' I said. 'One online conversation can do all that?'

'Indeed it can.' He paused for effect. 'Which is why he staged it.'

'Who, Daytrading Fool? Isn't he in trouble now? Or was it the XT Man?'

'It wasn't Daytrading Fool or XTXT Man,' Alec smiled.

'What do you mean?'

'They're the *same person*, Jamie.'

'What the fuck?'

'It was the same daytrader,' Alec explained, 'having a pretend argument with himself.'

'No way.'

'Yes way.' Alec smiled. 'He played both the bear and the bull. He let the bear win for a while so he could buy in. He picked up 80,000 shares while Daytrading Fool drove the price down. Once he had bought all he wanted, he let XTXT put a damper on the dive by challenging whether or not the conference call took place. Then, when he was ready to sell the next day—'

'He posted Daytrading Fool's confession!'

'Exactly!' Alec slapped the top of the monitor. 'And he did it simultaneously with two other aliases who were posting to different boards. He spent months developing the characters, then killed them in a single sweep. He made over $300,000 in the process.'

'I can't believe it. How do you know this for sure?'

'The guy is a client. He lives out in Hoboken and trades all day. We make the market in that stock.'

'Jesus Christ, Alec, isn't that illegal?'

'Not yet, it isn't. I mean, what *he* did is illegal, but we're just conducting his trades. How were we supposed to know?'

'But we did know. *You* know.'

'We know, but we don't know. We certainly have plausible deniability. We can't be expected to monitor every thread. There's hundreds of them.'

'You play the game, you take your chances?'

'Welcome to the wonderful world of e-trading.'

'But your name, your company name is on the bulletin boards.' I had returned to referring to M&L as 'you.'

'We put up disclaimers. 'M&L is not responsible for the information posted."

'That's kind of you.'

'Consider the alternative, Jamie. If Birnbaum gets his way, the firm will be held accountable for every posting. He'd institute processes and double-checks that would cost us more than our commissions.'

'But it couldn't be a good long-term strategy like your dad wants. Not if the majority of your traders are losing money.'

'They're not our real clients. These are idiot daytraders. And they're transacting more than ever. These kinds of episodes just make the house-wives reading them feel like they're in the thick of it. Like they're part of the game. They love it, so it must be worth money to them. Some people pay to go the movies. These wannabes pay for the thrill of swimming with sharks[116]. We got the idea from reading that Jupiter report on how community areas draw traffic to commerce sites. Since we put up the boards, transactions have gone up 175 percent.'

'I don't mean to insult the family business, but there must be better ways to drive transactions through your site.'

'Fine, Jamie.' He turned the monitors back to their original positions. 'You're the Internet guru now. Go think of one.'

116. Perhaps an allusion to a more dangerous variant of the late 20th century fad of paying to swim with dolphins for supposed therapeutic purposes.
—RAYGIRVAN

'I will,' I said, accepting the challenge.

'Well, you do that!' Alec punctuated his sentiment with an enthusiastic nod, just to make sure I knew he was amused, not offended, by my insolence. 'The limo leaves in an hour. You've got your bags, right?'

I nodded and took my leave.

I can handle this, I thought as I went back to my office. It's no different from game design. Just make online trading an entertaining experience, without resorting to the dark perversion of online community that M&L had relied on until now. No biggie. This might even be fun. And I'd actually be doing a good thing.

Hell, the Morehouses didn't even know the half of what was up my sleeve. I had an earth-shatteringly brilliant new technology to pitch. TeslaNet. A communications infrastructure based on the electrical charge of the earth itself. It could blow the lid off everything. And it was invented by kids from the neighborhood. That's why I was working amongst the suits, I reminded myself. This is why I was pretending to be one of them. I was an agent of change—a double-agent, in fact, using my position in the control room of corporate capitalism to subvert it.

This made me feel good enough about the state of my soul to call home and speak to my mother. She had a way of detecting the health of my psyche by the sound of my voice, so I only liked to speak to her when I was feeling confident. Otherwise she'd identify the gaps in my emotional logic and pry them apart until I couldn't live with myself any longer. Like that time I called her from Geraldo's green room. She made me feel so conflicted about condemning the Jamaican Kings on national television that when I finally went on the air I overcompensated and proclaimed the Internet a 'hacker's playground.'

Not that Mom supported the Kings in the least. Back then, she held them responsible for my downfall. But her persistent questions—honest, heartfelt, and non-judgmental—worked on me like a Chinese water torture[117].

'Howdy Mom!' I said cheerfully.

There was no need for the pretense. Sophie had bad news.

'I'm so glad you called,' she said. 'We haven't spoken since—'

'Yeah,' I pre-empted her reproach. 'It's been crazy.' I used the word 'crazy' whenever I felt a curse word coming on. 'I'm off to Montana tonight for some crazy meeting.'

'Oh.' She paused. 'I was hoping you would be here tomorrow. We'd go to services as a family. As a show of support.'

'Why? What's wrong?' I already knew.

'He called the Assembly this morning.' She meant the Rabbinical Assembly. The place rabbis call to find new jobs.

'Don't you think it's a little premature?'

'Of course I do,' she said. 'I think he should put up a fight.'

'Did you tell him?' Was it just me, or do all sons serve as intermediaries between their parents?

'He says I'm biased. I don't see him the same as the congregation does.'

'They think they'll get a more experienced rabbi on what they pay? Are they crazy?'

'I don't know, honey. But I think he would listen to you.'

'Me? He thinks I'm the enemy.'

'No, he doesn't. He's proud of you. You should have heard him kvell over the article in the paper.'

'You saw it?'

'Morris did. He came to services last week, just to show it off. You should have told us.'

'I saved a copy for you,' I lied. 'It's really straight out of the company press

117. Refers to the excessive water retention a person experienced after eating large quantities of Chinese food prepared with monosodiumglutamate or MSG.
—AMELIAB85

release, you know. I mean, it's no big deal.'

'Of course it's a big deal. The whole congregation was talking about it.'

'The same congregation that's trying to get rid of him.'

'Don't you see, honey? That's why he needs you. He'll listen to what you say.'

My mom was smart, if a little overanalytical. She studied psychology in college, and I understood where she was coming from. Dad was taking out his personal frustrations on his congregation. If he could make his peace with me, then maybe he'd make peace with them, too. But it was a stretch.

'Dad is just too good for those people,' I said.

'They need him, Yossi. We all do.'

She meant me. I guess I hadn't escaped her Freudian schema.

'Look, I can't come this weekend. I'm on my way out right now. But I'll come next week. And Passover.'

'Of course you're coming Passover,' she said, as if it was an obligation for me to attend, and not a favor on my part. 'You're bringing someone special?' She wanted me to work on making grandchildren, too?

'There's no one special right now, mom. But maybe I'll bring someone. We'll see.'

'How's the apartment?' She changed the subject.

'Look, I better get myself together here.'

'Could you take a moment to talk to Miriam? She loves to hear your voice.'

'Sure, but only for a minute—'

My mom had already put down the phone. I could hear her calling to my sister, and the extension being picked up.

'Hullo?' Miriam asked into the void.

'Hi Miriam.'

'Hi,' she said.

'I'm going away to see some cowboys,' I said, romanticizing the journey.

'Real cowboys or pretend cowboys?'

'Real ones, darling. With horses and everything.'

'On TV?' she asked.

'No, Miriam. Real ones.'

'The truck with the hay?' We had gone on a hayride at Lake George one summer when we were children.

'That's right,' I said, remembering the image for the first time in years. 'That was fun, wasn't it?'

'I finished the pot-holder for you,' she said.

'Thank you, Miriam. That's great! I'll come over and get it.'

'You're coming now?'

'No, Miriam. Soon.'

My mother's voice interrupted from the other extension. 'Jamie has to go now, sweetheart.'

'But he's not here,' Miriam said, incapable of experiencing telecommunications as genuine togetherness.

'He has to get off the phone,' Sophie explained. 'Say good-bye.'

'Good-bye, Jamie,' she said. 'I love you.'

'I love you, too,' I said, using this as my excuse to get off the phone without saying a separate good-bye to my mother, and hanging up.

I made a note on my organizer to call home from Montana. Not that I'd forget, but it made me feel better about taking off when my family needed me.

I used the next hour to insert some extra slides into my PowerPoint[118] presentation for the TeslaNet pitch. I stole a few graphs and charts from the *Wired*[119] and *Upside*[120] magazine web sites and changed their credits to read

118. Packaging was an accepted measure of quality. Successful sales pitches of the period utilized snazzy audiovisual accompaniment. Although these computer-aided presentations usually offered no additional information, the complexity of their technology was thought to indicate the technological level of the idea being pitched. It also kept the audience's attention away from the speaker, who might communicate unwanted information inadvertently through his body language.
—Sabina Samuels

119. At the time, *Wired* was a full-fledged magazine with articles—not the computer parts catalogue we know of today.
—Sabina Samuels

120. Another computer industry magazine.
—Sabina Samuels

'M&L Research.' It was a standard practice.

Just as the golden glare of the setting sun through my windows was making the images on my monitor all but unreadable, Alec appeared in the doorway, a suitcase in each hand and a cowboy hat on his head.

'Ready pardner?' he asked, pushing his hat down over his forehead.

'Sure thing.' I popped out the disk and placed it in my pocket. 'Let's go.'

Alec's festive attitude was contagious, and as we swaggered together through the passages leading to Tobias's office, I began to feel like the powerful young Turk I was. Our strides were long and we spoke to each other loudly, raising the heads of junior executives and secretaries in their cubicles.

'Have you been to this thing before?' I asked.

'My first year. He usually brings Mort or one of the fund managers.'

'Well, I'm a fund manager, now, I guess.'

'Not that kind of fund,' Alec belittled me. 'I'm talking about multi-billion dollar ones. Like the Platinum Fund, or the Circle Investors.'

'So why do you think he's bringing us?'

'To make up for lost time,' Alec said, turning a corner. 'The Bull Run has changed over the past ten years from a monetary-policy-interest-rates kind of thing to a media and technology soirée. My dad's got a reputation for being totally large cap, and anti-NASDAQ. Old school. He gets lost in their conversations now.'

'Doesn't he realize those guys don't know shit? They're all just faking it.'

'Which is why we're gonna do so well, sport,' Alec said as we arrived outside Tobias's outer office.

'He'll be with you in a moment,' Brad said, not realizing that Tobias was already coming out, suitcases in hand. Brad jumped up to take the bags from Morehouse, who hesitated for a moment before handing them over, as if to say, I could carry them easily, but what the heck?

We headed out towards the elevators, Brad leading, a suitcase in each hand. Tobias followed about two meters behind him, his wide frame taking up so much of the aisle that Alec and I, laden with our own luggage, had to walk slightly behind him. But our entourage made quite a sight. A valet, the general, and his two strapping young lieutenants. A path was cleared for us as we marched, young women pressing their backs against the walls and holding their papers up to their breasts to permit the convoy's passage. Just marching with Tobias made me feel powerful by association. I was part of the inner circle, and the key player in our firm's invasion of a new territory.

We entered one of the spacious lifts and Brad pressed the button labeled 'L.' As more people got on, it was impossible for them not to notice the assembled officers. I knew I was being stared at, and felt emboldened, almost aroused by their gaze.

We stopped again on the twelfth floor, and a bike messenger, about my own age, got on and leaned nonchalantly against a railing. He looked slightly ethnic—like a dark Italian or maybe Moroccan—with loose, light brown dreadlocks. He had a blue canvas bag strapped around his chest, and a bicycle wheel in one hand. He wore a torn red t-shirt and tight lycra pants over thighs defined by days spent pedaling. His tan skin was shiny from the sweat of his constant workout racing through New York's streets. He looked like he didn't have a care in the world.

I wasn't the only one staring at the messenger. All the women in the elevator were fixed on the young man. Their eyes were tracing the contours of his neck, the small of his back, the way he held his pelvis forward like a young colt, with his genitals pushing through his biker shorts. Suddenly, I felt stifled by my suit, and burdened by my bags. I had a PowerPoint presentation in my jacket pocket that could lead to millions, perhaps billions of dollars in revenue. But as far as the women around me were concerned, I was just another suit. The messenger was the real maverick. An unashamed slacker. He was free.

I wanted to shout. To let them know this wasn't really me. I was an athlete in college, and a good one. I had a decent chest, too, and strong arms— at least as strong as the biker's. I might even win if we had a fight to the death. But standing there, a corporate stooge in head-to-toe Armani, I felt like my dick wasn't even long enough to hang down. A putz.

No! The slacker was the loser, even if he was the object of every one of these women's fantasies. Bottom line, he was just a messenger, and could never support a family, or put kids through school. But who knew? Maybe he was in a band, playing weekends at the clubs, just about to break through. Or maybe he was an up-and-coming young artist, on the verge of a show at the Whitney. He certainly acted like he had a real life. Or life.

The limo was waiting just in front of the M&L tower. I knew enough to put my suitcases on the curb for Brad and the driver to stow in the trunk. Still, I couldn't fully trust them with my laptop, so I pretended to hold the car door open for Tobias and Alec in order to watch as my bags were safely packed with the others. I wasn't used to other people handling my things for me, and just couldn't believe that everything would be taken care of in the background.

How did the rich manage to trust their servants so much? And what happened when they made mistakes? Brad and the driver's heads were deep in the trunk discussing the optimum space-saving arrangement, while the row of expensive luggage just sat there unattended on the sidewalk! Would they be able to see out of the corner of their eye if someone tried to take one of them? Were they even aware? Did street people simply know not to steal this stuff? Was it some vestige of a sixteenth century understanding between street peasants and the servants of the nobles?

There wasn't enough room in the trunk for all the bags, anyway, so I ended up sitting next to the hand luggage, facing the rear of the car. A great expanse of unused stretch-limo-space separated me from Tobias and Alec, who sat in the real back seat.

'How about a drink?' Tobias said, gesturing with his head.

Only then did I notice the bar nested in one of the highly lacquered wood panels on either side of the passenger compartment.

'What would you like?' I knelt before the rack of bottles and glasses. 'There's Scotch, and I think vodka.'

'Scotch rocks,' Tobias said.

'Me, too,' said Alec.

I steadied myself against the carpeted bump running down the length of the floor and mixed the three drinks. I put one down on the bar, then climbed over to the Morehouses with theirs.

'Bring yours, too,' Morehouse said.

I did as I was told. It sounded like Tobias was about to shed some of his wisdom on us, and sitting on the floor at Morehouse's feet was a small price to pay for this kind of access to the Chairman of M&L.

But Morehouse just sipped his drink and stared out the window at the merging lanes of bumper-to-bumper traffic attempting to snake into the Holland Tunnel.

'I guess we should have taken the bridge,' I said, trying to start a conversation. If Tobias didn't pick up on the cue, I decided, I would return to my seat at the far end of the car. Morehouse didn't respond. As I sat there in silence, figuring out how to move away without appearing as though I didn't appreciate the intimacy of the moment, Alec's head fell back onto the rear dash, and his jaw dropped open.

Tobias's turned to the boy and, with great tenderness, maneuvered his son's body so that it was leaning, more supported, into the corner of the leather seat. He placed a folded suit jacket behind his son's neck as a pillow, and an overcoat on top of him for a blanket.

'He's a good kid,' Tobias said, 'especially with all he's endured.'

'Yeah.' I tried to empathize. But what had a privileged kid like Alec ever had to endure?

'Birnbaum put this family through a lot, you know,' Tobias said.

'Really? How's that?'

'Alec never told you?'

I shook my head.

'Figures.' Tobias smiled at his sleeping son. 'He takes everything in his stride. Even the accident.'

I assumed Tobias meant the boating accident at Princeton. 'It wasn't really that big of a deal,' I said, trying to downplay my own heroism. 'It was dark. He just got a little disoriented. It can happen to anyone.'

'Not that,' Tobias said. 'He can't raise his left arm past the shoulder, you know.'

'No, I didn't. I had no idea.'

'They used to tease him at Andover about it. He really never told you?'

'No. What happened?' I wasn't sure if this was such a good idea—talking about Alec while he slept unaware.

'Funny the way things work out.'

I had no idea what Tobias was talking about. I didn't even know how to ask. Morehouse saved me the trouble of figuring it out.

'Ezra and I had been friends since his days at Manhattan Savings and Loan,' Tobias began. 'M&L didn't even have a seat on the exchange, yet, and Birnbaum was still just authorizing business loans for the bank. He used to come over to our apartment at Lex and 83rd on Saturday afternoons, straight from temple. I remember he'd take the yarmulke off his head, fold it neatly in half, and stick it in his back pocket. Then we'd watch the game. Maybe shoot the shit over a few beers. Talk about how we were going to take over the financial scene.'

'I didn't know you two went so far back.'

'Yeah, well, we do,' Tobias said, holding his glass out for a refill. I obliged him with lubrication.

'Birnbaum was a real nut back then. Quite the neurotic. He was seeing a shrink[121] for it.'

'What was wrong with him?' I asked, carefully handing Tobias a glass filled to the brim with tongue-loosening Johnnie Walker Black.

'He used to imagine that things were falling on people's heads,' Tobias laughed. 'Or that they were about to. He couldn't make it through a cocktail party without warning someone that the chandelier looked like it was about to pull itself out of the ceiling and come crashing down on their head. Or, in the street, he'd always take a route away from construction because he thought a crane might fall or a scaffold would collapse. Remember when that helicopter crashed into the PanAm building?'

I stared at him blankly.

'Ahh,' Tobias shrugged. 'You're too young. The MetLife Building[122]. There used to be a heliport up there. And one time, a copter took a bad approach and knocked right into the top floor. Some debris fell to the street, and a lady was killed.'

'And Birnbaum predicted it?'

'No,' Tobias said. 'But he took it as evidence that these things do happen. He cut out all the newspaper articles about the tragedy—cut them out carefully with scissors—and kept them in his briefcase. He used to read them over and over to himself wherever he went.'

121. Refers to the profession of psychiatry or medical doctors of mental disorders. HMOs rarely approved psychiatric care, thus "shrinks" almost exclusively treated the upper class. Many "shrinks" were essentially drug dealers providing their patients with high quality drugs legally prescribed. —AMELIAB85

122. The Scientology Building, on 44th Street. —Sabina Samuels

128

'So, did the psychiatrist cure him?'

'Sure,' Tobias said. 'He cured him. He hypnotized him, and gave him a little whaddyacallit? A little mantra to say whenever he felt like someone was going to have an accident. Something like 'no one is in danger, nothing is wrong, everyone is safe, everything will be okay.''

'That's pretty simple.'

'And it worked, that's for sure. He was over one Saturday. We were watching the Jets. Alec must have been less than a year old. He was still crawling around on all fours.'

'It's hard to imagine the two of you sitting on the couch, throwing back brewskies with Alec crawling at your feet.' I delighted in imagining Tobias as just another middle-class Joe.

'It was worse than that,' Tobias joked. 'We'd sit there in these two La-Z-Boy chairs I'd bought against the decorating tastes of Alec's mother. God, she hated those things. Well, we'd get buzzed on Michelob and watch the Jets struggle, while Mary cooked up burgers or fried chicken in the kitchen.'

'I'm surprised Alec didn't become a big fan,' I said.

'I'm surprised he didn't develop a phobia of his own,' Morehouse responded. 'See, when Mary was in the kitchen, Alec was my responsibility. The house was child-proof, so we'd just let him roam free. Maybe throw him some popcorn. Ezra was always in such a state—he'd watch Alec's little mouth to make sure he wasn't choking on anything.'

'That is pretty weird, I guess.'

'But when he got cured, all that changed. He'd just finished his final week of hypno-therapy, and he was using his mantra all the time. You could hear him reciting it under his breath whenever he got into an elevator. It was like a constant babble. I learned to ignore it. He had actually seen it coming, but didn't say anything.'

'Seen what?'

'We were leaning back in our chairs. Full recline. Practically horizontal. And Alec had crawled under mine. Ezra saw all this and wanted to warn me, but figured it was his sickness making him worry. So he just recited that mantra, instead. 'No one is in danger, everyone is safe,' and all that. Then Mary called me from the kitchen. Something about helping her drain the fried chicken. I'll never forget. I put my hands on the arms of the chair to straighten up, and I saw Ezra's eyes close, and his lips vibrating with that mantra.'

'And Alec—?'

'Well, I pushed forward with my arms to close the chair. Just as the springs were pulling the leg rest all the way shut, I heard him scream. There was nothing I could do.'

'Oh my God.'

'I got it back open in a second, but Alec's little body was all twisted up. He wasn't even crying, just wheezing. Struggling to breathe.' Morehouse stared at his sleeping son as he spoke. 'We got him to the emergency room and they told us he had broken two ribs. They said his arm had been dislocated, but that they got it back in the socket and it wouldn't need surgery.'

'Jesus, you must have been shook up.'

'Yeah, but not as much as Ezra,' Tobias said, turning back to me. 'We didn't get back from the hospital until late that night. And when we opened the door, Ezra was still sitting there in his chair, repeating the mantra to himself, again and again. He had a complete breakdown. Took two months off to get straight.'

'And Alec?'

'Turns out they were wrong about his shoulder. He had torn a number of tendons in there. He could barely move his arm at all. We got him an operation when he was about three. He wore a stiff white plaster cast over his shoulder and arm for months. But he never got the full motion back.'

'Did you sue?'

'Who sued doctors back then? It was the early 80's. Malpractice hadn't come into vogue. But Birnbaum always did what he could for us after that. When he got elected to the board of the New York Reserve, he'd be sure to drop me an extra hint about which way the Fed was going to move rates. I mean, most everyone had a pretty good idea which way they were going, but it was nice to have his confirmation. It let me make bolder moves.'

'And what about Ezra now?' I asked. 'Is he still so neurotic?'

'Well, he still sees that same stupid shrink.' Tobias spit a bit as he spoke, relaxed by the alcohol. 'But I don't think that helps him half as much as his sessions over at Ms. Halstead's.'

'You mean hookers?' A guy who goes to temple every week sees hookers?

'Madams, more like it,' Tobias said. 'Or mistresses or whatever you call them. Girls in leather with whips and such. They tie him up, or he pretends he's a school boy and they spank him. That sort of thing. He's a mess. Imagine what'll go down at the Fed if that ever shows up on Page Six[123].' Tobias winked.

'Yeah,' I said. What else could I say?

Tobias turned back to Alec. He nudged him, to make sure he was asleep. Alec curled into a different position.

'That's the reason I'm bringing him along, you know.'

'How's that?' I asked.

'Birnbaum owes us.'

I should have realized then and there that these guys weren't playing around.

123. A gossip column in the now-defunct New York Post that originally focused on entertainers, but eventually became a scandal sheet dedicated to the exploits of the City's celebrity businessmen.
—Sabina Samuels

6. Failure

I woke up as Morehouse's Gulfstream 5 touched down on the airstrip. I had meant to stay awake for the whole flight, having never been on a private jet before, but my third helping of sushi and sake put me over the edge. There was no one to talk to, anyway. Tobias, who had flown navy war planes, spent most of his time leaning through the door of the cockpit trading near-miss stories with his two good-natured pilots, while Alec discussed decorating strategies with Aneya, a Czech airplane interior-designer who had been hired to bring Morehouse's G-5 up to the level of those belonging to the more demonstratively wealthy entrepreneurs of Silicon Valley.

'Eef you go wit da full hot tub, like Mr. Gates,' she explained, pointing one of her long maroon fingernails at the plans, 'den you need to build a substructure, here.'

Her services would end up never being used. At dawn, as Tobias took the co-pilot's controls to assist with the landing, he saw the fleet of planes belonging to the other executives lined up on the runway. A few were passenger jets, like his, but the rest were converted military aircraft.

'Jesus fuck!' Tobias said as they pulled the G-5 into a space between two MIGs. 'Has everybody here got a fucking war plane? How do they afford this shit?'

'They're not that expensive, Dad,' Alec offered. 'Army surplus sells 'em, I think.'

'Find out,' Tobias said, removing his seatbelt. 'If anyone's got a right to fly one of those, it's me.'

A black Lincoln Navigator[124] took us from the private airstrip to the ranch it served, a 40,000 acre spread originally owned by one of the last of the independent cattle companies but since taken over by a division of the Entertainink media empire, which made more money using it as a set for movies than selling its steer. The annual Billionaire's Bull Run was being held at the ranch long before it changed hands, though, leading to speculation that Entertainink's chairman Marshall Tellington, the former Rhodes Scholar, only purchased the property so that he'd be able to attend.

As our SUV passed over the cattle grate and up the hill towards the main compound, I was overwhelmed by the intense aroma of cows and dung. I popped a prophylactic dose of antihistamine[125], and loosened my tie.

'Not yet,' Tobias said. 'We'll change when we get to our rooms. Until then, spit and polish.'

I figured Morehouse was still in residual military mode following his three-point landing, and complied. We walked up the wooden steps to the porch (Aneya had been diverted to a nearby motel with the two pilots) and

124. One of several Sport Utility Vehicles, or SUV's. They were military trucks which had been adapted for use in urban (African-American) zones, where aggressive driving, profligate gas consumption, and a sense of insulation from potential attacks were valued.   —Sabina Samuels

125. Air pollution and artificial ingredients in processed foods had so compromised the human immune system by this time that many people would spontaneously launch antibody attacks against harmless natural agents such as pollen and animal hair. Such reactions were called 'allergies.'   —Sabina Samuels

then into the house, an enormous old Western ranch that looked like a movie set, which it was. In the foyer, in front of a life-size Remington bronze of a cowboy wrestling atop a bull, a table was set up for registration.

That's when I noticed the girls. The cutest one was handing a canvas bag filled with notebooks, proposals, and a variety of T-shirts, mouse pads, and other corporate 'shwag'[126] to a man in a trenchcoat. She had red hair cut in a bob, and huge green eyes that smiled knowingly as she directed the man to his accommodations. Although there were three girls behind the table, and two of them were free, I maneuvered myself around my colleagues, boxing them out with my back in such a way as to indicate that the red-head was mine.

'Jamie Cohen,' I told her, awaiting her eye contact as she perused her guest list. She blew the bangs off her forehead before looking back up at me, with the same knowing smile she gave the last registrant. It worked on me, in spite of myself, as if I were the first man she ever smiled at in her life.

'You'll be staying in cabin four,' she said, 'with Mr. Morehouse.'

'That must mean me,' Alec said, idling over. I involuntarily shouldered Alec away.

'Do you work here at the ranch year-round?' I asked, falling into my best appropriated Montanan.

'Oh, no,' she laughed, handing me my nametag. 'We're flown in for the event.' She made some notes on her papers and reached down for another canvas bag.

'Really?' I asked, desperate to keep the conversation going. 'From where? New York? That's where we're from.'

'Yeah,' she said, amused by my awkwardly forced flirtation. 'Technology advisor, Morehouse & Linney,' she read off my nametag.

'Right,' I laughed, trying to see around the stacks of notebooks to the tag

126. Free items with corporate logos. Many of these items are now collected in the Museum of Shwag in Barcelona.
—Sabina Samuels

134

on her lavender, pullover sweater. 'And that must mean you're...'

She arched her back, raising her chest above the pile of stuff on the table, and simultaneously pushing the curves of her breasts through the material of her sweater. Surely she knew the effect this had on people.

'Jenna Cordera,' I read. 'That's pretty. Spanish?'

'Way back, I guess,' she said. 'You're into nationality?'

I didn't know what to say. Had she pegged me for a racist? Could she tell that I was already evaluating the impact that a Catholic-raised girl of at least partially Hispanic descent would have on the Cohen lineage? My parents would adapt. Or maybe she would convert.

'It's just interesting, that's all.' I figured I'd cut my losses. 'I guess I'll see you around, then.'

'I guess so,' she said, smiling at me in a way that either meant genuine interest or simple self-satisfaction at having successfully entranced yet another one of the scores of businessmen who would have the very same interaction with her that day.

'Christ, Jamie,' Alec ridiculed me later in the cabin as we unpacked our bags. 'She's *paid* to flirt with you. It's her *job*. Most of these girls are professionals, receive my meaning?'

'Oh,' I said. Fun and games. Right.

Cabin Four, like all the others, had twin beds with identical cowboy motif headboards, matching dressers, and a bathroom between them with a horseshoe on the door. Tobias was staying in the main house, with the other old-timers. The possibility that any of these sixty-year-old-plus executives might suffer from embarrassing physical maladies[127] such as incontinence[128], colostomy bags, or worse, earned them the right to private rooms, no questions asked.

Alec sat on his bed. He'd already changed into faded jeans, a blue flannel

127. Prior to the development of organ cloning and tissue regeneration technology, people had to live with chronic physical malfunctions. Such malfunctions were socially awkward, as they reminded people of their mortality.

Today, of course, the only reminder of our mortality is the life-clock crystal[a] implanted in each of our hands.
—SHANKEL

a. Life Clock Crystal: This recalls an interesting example of clever but flawed historical prediction. The 1976 movie "Logan's Run" was remarkably accurate in anticipating the Washington Wilderness and the brain damage consequent on living in its poisoned biosystem, but assumed that life-clocks would dictate, rather than provide actuarial advice on, their owner's lifespan. —RAYGIRVAN

128. Traced back before the 20th century, this word described the quality of being uncontrollable. It evolved into the definition of a human condition in which the victim was incapable of controlling their excretory functions. After stem cell research altered this human biological process between 2004 and 2012, the word was forgotten. It was picked up again in 2234 to describe a new condition, this time a mental one, known in layman's terms as "Binary Plus."

For sufferers of Binary Plus, life's choices are narrowed so that the word's original definition takes meaning in society once again. An incontinent is not out-of-control, they are uncontrollable, and thusly free. —CASE_MAKER

shirt, and well-worn beige cowboy boots. He fit in perfectly with the shel-lacked logs that formed the cabin's wall. Did he already own these clothes? Did the Morehouses have such a property themselves? Alec seemed capable of rising to any occasion, fully costumed. They must train kids for this in prep school.

'Look at all this shit they gave us,' Alec said, picking through a pile of shwag next to him on the bed. 'Four T-shirts, two mouse pads, three base-ball caps, a yo-yo, five - no - six pens, a mess of pads...shwag city.'

'Tomorrow's landfill,' I said, opening my luggage.

'We could start a business selling shwag, you know.' Alec held up a T-shirt from a random web company. 'You know how much of this stuff is sim-ply discarded? Enough to clothe the whole world, I bet you. We could buy surplus promotional clothing from companies that go out of business, or over-runs from conventions and stuff. And then re-sell it as high fashion. We'd put our own label on it—somewhere really visible. Like right here on the tit. Or in random places. Different for every garment, but really con-spicuous.'

'What would our label say?'

'It'd say 'Shwag.' Get it? We'd rebrand generic shwag as Shwag. Recycled but new and ugly clothes, packaged as social satire.'

Alec had ideas like this all the time. I feared the day this boy would be running M&L, and had the power to implement them.

'Is there a schedule of events in all that junk? When's my TeslaNet speech?'

'I guess you're part of the 'new technologies' panel at three this after-noon,' Alec said, leafing through the pamphlet's mock rawhide pages.

'A panel?' I asked, more of the air than Alec. 'I can't do this kind of thing on a panel. It's not up for conversation.' Audiences tuned out for panels, because they were never about anything other than whatever company or product the panelists were there to pitch. Then again, who was I but a guy from some company, pitching a new product?

'You're lucky to be on it at all, Jamie,' Alec said. 'There's only two panels and a couple of speeches the whole weekend.'

'And the rest of the time...?'

'Cowboy stuff, Jimmy. And networking. Come on. Get dressed. What're you gonna wear, pal?'

I opened my suitcase. I had some casual wear, but it was all new, high-fashion duds I picked up at Armani and Prada[129] after Tobias's approval of my suit. Great. I finally went upscale, but at precisely the wrong time. I'd have been better off with my old college clothes. I scrounged for something manly or at least earthy and then lined up my proposed outfit on the bed: a pair of new black chinos, a T-shirt, and a gray hooded sweatshirt I brought along in case I had time to take a run.

'That it?' Alec asked.

'It'll have to do,' I said, sadly taking off my dress shirt.

'You won't even score a hooker in those, my friend,' he laughed. 'That's okay. More for me.'

The fifty-three men and two women who had arrived that morning were served lunch on the big house's sprawling back lawn. Fried chicken in giant wicker baskets, set onto picnic tables covered with red-and-white checked tablecloths. As I dug around for a drumstick, I couldn't help but think of the fried chicken that was indirectly responsible for mangling young Alec in the springs of that chair.

Or maybe I had subconsciously seen the old neurotic, himself, reflected in the glass of a lemonade pitcher as he slowly approached from behind.

Ezra Birnbaum. I recognized him immediately from his appearances on

129. Americans valued clothing made in other countries, especially European ones. Little did they know (or acknowledge) these clothes were not manufactured in Europe, but in Southeast Asian factories.   —Sabina Samuels

130. A television channel delivered through wire cable. Its programming, at the time, focused on the stock market.
—Sabina Samuels

CNBC.[130] As the wiry seventy-year-old struggled to get his cowboy boot through the opening between the bench and the picnic table, two of the hired young hostesses appeared from nowhere, each taking an elbow to steady him as he sat down next to me and across from the Morehouses.

'Another year, another fucking hoe-down,' Birnbaum said. He wore a crisp new cowboy shirt, still creased from the original package, and a starched white kerchief around his neck. Both contrasted sharply with the black plastic bifocals set atop his long, Semitic nose, and the few hairspray-pasted strands of gray spiraling around his bald spot.

'Good to see you, too, Ezra,' Tobias said, much more in his element than the feeble Fed chairman was. Morehouse's thick white hairline was visible beneath the brim of his black felt cowboy hat. Except for his bloodshot eyes, he looked positively virile. His fleece-lined suede jacket and tough denim shirt made the swollen capillaries in his face appear more like ruddiness than alcoholism. 'You're sitting next to our newest addition, Jamie Cohen.'

'Pleased to meet you,' Birnbaum nodded in my direction while keeping his eyes on the prize: a basket of chicken at least a foot beyond his reach. I rose to push it closer to my equally out-of-place Jewish elder. 'Thanks,' Birnbaum said, involuntarily licking his lips in the spasmodic manner of an old grandpa as he leaned forward to choose his favorite poultry part. This was my own true destiny, I thought, as Ezra tested the tenacity of the Polygrip before sinking his dentures into bird's flesh.

I'd have time to bemoan my DNA, later. For now, what an opportunity this was! The Chairman of the Federal Reserve, a personal friend of the President of the United States, was seated right next to me. And no one was speaking. I could start a conversation about anything at all—the nature of money, the impact of technology on world economics, the public perception of the World Bank. But what I knew about my own firm's strained relationship with the Fed's proposed investigation of online trading kept me from all but the safest of topics.

'It's good chicken, huh?'

'Mmm,' Birnbaum said. 'A little dry, maybe.'

'Remember how Mary used to buy kosher when you'd come over?' Tobias asked. He knew exactly the chain of associations he hoped to launch in Birnbaum's brain: chicken, football, LaZboy, crunch. Apparently, it worked.

'You went right to the firm from Princeton, Alec?' Ezra asked.

'Yes, sir,' Alec said. 'After a year in Europe.'

'That's good. Broaden your horizons. Sow some oats.'

'Sure did,' Alec laughed proudly.

'You know the Fed's decisions aren't mine alone to make, Tobias,' Ezra said, suddenly bringing the subtext into text. I'd heard this was his style. Take people off-guard. He was scheduled to appear at a Senate hearing next week, and everyone wanted some advance word on his comments—as well as the chance to influence them. 'They all have a vote. I'm just the messenger.' I admired this abrupt candor, and looked forward to Tobias's response. It was not to come.

'Ah, Jesus, will you look at that?' Tobias changed the subject. 'Those synapse guys are a fucking cult.'

At the next table, six young men sat eating their fried chicken with forks and knives. Two wore green polo shirts with a corporate logo, and another wore a green cap.

'Synapticom, Dad,' Alec corrected him. 'They're the leader in reactive architecture.'

Reactive architecture was the attention economy's latest version of stickiness. Instead of simply making it hard to leave a web site, Synapticom's interfaces exploited feedback loops and Pavlovian cues. The company's claim to fame was the sad 'bong' sound that was heard every time a user checked for mail and received none. While the arrival of a new message would lead to a happy three-note chord, the bong sound made users feel isolated and alone. The audio sample had been developed after two years of research into aural psychology, and was actually based on the sound of a finger being amputated with a hedge cutter. Synapticom had since developed a series of other audio and visual cues that rewarded transactions and punished non-compliance.

'A shame what happened to their CEO,' Ezra said. 'A real tragedy.'

'I heard they'll be announcing his replacement at the panel this afternoon,' Alec said.

'I hope you'll be able to make it, Mr. Birnbaum,' I added, a bit too eagerly. 'I'll be doing a presentation, as well. Something very new we're developing.'

'Oh really?' Ezra struggled violently with an ear of corn on the cob. About my presentation, he couldn't have cared less. Would anyone?

By the time the audience was assembling on a series of wooden benches set into a hillside amphitheater in the woods south of the main house, however, I began to think my presentation might matter to these gentlemen, after all. The circular stage was at the bottom of the hill, making me feel like I was about to address the Roman Senate.

Thanks to the revised schedule, I would have just ten minutes to explain how TeslaNet works, and how it would revolutionize networking access for the whole world, forever. In the process, I'd establish myself as the next great young new media visionary. Or, at the very least, as something other than a complete idiot.

I was the third of four presenters, just after the new CEO of Synapticom, who, in accordance with their new 'green and clean' campaign, had refused to fly and would appear instead by live satellite feed. Maybe capitalism would restore the environment, after all. I'd be followed by Ruth Stendahl, an ex-CIA operative who was now director of an investment consultancy charged with convincing Eastern European businesses to put their resources into NASDAQ.[131] She was a diminutive but forceful woman, who insisted on testing every facet of her own audio-visual presentation, leaving little time for me to get my own ready. Screw her. TeslaNet would crash the stock-market pyramid altogether.

I went over my notes and timed my slide changes as the first speaker, Ty Stanton of IDPP, announced his breakthrough business concept, 'The Meta-Incubator.' Of course Ty had already leaked the idea to nearly everyone in attendance, so no one bothered to listen. The noise of the crowd, busy networking among themselves, drowned out Ty's presentation in spite of his lapel mike. Only the occasional burst of feedback from the speakers penetrated the din of deal-making. Ty finally left the stage, garnering no applause. These men were too important to bother with being polite. From his seat in the stands, Alec mouthed to me, 'Don't worry.'

I wasn't worried. Ty flopped, but I wouldn't. The video presentation by Synapticom would be a perfect transition into my own speech. The audience will welcome a dynamic young speaker standing before them in the flesh after enduring the flatness of a satellite feed.

But as the green-adorned young executives of Synapticom took the stage, I feared I was destined to play into an anti-climax. What seemed like a thousand lasers suddenly blasted from throughout the surrounding woods towards the stage, creating a crisp, swirling, luminescent rainbow in the day-lit air that eventually resolved itself into the bright green Synapticom logo. Music, as if from the heavens, burst through the amphitheater's speakers:

131. By filling in yet another level on the Great Pyramid's base, Stendahl's efforts would allow the international investment scheme to build for another 18 months before it sank. Her former contacts in the Eastern Block governments were now directors of their countries' telecommunications monopolies, and although she lacked the leverage that the State Department afforded her in her earlier incarnation, the kinds of ROI she was promising these Eastern Europeans meant much more to them than any of their former Politburo sympathies.
—Sabina Samuels

thick, orchestral chords with no discernible melody, but that seemed to resonate with joy, optimism, and hope. I could feel myself getting swept into the enthusiasm of the moment, as did the assembled great men. When the music reached its final crescendo, the lasers simultaneously shot directly into the sky in a brilliant white, bringing the audience to its feet. A pulsating wall of light surrounded the amphitheater, reaching to the skies. Everyone—myself included—cheered the display.

The greenshirts took positions in front of the main screen as the video began. It traced the history of Synapticom in breathtaking graphics, from the evolution of the sticky web site to the introduction of the trademark 'no mail' bong. A computer-generated female voice narrated Synapticom's role in lobbying for looser restrictions on Attention Deficit Disorder[132] medications, which led to a 45% increase in the number of eyeball-hours that America's youth spent focused on commercial web sites, and a tripling of the e-commerce dollars they spent. By the turn of the century, the company had acquired the American Association of Hypnotherapists in order to establish its feedback and compliance division, and complete the testing of its new Reactive Architecture[TM] line of turnkey web-site solutions. By adapting the fundamental hypnosis principles of pacing and leading to the one-to-one information space, Synapticom was now on the brink of helping its clients create web sites that could track the behavioral patterns of each user, mirror them precisely, earn their trust, and then lead them towards more consumption-based expressions of their underlying psychological needs[133]. The 'buy' button itself would be able to activate serotonin production in the brain.

Then, the soundtrack became more discordant. Television footage of Synapticom's dashing 26-year-old CEO, competing for America's Olympic snowboarding team last January. In a news clip all-too-familiar to everyone present, the young man somersaults over a ravine but misses his landing, dig-

132. A diagnosis used to describe young men whose brains had developed resistance to corporate programming.
—Sabina Samuels

133. The early 21st century saw the true convergence of psychology, economics and patriotism. In the aftermath of the destruction of the First World Trade Center in September 2001, the American market teetered on the edge of collapse and national confidence was shaky. After initial appeals for food, medicine and charitable donation, the President and Congress called on the American people to spend their remaining disposable income on personal consumer goods. "This will re-emboldenify the American Spirit," said then President George W. Bush. "We must not let the enemies of freedom disrobe us from our great cause."

In subsequent days, White House aides made a number of efforts to clarify Mr. Bush's statements, but his original words are still as inspiring today as they must have been at the time. —SHANKEL

ging the tip of his board into the wall of rock just short of the other side. His arms flail desperately, as if to propel himself to safety as he careens down the cliff, slamming repeatedly into the jagged rocks, his board flying free behind him. The audience gasps in unison as his head hits one of the protruding rocks, snapping his neck back so far, so fast, that his chin smacks against his own back. The micro-moment of agony is repeated again from a closer angle, then again, even closer, before the video resumes and the limp body continues its descent, landing lifeless in the stream at the ravine's bottom.

Silence. The lasers faded to an orange glow as the synthesized female voice resumed. 'The company's board of directors initiated a global search for a new executive capable of continuing the Synapticom mission into the next millennium. Hundreds of candidates were interviewed, but when they met the man you are about to meet, they knew instantly that they had found a candidate so unique, so prescient, and so fully aware of the impact of technology on the evolution of the human spirit, that Synapticom would be shepherded to even greater heights.'

'Ladies and gentlemen,' the computer intoned, 'it is with great pleasure that I introduce the new CEO of Synapticom, coming to you live from his mountain villa in his native Stockholm, Thor Thorens.'

Of course! He was a legend in the gamer community. Thorens Interactif made wildly popular games that taught kids about ecology and nature. The company had been absorbed by Viacom back in the nineties, in a stock swap that made Thorens a billionaire. After that, he spent his money funding environmental causes. He even worked for the UN, then volunteered as a consultant to the G8's developing nations program. Word was he became a Buddhist after that.

Before anyone had a chance to applaud, Thorens' image appeared on the giant screen. He was about 45, with straight brown hair and crystal blue eyes.

The hunter green shirt beneath his off-white suit jacket explained from whence his company's fashion trend had emerged. Thorens smiled humbly, and cleared his throat.

'I am delighted to be with you all,' he said calmly, with a slight Scandinavian accent. 'I'm sorry I could not be with you in person, but we only negotiated my options package this morning.' He laughed, and the audience chimed in. I did, too. The joke only worked because Thorens' reputation was so to the contrary. I felt myself empathizing with the new CEO's plight, and hoped the well-principled European would be up to the challenge of competing with the assembled robber barons. If the column of green-shirted young men staring at their new leader with rapt attention was any indication, Thorens would have no problem.

'Our team will now be distributing a demonstration disk of Synapticom's new prototype technology, what we affectionately refer to in-house as Version 6.'

The Synapticom troops dispersed through the crowd, handing out stylish black plastic envelopes, each containing a single CD-Rom[134]. The black plastic was something my friend El Greco had always talked about as the ideal CD wrapping. Jude said he was working there—maybe he was the one who had designed it, I mused, fingering the envelope. I scanned the green shirts, but couldn't find El Greco among them.

'As you'll see,' Thorens explained, his own video image receding to the upper-right-hand corner of the screen in order to make room for the graphics demonstration, 'Version 6 operates in any dynamically driven web site environment. As long as your site assembles itself in real time, and has the ability to track the user's responses as they are made—and if it was built this century, it better...' There was more laughter from the crowd. This time, nervous laughter from executives who had no idea whether their own com-

134. A digital storage medium quite popular at the time, even though its data degraded quite rapidly by today's standards. —Sabina Samuels

pany's web sites were dynamically driven. Tobias turned to his son, who shrugged. Thor waited for everyone to stop shrugging, and continued. 'As long as it does, you'll be able to exploit the impulse-response algorithm of Version 6.'

Several of the old men dressed as cowboys suspended the pretense to put on their glasses for a better view of the screen.

'For example, once a user logs into this sample e-commerce site, his identity is noted by the server, and cross-referenced with his other Internet use, as well as any other consumer information we already have, including credit card purchases, insurance records, library activity, brain scans, what have you.'

The list of possible databases with information on the consumer appeared along the left side of the screen. As each database name was highlighted, the appearance of the web page changed.

'This user owns two dogs, sees a Jungian psychologist, takes natural vitamins, lives in a two-bedroom split-colonial, earns 142,000 per year, etc. Thus, the text and images on the screen, as well as the offerings and price points, adapt and arrange themselves to maximize probability of click-through. Further, the information recorded during the session itself becomes part of the greater database, not just for this user, but for all users with profiles containing similar or analogous consumption parameters. And it's available to all Synapticom-enabled media properties.'

In spite of the enthusiasm with which Thor spoke, his presentation amounted to little more than an extension of one-to-one marketing, albeit with a little psycho-pizazz thrown in for good measure. A customized web site based on cross-referenced user data. Whoopee. Mine was better.

'Where it gets interesting, though,' Thor predicted my response, 'is when we begin interpolating the moment-to-moment analysis of our reactive architecture program, in real time. For instance, how long did it take the user between clicks? Did he utilize the right half of the button, indicating rational left-brain activity, or the left half of the button showing a propensity for more emotionally based decision-making? Once we establish a preliminary neurolinguistic template, we can begin to utilize real-time entrainment techniques, such as altering the frequency at which the cursor blinks in order to target particular brain-states, pulsating menu bars subtly along the color spectrum, and, of course, utilizing images and sounds that appeal to or stimulate the underlying psychological propensities for sex, survival, profit, or even personal fulfillment, depending on the user's mindset at that moment. Secondary reinforcement.'

As he spoke, the web page slowly adapted itself to the fictional user's psychological profile. It looked like an organic wall of graffiti, a near-psychedelic display of colors, images, and pulsating light, all directed towards the 'buy' button.

'Once the user makes a return visit, we can proceed using the earlier calculations as a starting point. Our preliminary tests of consumer confidence and personal wealth optimism following reactive architecture immersion have been most promising. In fact, subjects in our focus groups regularly refused compensation altogether. Over ten percent of them applied for jobs at the company just so they could work with the interface on a daily basis! It appears that the program actually induces such a profound state of well-being that consumers feel rewarded simply for interacting with it. But not so rewarded,' Thor added with a brilliantly executed smirk, 'that they don't feel compelled to come back for more at the earliest possible convenience.'

The entire crowd laughed. I heard myself laughing, too.

'And best of all, gentlemen,' Thor said as his image enlarged to fill the entire screen, 'the data we gather for our concatenated consumer database, not to mention information we gather about transactional psychology, is more than enough to make this venture into reactive architecture a veritable cash cow of intellectual property. This is why Synapticom is prepared to make our program available to the networked sales industry...for free.'

All at once, everyone rose from their seats and applauded. All but a few of the older men, including Birnbaum, an Asian man in the second row, and Tobias Morehouse, who just sat amidst the cheering crowd, scratching his head. Maybe they were outside the parameters of the target audience for whatever compliance techniques Thor was using in his demo.

'Thank you for your attention,' Thorens concluded as his image faded to black and the Synapticom logo rendered itself onto the screen in trade-marked green. The same hue as money, but brighter. Almost neon.

It was brilliant. Only a card-carrying humanist with the Third World and environmental credentials of Thorens could pull off a technology as blatant-ly de-humanizing as Synapticom. But why had he chosen to do it?

No time to worry about that, now. The announcement of my presenta-tion was lost under the still-tumultuous applause for Thorens. What could I possibly do to compete with that, anyway? Show my ripped-off slides track-ing consumer uptake of new technology? I decided to go for broke. Thor exploited every piece of presentation technology known to man—from lasers to God-knows-what sorts of hypnosis techniques embedded within that video presentation. I'd dispense with the PowerPoint altogether, and adopt the fireside chat technique I used that time when I appeared on Oprah[135] as a reformed hacker telling parents the ten warning signs of Internet addiction.

'Hi,' I began simply, pretending that the tail end of Thor's applause was meant to welcome me up to the podium. 'Thanks a lot.'

Alec looked worried. He motioned towards the big screen—trying to tell me the presentation wasn't up. I demonstratively put my remote control

135. An African-American woman who hosted a popular television program about spirituality and obesity.
—Sabina Samuels

147

down on the table, then slowly gripped the sides of the podium. I leaned in towards the microphone—much in the way my father did at the pulpit on high holy days, when he'd implore the congregation to feel guilty for all their transgressions[136]. This was my opportunity to reach to the most powerful men in the world—and to change the way they thought about the Internet, forever.

'I used to be a hacker.' It was a daring opening, I thought. I proceeded to recount my personal history with computers. How I played with them as a kid, and reveled in the freedom they offered. How I hacked through networks, got in trouble, and eventually designed games through which people could experience some of the thrill of a networked environment without the legal consequences. My laugh line didn't get the response I expected. They all just sat there, confused.

'The beauty of networks is the freedom they afford us,' I continued. 'It's about liberation, autonomy, and the ability to communicate with anyone, anywhere, at any time.' Alec made a circular motion with his finger for me to get on with it. 'And that's why I'm proud to announce the arrival of the Internet's first truly wireless, cell-free, absolutely infrastructure-independent network: TeslaNet.'

That got them. Several of the businessmen murmured questions to the younger technology advisors at their sides.

'That's right,' I went on, 'no modem, no satellites, no cell towers. TeslaNet is a piece of software that allows any device to access the net through the ground itself. Just install the program, connect the computer to any grounded electrical outlet, or even just drive a metal spike into the ground itself, and you are online. It will make paying for Internet access a thing of the past.'

The audience was hushed. Stunned. I decided to leave them wanting

136. Given the importance of consumer behavior in the culture of the day, it is reasonable to assume that these so-called "transgressions" involved the failure to spend money. The High Holidays were most likely a marketing/promotional period when increased consumption was encouraged (see "Christmas In July," "Back To School," "Dads 'n' Grads").
—SHANKEL

more.

'I'll be available to speak to any of you about it at your convenience.' I smiled and gave a little bow of the head. 'Thank you very much.'

As I returned to the table in self-appraised victory, Ruth Stendahl, the ex-CIA investment analyst, leaned toward her microphone on the dais.

'That's an impressive technology,' she complimented me, 'if it works.'

'Oh, it does.' No one heard me. I pulled a microphone across the table towards me. 'It does work.'

'But what I want to know,' she intoned from the top of her register, 'is what sort of revenue model you've developed.'

Revenue? I thought no one was supposed to talk about revenue.

'Why I'd be happy to explain.' I spoke as politely as I could, even though I was stiffening from her attack. 'We sell the software, for money.' I loved using sarcasm on people like Stendahl, who used it so often themselves. 'We're anticipating a price point of about 50 dollars, and a viral marketing strategy that will cost us under a million dollars, total.'

'But, if you'll pardon me for asking...' Stendahl spoke as if ripping me to shreds were a terribly painful procedure for her. 'How do you think such a technology would impact the viability of the telecommunications industry?'

I shouldn't have let myself get so provoked. 'That's *their* problem, don't you think?'

The audience shuffled uncomfortably. Morehouse had closed his eyes. One of the other men in the rows of benches raised his hand. A girl ran to him with a microphone.

'Mr. Cohen,' the man said, scratching his moustache uncomfortably, 'I'm sure you're aware of the Telecommunications Industry Consortium...'

I was utterly unprepared for the assault that followed. One by one, businessmen dressed in cowboy clothes rose to condemn TeslaNet as a 'category killer,' an 'irresponsible act of piracy,' and 'just another open-source night-mare.' The only thing that saved me was the clock.

Ruth Stendahl restored the crowd's enthusiasm with an optimistic assessment of the Eastern Bloc's cash flow potential, after which the men dispersed to ready themselves for the evening's barbecue. I just sat at the dais with my head in my hands, hoping no one would try to speak to me.

I felt a big hand on my shoulder. 'It happens to everyone, kid.'

It was Tobias. He pulled me up out of my chair and gave me a hug. It was good.

'You're going to be okay,' he told me. I felt even more profoundly sorry for letting him down.

'But the technology really works,' I said. 'It could change everything.'

'I know, Jamie,' Tobias said with compassion. 'I know. But sometimes doing good business means not changing things too much.'

'What do we care if we fuck things up for other companies?' I asked. 'That's called competition. It's how technology evolves.'

'Then why do you think no one's manufactured a solar-powered car? Or even a decent electric one?' Tobias asked. 'You think the kids at MIT[137] don't come up with new ways of doing that every year?'

'But if they do...'

'Then one of the oil companies buys it from them,' Tobias smiled. 'For good money, too. Just to keep it from reaching the market.'

Alec sidled up next to us. I think he was surprised to see his dad's arm around me. 'You two okay?'

'We're going to be just fine,' Tobias said. 'We've got a trump card, now. Let's use it wisely.'

137. Massachusetts Institute of Technology, like Harvard Business School, became a technology incubator early in the 21st Century. Students paid no tuition, but all their research and business plans became property of the schools, with the condition that the inventors had first right of refusal on serving as CEO of any resulting spin-off company.
—Sabina Samuels

7. Prairie Oysters

I rocked back in my chair and looked up. Something about the altitude, the general flatness of the high plains, or maybe just the country[138] air made the sky look genuinely bigger than it did in the city. And now, at night, the stars looked more like a substance than little lights. Sugar on slate. This is why the rich come here, I thought—or to Aspen, or Sun Valley. Summers at the Concord couldn't compare with this.

Dad. Shit. I'd forgotten all about him and now it was too late to call. Well, good. That's what trips were for: to forget about real world concerns. Besides, I had work to do.

'You going to the bonfire?' Alec joined me on the front porch of Cabin Four, holding one hand over his stomach as if he had eaten too many ribs at

138. Advertisers perpetuated a mounting conflict between urban and rural attitudes, by insisting that country air was of a greater quality than urban air. Marketing professionals exploited this to their advantage by associating products with the country such as butter, juice, and cars, all unrelated to air.   —RABBITROAR

138b. Ironically, in many rural regions in the early 21st century (notably England), country air was of worse quality than city air, due to high ozone and nitrogen dioxide levels ('photochemical smog') caused by the action of sunlight on pollutants from adjacent urban areas.

—RAYGIRVAN

the barbecue. In the other he held a joint. A bloated, preppy, pot-smoking cowboy. The screen door clacked shut, and the planks creaked beneath Alec's feet.

'I guess I'll check it out. You?'

'I dunno. It's mostly the older guys. But I hear it might be the last year they do it. And it is, well...'

'The thing to do?' I finished for him. He handed me the joint, and I took a hit.

'Cheer up, Jamie, okay? Everybody's been talking about your presentation, you know.'

'They're probably angry you guys brought me along.'

'You say that like it's a *bad* thing,' he joked.

'Ah, fuck. What am I gonna tell the guys?'

'The truth. It's better to find out now something's not going to work than after we've put money into it, right?'

'But that's the whole point,' I could feel myself whining. 'It *does* work. It's probably the only thing developed in the last three years that really does.'

'If the people here don't want it to work, Jamie, then it doesn't work.'

'The people here have nothing to do with it. We release a program like TeslaNet, and it will spread like a virus. No one can stop it. Welcome to the networked world.'

'Well then, why did your friends turn to you for help?'

'Maybe they shouldn't have,' I tested his premise. 'Maybe I'm just insinuating myself into something. Teslanet is part of a revolution, Alec.' I tempered my rhetoric by exaggerating it. 'The revolution will not be monetized.'

'It already has been, Jamie. The chaos of the nineties is over. Order's been restored. Where were you? It's not a networked world, anymore, it's a networked economy.'

'Technologies still spread by the laws of evolution, Alec. Survival of the fittest. Ideas compete for dominance.'

'Technologies spread based on their ability to generate a better story—for *everyone at the table*. It's a team sport. What do you think this Bull Run is all about, anyway? It's to set the rules.'

'Then why wasn't Bill Gates ever invited here? He's set more rules than anyone.'

'He *was* invited. He just didn't show up. He thought he could make it on his own. And he had a good run of it, too, until the Justice Department was convinced to take him down. No one dared try it, since.'

'Come on, you're saying that the men here pull strings at the Justice Department?'

Alec just raised his eyebrows.

'There are still plenty of monopolies, though,' I said. 'AOL-Time Warner? Viacom-Disney?'

'Sure there are. But as long as everyone else is kept in the loop, everybody wins. No one says 'boo.''

'What about the press? There's still a fourth estate[139].'

'The press is protected from government, Jamie, not corporations. These people own the press. The airwaves were auctioned off to them years ago.'

'But not the individual reporters and journalists.'

'And what would possibly motivate them to rock the boat? They're getting half their salaries as stock options, anyway. Marshall Tellington puts real-time NASDAQ tickers on his writers' computer desktops, just to remind them of that fact. Think anyone's going to write an article decrying the state of the media business when their kid's Brandeis education is depending on that little number in the corner of the screen?'

139. The government of the Old United States was divided into three branches: the legislative, executive and judicial. The so-called free press (which the author points out was hardly free, but rather owned by corporate interests) was referred to as "the fourth estate" because it ostensibly monitored the activities of the three formal branches of government. By the early 21st century, the fourth estate had all but abdicated its watch-dog responsibilities, having become little more than a delivery system for lurid entertainment and corporate propaganda. Many media critics of the day agreed that the final nail in the coffin came in the early 2010s when, upon Dan Rather's retirement, the CBS Evening News was taken over by comedians Jon Stewart and Aisha Tyler and re-titled "Infotainment Tonight".
—SHANKEL

'You make it sound like a fucking conspiracy.'

'But at least you're in on it, now, eh?' Alec put his hands on the arms of my chair and leaned into my face. 'Wanna go back to writing game stories from a one-bedroom in Somerville, or are you ready to join the party? It's time to move up-campus again, pal.'

Alec was good at what he did. Every last word of his argument was calculated for its ability to generate an emotional response in his target audience. Even the choice of Brandeis. I knew full well what he was doing, but it still worked.

Maybe all that humiliation I endured during the afternoon would serve as my initiation into the Coachmen's Club, I mused as we followed the path of tiny lanterns that had been placed through the woods.

'Think we'll get to see your father's legendary tool?' I asked Alec.

'You wish,' he teased back, grabbing his crotch. 'It runs in the family, you know.'

'They don't really do that sort of stuff, anymore,' I asked, 'do they?'

Alec stopped and stared off into the woods. Then I saw it, too. In the clearing ahead, a huge bonfire raged. Around it, unmistakably, the forms of dancing girls.

'Come on!' Alec suddenly shouted, tugging my sleeve and drawing me forward.

The orange light from the roaring fire made the whole clearing seem like a scene out of Dante's *Inferno* (which I'd never actually read, but imagined this is what he meant). Seven girls, by my count, leaped around the fire, dressed in various combinations of black leather, white lace, and what looked like vinyl swimwear.

'This is kind of intense, Alec.' I backed away. I wanted to watch from a safe distance. With binoculars.

'Come on, man, what are you talking about? This is great!' Alec ran into the fray.

But there wasn't really any fray to jump into. Gathered in a big circle around the fire, about thirty men sat on tree stumps fitted with velvet cushions to shield their aging buttocks. Amazingly, they seemed indifferent to the proceedings, and talked among themselves, smoking cigars and drinking beer from over-sized urns.

Tobias was there, too, sitting between Ezra Birnbaum, who had traded in his stiff cowboy clothes for a pair of sweats, and his old Coachmen's Club nemesis Marshall Tellington, the chairman of Entertainink. If a bomb went off here right now, I mused, the government, economy, and mass media would be decimated. Especially now that they were, for all intents and purposes, the same thing.

Alec waved his hat in the air and danced with the girls, oblivious to the fact that he was the only spectator in the action. He looked pathetic, but I envied his abandon, all the same. I found a safe spot in Tobias's little cluster. My presence wasn't even acknowledged. It reminded me of my job in college waiting tables at weddings for wealthy drunks who'd only address me when they wanted help getting to the bathroom to throw up. They treated me like a non-entity, as if they wouldn't feel comfortable vomiting in front of a stranger unless that stranger were less than human.

But for now, I preferred playing fly on the wall. This kind of celebration was pictured in the Jewish dictionary right next to 'Goyim Naches.' I'd always known what sin they committed in Sodom. Gomorrah had been a mystery, until now.

Three more girls in tight black leather outfits entered the open area between the bonfire and the onlookers, pulling a long chain attached to a collar around a tall man's neck. He was completely naked except for a black leather mask over his head. The girls led him towards a metal contraption with a big crank. It looked like the mechanism that's used to lower a bucket of water into a well.

I took a position behind Tobias, to make it clear to anyone who cared that I was affiliated with M&L, and on the job. Only a few of the younger men were present at all, actually, and those who were looked about as bewildered by the goings-on as I was. One or two joined in with Alec, in the hope of brushing against one of the scantily clad performers, but the rest seemed more disgusted than titillated. As if the whole thing were a waste of time, especially when there were deals to be made.

The naked slave wrapped his arms and legs around the horizontal cross-beam of the metal mechanism. The girls gathered near him, pulling short leather straps from their waists, and using them to tie their slave to the post.

'Bet you wish it was you, huh Ezra?' Morehouse elbowed the Fed Chairman.

'Ahh, the joys of the pro-sexual movement,'[140] Tellington chortled. 'In a world where the President of the United States can't even get his dick licked by an intern, at least we still have this.'

'You can join in at any time, Birnbaum,' Tobias teased. 'I'm sure no one would object to an additional slave.'

Once the victim was securely tied to the horizontal pipe, the leather-clad mistresses wheeled it slowly towards the fire. Even the most hardened of the observers were distracted enough by this upscaling of stakes to take notice.

'It's a spit!' I exclaimed involuntarily as I realized what was happening. Tobias and Tellington laughed out loud.

The naked man was now dangling over the bonfire, flames lapping against his back. While one girl doused him with oil, the others slowly turned the crank, spit-roasting their slave as if he were a stuffed pig. Alec

140. Since the 1970's, the most extreme forms of objectified or polarized sexual behavior, such as inquisitor's garb, torture, and bondage had been re-contextualized by their practitioners as a path to sexual freedom. It was believed that by surrendering to one's most fetishistic desires and dualist fantasies a person liberated him or herself from the social and religious taboos inhibiting healthy sex. This was a time, you must remember, when pornographer Larry Flynt and fundamentalist minister Jerry Falwell were thought to be on opposite ends of the sexual liberation spectrum; of course, both media personalities actually objectified females to an equal extent.   —Sabina Samuels

wandered back to his father's side. He didn't want to be mistaken for the dominatrices' second course.

'They're not really going to cook the guy, Dad, are they?'

Tobias and Tellington smiled knowingly at one another.

'I guess we'll have to see,' Tobias said ominously. 'Isn't that right, Ezra?' He nudged the old man's elbow, knocking it from its position on his knee. Ezra quickly covered his lap with his hands and crossed his legs. But not before we had all seen the erection pointing up through his sweatpants.

Morehouse and Tellington exploded in loud, raspy, cigar-throated guffaws.

'I knew there was a reason we still bothered with this!' Tobias managed to say through his hysterics. Tellington couldn't even speak. His face was beet red, and his eyes bulging out. Alec laughed along, too, although he wasn't sure what had just transpired.

'At least I can still get a woody, Tobias,' Birnbaum finally countered with a grin. Morehouse turned a different sort of red, as Tellington fell off his stump.

I wished I were somewhere else. Anywhere else. I could feel myself withdrawing from the orgy. Imagining my dad back in shul at the pulpit, looking into the faces of congregants, trying not to count which ones were still on his side.

I sensed it coming on this time. As I brought my attention back to the raving throng before me, the motions of the assembled satyrs took on an almost supernatural quality. In the flickering light of the fire, their skulls took on new proportions. Dark shadows around their brows, deep, inhuman sounds emanating from their huge, gaping mouths. Wild bulls, a pack of them, reveling in mindless ecstasy.

They laughed like real people, and even had the facial expressions of humans, but their heads were transformed. They stamped their feet on the ground. Smoke emanated from their huge nostrils. They were all bulls. All of them. Everyone except the man on the spit, whose eyes, staring in terror through the holes in the mask, were my own.

I pulled myself out of the trance. The Greek chorus started up again. *What are you doing here? Who do you think you are?* Shut up, Goddamn it! I shouted them down. Everybody else here is having fun with this. I can, too. It's just a fucking show. Entertainment. Nobody's getting hurt. Why do I need to be the judge? Am I supposed to be better than these men? I'm here, aren't I?

Yes, I *am* here. Right here, right now. In fact, I'm the first generation of my family to make it to this level. The very top. As inside as it gets.

I tried laughing, just to see how it felt. If it fit. And it did. I tried it again, and it sounded a bit more natural. It resonated in my chest. I hollered. 'Yee-haw!' Just like those bubbas I rowed with on crew at Princeton. 'Yee-haw!' I raised my fist in the air as the dominatrices pulled out their whips and punished their roasting slave.

'Burn, baby!' I was propelled by a greater force. No matter how badly my presentation went that afternoon, no matter how cruelly I'd supplanted Carla, no matter what I might be called upon to do, or what dastardly plot I might concoct myself, no matter how goyish these naches—the madness I was a part of now made it all fade away. The fire burned it off. Don't look back, Jamie. Just go.

'Go! Go! Go!' I could hear myself screaming now, at the top of my lungs. And I didn't care who heard me. I was one with the stampede. Included. And it felt good.

For we were all in it together. Running wild. Each one of us as complic-it as the other. And every man as vulnerable as Birnbaum and his boner.

Suddenly, people who were ashamed of their boners seemed like the fools. We were men, weren't we?

The louder and more outrageous we got, the deeper our bond. Galvanized in our bravado. There was no turning back.

I rolled my head back and howled at the Montana stars. Every ounce of doubt pulverized and evaporated by the sound of my own whoops and hollers. The collective cacophony absolved my sins. This is the sensation Jews aren't supposed to have, I thought. That power released in the sacrifice of one's first-born son to the pagan god Molloch. Abandoning the fear-based laws of our fathers. Relieved of the obligation to stand back and judge. No longer God's chosen and the object of man's contempt. Just one of the beasts, now. And one with them all.

Then I noticed it. The masked slave was frantically shaking his head, and struggling to get to free. Was it part of the act, or was something truly wrong? And how would one tell the difference? I debated whether to shrug it off, but something inside told me that there was a problem. Things had gone too far. Even one of the torturers seemed to acknowledge the victim's panic as real. She desperately tried to alert her co-workers. But they were so caught up in the heat of the moment that they mistook her agitation for frenzy.

I wasn't the only one who had stopped to take notice. Some of the other men in the audience now began to shout for the girls to stop, but it was impossible to distinguish these warning cries from the encouraging chants of their fellows. The skin on the poor slave's naked chest and back had taken on a bright, reddish hue, as the flames danced against it. There was the unmistakable scent of burning hair and fried fat. Through the mask, the slave's mouth screamed in pain.

The revelry decayed into pandemonium as the other performers came to realize they were cooking the man alive. They tried to lift the metal spit but it had grown too hot. They waved for the men to come help them, but no one made a move. Finally, I grabbed Alec, and we plunged into the flames, followed by another of the younger men. I took off my sweatshirt and used it as a pot-holder to grab one end of the spit. Between the three of us, we managed to drag the poor slave to safety. His back was charred and bloody. Alec fell to his knees, and vomited into his cowboy hat, as the dominatrices released their fried companion from his bonds.

But they were smiling! I was aghast. I moved slowly backwards, horrified. The slave, too! He was smiling now, in no rush to escape or tend to his wounds.

Then I heard applause. I looked at the circle of men around me. They were clapping and laughing. The dominatrices were standing in a line now, their slave between them. They were all holding hands and bowing together.

I helped an even more shaken Alec to his feet, and we returned to our places in the circle.

'They got you, kid,' Tobias said, swigging back his beer. 'They got you, good.'

'It was all an act?' I asked.

'Jesus,' Alec said, wiping a dribble of vomit from his lips. 'I thought they were—'

'Yeah, I bet you did,' said Tellington.

'Ahh,' added Birnbaum. 'To be young again.'

I was incensed. 'I can't believe you guys!'

'Don't worry, Cohen,' Tobias smiled. 'Next year, you'll be on the other side of the joke.'

'Everyone's gotta pay his dues,' Tellington wheezed. 'Everyone pays his dues.'

The three men laughed together, as two young women dressed in feathers emerged from the woods for the next act, to the sound of exotic music.

I wanted to stomp off in anger. Let them know I didn't appreciate being toyed with. Duped. Abused. But I couldn't bring myself to do it. Tobias patted my back and nodded at me. He knew what was going through my head. He was reassuring me. The worst was over. I was in.

I know it sounds silly, now, but it meant so much to me, then. The whole thing had been staged for me. Just like Tobias's initiation at the Coachmen's Club. To think of all the trouble they went through! It wasn't just for their sick amusement, but for my benefit, and the benefit of the other initiates. To let us in on the game. The whole thing was just a game, and only people who realized this could be allowed in. I finally knew what it meant to be a player. There's no words for it. You have to *be* one to know.

Alec was still shaking. He turned back towards the path. 'Let's go, Jamie. I've had enough.'

'Come on, man.' I stopped him. 'You're gonna leave now? That was the hard part. Now we're in.'

He just shook his head. He was still green from throwing up. His bottom lip was quivering.

'Maybe it was the joint, Alec,' I tried to console him. 'That stuff was pretty strong. Maybe it's making you a little paranoid.' I felt like I was talking someone down off a bad trip.

'Of all people, Jamie...' Then he ran off. Tobias looked up, concerned.

'I'll talk to him,' I said, chasing after Alec.

He was following the path of lanterns, making his way back to the cabin. I shouted after him, but he ignored my calls. Fine. Let him stew. He just took it a little harder than I did, that's all. When the pot wore off he'd be fine. Besides, it looked like something was going on down by the amphitheater, the site of my previous humiliation. The bonfire games had given me enough confidence to return to the scene of the crime and see what was going on there.

On the stage, a number of young men talked quietly amongst themselves around the dais. Drinks were strewn about, and citronella candles served as ashtrays. A mellow scene. No initiation necessary. Only a couple of them had bothered to wear the cowboy get-ups, and they were the ones who looked out of place, here.

'You've got to have faith,' one of them, a Synapticom greenshirt, was saying. He'd probably been here since this afternoon, answering questions. 'It's not a bubble unless people believe it is. It'll keep growing forever. The universe expands forever, right?' These poor kids took their work so damn seriously. Or maybe they were drunk.

'You still have to position yourself for the possibility of another crash,' one of the guys in cowboy clothes argued. The greenshirts stared at him as if he had violated a sacred Masonic pact. "Okay, correction. All right? There could be another correction, which is why it's only smart to hedge your bets, even just a little.'

'Every bet you hedge is an opportunity missed,' another, smaller greenshirt explained. 'And it contributes to the perception of fear. And that costs us all.'

'Gimme a break,' the cowboy said. 'My keeping a balanced portfolio doesn't cost you any business.'

I pulled up a seat and straddled it from behind, crossing my arms casually on the chair back, while I decided whether to join in the debate.

'Sure it does,' said the smaller of the Synapticom guys. 'If you keep potential energy locked up in old paradigm large cap stocks, there's less fuel for growth. Those companies don't take risks. They don't invest in change.'

'Worse,' the other added, 'value investing is intrinsically contrarian. It's a betrayal of the market the feeds you.'

'Traitorous,' the little one added.

'We're not being too hard on him,' the third one said. 'Are we, Jamie?'

They knew my name. They must have seen my pitch. I could use this status to my advantage.

'Forgive me,' I said. 'I didn't catch your name.'

'You don't recognize me, Cohen?'

I looked at the dashing young man in the gray suit and green shirt. I was at a loss.

'You went to Princeton, right?' I asked.

'Jamie, it's *me*,' he said. 'Clive Vahanian. Remember?'

'El Greco! Jesus fucking Christ, man!' I shouted, standing to embrace the slender man who I remembered from my youth as the fat kid. The boy who'd get stuck on the chain link fence when we were running away from the Radio Shack[141] manager, stolen diodes in our knapsacks. 'Jude told me you were at Synapticom. Shit, you look great.'

El Greco seemed a tad embarrassed by my display of affection, or maybe he was afraid of what I might reveal about our childhood together. He shook my hand. Warm, but cool.

'I've been taking a lot better care of myself,' he said. 'The company's helped me with that. Nutritional guidelines, a gym and pool right in the building. We're all pretty healthy as a result.'

'I'm impressed. I really am.' I was a little concerned, too. Perhaps El Greco would loosen up if he were removed from the green organism of which he'd become a component part. 'Come on, let's take a walk.'

'Sure,' El Greco said, turning to his fellows. 'I'll be right back.'

We hiked down the hill behind the amphitheater, the moon lighting our

141. Throughout most of Jamie's youth, this chain of retail electronics stores sold transistors and circuitry that, in the hands of a knowledgeable hacker, could serve as the component parts for media devices that could not be purchased legally in their assembled form, such as the tuners that allow people to descramble encrypted television signals. Oddly, though the radio waves were passing through their bodies, people were not permitted to access the content without paying. Radio Shack eventually became a cellular telephone distribution outlet, before being absorbed by an office supply chain.
—Sabina Samuels

path. It had been a long time—since my trial for the DeltaWave Virus—and neither of us was sure if the other was still pissed.

'So,' Greco said. 'You've been hanging out with Jude, then?'

'Yeah.' I was glad to hear Greco talk about something from the real world. 'He said you were in on TeslaNet at the beginning.'

'I was. Such as it is.'

'What do you mean?'

'You're in on it, right?' Greco asked.

'I'll get a cut. Well, the company will. Sure.' He didn't seem to understand what I meant. 'It's not like I'm going to ask Jude for a kickback.'

'Funny seeing Jude get into business, isn't it?' Greco mused. 'He was always such a commie.'

'We all were, then,' I said, testing his ideological compass. 'Remember? No personal ownership, no personal fame.'

'Well, I guess we both grew up a bit.' He gave me my answer.

We came upon a stream. I found a stick and threw it in the water. It was carried a few meters before it got caught against a rock and wiggled in the current to get free.

'So you're really into all this now?' I asked.

'Come on, Jamie, you're one to talk. You're at a brokerage house.'

'I didn't mean anything by it, Greco,' I lied. 'It's just freaky, isn't it? How crazy everything's gotten?' I was wary not to reveal my misgivings too directly, lest I be outed.

'A little cognitive dissonance is only natural, I suppose,' Greco said, using language that surprised me.

I carefully edged nearer to the water, stretching my arm out towards the imprisoned twig.

'I mean, sometimes you just have to stop trying to change the world,'

Greco finally admitted, 'and learn how to change yourself, instead.'

I picked up a small stone and tossed it towards the stick. It missed.

'So, how have you changed then?' I asked. I found another rock and threw it, a bit harder this time. Missed.

'You know what I mean, Jamie. Taking a real job, learning about business.'

Both of us were looking for stones, now, committed to the task of freeing the stick.

'Sure, but you were an artist. A graphics genius. I can understand you working at Synapticom, but what are you doing here with the money people?'

'The program takes care of the graphics by itself, now,' Greco said sadly. 'I came up with the basic routines—the screen-blitting, the bitmaps, self-customizing fonts, even a few analog graphics generators. The program uses them to render the images now. It all happens automatically. And then the algorithm evolves based on success rates.'

'So why didn't they just give you severance and let you go?' I tossed a stone that grazed the stick, but not square enough to dislodge it.

'I finished the job,' Greco explained, 'but I'm still on contract. They put me in sales with the other guys.'

'What do you mean, 'the other guys'? There's got to be a division there closer to your skill set. Interface design? Research and Development? HTML coding?'

'They're all gone, Jamie. There's only twenty-six employees, now. Plus some support staff we job in from the temp agencies.'

'But Synapticom has offices all over the world. Amsterdam, Sydney, Cairo...'

'They're all just servers, Jamie. Virtual offices. We send a team over to do face-to-face negotiations and press conferences when we have to. It's much cheaper that way. Our burn rate is less than two million a year now. And our market cap broke the forty-five billion mark last week.'

'You guys must be raking it in.'

'It's a unique business plan, actually. We've got no clients, and no real revenue stream. We just give away the technology, and then—because we know it works—we invest in the companies that take it from us. It's an extended accelerator model, really.' Greco tossed another stone. It missed. 'Then, the program uses the feedback from user response to improve itself, so our R&D department became superfluous.'

'You gotta admit that's kind of scary,' I said, moving to a better vantage point from which to attack the branch.

'I don't know. Sticky web sites and non-reactive coercive architecture looked a lot scarier to me. The user symptoms were identical to end-stage amphetamine psychosis. All stimulus, and no positive feedback. It would have driven everyone crazy, eventually.'

'Like Synapticom's 'reactive architecture' won't?' I asked. 'You're putting your users in an environment that creates aspirations and behaviors. You pay them to make the right decision, like you're tossing them Reese's Pieces.[142] They don't even know they're being led around by their noses.'

'I suppose they don't.' He paused, then added, as if thinking aloud, 'I guess that's what makes them customers.'

'I guess.'

Greco suddenly skipped a stone along the surface of the water. It ricocheted off a rock and then wedged itself under the branch, releasing it. The current carried it away into the darkness.

'They're all deluded, anyway,' he said. 'None of them see what's really going on.'

142. A peanut butter candy made famous by its paid placement in a Steven Spielberg film about a friendly alien. This was long before extra-terrestrials' true nature had been determined.
—Sabina Samuels

'It's all how you look at it,' I laughed, echoing one of Jude's constant refrains.

Maybe, deep down, Greco understood things the way I did. He was a gamer, too. Once.

'You should come over to the office, sometime,' he said. 'You'd get a kick out of it, I think. It's really not as heinous as you're imagining.'

'No, no,' I insisted. 'I'm not saying it's heinous at all. It sounds like a great gig, as long as you don't take it too seriously.'

'What do you mean by that?'

'Nothing.' This was a weird situation. I wanted to relate to him as an ally, but of which camp? Hackers against the system, the businessmen within it, or true players who transcended both? I had no basis for a knowing wink, so I went for sympathy. 'I'm probably just bummed about how badly my presentation went this afternoon. Jealous of you guys, even.'

'Oh.' Greco was unconvinced. This made me nervous. As if he could push a button on his belt, summoning a squadron of greenshirts.

'Really, Greco. I'm impressed. I wish there was a way I could get involved. Maybe we could implement the Synapticom interface on the M&L trading site. You know, create an interface that would make people trade more.'

'I suppose it could be ported there.' Greco tasted the saliva in his mouth as if he were considering the possibility.

'They've been asking me to come up with a legal way to get trading frequency up,' I said. 'The Feds are cracking down on the community areas. Too many day traders making up scams. This could be a perfect alternative.'

'I think we tried it before. It's a regulated space. Lots of government intervention.'

'I can make it work. Morehouse is old friends with Birnbaum.' I was excited by the possibility, now. 'They go way back. Kinda sick stuff. Tobias has him by the balls. Birnbaum will do what we tell him.'

'Great, then. I'm sure we can set something up.'

'It'll be like old times,' I smiled.

'Let's hope not,' Greco laughed, starting back up the path. I didn't press it. An exclusive with Synapticom would more than make up for the afternoon's gaffe.

'So tell me,' I said as we climbed the embankment. 'What is it with these green shirts?'

'Funny,' Greco said. 'No one ever asks us about it.'

'Well, it is a little intimidating, you know.'

'It's not meant to be,' Greco said. 'It kind of started as a joke, after we saw Mr. Thorens wearing one. And then, with the environmental campaign and all, it sorta caught on. It's a fascinating color, if you do the research.'

The research on the color green? Too late to ask. We were back with the others now and El Greco was already being re-assimilated by his squad. Still, I felt I scored a double victory. I was halfway to a deal that justified Morehouse's decision to bring me along, and I'd re-established a connection, however tenuous, with another of the Jamaican Kings. Maybe everything would be okay after all.

'So,' the leader asked Greco, 'is our friend from M&L on the team?'

On the team? Was that whole thing planned? Had El Greco been instructed to work me over?

'Jamie's going to see about an implementation on M&L's trading site,' Greco said, somewhat sheepishly, proving that he still had enough of a soul to feel ashamed.

I wanted Greco to know that I understood his pressure to perform—that I would play along, for his sake.

'He's really enthusiastic about the program,' I said, hoping he would recognize my efforts on his behalf. 'Captivating when he speaks about it.'

The leader wasn't having any of it. 'You don't have to make a case for your friend, Jamie. We're all well aware of Vahanian's talents.' He knew what I was up to, and wouldn't let me forge an alliance at his expense. El Greco was on his team, not mine.

'No, really,' I insisted. 'He makes a convincing case.'

'If you knew you were being convinced,' the leader said wryly, 'then he wasn't doing his job.'

'He wasn't pitching me or anything,' I back-pedaled. 'It just sounds like a great addition to our site. Something that will help us a lot. He made it really clear.'

'Well, good, then,' he said. 'We'll be glad to have you aboard. My name's Parrot. Simpson Parrot.' He shook my hand. And then, just to make sure I had no doubt about having been played: 'Hopefully you'll be able to use your pull with the Fed to get past the regulators.'

Okay, fine. The whole thing had been a set-up.

It didn't really matter, I told myself as I stepped onto the porch of Cabin Four. I'd let them maintain their smug contention, if it made them happy. They were the ones giving away their technology, and we were the ones who'd profit from it. As for El Greco, well, he was certainly in better shape than when I last saw him. And something felt good about making contact with another Jamaican King, even under these circumstances. *Especially* under these circumstances. Compared to El Greco, I was still a free man. If only there was a way to play rainmaker[143] for Jude and Reuben, then everything would be perfect.

As I quietly opened the door, I could hear Alec stirring in his bed. Poor kid. I left the lights off, and tried to feel my way around in the dark. I got my pants off, laid them on the dresser, then made my way to the bed and sat

143. "Rainmaker" had a different connotation back in 2008. Back then, a rainmaker was someone who secured high-paying clients for a business. It was only with the advent of global climate change and the increase in EWEs (Extreme Weather Events) that the term "rainmaker" took on its current meaning (a bringer of destruction and misery).

There were, of course, negative images of rain[a] from this period (see "Nobody Better Rain On My Parade," "Gray Skies Are Gonna Clear Up"), but these tended to treat rain as a trivial inconvenience or an expressionistic symbol of glum mood. Rain was rarely treated as the horrific threat to human life we know it to be.

The phrase "Rain Rain Go Away; Come Again Another Day," which officially replaced "In God We Trust" on our currency in the late 2080s, actually originated as a simple children's rhyme. —SHANKEL

a. negative images of rain: Nevertheless, a few examples indicate the horror. "Hard Rain" and "Purple Rain" were especially prescient. Contact with contaminated rain caused mutation characterized by accelerated bone growth so that victims literally grew out of their skins, accompanied by mental confusion and bleeding from the eye sockets.

A song of the period, akin to the Ring-a-Ring-a-Roses nursery rhyme describing the plague of an earlier era, chillingly recalls the symptoms:

"Raindrops keep falling on my head, and just like the guy whose feet are too big for his bed, nothin' seems to fit ... So I just did me some talkin' to the sun... Raindrops keep falling on my head, but that doesn't mean my eyes will soon be turnin' red." —RAYGIRVAN

down. There was something soft all over the comforter. Like goose down. I felt around to find the source of the leak. There was a thick pile of the stuff, a mound of feathers. Suddenly, it moved.

'Hey!' a female voice shouted.

I leaped up and turned on the light.

One of the feather-dressed dancers was sitting up in my bed. It was Jenna—the redhead from the registration desk.

'What the—?' I gasped, as she gathered her things together. There was a bottle of bourbon on the floor, and the telltale residue of powder next to a rolled-up hundred-dollar bill on the nightstand.

'Hi Jamie,' Jenna said. 'What time is it?'

Alec sat up in his bed and tried to steady himself against the wall. He was trashed. 'I'm sorry, Jamie,' he slurred. 'I figured you...'

'It's okay, Alec,' I said, trying to make sense of the situation. 'I can find a bed over at—'

'Never mind,' Jenna said, gathering her things. 'It's not what you think. I've got work in the morning.'

'Okay, then,' I said. 'Umm. Good night.'

She stood by Alec's bed for a moment. 'You sure you want me to take this money?'

'Just shut up and go, okay?' Alec said.

'I'll never understand you college boys,' she said, allowing her huge, feather-encased bust to brush against me as she left. I closed the door behind her.

I wiped the feather lint off my bed, turned over my pillow and switched off the lamp. 'Why didn't you go for it, Alec? She was hot,' I offered, even though I thought she was embarrassingly garish—and even though I had wanted her for myself. 'She was definitely into you.'

'That's not what I paid her for. I wasn't moving in on her. Not like that.'

'Whatever, Alec.' I let it go. 'Are you okay? How much did you drink?' I wasn't going to mention the blow[144].

'I'll be okay,' Alec said. 'I've seen rooms spin a lot faster than this one.'

'All right, then, good night.'

'Yeah.'

We lay in silence for a while.

'I could have made it back, you know,' Alec finally said.

'Huh?'

'To the docks. When the boat tipped over. I could have made it back without you.'

'There's nothing to be ashamed of. You were drunk.'

'Not that drunk, Jamie.'

'Look, your dad told me about your arm,' I admitted. 'Between that and the booze—'

'I could have made it back,' he slurred.

'Just try to get some sleep, Alec,' I said. 'We can talk about it tomorrow.'

He was out. I felt an odd sense of remorse as I lay there. Like I had taken him down and replaced him in the pecking order. Another video game character's energy absorbed.

When I awoke, Alec was gone. So much the better. There'd be more of a buffer before I saw him again. Maybe that's why he left.

I scrounged around for my watch on the floor. It was only 7am. How the hell did Alec wake up? I pulled open the curtains, and the bright white Montana sun blasted me with a light more intense than anything I ever had to contend with in the city—where I'd be gladly returning that afternoon. This ranch stuff was entirely too weird. It brought out people's dark sides.

I showered and shaved, then put on the clothes I wanted to be wearing all

144. Slang for cocaine and oral sex. Presumably, he is referring to the former, but several editors on our staff insist this is a homo-erotic reference, in light of the passages immediately following.
—Sabina Samuels

along. A Brooks Brothers button-down shirt, corduroys, and a v-neck sweater. The cowboys be damned.

I walked to the main house, but no one was eating breakfast. A few of the support staff sat at a table, checking off lists on clipboards. One of the women turned around. It was Jenna.

'Well, good morning, Mr. Cohen,' she said.

'Where is everybody?' I asked. 'Is breakfast over already?'

'No, silly,' she said, gently slapping my hand. 'It hasn't even started yet.'

'Then where— ?'

'You've all got to work for your breakfast today,' she said. 'They're all assembling by the west pasture.'

'The west...?' I had reviewed the map I got with my orientation pack, and knew perfectly well how to get to the pasture, but I wanted a chance to find out just who this Jenna was, and what had transpired with Alec. Or maybe get somewhere with her, myself.

'It's up that way,' she pointed. 'Past the barns. Just keep following along the base of the hill.'

'Can't you show me?' I asked.

'I don't go out with freshmen,' she laughed. 'However loud they can howl.' She winked at me. Of course. I guess we had both seen one another's darker sides. I blushed and was on my way. God[145], I thought, these women have a lot of dirt on a lot of very important people. Best not to make any of them mad.

As I made my way past the barns, I came upon several ranch hands—real cowboys—struggling with a bull in a corral. They were pushing at him with steel prods, sending him towards an anxious cow in a tiny pen. One of them noticed me and stared a moment. I felt like an intruder. Like a summer camp kid coming upon a townie.

145. Contextually the God of the Israelites. Believed to be sovereign creator of the universe. Also blamed for many acts of destruction: "acts of God." But for the most part is a name that is used to explain the unexplainable.
—JACOBYACOV

The ranch hand suddenly looked up towards the sky. He must have had better ears than me, for only a few seconds later did I hear it, too. A helicopter was heading up towards the meadow.

'What the fuck are they gonna do now?' the hand said to his partner.

Whatever the fuck it was, I wanted to find out, and so I ran after it. The copter was hoisting a huge wooden crate suspended by long steel cables. I followed it all the way to the west pasture, where I found my fellow campers, hanging onto the wooden post. Tobias was waving his hat in the air.

'Just in time, Jamie!' he shouted. 'They're bringing'm in now.'

'Who?' I asked, as I pulled myself up next to him on the fence.

'The bull from New York. The one they were supposed to kill. Tellington bought him, the rascal!'

The helicopter, painted in the style of Entertainink's bright orange corporate seal, was hovering over the center of the pasture. Cows were running everywhere, in spite of several ranchers' efforts to calm them, as the giant crate was slowly lowered.

'I've got some good news, Mr. Morehouse,' I said, unsure if this was the very best or absolute worst time to bring it up.

'What'dya got, kid?' Tobias said, jovially. 'Did you get laid? Did Alec?'

'No no, not that. I mean, I don't know if Alec got laid.' I already felt a need to cover for my fallen friend. 'He may have. I was, well, I had a little meeting with the Synapticom guys last night. About using the program on our trading site. I think it would be a great addition. And they're willing to make it available to us.'

'Sounds good to me,' Tobias said, still watching the crate. 'Great work. Make it happen.'

'Well, yeah. We're going to. It's just a matter of the regulators. Part of the reason they're going with us, frankly, is your relationship with Birnbaum.'

'Figures,' Tobias said. 'But they're right. If anyone can open that door, it's us. Just make sure they give us an exclusive if we're the ones who have to go through the trouble.'

'I don't think that will be a problem.' I'd already taken that into account.

'Done, then,' Tobias said, returning his attention to the crate. 'You gotta see this.'

Amazing. This is the way deals are made. Right in the midst of everything. When something is supposed to happen, it just happens. It simply falls into place.

The crate was lowered very slowly from the helicopter's winch, but it still hit the ground with a tremendous thud. We all applauded.

Tellington spoke to the crowd through a megaphone.

'Gentlemen, it is with great pleasure that I introduce to you, straight from the wilds of New York City, a creature whose execution was stayed by the governor himself. Otto the bull!'

There was a tremendous collective cheer as two cowboys opened a panel on the side of the gate and ran for cover. But nothing happened. The cheers died down as everyone waited for the bull to emerge. But still, the crate just sat there.

One of the cowboys carefully ventured towards the opening on the side of the crate. He peered inside, then scratched his head. Suddenly, a black blur filled the opening. The stunned cowboy dodged for cover as Otto stormed from his tiny prison. He charged about ten feet then stopped, and turned. The cowboy lay on the ground with his hands over his head. The bull just stood there for a while, then casually turned away and limped off towards the other end of the meadow.

We were all unsure of what to do, until Tellington motioned for us to clap, which we did tentatively at first, then with greater bravado. Just as the applause reached a peak, Tellington raised his megaphone.

'Gentlemen: find a hand, and go get your breakfast!'

Tobias tapped my shoulder. 'Come on, kid, let's go!'

With a young ranch hand at our side, Tobias and I ran out into the meadow, along with a dozen other such trios.

'What are we doing?' I asked as we ran.

Tobias ignored the question.

'Look,' he said to the young hand. 'Over there.' A young calf stood alone by a bail of hay. 'Is that one of them?'

'Yes sir, it is,' he said. 'Want me to drop him for ya?'

'You want to drop him, Jamie?'

'I, uh—' I had no idea what was going on.

'You better do it,' Morehouse said to the hand. 'Come on, Jamie.'

The ranch hand pulled a length of rope off his belt and slowly approached the young animal, taking small steps and swinging the lasso over his head. He made a kissing sound, causing the calf to turn its head towards him. At the same moment, he threw the loop over the calf's neck and in one smooth motion lunged forward and tackled it to the ground. He wrapped the rope around the calf's limbs in a practiced set of twists and knots that incapacitated it in seconds.

'Come on,' he said, pulling a small pack off his shoulder, and motioning for me to take it.

'Go on,' Tobias said, pushing me towards the cowboy's pouch.

I took it and looked inside. There was an empty jar and a bottle of disinfectant.

'Okay, now,' the cowboy ordered calmly. 'Open the bottle and bring it over here.'

I did as I was told. I unscrewed the cap, which was attached to a long swab that dripped with the brown fluid.

'Bring it here,' the cowboy said. 'And wet it good.'

The cowboy held the young bull so that his testicles were exposed. Only then did I grasp the reality of what was occurring. We were going to cut them off.

'Umm...'

'It's okay, give it here.' The cowboy took the swab and doused the animal's scrotum. 'That'll do.' From a leather sheath on his thigh, he removed a long, shiny knife. 'Now who's gonna do it?'

'He is,' Tobias said.

'Where's Alec?' I asked. 'Don't you think—?'

'Come on, Cohen. There's nothing like working for a meal.'

I took the knife from the young rancher, and regarded my victim from the animal kingdom. I just knew I wasn't going to be able to do this, but stalling would only make it worse. And things with Tobias had been going so well.

I formed the words in my head. 'Sorry,' I'd begin, 'but I'm just not—' Then, as if guided by the force of an unseen hand, I gripped the knife tight and leaned in towards the frightened beast.

'You hafta clean the blade!' the rancher said, pointing at the bottle.

A reprieve. I applied the disinfectant to the blade, slowly and carefully.

'Come on, now. Right at the top here,' the cowboy said, touching the base of the scrotum. The calf suddenly bucked, trying to wriggle free. 'Hurry up, now.'

I'd have done it just a moment ago, but now I couldn't move. I couldn't even speak. I just crouched there with the knife in my hand, frozen in place.

'It's okay, sir,' the young ranch hand said. I looked him in the eyes for the first time. He couldn't have been more than fifteen. 'How 'bout you just hold him down.'

He took the knife from me and slowly released the calf so that I could get hold of it. I grabbed the animal's leg with one hand and the rope with the other, holding apart the calf's thighs, as the boy had done. I breathed a sigh of relief, thankful for the lesser task, and anxious to do at least this job right. The boy knelt down and leaned in.

'Well, shit,' Tobias huffed. 'Let *me* do it, then.'

The boy surrendered the knife to Morehouse.

'Just at the base,' the boy said.

'I know what I'm doing.'

The blade approached the soft pink flesh. It seemed as though time were standing still. I was at my young cousin's bris[146]. Samuel, who had been named Benjamin's godfather, was supposed to be the tzondik[147]. But he had gotten called away to a congregant's deathbed, and—though I was only fifteen at the time—they asked me to take his place. I was filled with dread, but the mohel was a charming old Hassid with a great long beard and kind, twinkling eyes. He gently but firmly talked me through the ritual, five thousand years of Jewish tradition behind him. I held the infant's thighs open from the foot of the table while the mohel worked on the foreskin.

As my baby nephew screamed and struggled, I just stared into the knowing eyes beneath the brim of the big black hat and felt reassured. I had the sense that standing behind the mohel, stretching for miles, was a line of mohels from generations past. It wound all the way back to Abraham himself. The bris was as much an initiation rite for me as it was for Benjamin. I had felt bonded to the boy ever since.

On the prairie, as I stared into the old face beneath the black cowboy hat, I found none of the same solace. The veins in Morehouse's forehead were protruding and pulsating. His teeth were clenched and his eyebrows furrowed. For this wasn't a bris at all, it was a sin. Jews aren't allowed to cut off

146. Male circumcision was practiced by a majority of Americans until halfway through the 20th century. Called a 'bris' by Jews, the ritualized removal of a baby's foreskin eight days after his birth was thought to serve as a covenant with God, guaranteeing the child's, as well as the father's, future prosperity.
—Sabina Samuels

147. The Tzondik, usually a relative, held the baby while a professional 'moyle' actually performed the ritual mutilation.
—Sabina Samuels

the parts of a living animal. It's not kosher. Jews aren't even allowed to hunt.

As the blade penetrated the calf's tender skin, it flailed its legs and bucked its head back. I held on tight. If I slipped the animal could be hurt even worse. Tobias used a sawing motion to make a slit about three inches wide at the base of the scrotum. He reached his fingers inside the sack and withdrew a network of red veins and white membrane.

I looked away and tried to concentrate on something else. What had I been thinking about before? Oh yeah. Kosher laws. To bring mankind out of its hunter-gatherer stage. We were shepherds and farmers, not hunters. We created laws to minimize our cruel impact on other life forms. To thwart the rule of the wild. Interventionist regulations to ensure we killed humanely. Although a chicken having its neck slit the kosher way might experience no less pain than one whose head was simply chopped off, at least someone was worrying about it.

The smelly steam rising from the calf's groin pulled me out of my intentional trance.

'Just pull it all out, now,' the boy was saying.

Tobias removed one, and then the other red, bloody ball through the incision. They were still attached to the calf by a cluster of stringy veins or arteries or something. Tobias held the balls in one hand, and pulled on the cords with the other. He pulled and pulled but the cords were endless. It all piled up on the ground in a bloody tangle. Finally, Tobias found their origin, deep within the sack, and began to cut at them with the knife.

Only then did the young bull begin to scream. It wailed in long, doleful whines. Blood spurted everywhere, as Tobias hacked away. A dark red stream arched in the air like a Roman fountain. Some of it landed on my corduroys, where it spotted the fabric like warm ink. Tobias took a moment to wipe the sweat off his brow with the sleeve of his suede jacket, then continued the butchery.

The carnage was everywhere. The calf bucked furiously, blood pooling beneath him. I was getting dizzy, and tried to look up at the sky. But as I averted my gaze I felt the calf wriggling free. I tightened my grip on the rope but lost hold of the calf's leg in the process. The desperate animal managed to right itself and leap almost a full yard away until the rope went taut, spinning himself around and splattering all of us with his blood.

The calf darted this way and that, trying to run, but I dug my feet in the ground and yanked on the rope. The animal went berserk and ran the only way it could: in circles around its captor. In seconds, I was tangled in my own rope. As the young bull continued to encircle me, the rope got shorter and shorter until the animal and I were tied to each other—him bleeding, both of us screaming. As the animal struggled against me, the rope slid up around my neck. I couldn't breathe.

'Don't move!' Tobias shouted, diving in to finish his botched surgery on the now two-headed beast. I gasped for air as my face was pressed down together with the poor calf's into the mud. I could feel the animal's wet breath against my neck as it whined.

'There!' Morehouse said, plopping the blood-red testicles into the glass jar and panting with relief.

'Help!' I gasped, my face submerged in the bloody mess by the force of the young bull rolling frantically on top of me.

The ranch hand took the knife from Tobias and cut the ropes tying us together, two panicked mammals. The moment he was free, the calf quickly hobbled off towards the other end of the meadow, leaving a trail of blood behind him. I fared only slightly better. The cowboy sat me up and patted me on the back, helping me cough up a mixture of dirt and cow blood. I still couldn't breathe.

'Take your time, sir,' the boy said. 'You just got the wind knocked out of you, that's all.'

I wheezed and hacked for a while until I got some air. As I felt my full awareness returning I realized I was sitting in a puddle of hair, entrails, and blood.

'Whooey!' Tobias exclaimed, his face dripping with red-soaked sweat. 'That was a tough little feller, eh?'

I just sat there, panting pathetically.

'Better get changed before breakfast, kid,' Tobias said, putting a hand out for me.

'Yeah,' I finally said, letting him pull me upright.

'You okay?' the young cowboy asked me.

'Yeah.' I thought maybe I was supposed to give the kid a tip. 'Thanks.'

I made it back to the cabin, grateful that this whole ordeal would soon be over. Anticipating the flight home (as well as to guarantee not being dragged into any more bull bunkum) I got changed into my best Prada suit. I wore a pale green polo shirt underneath, to intimate my fledgling alliance with Synapticom.

Their whole team had already left for Nepal that morning, though, I learned when I arrived at breakfast. About twenty-five men were gathered around six long tables on the back porch of the main house. They were mostly the old bankers and investment barons who'd been coming to the ranch for years.

'Only the men who brought back something get to eat here,' Tobias said, patting on a seat for me to sit down.

'We got four,' Alec gloated from across the table. 'Me and Tellington and Mr. Newman.'

'Oh, you were out there, too?' Morehouse asked.

'Sure I was,' Alec answered, as if his honesty were being questioned.

'That's great.' I tried to be supportive. 'Four? We had hell just getting one. Or does one pair count as two?'

Tellington laughed. 'It counts as one, Cohen. Just one. But with that old clown as your partner I'm surprised you got even that!'

'He did all the work, sir, really,' I admitted on behalf of my benefactor, and Alec.

'Nah,' Tobias shrugged. 'Cohen proved himself out there, there's no doubt about it.'

'Good to hear it,' Tellington said. 'I like your style. You had real spunk on stage, yesterday.'

'Yeah, well...'

'No, really. I'd like to help you guys out.'

'How's that, Marshall?' Tobias asked casually, pretending to be involved in the cornbread.

'That project of yours, what's it called?'

'TeslaNet,' I quickly filled in.

'Yeah, TeslaNet. I thought maybe I'd take it off your hands. Keep it in development at Entertainink.'

'What do you mean by development?' I asked.

'He means development, Jamie,' Tobias cut me off. We all knew that 'development' meant cold storage.

'I'd be prepared to offer you four million if you sign off by the end of next week,' Tellington said.

At the industry standard thirty percent commission for the brokerage house, this would mean over two million for Jude and Reuben. It would also mean the end of their TeslaNet project.

'But the development team—'

'They'd participate in back-end revenues,' Tellington cut me off. Of course if the program were never released, there would be no back-end revenues.

'Make it six and throw in a few positive network news stories about online trading and you've got a deal,' Tobias said, spreading butter on his cornbread. I was impressed. Tobias was already thinking about how to push the Synapticom alliance through the SEC.

Tellington scrunched his face.

'The offer's only good until the omelets get here,' Tobias added.

'Done.'

As I wondered whether and how to disclose to my former hacker buddies that accepting two million each for their life's work would effectively bury the project for good, a ranch hand placed my meal before me. An omelet, grits, and fresh, pan-fried, young bull testicle, smothered in onions.

The men all voraciously consumed the product of their earlier labors, grunting and slurping as they did. I just stared at the trafe[148] on my plate.

'Don't be scared, Jamie,' Alec said. 'It's just meat. Like sausage.'

I put my fork into the veiny little meatball and brought it to my face. No one was watching, but where could I get rid of the thing? I closed my eyes and put the morsel of genitalia in my mouth. It was gritty. Stringy. Hard-to-chew. But as my teeth crushed the life-giving gland, I thought I felt an inkling of how a tradition like this got started. Or why it survived.

These little balls were all that was left. This grown-up version of cowboy games. There was nowhere for these old sports to be men. They had no wars to fight for real, and now business battles like mergers and acquisitions were being arranged by math geeks. Even the glass ceiling had begun to crack, and someday soon there'd be as many women in the Forbes 500[149] as men. The game, as they knew it, would be over.

148. Non-kosher food. —Sabina Samuels

149. A list of the wealthiest humans in the world, published in a magazine founded by one of those people. —Sabina Samuels

But that didn't explain why Ruth Stendahl, the Internet investment queen, was allowed to sit at the table munching on bull balls with the rest of us.

'Hey,' I whispered to Morehouse. 'What's her deal? She wasn't out there, was she?'

Tobias laughed, and then with his mouth full shouted, 'Marshall! The kid wants to know why Ruth's allowed to eat.'

'Why don't you ask her?' Tellington said, loud enough for Stendahl to hear from across the table.

'What's that?' she said.

'He wants to know why you get to chow on the oysters!'

Ruth just smiled, then toasted Marshall with her orange juice.

I figured I'd give up, but Alec's curiosity had been piqued, too.

'Why *does* she get to eat with us, Dad?'

Tobias and Tellington regarded one another for a moment, silently deciding who would have the honor of explaining. Tobias won.

'If you please,' said Tellington.

'Until the early nineties,' Tobias began. 'There had never been any women at a Bull Run.'

'None except the performers, of course,' Tellington added.

'You want to tell it?' Tobias asked. Tellington raised his hands in surrender. 'Okay, then. Well, when biotechs started to hit, and then the chip companies, most of us were left in the dust. Stendahl had seen it all coming. She used to work with the spooks at the State Department, and she was crafty enough to spin off a division of the National Science Foundation into the private sector and then run it herself with some old Defense Department cronies of hers. It got so you couldn't open a dot-com without registering through her company.'

'We know that, Dad,' Alec interrupted. 'It's the history of the Internet. But why does she get to eat the prairie oysters?'

'I'm getting to that. It was back in ninety-four or ninety-five, right Tellington?'

Marshall nodded.

'Ninety-five I think,' Tobias continued. 'And we were all getting ready to do the oyster drive—that's what we called it then. And she looked at us like we were fucking imbeciles. She'd made it through the bonfire the night before and hadn't fallen for anything. She must have thought we were gonna give it one last try. So she stayed behind, and we figured that was fine. We'll leave her out of it. Save something for ourselves. And just to rub her nose in it, when we got back we put all the balls we'd collected in a big bucket, and left it on the kitchen table right over there. And we all sat around waiting for her to look in there and run screaming. They looked God-awful. A bloody pail of bull nuts. It made your skin crawl.'

'So what happened?' I asked.

'She ambles on over to the table and says something like 'you boys done?' And we just sit there grinning our best shit-eating grins, ready for her to show her true stripes.'

'And then?' Alec asked. He was on the edge of his seat.

'She looks down into the bucket and sneers. Didn't blanch at all. Then she reaches in and pulls one out. She holds the raw, dripping thing in front of her face, dangling it by the little vein. And she looks around the table at us and, totally deadpan, mind you, and she asks 'whose is this?''

'Gross!' Alec shrieked.

'None of us knew what to say. We were in awe. Guys were crossing their legs and looking down. Then she swings the ball around like a little lasso, tosses it in her mouth, and swallows it whole.'

8. Contracts & Covenants

In anticipation of their victory on my father's contract referendum, the Executive Board of Whitestone Temple had kindly prepared a settlement offer that they delivered to him, by FedEx[150], the Monday before the web vote was scheduled to take place. If Samuel resigned his position effective immediately, the temple would pay him a severance of one year's salary.

Of course, the only reason they made the offer was to keep themselves in good standing with the Hebrew Union[151]—the puppy mill for new rabbis, to whom they'd be applying for a more liberal leader once my dad was gone. The quieter this went down, the better for all.

They were asking my father to take the kind of self-effacing step that I suspected gave people cancer, and I didn't want him to have any part of it.

150. A delivery company of the period. Most remembered for its association with the Tom Hanks character in the film *Castaway*.   —Sabina Samuels

151. Hebrew Union was actually a college for rabbinical students. It closed in 2079, after the reform, conservative and orthodox 'movements' in Judaism finally merged.   —Sabina Samuels

On the other hand, it was a bit gratifying to see him finally buckling under to the wave of economic expansion that I now had the power to surf for sport. I, more than anyone, knew what it was like to wither under his self-righteous gaze. Why would anyone subject himself to it voluntarily every Sabbath? We weren't Catholic Mafiosos with a need to confess the hits we'd ordered. Just successful people, having a bit of fun.

I had been visiting home so infrequently that I was half-afraid my appearance would make my father think there was even worse news we were keeping from him—like when a famous baseball player shows up at a kid's bedside in the hospital, signaling by his very presence that death is imminent. So I scheduled a meeting with Jude and Reuben at home that same afternoon, as my mom suggested. It would give me a pretext to see my dad, and the domestic location might lend an air of sincerity to my business dealings—which were anything but.

Predictably, Sophie ordered a box of cinnamon rugelah from Silverman's, and a full plate of the dense pastries was awaiting my arrival that afternoon. While Samuel composed a sermon on legal pads in his customary fashion, thick volumes of Midrash spread out all around him, my sister and I enjoyed the refreshments at the other end of the dining-room table.

'So what're you gonna talk about, Dad?' I asked.

'You really want to know, Yossi?'

'Sure, I do. Tell me. It's gonna be about Pesach, right?' I knew my dad would appreciate my use of the Hebrew word for Passover.

'You were never interested before.'

'Before what?' As if I didn't know.

'I want to hear, Daddy,' Miriam pleaded.

'Very well,' Samuel said, putting his pen down. 'I'm going to explain why God didn't let Moses into the land of Canaan. Do you remember why that happened?'

I always hated when my dad treated us like bible students, but today I actually felt myself enjoying Samuel's patronizing tone.

'Didn't it have something to do with not having faith? Or breaking a rule?'

'Close, Yossi. It had to do with his faith, but it had even more to do with his age.'

'What? He was too old? Those guys lived, like, four hundred years.'

'It wasn't old age. It was old thinking,' Samuel said, drifting into his practiced, oratory style. 'The Israelites were in the desert, at Horeb. Exodus. They're tired, sick, hungry, and, most of all, thirsty. 'Why did you bring us out of Egypt just to die of thirst here in the desert?' they asked him. It was the first Jewish joke: 'We could have died just as easily in Egypt, and there, we'd have water!' So God told Moses to raise his staff and strike it against a rock, for water to come rushing out. And he did so. He tapped his staff against a large rock, and out gushed water for all the people and their herds.'

'Yeah, Moses did miracles like that all the time, right?'

'Moses parted the Dead Sea!' Miriam said.

'The *Red* Sea.' Samuel lovingly corrected her. How will they take care of her after he's sacked, I wondered. I could probably help out, if they'd let me.

'But later,' my dad continued, 'years later, the people cried to Moses again, 'we have no water. Surely we will all die of thirst.' And God told him, 'Speak to that rock before their eyes and it will pour out its water.' But Moses didn't do as he was told by God. He didn't speak to the rock. No, he raised his staff and then struck the rock twice. And the water came gushing out as it had before.'

'What's the big deal with that?' I asked. 'He used the proven method.'

'It worked, sure. But he didn't do as God had instructed him. And God told him so.' Samuel found the appropriate passage from his notes. 'And God said, "Because you did not trust in me enough to honor me as holy in the sight of the Israelites, you will not bring this community into the land I give them." '

'That's pretty rough, though. Banging on the rock with his staff is still a major act of faith. Besides, it worked before. And it sounds like he was under considerable pressure to perform.'

'But Moses was relying on his experience, rather than the word of God. He didn't have faith that his words, alone, would bring forth the water.'

'And God got mad over that? After everything Moses did?'

'I don't know that God was mad, exactly,' Samuel said, pensively. 'I don't think God was testing Moses as much as proving something to him. That Moses was of the wrong generation to lead the people in their new land. He still understood things in the old way. He understood the power of his staff, but not of his words. That's why he couldn't lead the younger generations. He wasn't one of them.'

'Sounds like an upgrade problem,' I tried to make light. I knew my dad was talking about himself. He was preparing a farewell speech.

'Explain it to me,' he asked, innocently.

'Well, legacy systems, they.... When you want to use a new piece of software, it...' I couldn't find a way to bring him up to speed.

'I guess that makes me a bit like Moses, too,' he smiled. 'You can't even explain to me what's going on in that virtual head of yours in a way that I can understand.'

'No, Dad, really—'

'Don't worry about it, Jamie. It doesn't make me feel bad. Just ready to move on.'

'You're not getting fired, dad. We'll work this out.' He used my American name. He must've been really depressed.

'Sometimes we have to trust what life brings us.' Samuel motioned to the plate of rugelah. I passed it across the table to him. He took a piece and ate it in several small bites.

'I know I've been hard on you about your job. Your choices,' he said.

'You haven't, Dad,' I lied. 'You've tried to be supportive.'

My mom, who must have been listening in from the kitchen, stood in the doorway to better hear our exchange.

'No, I haven't been supportive at all,' Samuel said, shaking his head. 'Not like Morris. But it's not because I don't trust you. It's just because I don't understand. All this talk of networks and money and business. I only fear it because I don't understand it.'

'But it *should* frighten you, Dad. It's scary stuff. I don't want you to accept it like Uncle Morris does. No one knows where it's all going. And no one's in charge.'

'You're in charge, Jamie. That's what I have to accept.' He looked around at his books. 'Sometimes I think the Torah was written for parents. Or rabbis.'

I wanted to confess to my father right then and there. That I'd gotten into something beyond my control. That I had eaten the testes of a baby bull. That I was about to sell my friends up the river. That I was going to help Tobias Morehouse launch a stock-trading web site that could hypnotize its users into making more transactions. That I was part of a band of market fascists who meant to monetize humanity itself. But the doorbell rang before I could say another word.

'Somebody's at the door!' shouted Miriam. She ran to open it.

'That must be the Epsteins,' said Sophie, nervously running after her daughter.

The Epsteins were what are known in rabbinical circles as 'returnees.' Wealthy, bored, and in existential despair following the death of Mr. Epstein's mother, the couple had returned to the religion of their youth in the hope of finding a sense of connection to something more authentic than the faux-antique facades of the South Street Seaport shopping mall. A forty-thousand-dollar donation to renovate the sanctuary earned them seats on the board, and Samuel hoped their commitment to traditional values would swing a few votes to his favor.

But returnees do not return without bringing back problems of their own.

'Good afternoon, welcome!' Sophie greeted them as she opened the door.

'Shalom, Rebbetzen,' the middle-aged man said, 'Shalom!'

'Why of course, Mark,' she corrected herself. 'Shalom!'

'Actually,' he said, kissing the mezzuzah on the doorframe, 'I've decided to use my Hebrew name from now on. Meyer. Meyer Epstein ben Moshe v' Rivka.'

'How wonderful!' Sophie clapped. My mom knew the drill. 'Shalom, Meyer Epstein!'

'You know my wife,' Meyer introduced her formally, 'Shoshana Irit.'

'Shalom, Rebbetzen.' The woman bowed like a sushi chef. 'I never learned my real Hebrew name,' she said sadly, 'but we looked in a book and picked out the ones closest.'

'Well please come in Shoshana Irit, Meyer,' Samuel said, rising from his chair. 'You've met my daughter, Miriam?'

Miriam took Meyer's coat, revealing the white fringe known as 'tzi-tzi' sticking out from the front of his pants.

'Chabad!' she exclaimed, innocently mistaking him for one of the Lubavitch[152] orthodox who usually wore such garb.

152. A Jewish cult that grew in popularity in the late 1990's when it claimed that it had found the messiah in the personage of its own head rabbi. They disbanded after a scandal in which forty of their rabbis were revealed to be selling psychedelic drugs to non-Jewish children.
—Sabina Samuels

'No, no,' Meyer said sweetly. The whole congregation knew of her disability. 'Just a good Jew.'

'Come, come.' Samuel gestured to the dining room. 'Let's sit down and get to work.'

Mr. Epstein had decided to get bar mitzvahed a second time, now that he knew what the ritual was 'really' about. His superfluous ceremony would take place in a week in front of the whole congregation, and my father was preparing him privately from home rather than at temple with the thirteen-year-olds. Meyer had taken a crash course in reading Hebrew at an orthodox shul in the city, and now proceeded to race through the text of his torah portion, holding his hand over the English transliteration just to prove he was reading from the real Hebrew characters[153].

'Excellent job,' Samuel praised him when he was finished. 'Terrific, really. You know, Judaism is the only Western religion where the initiation, the bar mitzvah, amounts to a demonstration of literacy.'

'Of course I still have no idea what I'm actually saying,' admitted Meyer.

'It's still very commendable, Mr. Epstein,' Samuel said. 'It's a fascinating passage,' he continued, demonstrating his rabbinical expertise, 'because it shows that the slavery in Egypt actually symbolizes an enslaved state of mind.'

'But we were really slaves in Egypt, too,' Shoshana Irit added as she nibbled on a rugelah.

'Some Israelites most likely were, in a sense,' Samuel said, 'but the release from slavery is presented here more as a culmination of Abraham's covenant with God. People often take the plagues quite literally, but they are meant more symbolically. The slaying of the Egyptian first born really represents the slaying of the first born civilization. The Hebrew word for Egypt, 'Mitzrayim,' translates as 'a narrow place.'

153. Hebrew characters, as we know today, aren't really Hebrew at all, but Aramaic. The Torah was, itself, a transliteration for a population of Jews who could no longer read Hebrew. But most Jews of the 21st Century did not know this, or pretended not to know. —Sabina Samuels

'But the plagues really happened, right rabbi?' Epstein insisted.

'Well, the story we read in the Haggadah was written during the Roman occupation,' I came to my father's aid. 'The Jews needed the tale of revolution to give them hope of overcoming their oppression and winning back the temple.' I surprised myself with that one. Maybe I was still a Jew, after all.

'That's quite right, Jamie,' my dad said. 'The Haggadah was regarded as a subversive document. But, more importantly, it's a lesson on how to escape slavery of the mind. Or the soul. The way we can enslave only ourselves—by building pyramids to false gods.'

Meyer seemed quite unsettled. He hadn't paid $40,000 to be thrown into doubt about his heritage.

'Now, of all times,' he complained, 'isn't it important that we affirm the literal truth of our history? Many people calling themselves Jews don't even believe that Moses existed!' Shoshana Irit nodded emphatically with each of her husband's words.

Samuel took a deep breath. He was torn between serving as a genuine rabbi for these overzealous returnees—which would mean helping them temper their extreme views—and exploiting their conservative bias in order to secure his own position at the shul. As always, Samuel's higher obligation won out over self-interest.

'Okay, Meyer,' the rabbi said. 'Let's look at the story a little more closely, then. Why were the Israelites down in Egypt in the first place?'

'The famine!' Miriam shouted.

'Excellent, Miriam,' Samuel said. 'And why is it they were allowed to immigrate to Egypt?'

'Because Joseph was Prime Minister,' Meyer answered quickly, as if he were competing with Miriam on a game show.

'Right. He had been betrayed by his brothers and sold into slavery. But his ability to prophesize earned him a place as Pharaoh's right hand man. He lived like one of the Egyptians. And his people followed him into what eventually became slavery, building pyramids to the Egyptian gods.'

'That's terrible!' Shoshana said.

'He forgot he was an Israelite. But four-hundred years later, Moses—an Egyptian nobleman—remembers. When he sees a slave being killed by a guard, he is inspired to act.'

'Damn right, he acts!' Epstein clapped his hands. 'He killed the guard on the spot!'

'True enough. He witnessed such cruelty that he was pulled from the dream. He was liberated, and he set to liberating his people.'

'And now you're saying this never happened?' Meyer looked up at the ceiling, as if God were witnessing this blasphemy.

'No, Mr. Epstein,' I tried to bring it all home for my dad. 'He's saying that it's still happening. It's happening every day.'

My dad and I looked at one another for a moment, Samuel's eyes beaming with newfound respect for me, while I tried not to cringe from the undeserved admiration. I liked it better when my dad criticized me. His faith made me feel suddenly adrift.

I was saved by the bell. Miriam again rushed to answer it.

'Who have we here?' Jude bowed to her from the threshold. He took her hand and kissed it as if she were a queen. She laughed and curtsied.

He came in with young Benjamin.

'So, are we celebrating or what?' Jude asked.

'I think so,' I said. 'Let's go upstairs where I can tell you the whole story.'

'Hello, Rabbi, Mrs. Cohen,' Jude said. 'Good to see you again.'

My parents nodded at their son's childhood role model.

'Come on,' I said. I didn't want these two worlds mixing any more than necessary. As we went up the stairs, Miriam grabbed the plate of rugelah from under Mrs. Epstein's nose.

'Bring this with you, Jude!' she shouted, running with the plate and losing a substantial portion of its contents in the process. 'For you to eat!'

'Funeral food! Cool,' Jude joked of the pastries. Then, to Samuel, 'I didn't mean, you know...'

'It's quite alright,' Samuel said from the table. 'Enjoy.'

As I went up the stairs, I felt like I was leaving him behind.

With every opportunity in the world to do otherwise, I pitched my heart out to Jude. I made no mention of Entertainink's intention to bury TeslaNet forever. I focused instead on how the first six million dollars would be split, and how revenue would be assessed after that. Jude didn't seem at all surprised or even impressed that we were talking about millions of dollars. He nodded along as if he already expected it. Not even Benjamin batted an eye. In fact, he looked positively morose about the whole deal. Did he sense my ambivalence?

Finally, when I was done, Jude asked just one question.

'So you think this is the right way to go?'

I didn't know what to say. I had been basically honest with Jude, if not absolutely forthcoming. He didn't deserve any better, really. This was the guy who had fucked me—the fact that it ended up serving my goals not withstanding. Besides, I was on a new team now, and that team was depending on me. A whole industry was depending on me. But I couldn't give my unconditional recommendation and live with myself. Not after all that Bible stuff downstairs.

'I think it's a good deal,' I said. 'A really good deal.'

'You're saying we should take the money?' Jude pressed. Why was he letting me make the decision for him? My Greek chorus began rustling their sheet music.

'If you don't mind losing control of the project,' I edged toward disclosure, 'yes, I do.'

Tell him! Tell him! The chorus chanted.

'Well, TeslaNet is beyond anyone's control once it's released, right?' Jude asked rhetorically.

'That would be true,' I said, wording my sentences as carefully as a President giving grand jury testimony[154].

'And they'll release it, right?' Jude asked.

We'd finally reached the juncture I was hoping to avoid. Jude had an incredible knack of digging down to the weakest line of code.

'Well,' I managed, 'they're paying an awful lot of money if they have no intention of actually releasing the program.' There. I mentioned the possibility. It was a throwaway line, but it would serve to alleviate me of responsibility later on.

You are lost, Yossi! Lost!

'Cool, then,' Jude said, satisfied. 'We'll do whatever you say.'

'Well,' I smiled as best I could. 'It looks like you're the next Internet millionaire.'

'Correction: TeslaNet millionaire.'

We toasted rugelah. *How could you??*

I went over the details of transferring the patent application to Entertainink and had Jude sign a few preliminary documents making M&L the broker of record for the deal. Benjamin seemed to be getting more withdrawn. When Jude left to debrief Reuben, I asked Benjamin to stay for a moment. He obeyed, as if he were following a teacher's orders.

'Aren't you excited about what's happening?' I asked.

'Yeah, I guess.'

154. Political parties of the period competed through a complex process of accusation and recrimination, usually about sexual misconduct but occasionally with reference to campaign financing. (Candidates raised money from corporations and then purchased advertisements on television and elsewhere.) Although feminism was given lip-service at the time, most politicians still practiced blatant sexual harassment, making themselves vulnerable to scandal. In many cases, however, a politician's post-scandal contrition could earn him higher poll ratings than he would have achieved had the sexual misconduct never been unearthed. See biographies of William Jefferson Clinton for more on this phenomenon.
—Sabina Samuels

'You're in on it, too, you know. Five percent. You're gonna be the richest kid in your grade.'

'That's cool,' he mumbled, flatly.

'Jude hasn't done anything to freak you out, has he? Those guys play rough, sometimes.'

'No.'

'That's good.' I was secretly hoping that Benjamin's sentiments toward Jude might have changed.

'Is that it?' Benjamin wanted to leave.

'No.' I was searching for something to say. 'How's the game emulator working out?'

'It's cool,' he said. 'I downloaded a bunch of stuff for it.'

'It still works?'

'With the older stuff. Yeah.'

'El Greco wrote most of the graphics code, you know. I just saw him again. He's not fat, anymore. Do you remember him?'

'No.'

Benjamin just sat on the edge of the bed, the points on his little bony frame showing through his striped T-shirt and his big brown eyes staring into space. It made me felt dirty. Like an adult.

'What's wrong, then?' I asked. Surely the boy couldn't see through to my compromised soul, could he? *Yes he can!* Besides, I had just made them all millionaires. *You made them all slaves!*

'Nothing,' Benjamin said. 'I better go.'

'Did they do another jock check[155] at school or something?'[156]

'I'm not afraid of jock checks, anymore, Jamie.' He went to the door. 'I gotta go.

'Hey!' I followed him down the stairs. 'I've got Knicks tickets for Friday

155. Not to be confused with the 'jock check' neo-tartan designs popularized in the 2080s by the Scottish Federation costumier Ieuan Kwezi McFadyen.
—RAY GIRVAN

156. We're not sure exactly what is being referred to here. Most likely, it refers to an obscure ritual practiced on adolescent boys by physical education teachers, in which the wearing of protective undergear is enforced through some sort of inspection. —Sabina Samuels

night. Wanna come?' This was a major invitation.[157] I got them from Morehouse, personally, and they were supposed to be for clients, not cousins.

'Nah,' Benjamin said, already outside and getting on his bicycle. 'I got lots of homework.'

'Okay,' I called after him as he pedaled away. 'You got my new email address, right?'

Benjamin's odd behavior made me feel all the more like I was spreading poison in Queens whenever I went home—as if my briefcase contained toxic contaminants from the business world. But they weren't really toxic; it was just a matter of context. I had made my friends six million dollars, I had laid the groundwork for Entertainink to promote the next crucial iteration of a free market economy, and I had developed a way for M&L's trading sites to generate traffic without relying on illegal day trading scams. A pretty complex set of potentially conflicting agendas, now working in concert. Not bad for a rookie.

And as I passed through the dehumanizing revolving doors into the M&L machine the next day, a neatly tied box of rugelah in my hand, I felt like I was bringing a macrophage into the very heart of the system. My ethnic heritage, now served as a secret weapon. The kosher treats themselves were a symbol of virtue—my connection to something outside the casino. I could play both sides of this game, now.

I strolled over towards Alec's office then bowed in the threshold, holding the open box up as if it were a peace offering. Maybe it was.

'Work now, Danish later,' Alec said, gliding briskly across the busy floor towards Morehouse's office. 'Birnbaum's gonna be on any minute.'

Advance word was that the Fed would be coming down hard on the recent surge (within-the-surge) in electronic trading.[158] Computer monitors in offices and cubicles all over the building were lighting up with in-screen

157. From the way they were coveted, it appears that basketball tickets hadn't been available to the general public for several years. Only companies like M&L, television actors, and extremely wealthy individuals had access to seats in Madison Square Garden. In addition, games were not broadcast on free television, making the sport virtually inaccessible to the lower classes (except those who played, of course).

158. Electronic documents from the recently decrypted SEC archives indicate that shortly after the turn of the century, online brokerages had discovered (or created) a particularly complex, multi-part tax loophole. It allowed corporations to save enormous taxes if they deposited their employees' payroll checks directly into their online trading accounts, as stock purchases. Employees who opted for these 'direct investment' plans were, in turn, incentivized by much better terms on their margined securities. So, instead of being held to a borrowing limit of 80% against current assets, account holders whose paychecks were invested automatically were free to borrow against the full value of their next twenty-four months' salary. It led to an average margin of 600% against savings, and accounted for the last few pumps of air into the NASDAQ bubble. Worse, every extended downswing in the NASDAQ threatened a cascade of margin calls that could wipe out two-thirds the valuation of the entire index. As a result, even those who originally had concerns about the practice were soon depending on it for the market value of their own investments. —Sabina Samuels

159. What follows is a direct transcript of Ezra Birnbaum's videotaped Senate testimony:

Senator of Louisiana: These 'frenzied paroxysms' you speak of, Chairman Birnbaum. Are you suggesting some kind of Biblical retribution for our citizens' faith in what always struck me as the American Way?

Birnbaum: No, Mr. Senator. With all due respect, I simply mean to suggest that investments of various kinds will provide varying levels of long-term protection of capital. Many of the gentlemen in this very room, in fact, have—irresponsibly and to the detriment of the individual investor—recast the bear market of 2001 as a sustained correction. Further, if working, non-professional investors are routinely exposed to what could only be considered self-promotional trading systems, they may very well lose sight of the relative value of cash and bond savings vehicles in light of the more speculative allure of high-flying technology issues.

Senator of Louisiana: If I understand you correctly, and I'm not sure I'm quite educated enough to do that [laughter from other Senators]. I understand that the Fed's job is to protect the value of money. Of the currency of this great land. But also, and please correct me if I am mistaken, that the Federal Reserve is, in fact, a private corporation with no direct accountability to any elected authority.

Birnbaum: That is correct, sir. But that is merely to insure that—'

Senator of Louisiana: Please allow me to finish, good sir. [pause] And that as a spokesman for the Federal Reserve Bankers, whose primary asset is US currency, you have what could only be understood as a vested interest in the worth of the dollar.

Birnbaum: Yes, but it was set up this way to insure that—

Senator of Louisiana: You'll have a chance to speak. [Senator toys with his

streaming video images of Birnbaum's live testimony.

A hush came over brokerages, businesses, taco stands and taxicabs throughout New York as the old man adjusted his bifocals and looked down at his prepared remarks. Not that the Fed would announce a policy decision—he hardly did that at all, anymore, now that Congress had taken away his ability to adjust interest rates without their approval. But the Fed's words still exerted some influence over an intensely emotional market. No one expected his own psychology to be changed by Birnbaum's often dour predictions—but everyone did fear what the Fed's pronouncements might do to the psychology of others. And this secondary fear, in turn, dampened market sentiment as much as if people actually believed what he said, themselves.

We made it into Tobias's conference room by the time Birnbaum had gotten through his customary admonition against making investment decisions based on the 'specious commentary of online traders.' In language pulled from his previous testimonies, he claimed 'those who exploit the anonymity of the Internet to commit securities fraud must understand that the online world offers them no insulation from law enforcement.'

'No news is good news,' Tobias said, leaning back in his armchair. 'It looks like he listened to us.' As long as Birnbaum made it sound like the Fed was on the case, he was tacitly approving of online trading for the American public.

'But even with our current ability to enact oversight,' Birnbaum continued, 'the prevailing perception of online trading as a substitute for cash savings, and technology securities as a de facto Social Security system[159], can lead only to an escalation of risk with potentially disastrous results for the uneducated investor.'

'Here he goes,' Alec said, leaning in towards the rear-projection monitor at the end of the conference table. 'Uneducated investors?'

'Shh!' Tobias silenced him.

'A new generation of online trading programs promises only to exacerbate this trend, lulling the public into an evermore frenzied paroxysm of optimistic transactions.'

'Huh?' Alec said.

Tobias slapped his open hand on the table for his son to shut up. It was much louder than his fist had been the week before. He was learning.

But we may as well have turned off the broadcast right then. Birnbaum had made his stand, and our course was now clear. By the time the old man was done—an hour and forty-five minutes later—he had cast himself as the guardian of rational thinking in the midst of a nationwide, computer-aided psychosis. He warned that the events of just a few years ago could well repeat themselves. Even the Senators seemed horrified by his stance, and did their best to protect the interests of their campaign contributors.

It went on all afternoon[160]—senators on both sides of the aisle[161] attacking Birnbaum for his attempts to manufacture skepticism in an otherwise contented citizenry, and to put the personal concerns of an elite cabal of bankers over the priorities of a nation of individual investors struggling to compete in an increasingly open international economy. Still, the damage had been done. Birnbaum declared himself committed to exposing the questionable practices of the online trading companies, and M&L's impending adoption of the Synapticom system was directly in his line of fire.

'We can get ads broadcast by tomorrow night's newscasts,' Alec said, spreading his storyboards across the table.

'We're going to need more than good advertising, Alec,' Tobias grumbled. 'He's declared war. I can't believe he'd do this to us. That motherfucker.'

'He's old,' I said. 'He's got nothing to lose.'

pencil] It seems to me that you are challenging the American people's faith in the investments that make this country grow, the ones that stand a chance of providing us with new prospects for education and opportunities for advancement across all race and class boundaries. And you are doing this so that they will keep more capital tied up in your dollars.

Birnbaum: They're not my dollars, Mr. Senator.

Senator of Louisiana: I think I understand your position, Mr. Birnbaum. I surrender the balance of my time.'
—Sabina Samuels

160. Social Security was system that redistributed wealth from the young and able-bodied to the elderly and disabled. It is a curiosity of 20th century America, which was usually disdainful of social welfare programs. Its survival into the 22nd century is widely attributed to the fact that it benefited primarily the old and that the old, more than any other population cohort, voted.

To this day, despite the abolition of formal currency and the free provision of every conceivable human need or desire, Social Security technically remains the law of the land, alongside the 2nd Amendment and the ban on bathing one's horse on a Sunday in Boston's public square.

There have been a number of attempts in recent years to discontinue the now completely meaningless program, but they have always met with strong resistance by centarian and bi-centarian citizens' groups, who have been convinced by hysterical Talk Space hosts that they will no longer receive their gerontological treatments if Social Security is abolished. —SHANKEL

161. The Congress used a two-party system based on an ancient French parliament, whose designations as 'left' and 'right' referred to their positions relative

199

note continues on page 200

to the Speaker. Once the two chief American parties became indistinguishable and were subsequently joined by countless others, such designations were abandoned.   —Sabina Samuels

'What do you mean by that?' Alec asked.

'I just mean he feels free to say what he really thinks. There's not a lot we can do to stop him.' I felt surprisingly light about everything. Like I had no stakes in the matter.

'I'm not so sure about that,' Alec said.

'Never mind,' Tobias stopped us. 'If we're going to launch a PR campaign, it better do more than show people happily using our system. We've got to attack Birnbaum directly. Where's his vulnerability?'

'Let's see,' Alec said sarcastically. 'Frequent use of professional dominatrices, an unnatural attraction to his own daughter...'

'Seriously. Something we can use.'

'We could use that,' Alec suggested with a shrug.

'How about his bizarre language?' I said. 'Evermore frenzied paroxysms...'

'Of optimistic transactions,' Alec finished for me. 'Yeah. That was weird.'

'What if we attacked him from a populist perspective?' I said, amazed by my own cunning in this regard.

'I get it,' Alec joined in. 'Something like 'They've made their money, now they want to keep you from making yours. Protect your right to trade."

'Exactly,' I said. 'It's consumer protection.'

'But Birnbaum's the one arguing for consumer protection,' Morehouse objected.

'That's why it's his vulnerability,' Alec said. 'We take his words right from him, but reposition him as the enemy of the people.'

'It's perfect,' I agreed. 'He's the one saying that non-professionals are too stupid to make decisions for themselves. We, on the other hand, we're defending the little guys from regulations meant to keep them out of the game.'

'I like it,' Morehouse said. 'It'll kill him. When can you have something on the air?'

'I've got studio time booked tomorrow afternoon,' Alec said. 'And a set of focus groups in the morning that we can use for 'people-off-the-street' footage[162].'

'Great. You two work on the strategy tonight and get the agency in on the execution tomorrow.'

'I really think this is more Alec's forte than mine,' I said, as much to avoid stepping on my friend's professional turf as to protect my first night off in what seemed like weeks. 'I'm sure he doesn't need me looking over his shoulder.'

'It's your idea, I think you should be there,' Morehouse said. 'Don't you, Alec?'

'I—' The speaker phone beeped before Alec could finish.

'What?!' Tobias shouted into the contraption. 'I said—'

'It's the Russian. He's found one,' squawked Brad's voice. 'You told me to—'

'Put him on,' Tobias said. 'Sorry. It's about my Ilyushin," he told us. Then, back to the phone, "Hello, Uri? How's the weather in Leningrad? What's that? St. Petersburg, now? Yeah, whatever.'

'His *what*?' I whispered. Maybe Alec and I could bond somehow in this brief moment alone.

'His Ilyushin,' Alec said. 'He's getting one of those fighter planes like the Valley guys have.'

'Oh Jesus, not really?'

'Yup. He says he knows how to fly one.'

'He's gonna get himself killed.'

'And whoever happens to be sitting in the other seat,' Alec said, rolling

162. This was a popular means of gathering opinions of 'real people' for news programs and advertisements. It was used especially for selling services or products because the concept of seeing a satisfied customer was a powerful persuasive message in an era of widespread "personal injury claims." Ironically, much of this footage was actually made using actors.
—BMXEDD

his eyes.

'Which is most likely you.'

'Or you,' Alec shot back, with a bit too much spin on the ball.

I took this as an opportunity to break the veneer. Tobias was too wrapped up in negotiating transport costs with the Russian government to take notice.

'Look, Alec, you want me to hang back?'

'What do you mean?' he asked nonchalantly.

'You know, give you some room. I feel like I'm cramping your style.'

'If you feel that way.'

'Besides,' I offered, rolling my chair closer to his, 'I've got to work out the new web site architecture this afternoon.'

'Whatever.'

Tobias hung up the phone and grinned broadly.

'Just wait till they see what *I've* got,' he said to the air before returning his attention to us. 'So, who's on this tonight?'

'I'll handle the campaign, dad,' Alec said. 'Jamie's got to do some coding tonight.' I hated the way he said 'coding.' As if it were a menial skill, for working class techies. He was just jealous that I'd become his father's new favorite son.

'Okay,' Tobias agreed. 'As long as he's involved in the process tomorrow.'

Tobias didn't want to make a move without my approval. I was his right-hand man. I realized I was running the whole show, now. Weird, seeing as how I didn't really believe any of it. But I liked feeling responsible for so many people's fates. Depended on. It was just a matter of holding it all together.

My magnanimous surrender of the PR to Alec only magnified my power to do so. Besides, I'd already come up with the strategy. Now it was just a matter of implementation. Besides, I was too busy. I had an appointment at Synapticom that afternoon, and Birnbaum's performance on TV hadn't demonstrated M&L's famed muzzle over the Fed very well at all. I'd have some cleaning up to do. But it'd be no problem. I was in my stride.

I stopped by my office to check the phone log. Carla Santangelo had left a message—something about my meeting her at the focus group tomorrow. How did she know about it, already? No matter. I wasn't going to let her muscle in on the territory I had stolen from her a week before. Then again, I'd been thinking it might be good to see her again. Perhaps things would be different now that I wasn't her slave boy. Or maybe she was only on my mind because she was the last woman I'd slept with. Supply-side sexual economics. I didn't return the call.

I opted for the hovercraft across the Hudson to the Synapticom pier[163] in Fort Lee. It was a fun ride, and I wished Benjamin were with me on the deck getting his face pelted with spray as the deafening noise of mechanical wind rumbled underneath the vessel. Sunlight glinted across the building's glass facade as it approached, reminding me how long I'd always wanted to take a look inside that shiny oval.

I was still in college when they broadcast the first tour of the building on CNN. Feng Shui[164] was in vogue, and a dozen masters of the art attended the opening ceremony, burning sage and praying to the various forces of nature. A year later, the wraparound hologram on the building's roof was lit for the first time, making Synapticom the only man-made structure in New York City visible from the space shuttle (other than the Staten Island land-fill, which wasn't really a structure at all).

A giant photograph, shot from space and hanging behind the reception desk in the circular lobby, was meant to remind visitors of this fact. Next to a black blob representing Manhattan was a tiny green dot. For anyone who couldn't find it with the naked eye, every ten seconds a laser from the ceiling shot green arrow at the dot with the words 'you are here.'

163. The Synapticom building was located at a pier in Fort Lee, New Jersey. Office rents had skyrocketed in New York. Development of new properties had been successfully thwarted for years by a powerful group of real estate cartels. But once the hi-tech and bio-tech billionaires realized they could bribe government officials for half of what they were already doling out to their landlords, red-lined areas like Harlem, Washington Heights, and the Lower East Side were razed for office space. Before that happened, though, even the wealthiest new companies were forced to find creative solutions to the real estate shortage.

Synapticom's answer was a free-floating barge, designed and constructed in Singapore, then towed all the way to Fort Lee. Visitors were flown to the facility in bright green helicopters that took off every fifteen minutes from Manhattan's East Side, or carried on a hovercraft from the 79th Street boat basin. Employees simply drove across the George Washington Bridge and parked in a lot at the pier. —Sabina Samuels

164. A set of supposedly ancient Chinese architectural principles based on astrology and geography, which were later revealed to be the invention of an interior designer from San Diego. —Sabina Samuels

'Mr. Cohen,' a gorgeous, slender black model wearing a tight green turtleneck greeted me from behind the stone counter. 'Welcome to Synapticom. I'm Monique. Is this your first visit?'

'Um, yes, ma'am. It is.' If she knew my name, then why didn't she know it was my first visit? Or was the question meant to put me at ease, to relieve me of the fear that my privacy was being invaded? I made a mental note to ask Greco about this tactic, later.

'Won't you please come with me?' she asked.

Monique rose to a statuesque six-feet-plus and escorted me through the circular lobby to a Zen-white changing room. The walls were lined with pale wood cubbyholes, each containing either a pair of shoes or small burlap sack. She removed one of the sacks and opened it.

'You can put these on,' she said, handing me a pair of muslin slippers. 'Then place your shoes in the cube.'

'Does anybody ever refuse to change their shoes?' I asked as I slipped off my loafers.

'That's a good one.' She smiled, her beautiful white teeth distracting me from her evasion. She slid open a frosted glass panel in the wall revealing a neat row of dark green smocks on hangars. 'Would you like a robe?'

'No thanks,' I winked. 'I'm just getting a trim.'

She either didn't understand the joke or had heard it too many times before. Monique handed me the robe and I put it on as I was instructed.

'Hello, Jamie, glad you could come.' The sight of El Greco standing in the doorway relieved me, greatly. This, in turn, alerted me to how anxious I had been all along which, in turn, made me feel anxious all over again. At least this time I knew it.

'Good to see you, man,' I said. 'Are you my tour guide today?'

'That's a good one, Jamie. Come on.' He spoke in a friendly, but overly precise way. That Synapticom way. Must be because he's at work.

Greco took me back through the main lobby towards the elevators.

'We're assuming a good faith non-disclosure on everything you're about to see,' Greco said as the doors opened. 'That okay with you?'

'Sure, you've got my word.'

'On video, as a matter a fact.' Greco smiled. 'All activity in the building is digitized, compressed, and stored.'

'It must take up a tremendous amount of resources.'

'Not as much as it saves in legal fees,' Greco said, pushing a button. 'Since we're on a barge there's no basement, obviously. The first floor is just reception, the auditorium, changing rooms, and the cafeteria.'

Two other greenshirts were standing in the elevator with us. They didn't speak, or even acknowledge Greco's presence.

We proceeded along one of the building's many circular corridors to a set of glass doors. Greco stood still for a moment. 'The face recognition software still takes a second.' Then the doors opened and the sounds of animals echoed from within.

'Sounds like a pet store in here,' I said.

'We call this the Skinner Suite,' Greco said as we made our way through a maze of plexiglass cubicles. 'It's not really needed, anymore, so we're phasing it out.'

We stopped at a wall of clear plastic boxes, each containing a single white chicken. The birds were pecking at buttons beneath red and green light bulbs.

'What are you doing to them?'

'It's more of a demonstration than an ongoing experiment,' Greco explained. 'We have three scenarios at play. See the chickens in the row on the left? They can peck at the button whether it's green or red, and food will be dispensed, no matter what.'

'They look pretty fat and lazy.'

'Exactly. They eat the most, but have poor reflexes and shortened life-span.' He pointed to the row in the center. 'This sample in the middle, they have to peck at the button for food, too, but they may or may not get a pellet. The light may be green, or it may be red. It makes no difference. They have no way of knowing if their efforts will yield a pellet. Sometimes, we even dispense a pellet when they've done nothing.'

The poor birds looked frazzled. Some cocked their heads frantically, while others just lay in their cages, twitching.

'Ironically, they're fed more total pellets than these specimens on the right,' Greco continued. 'The ones we call the Synapticom sample.'

'And what do you do to them?'

'Simple. If the light turns green, the bird has two seconds to peck the button and it gets a pellet. If it pecks when the light is red, it gets an electric shock.'

The chickens looked robust. Attentive. They had to be.

'So it just sits there all day, waiting for the light to turn green?'

'Right,' Greco said. 'This scenario leads to the greatest alertness, and the longest life-span.'

'And an acceptance of absolute powerlessness,' I added.

'It does have power. For a moment. What does a chicken want with power, anyway?'

We proceeded through a series of similar experiments using rats that chased food through mechanical mazes, dogs that leaped about their cages to avoid electric shocks, and chameleons that responded to ever-changing background colors. Finally we came upon a wall of monkeys with tiny plungers in their hands and electrodes in their skulls.

'What are the chimps doing,' I asked. 'Playing the Synapticom version of Jeopardy?[165]'

'Not exactly,' Greco answered. 'Depressing the plunger activates their brain in such a way as to induce orgasm.'

'You're shitting me.'

'Not at all. The first group, in the cages on the left, are able to produce an orgasm whenever they press the button.'

'But the cages are empty,' I said. 'Where did they go?'

'Well, predictably, the entire sample died. They gave themselves continuous orgasms at the expense of food.'

'That's scary.'

'In a way,' Greco said. 'The second group, in the middle cages, they are entitled to six orgasms in each 24-hour cycle. The light stays green as long as they have any orgasms left, then it turns red. Invariably, they use up all their orgasms in the first five minutes, then mope around the rest of the day. Notice the low body weight and non-responsive demeanor.'

The monkeys in this row looked a bit lethargic and suspicious.

'Now these subjects in the last row,' Greco pointed to the rightmost column of stacked monkeys. 'They have a red, yellow and green light bulb in their cages. Red means the orgasm button won't work. Yellow is a warning cue, meaning that the plunger will be activated in five minutes. And green means the plunger is functional. We cycle through to green six times in each 24-hour period.'

'And these monkeys are the happiest?'

'Well, their bodyweight is the best, and their reflexes test well ahead of the others.'

'Hmph.'

'But what's more interesting, really, is the way they've begun to respond

165. A television game show developed by a former talk show host and casino owner named Mervyn Griffen, in which contestants won prizes by reverse-cognating the questions to a series of answers. Its long-term psychological effect on players and audience was to stress inevitability. We still do not understand the origin of the program's title, or who is actually thought to be in jeopardy as the game is played.   —Sabina Samuels

to the colored lights. During the red phase, they eat, sleep, even mate. When the light turns yellow, they stop whatever they are doing and grab the plunger. Even if they are in the midst of coitus, they stop to ready themselves.'

'That's pretty weird.'

'But that's not all,' Greco went on enthusiastically. 'During the five minutes of yellow light, the monkeys reach full excitement.'

'They get boners?'

'Exactly. Big ones. And after the five minutes of yellow light, as soon as the bulb switches to green, the monkeys spontaneously achieve orgasm, whether or not the plunger is activated! Sometimes they even have the orgasm before they depress the plunger. A purely conditioned response.'

'Does it work on girl monkeys? That could be useful.' My joke was ignored.

'In each case—from chickens to monkeys—the animals who did the worst were offered the greatest control over their choices. They all reached a state analogous to the psychosis of a sticky web-site addict.'[166]

I had a friend from college who was still in therapy for that.

'And those who invariably fare best are the ones whose interface offers them predictable results at the expense of autonomy,' he explained.

'So what are you trying to prove?' I asked. 'That people like being told what to do by machines?'

'It's really our company's effort at due diligence. We're looking at the long-term effects of our interface philosophies. Because once our systems are put into place, they become essentially self-sustaining. It's a form of techno-ecology, conceived by our first CEO.'

'The snowboard kid?'

'Right. He foresaw that much of what we develop here today will become

166. Aggressive military psyops tactics were applied to attention retention protocols on e-commerce websites. Many users, particularly in the highly targeted 16-24 demographic, were inadvertently terrorized on a subconscious level, leading to a series of symptoms—paranoia, aural hallucinations, convulsions—normally associated with end-stage amphetamine psychosis. —Sabina Samuels

embedded in the civilization of tomorrow. The program will modify itself without further intervention. We are actively participating in the evolution of our species.'

'Wow. That's a highly developed social conscience,' I said, raising my eyebrows a bit too high.

Greco spoke plainly for the first time. 'Are you being sarcastic, Jamie? If you don't believe in what we're doing, maybe you aren't the right—'

'Chill, Greco, okay? This is just an e-commerce interface we're talking about here. Not a new society.'

One of the monkeys' lights changed from red to yellow. It ran to its plunger, then squatted expectantly.

'But since we are developing reactive, self-mutating interfaces, it is the programming itself that will be driving evolution from here on. The Synapticom Algorithm is interpolating the feedback from users in order to drive that behavior.'

'Drive it how?'

'Towards whatever ends we program into it, now. Think of it like a series of intelligent agents.'

'What? Shopping assistants?'[167]

'Yes, but a Synapticom Algorithm shopping assistant would use the information it gets about you when you interact with it in order to influence your future behaviors. Each time you accept or reject a deal it proposes, the agent adjusts its style of offering. Eventually, it learns how to get you to buy.'

'You mean it learns what kinds of products I like.'

'It's less significant to the agent that it find what you wanted it to, so long as it can convince you it did a good job and get you to accept its suggestion for action. This way, it can create or alter demands as easily as it meets them.'

'But there's a difference between getting what you want and thinking

167. The first application of intelligent agent technology was for product selection in online shopping auctions. Customers would launch agents through the online shopping malls to find the kinds of products they wanted, at the best deals. —Sabina Samuels

209

you're getting what you want.'

'And just what would that be?'

I had no answer that didn't involve theology in one way or another.

'But what does all this do to the end user?' I asked. 'Turn him into a reactive machine?'

'Not at all,' Greco said, tapping on one of the windows in the wall. 'It turns him into one very happy monkey.'

The monkey sat staring at the yellow light bulb, panting. A huge erection was emerging from his furry loins.

We left the animal labs and proceeded towards a human work area. Nominally human, at least. Greenshirts sat in rounded cubicles positioned along a curved glass wall overlooking the Hudson River. They seemed happy, if a bit too perfectly so. Nothing was out of place. Not a single pencil or paperclip. There weren't even any pencils or paperclips there. Just keyboards, headsets, and flat-panel monitors.

'That's some view they've got,' I said.

'You like it?'

'Sure. You can see the whole city.'

'You think it's real?' Greco asked, crossing his arms.

'Well, sure, isn't it?'

'It may be,' he said. 'We installed hi-def liquid crystal displays into the windows. When the displays are turned off, the glass is transparent. When they're on, they render a fictional view, generated completely artificially using analog algorithms. It's a screen-blitting routine that I developed myself.'

'That's amazing!' I put a hand on the glass. 'Remember that screen-blit you wrote back in school? For the game emulator?'

'Of course. This is based on the same code.'

'Does it still flake out into those little squares when the rendering freezes?'

'Yeah!' Greco said, the memory drawing him out of his Synapticom-speak for a moment. 'It still has that little twitch to it. I like to think of it as a feature.'

I felt a hand on my shoulder.

'Admiring the view?' It was Parrot, the lead greenshirt from the night at the ranch.

'Yes,' I said. My muslin slippers suddenly made me feel vulnerable. 'I'm just trying to figure out if it's real or one of Greco's simulations.'

'You should join the pool, then, Mr. Cohen,' he said.

'What pool?'

'Why don't you explain it to him?' Parrot said as he left us and continued on his way around the arced workspace.

'At the end of each day,' Greco explained, his courteous but impervious persona restored by his superior's brief appearance, 'everyone in the office registers whether he believes the view was real or animated. The winners get to stay late and play networked games.'

Get to stay late? I didn't pursue it. 'And how many people work here, exactly?'

'Honestly, almost everyone has been phased out,' Greco said. 'The staff is down to under twenty regular employees now. They're all on this floor. The rest are temps.'

I noticed how scarce human life was in this environment. And the humans who were there seemed pretty mechanical, at that.

'Don't people complain? I mean, don't they want better job security?'

'They leave with their options,' Greco explained. 'And they fully understand that once the algorithm has successfully integrated their function, their presence is redundant.'

'So eventually there'll be no employees,' I said. 'Just a program. And a corporation.'

'That's the idea, yes.'

'Doesn't that scare you?' I asked, trying to see through my friend's eyes to the Greco I knew as a child.

'Where is it written that people have to work for a living?' he asked plainly. 'Come on. Mr. Thorens should be ready to meet you in a few minutes.'

He took me to a round, windowless conference room at the center of the office floor. We sat at a large, circular table.

I was excited to meet Thorens. Maybe a Buddhist environmentalist like him would restore some humanity to this place. Knowing he was ultimately in charge put me at ease.

'I had no idea he was in New York. Does he come often?'

'Oh no. He's only scheduled to be here once a year. Otherwise he stays in Sweden. He insisted on telecommuting in his contract. He did it on environmental grounds. To save jet fuel. And to prove that it could be done.'

A gentle gong sounded from speakers in the ceiling. Greco pushed down on the tabletop, causing a flat-panel display with a green Synapticom logo to raise up from the surface.

The logo dissolved and was replaced by the slightly grainy satellite image of Thor Thorens, sitting at a large wooden table on a rustic outdoor deck, a beautiful lake in the background. Papers were strewn about, held in place against the wind by rocks, books, and earthen coffee mugs.

'Hello Mr. Vahanian!' Thor said. 'Is that Mr. Cohen with you?'

'Yes, sir, it is,' Greco said. His eyes were wide with admiration and readiness.

'Good to meet you, Mr. Cohen.'

'Jamie,' I said. 'And it's great to meet you, too, Mr. Thorens.'

'Thor,' he responded, warmly. 'I'd say I'm sorry I can't be there myself to meet you, but I'm not.' He gestured to the lake behind him. I nodded and smiled. 'And I'm sure Mr. Vahanian is showing you anything you need to see.'

'Oh certainly he is, yes.'

El Greco just sat there, smiling.

'Well, I just wanted to make the human connection with you, Jamie. And let you know I'm always available if you have a problem. The buck stops here, as you Americans like to say. Is there anything else you need from me?'

'Um, well, I just wanted to reassure you about the Fed. I know today's testimony—'

'Excuse me, Jamie, but I asked if there's anything you need from me. I'm not asking for anything from you. I'm fine.'

'I thought maybe you'd seen the TV reports, and I just wanted you to know that we're on the case.'

'I've got every faith in you and your people, Jamie. Really. And if this arrangement is just not meant to be, we'll find out soon enough. I'm not worried.'

'Well, that's good to hear. I suppose I just wanted...'

'To make sure I'm okay and reassured. I got it. Anything else?'

'I guess not. It certainly is a pleasure to meet you. I've been a fan of your work for years. And I'm especially glad to know a man like you—'

'Whoah!' Thor shouted as the wind knocked over one of his makeshift paperweights, sending a stack of pages into the air. 'That's the quarterly earnings estimates!'

Greco and I waited for Thor to recover.

'Where were we?' he asked. 'Oh, yes. My work, your pleasure. I do appreciate your kind words. They're not at all necessary. We're partners, now. And like any new relationship, let's just try to have some fun, and see where it goes, eh? Can't ask for anything more than that.'

'No, I guess not,' I said.

'Well, good, then.' Thor smiled, as another gust of wind disturbed the objects on his desk. He struggled to rearrange his makeshift paperweights. 'I better get some more rocks. See you when I'm in New York!'

He pushed a button on his table and disappeared.

'Wow,' I said. 'That's him?'

'The one and only.'

'Even better than I expected,' I said. 'He's so personable. Wholesome. Not a typical Internet businessman at all. He's got values. Even a sense of humor about all this.'

'I'm glad you liked him,' Greco said. 'He's very special. It's great to meet one of your idols and not be disappointed for once.'

I nodded to my old friend, empathizing with his great devotion. It was touching, in its way, and I felt downright cynical for my earlier suspicions. What's so wrong with someone loving his job, company, and boss? I knew I'd never feel quite the same way about Morehouse, however much he came to respect me.

Greco pushed down on a different section of the circular tabletop, and a control panel slowly rose up and into place.

'Let me show you the algorithm.' Greco depressed a few keys and the room darkened. Then images appeared on the walls all around us.

'We tested it first in games,' Greco explained over film footage of teenagers playing shoot-em-ups. 'We learned how to integrate reward and punishment into the interface, generate interest, create compelling goals, and so forth.'

The images changed to those of slightly older young men, playing military games. 'Our contracts with the Defense Department enabled us to apply these same principles to time-sensitive and highly reflex-intensive applications like missile guidance, aircraft navigation, and combat scenario analysis.' All around the room, video of bombs following computer graphic trajectories and hitting their targets. PowerPoint on psychedelics.

'Ultimately, we began to work on automating and accelerating the human responses to match the calculations of the computers. The trick was getting the human neural activity to anticipate the computer's requests.'

'You mean get the people to respond to the will of the machine?'

'The machine doesn't have a will, Jamie. It's simply obeying its programming.'

'But then the user obeys the machine?'

'Well, of course, assuming the machine has been properly programmed.'

'But then why have a human being in the equation at all?'

'Good question,' Greco said. 'For now, in military applications, it makes people more comfortable to know there's a human being in the sequence. That there's a safeguard of some kind. But once they're fully immersed in the algorithm, they may as well be part of the machine. They experience the emotional throughline of the activity—that's what we learned to simulate in the gaming experiments—but they really have no impact at all on the outcome. Except to add some time lag, and the occasional inaccuracy. But we're working on that.'

'So what's the application in shopping or, as in our case, trading?'

'I'm glad you asked, Jamie,' said Greco, sounding like the bad actor in an industrial hit documentary. He hit a few more keystrokes. 'It's a four-part process: Increase, Entrain, Reinforce, and Evolve.' The words appeared on the screen as he spoke them.

'The first objective is to increase the surface area of available human attention. This can take the form of environmental alterations—finding new opportunities for transmission such as marquees, embedded screens, multiple images...'

The pictures on the walls changed to images of advertising on cell phone displays, stock market reports superimposed on car windshields, and monitors over urinals.

'Or we can work to increase human reception capacity.' An image of the human brain appeared on one side of the room. The tightly wound strand of gray matter slowly unraveled like a ball of yarn around the wall. Iconic images of cars, numbers, and symbols laid themselves on the snaking membrane. 'This can be done with chemicals, cortical stimulation, high frequency stroboscopics, or aural manipulation.'

'You're changing people's brains?'

'Everything changes people's brains, Jamie,' Greco said condescendingly. 'A pizza, a carwash, a ferris wheel. They all change your brain. We just do it consciously. With purpose.'

'Okay,' I swallowed my misgivings. 'Then what?'

'After increase comes entrainment.' The images changed to those of people using computers to navigate the World Wide Web. 'This is the easy part. Simply test and implement the colors, frequencies, and architectures that generate the highest response rate. This could be measured in click-through, purchases, or whatever the desired goal. It's no different from direct mail testing.'

'Maximize user response,' I said, trying to make 'entrainment' sound more like a simple sales technique. 'Okay, then what?'

'We reward and, hopefully, accelerate the desired responses with secondary reinforcement.' The sounds of happy bells accompanied Greco's description, and the images on the wall showed people smiling; an Asian couple finding extra credits in their online bank account; an old man opening an attachment on an email message and finding a picture of a naked woman. 'We've found sex and violence to be the most compelling secondary reinforcements, but we're trying to steer these people towards more consumer loyal inducements such as rebates, air miles, and point systems. Keep it all directed back towards more spending, or more interaction with the program.'

Out of the corner of my eye, I thought I saw an image of a giant robot with a McDonalds logo for a head. The Prime Network Enforcement Vehicle from my dream! I spun around in my chair, but it was only a little girl opening a bag of McDonalds fries, and pulling out a plastic coin stamped '5 Points!'

'After that, the program is on its own,' he said. 'It simply evolves based on user interaction.'

Greco got up and the lights in the room rose with him.

'Evolves towards what?' I asked.

'What do you mean? You think of evolution as goal oriented?'

'Well, yeah.'

'And what's the goal?'

'I don't know. I like to think we're striving towards better means of survival, or consciousness. Or maybe some ethical truth.'

'You might want to check your science on that,' Greco said, leading me out of the room. 'I think they've figured out that consciousness is a by-product of evolution. Not its goal.'

'But you said the Synapticom algorithm evolves. In what direction? What does it want? Higher number of purchases? What metric does it use?'

'Oh. We don't use metrics like that anymore. The only metric the algorithm is still programmed to measure is user interest. It's more of an entertainment paradigm. We measure the level of engagement with the program itself. It modifies its behavior for each user according to the consistency and duration of their interaction.'

'Like a puppy dog,' I said.

'In the case of consumers, maybe,' Greco said, looking out over the work floor. 'But not in all situations. Here, for example, we think of it more like a coach.'

'Here?' I asked. 'You mean you're using it here? On yourselves? At Synapticom?'

'Sure we are,' said Greco. 'It's the easiest way to test the program's effectiveness. And since it creates a competitive advantage in terms of employee loyalty and worker efficiency, we'd be foolish *not* to use it.'

I watched the greenshirts at their work stations. They were absolutely fixed on their screens, and had smiles on their faces. They typed furiously, but effortlessly. There were no family pictures on their desks, no trinkets, plants, or stuffed animals. Nothing to distract them from building and selling their programs.

'You use it on yourselves, to make yourselves work harder?' I asked. 'Isn't that a little weird?'

'Only if you subscribe to old, Marxist oppositions between labor and management. Here, labor *is* management. We all want the same thing.'

'That's a great theory, Greco...'

'It's not theory, Jamie,' he said, putting a hand on my shoulder as if to heal me. 'Let's see if your disk is ready.'

He led me around the bend towards a cluster of three young programmers—two men and one woman, dressed in identical green shirts and ties.

'Hello, Mr. Vahanian!' the trio said in unison.

'Hello!' he responded in sing-song. 'How's it coming?'

'Almost done,' said one.

'—compiling the algorithm,' chimed in another.

'—with the customized protocol,' the girl finished.

'Terrific!' Greco cheered. They acted as if they were all components of the same, well-oiled machine. I was repulsed and intrigued.

'What's it like working here?' I asked the young woman. I figured she was the most likely to evince some emotional honesty.[168]

'You need to ask?' she said, smiling.

'Couldn't be happier,' said one of the boys.

'Here's the disk!' said the third, ejecting a freshly burned CD from his console and slipping into a black plastic sleeve. 'We had a great time testing it.'

I noticed the boy's head phasing out of focus for a moment. It became almost transparent, then faded back in as a smiling, black bull. Was this a side-effect of the program?

No. I wasn't going to let myself see this. Not here. I stared into the bull's eyes, and pinched my own thigh through a pants pocket, as if to wake myself from a dream. The animal head went fuzzy as the boy's human cranium slowly faded back up—a faint image at first, until it regained its normal opacity. The boy was handing the disk to Greco, who handed it in turn to me.

'Here you go,' Greco said. 'It's self-installing, and should automatically adapt to the coding on your site. Just give it a couple of minutes.'

'What do I tell our engineers? They're going to want to know how it works. I mean, how do we prepare the site? Where do we put in the hooks?'

'It self-installs,' the girl said.

'And adapts to your configuration,' continued one of the boys.

'Using a polymorphic virus,' said the last.

168. People still believed that females had a greater capacity for empathy and greater propensity for honesty than males. —Sabina Samuels

219

'Just pop it in like a videogame cartridge,' Greco capped it off. Then they laughed together.

'Well, thanks.'

'Thank *you*,' they sang in unison, returning their attention to the work stations.

'Come on,' Greco said. 'We better let them get back to work.'

But they were already so far engrossed in their next tasks that nothing we said or did could have distracted them.

We descended in the elevator back towards the lobby.

'So you're happy here?' I asked. I knew we were being recorded, but I thought I'd be able to gauge Greco's response by his tone of voice.

'It'll be hard to leave, yeah.'

'They're phasing you out?'

'There is no 'they," Greco chuckled. 'I've done my part. The graphics protocols have been fully interpolated.'

'That's why they moved you to marketing?' I asked as the doors opened.

'Everyone gets moved to marketing before they're released back into the general population,' Greco said. 'It's the healthiest way to make the transition, and teaches us new strategies for ongoing advocacy.'

'You mean, you basically sell this program for the rest of your lives?'

'It's more like promoting a culture. Like we did with the Macintosh as kids, remember? It feels more like a means of bettering society.'

'And increasing the value of your options, I imagine.' I stepped out of the elevator into the lobby and tried to remember where that room with the shoes went.

'Share-value is a secondary incentive, sure,' Greco said, pointing me to the left. 'But I don't think you have to cast it in such a cynical light.'

He was right. Why was I being such a curmudgeon? Greco was just playing the game, too, and from a better position than me. He couldn't lose. How dare I wish that this svelte, confident man be replaced by the fat little Greco I pitied as a kid? Did I really need to condemn him as an android just because he had found a strategy that worked for him? Greco wasn't really an automaton at all. He had simply grown up.

We entered the changing room. I sat on a bench and removed my slippers.

'You know I got Entertainink to buy Jude's TeslaNet program,' I said.

'I heard. That's great.' He looked at me a moment. 'I'm in on it, you know.' He raised his eyebrows.

'You mean they're cutting you in? For doing some of the code? That's great!'

'Yeah. We're all really happy about it.'

'For now, anyway.' Strangely, I felt like I could confide in El Greco. It had less to do with our history together than El Greco's Synapticom-inspired clarity and peace of mind. I wanted a mentor.

'What do you mean, 'for now?"' Greco asked, sitting down next to me.

'Nothing.' I couldn't tell him. 'I just think Jude's going to resent the loss of control.'

'Control is an illusion, anyway,' Greco said plainly. 'I'm sure Jude will see it that way. If he doesn't already.'

Maybe he would, I thought as I climbed into the bright green Synapticom helicopter and took off across the Hudson. How weird to depart like this— like I'd been a guest on Fantasy Island[169]. The other six passengers all seemed content, too, as if they had just visited a health spa. One of them, a guy in a black suit in the back, had a full bull head but I decided to ignore him and face forward. *Just don't think about it, and it will go away. If I still see bulls in a week, I'll find a shrink.*

Besides, there was another, more pressing sensation in my chest. It felt

169. A 1970's television show that, along with many other canceled series, enjoyed a cult comeback when streaming media came to the Internet. Fantasy Island was a one-hour network drama in which a white-suited Spanish therapist and his dwarf side-kick combined obsolete applications of Freudian dream interpretation with deluxe vacation packages in order to heal their clients from the lasting effects of childhood traumas. —Sabina Samuels

like the Reactive Architecture Algorithm disk was burning a hole in my breast pocket. I touched it, but it wasn't hot. Just another trick my mind was playing on me, that's all. Still, I didn't know if I wanted to rush home and load it onto my laptop, or simply throw it out the window before it turned the entire world into stock market bulls. Well, if I didn't implement it, someone else would. Besides, people everywhere were turning into bulls, anyway. Like the guy in back. And he seemed happy enough about it.

9. Focus Groups

'Hello?'

'The people, united, will never be defeated!'

Alec sounded oh so chipper on the phone that next morning. Chipper enough to wake me with a call at 6:15, just to make sure I'd be at the ad agency's studio on time.

'You're in a good mood,' I said sleepily, as I pushed a button on the remote control by my bedside, changing the tint on my plasma windows from black to clear. The sky was still only medium blue.

'You betcha,' said Alec. 'Everything's going according to plan.'

'I guess that means you're ready?'

'More than ready. See you at ten. You've got the address?'

'Yeah, yeah.' I could always look it up, later. 'I'll be there.'

'Jawol!'

I put the phone back under my pillow and debated whether to drag myself out of bed or reset the windows to night mode and get another hour of sleep. My morning hard-on was already in full bloom—a sign that things were right in the world—so I figured I might as well greet the day.

I padded across the white bedroom carpet to the bathroom, set the shower to 'very warm' and got in.

I looked down at my full-masted member, its slit of an eye squinting right back up at me, demanding service. Carla was the first sexy image that came to mind, but I didn't want to give her the satisfaction. The girls at the ranch, maybe? Nah. They probably had diseases, anyway. Still, that Jenna was awfully hot.

I imagined myself video-conferencing with her. It was a bizarre image, but I went with it. She was in a studio apartment, and I was in my office with the blinds open but my desk obscuring anything below the waist. My sexual fantasies never had computers or networks in them, before. Strange. I imagined myself pointing the camera down to my crotch, and watching her as she stared into her monitor. I saw her getting turned on by my image, by my body. It was the first time I had ever masturbated to a fantasy about someone else masturbating to me. I was an object of desire.

I got myself dressed as my spirit swirled down the drain and a CNBC anchor analyzed the S&P futures from Chicago. Yesterday's three percent downswing looked like it was going to be matched in the first hour of trading. Normally, people saw dips as buying opportunities. As long as traders could be convinced to borrow more money, they would use their new capital to erase losses within minutes of the opening bell and make a bundle in the process.

That's why Birnbaum's testimony was so devastating. By suggesting a need for government oversight on electronic trading, he was questioning people's ability to invest for themselves. And without a retail trading market, there was no one to fill in the bottom levels of the securities pyramid. One of the television analysts even suggested that Birnbaum might call for a curb on margin borrowing. The death blow.

I put on my tie while I watched a clip of reactions from the street. 'Why would the government get involved unless there was something very wrong?' a woman standing in front of a department store asked. 'I hope this doesn't start a selling panic,' a businessman added, 'I can't afford a margin call.' A man in a hardhat seemed to take delight in the controversy, saying 'it's about time someone finally pulled the plug.' This was a public relations disaster.

Who'd have thought that my college pal and I would one day serve as the market's last, best hope for salvation? With Birnbaum using his position to cast doubt on the online trading system, the Synapticom algorithm was a necessary countermeasure. Even I could see that. An unencumbered market was the most efficient path towards the creation of wealth. There were already more than enough resources for everyone in the world to be happy. Market forces worked together as a self-adjusting dynamical system—the perfect means to distributing capital based on innovation and need. It was the way civilization evolved.[170]

That's why interventionist naysayers like Keynes weren't even taught in economics classes, anymore. His theories had been disproved by Nobel prize winners. All you have to do is treat the economy like nature, and everything healthy will continue to grow. It's the organic farming principle. The more pesticides you use, the weaker your plants get.

I arrived at the DD&D agency (or, more exactly, since the latest merger, WP / DD&D / Whyte-Werner-Whitfield / DSDL Group Limited,

170. It appears clear that the narrator was familiar with and influenced by the works of 20th century novelist Ayn Rand. See her novel, *Fountainhead*, for a fuller, if non-sensical deliberation on this philosophy. In fairness, we must remember that these outrageously inane ideas were generally accepted principles of the silicon culture. And due to the society's fascist nature, dissenting views were frowned upon, or even forcibly discouraged.
—Sabina Samuels

International) and was met in the lobby by an energetic junior account planner who brought me up to the focus group suites. She opened a door marked 'OBSERVATION.' Inside the long, thin chamber sat Alec with two market researchers, drinking coffee, munching on pastries, and analyzing information on a bank of computer monitors.

'Glad you could make it, Jamie,' Alec said. 'Have a seat.'

I closed the door behind me and the chamber darkened, revealing three large panes of glass that looked out onto three separate conference rooms.

'Don't worry, they can't see us,' said a middle-aged woman whose headset held her white curly hair in place. 'These are two-way mirrors.' She held out her hand. 'I'm Martha.'

Alec flicked a switch on a console and the sound from the room on the left played through a speaker over the window.

'Not that I'm afraid of trading for myself, mind you,' a young woman was saying. 'But I just don't feel intelligent enough to make intelligent decisions.'

'She's lying,' said Martha. 'Look at her basal skin response.'

She pointed to a wavy line on the monitor.

'Good catch,' said Alec.

'What are you looking at?' I asked.

'She's got electrodes on her fingers,' Alec said. 'Everyone in Room A does. See?'

I put a hand on the glass to shade the glare. Sure enough, each of the volunteers around the table had wires coming from the tips of their fingers, attached by tiny rubber cups.

'Is that really necessary?' I asked.

'Sure is,' Alec said. 'It's the latest thing.'

'We found that focus group members tend to see their interviews as an opportunity to voice consumer discontent. Over seventy-five percent of

Americans have participated in a consumer research study of one kind or another. They're jaded.'

'So you attach them to lie-detectors?'

'Biofeedback monitoring of all kinds, actually,' she answered. 'Galvanic skin response, basal variations, even electroencephalogram brain-wave measurements, in some cases. It helps us determine emotional trigger points, subconscious activity, and neural inconsistencies.' She pushed a button and spoke into her headset. 'Number four is showing signs of prevarication, Tony. Try pursuing along a delta trajectory.'

'What's that?' I asked.

'Watch and learn,' Alec said.

The interviewer in room A, the man in a headset at the head of the table, got up from his chair and approached the young woman they called Number four.

'Do you think that your children...' he looked at his clipboard, 'Bertrand and Serena. Do you think they look up to you?'

'That's good, Tony,' the white-haired woman transmitted through her headset. 'Her wave functions are equalizing.'

The young interviewee hesitated then spoke. 'I like to think they do.'

'And do they watch you when you make your trades at the computer?' he asked.

'They've seen me at the terminal,' she said, trying to picture the scene. 'But I don't think they know quite what I'm doing.'

'But their impression of you,' he pursued her. 'Do you think they see a confident woman?'

'He's got her,' Martha said, switching off volume to Room A and simultaneously opening a channel to Room C.

Through the window on the right, I could make out five men and women sitting in front of a large TV monitor. They were all wearing metal head-bands with rubber antennae.

'Now as you watch this next tape,' an Asian woman standing before them was saying, 'I'd like you to listen to the speaker's words carefully.' She pressed a button on the remote in her hand, and the image of Ezra Birnbaum appeared on the monitor.

'Are you recording this, Dan?' Martha asked a technician at the far end of the observation booth.

'I'm getting it all,' he said.

As Birnbaum spoke on the TV, a screen in the booth displayed five wavy green lines. They remained steady as Ezra explained how the stock market had become a 'de facto Social Security system.' The white-haired woman made some notes. Then Birnbaum got to 'a new generation of online trad-ing programs promises only to exacerbate this trend, lulling the public into an evermore frenzied paroxysm of optimistic transactions.' Four of the lines on the screen went from smooth to spiky, and one stayed the same.

'What's that mean?' I asked. 'What are they thinking?'

'We'll give you the analysis, later,' explained Martha. 'Dan, do you have number three's baseline encephelograph handy?'

The technician handed her a piece of graph paper.

'No wonder,' she said. 'He's a fucking epileptic. How the hell did he get through screening? Remove his data from the mean response.'

Alec leaned back and smiled at me. The boy was in his element, now. In absolute control of the human psyche, safely protected by three two-way mirrors. I smiled back. Everyone should have a role to play. At least Alec had found his.

'Mind if I take a look at Room B?' he asked.

Martha flicked a switch, opening the monitor to the third torture chamber.

Three subjects sat in chairs with their eyes closed, as an elderly man paced in a slow circle around them.

'Good, Natalie,' the old man was saying. 'Now tell me what you see there.'

'No electrodes?' I joked. 'What's going on?'

'They're all under hypnosis,' Alec answered. 'It's an experimental technique.'

'I'm in a dark tunnel,' said one woman. 'There are numbers on the walls.'

'Can you make out the numbers? Read them to me.' The old man led her gently through the subconscious vision.

'There's a three, an eight, and a six,' she said. 'And then they get blurry.'

'Can you tell me why they are blurry?'

'I don't know,' she said, her voice breaking. 'I'm afraid. It's dark.'

'Everything is okay,' the old man reassured her. 'Go back to your safe place and wait for me there.'

This was a bit much. I felt like a voyeur.

'I gotta go 'Free Willy.[171]" Even Martha laughed at my euphemism.

'I'll go with you, Jamie.' Alec put a hand on the woman's shoulder. 'This is great work, Martha. We'll come back for the analysis.'

I waited for the door to close behind us.

'It's like the CIA in there. I had no idea.'

'I know.' Alec beamed. 'Isn't it great? Nothing is left to chance.'

I looked down the identical corridors—equal probability of a bathroom.

'Come on,' Alec said. 'It's this way.'

We walked down a long white hall, past colored doors with makeshift signs on scrap paper. 'Soap Study,' 'Kids and Bacon,' 'Arthritis Group,' and 'School Voucher Feedback.'

171. A pun on the title of a series of movies about a whale, made before the sea mammals went extinct. Jamie means that he needs to urinate.
—Sabina Samuels

229

'Jesus, there's a focus group for everything,' I mused aloud.

'This is a democracy, Jamie, so there'd better be.' He held the bathroom door open and followed me inside. I picked a urinal while Alec went to the sink. 'Focus groups are the keenest articulation of public desire. The ultimate voting process.'

'In a market economy, people vote with their dollars,' I said as my bladder relaxed. I liked the sound of my forceful stream against the plastic tray.

'Why leave everything to trial and error?' Alec asked as he washed his hands. 'A properly conducted focus group gets down to the very core of human need, before that need even reaches full consciousness. It allows us to address what people don't yet know they want.'

'So then you can make advertisements addressing those needs?'

'So then we can make products and offer services that satisfy people,' Alec said, drying his hands. He tossed a paper towel in the trash bin, crossed to the urinal next to mine and unzipped. 'If that need can be satisfied with a brand image, then so be it.'

I zipped up and went to the sink.

'But lie detectors[172]? Brain scans? Hypnosis? Does that really give you a better picture? Do we really want the market to be driven by the subconscious?'

'Absolutely. It's the only honest way. The real human spirit. Before it's corrupted by societal and neurotic filters.'

'You really believe that?'

'It goes down to what we all have in common. It's what makes us part of the same team.'

'Come on, Alec,' I said, washing my hands in the infrared-activated sink. 'That's a bit backwards. Human reason should be part of the equation. It's what makes us get married, build schools, write laws. Nature can be a cruel

172. These primitive machines were never able to prove anyone's guilt or innocence. Towards the end of its existence, the lie detector ended up being a tool used for mere entertainment, showcased by radio pioneer Howard Stern in "What's my sexual orientation" segments as well as on a short lived Regis Philbin game show called "Who Wants to Tell a White Lie?"
—IHATEGWBUSH

230

place. Rationality and conscience[173] are what keep us from killing each other whenever we want.'

'I beg to differ,' Alec said, zipping up. 'I've got faith in the goodness of people, just as they are. Rationality and judgment are precisely the things that make us kill one another. Re-read your Rousseau[174] and get over that nasty guilt complex already. It's going to hold you back.'

Alec was holding open the door for me, again.

'You're not going to wash up?' I asked.

'I washed before I pissed. My dick's the cleanest part on me.'

I pondered the deep sense of that remark as we made our way down the hall. I was washing my hands to protect others from myself, rather than protecting my own genitals from the filth of others. Might Alec be right about everything?

'Jamie!' a woman's voice called from behind us. It was Carla. Shit. What was she doing here? Sabotage?

'Hi, Carla,' I said. 'Sorry I didn't return your call. I've been swamped.' She looked good. More relaxed than in the pits.

'That's okay, I'm just glad you came. The group already started. Come on.'

'Group?'

'My focus group,' she said. 'Didn't you get the memo? I've hired DD&D to conduct a study with everyone I've dated in the last twelve months. To get their impressions. Their feedback. It'll only take an hour.'

'I read an article about that in the *Times*,' Alec said. 'It's the latest thing.'

'I'm kind of committed here,' I apologized. 'Alec and I have to create two spots by the end of the day.'

'That's okay, Jamie,' Alec said mischievously. 'We won't have the analysis done until noon, anyway.'

'Thanks, Alec,' Carla said, taking my hand. 'It's right this way.'

173. Around 2000, philosophy was still dominated by a religion called "psycho-analysis." Note these men only discuss on pre-rational and rational frames. Another religion called "new age" taught trans-rational frames.

According to Ken Wilber [a boring philosopher/guru of that age] most of people calling themselves "spiritual" were trapped by a "pre/trans fallacy."

Wilber's central thesis is the "pre-trans" cycle of involution and evolution. This is the idea that in it's development the psyche begins in a state of undifferentiated unconscious universalism. From there it passes through stages of increasing individualization and ego-development whereby it is able to recognize itself as a separate entity. Only after having attained this state is one able to progress on the mystical path and transcend the ego in order to consciously return to the undifferentiated One. —COSMODELIA

174. An 18th Century Swiss philosopher who had come back into vogue for his contention that the Noble Savage, untainted by institutional influences, was morally superior to civilized man. We must not judge such phenomena too harshly. These were victims of a media-generated mob psychology.
—Sabina Samuels

She took me down the long corridor as Alec threw me a you-fucked-her-not-me smirk and went back into his monitoring paradise.

'You really think I qualify for this, Carla?' I pleaded. 'I mean, we didn't really date. Except for that one night. I'm not sure how much I'll really add.'

'Don't be silly, Jamie. I could really use your honest feedback. Truly.'

'You could just take me for a coffee and ask me anything you like. I'll be honest. I was actually thinking about the whole thing just this morning—'

'Save it for the group,' she said, opening a door with a sign that read 'SANTANGELO FEEDBACK.'

Around the table sat three other men. One couldn't have been older than eighteen, and another was at least sixty.

'Hi,' I greeted the other men who had penetrated Carla Santangelo over the past year.

'Jamie?' The third one swung around in his chair. It was Jude!

'You? You slept with Carla?'

'Yeah,' he shrugged. 'I met her while you were away in Montana. She wanted to set us up with an IPO.'

'But did you know that she and I—'

'Not until after. It just kind of happened...'

'No crosstalk until we've begun,' interrupted a young female researcher entering with a clipboard. She adjusted her headset. 'After the session is completed, you can converse freely.'

'But ma'am,' I interjected, 'the two of us know each other. Are you sure that won't interfere with—'

'We have analytical filters to account for the influences of camaraderie and competition,' she said calmly. Competition? 'Just answer as spontaneously and honestly as you are able. As long as you answer the questions as best you can, you'll each get your thousand-dollar check.'

I watched, perplexed, as Jude leaned back in his chair. Why hadn't he ever told me? Did they talk about me when they were together?

Before I had a chance to determine my role in the triangle, the interviewer commenced our interrogation. 'Now let's begin with styles of seduction...'

Each of Carla's four sexual partners were asked to relate which of her actions turned them on and which didn't. I was surprised to learn that her hand-in-the-pocket maneuver had been used on all four of us, and worked on everyone but the youngest, who said he felt intimidated by it. When the interviewer pursued the line of inquiry, however, the boy admitted that he did get an erection in spite of his fears.

'What about styling?' the interviewer continued. 'Which seems more available to you—hair up or hair down?'

Carla's assembled ex's discussed the relative merits of her hair up ('invites you to let it down' and 'librarians are hot') versus hair down ('didn't know she had so much' and 'looks more natural and ready for sex.') On and on the impassive interviewer went, inviting us to rate each of Carla's actions and traits as if they were product attributes. I felt strangely reassured by our largely unanimous responses to the questions posed. Especially when it came to the morning-after.

'She made it seem like we had conducted some kind of business transaction,' Jude said. 'Like we had closed a deal.'

'Yeah,' I agreed. 'I mean, I would have done it again that morning, but she just read her paper. It made me feel, well, kind of cheap.'

'You didn't interpret it as a relief from responsibility?' the interviewer asked.

I looked at the one-way mirror. I knew Carla was back there. Is that what she was trying to communicate? That I was free of obligation?

'I *wanted* to take responsibility,' said the older man, the CFO of a chip company. 'I thought maybe she wanted to be kept. I've done that, before. Then I assumed that in the light of day I was just too old for her. Or that she looked at our quarterly earnings and determined I wasn't rich enough.'

'Very well, gentlemen,' the interviewer said. 'That just about concludes our hour. Just one more question for the group: why didn't any of you ask her out again?'

Wow. None of us. Poor Carla. Reduced to conducting a focus group in order to find out why she didn't get any repeat business. Maybe I had misinterpreted that whole morning routine of hers. Perhaps it wasn't abuse, but some weird defense mechanism. Her way of making it clear that she wasn't going to make any demands. I felt compelled to be honest with the interviewer. To give Carla some heartfelt feedback, even if it hurt her.

'She was acting like such a fucking bitch,' I said. 'That's why. I didn't feel safe with her. What did she want? A boy-toy? Or someone to dominate her? I could have gone either way, but she just closed up.' The interviewer was using some sort of technique on me. I couldn't help myself. 'Maybe I didn't really want to fuck her at all, okay? I just wanted her job.'

I was completely unashamed to have admitted the darkest truth. They hadn't attached me to any electrodes, but something in the interviewer's pacing of questions made me open up like I hadn't in months. Maybe Alec was right about focus groups. What was wrong with honesty, after all?

'I'd go out with her again,' Jude said. He was the only one who took this position. 'If it weren't for her thing with Jamie. I think she's kinda hot. And smart. I'd definitely see her.' Had Jude been drawn into an honest response, as well? His wanting her made me want her, too. But I had no chance to register my new conviction.

'Thank you, gentlemen,' the interviewer finally said, opening the door.

'You can pick up your checks at reception on your way out.'

Jude and I stayed in the conference room after the others had left. In real life, I had always played the part of the innocent, and Jude the hacker-derelict. The focus group had revealed something else about us to one another.

'So, you fucked her for her job?' Jude asked.

'It wasn't like that.'

'It's what you said.'

'She was the one who came on to me, anyway.'

'Whatever. I'm not judging you.'

I checked my watch.

'You have somewhere to be?' Jude asked.

'We're doing another group down the hall,' I answered. 'Then we're going to shoot a couple of commercials. Public relations stuff.' I knew I should say something about the TeslaNet deal, but I hadn't really been following its progress too closely. 'We should close on TeslaNet sometime next week. They're drafting up the paperwork.'

'That's cool,' Jude said. The fact that he didn't say anything more was driving me crazy.

'What did Carla offer you?' I finally blurted out.

'She thought we should launch TeslaNet independently. She said you'd be coming back with a big deal, but that if we believed in the product, we'd be better off taking it to market ourselves.'

'She did?' I knew she was probably right, but positive press on the Synapticom deal from Marshall Tellington's massive media empire was now depending on my delivering TeslaNet to Entertainink. It was a house of cards.

I figured that giving Jude an out would make him more confident in his

175. A case history of the research conducted for the M&L campaign appears in Martha Babcock's 'Ascent of the Icon: Man, Myth, and Money,' New York: Rutledge Press, 2009.

'In an effort to appease the many forces of nature they did not understand, ancient men customarily sacrificed their first born sons to the gods of chaos. The myth of Abraham introduced a kinder, gentler method of reparation, to a single, benevolent, and contractually obligated Lord. A mere piece of foreskin would satisfy his lust for flesh. That, and a few goats at regular intervals.

'But people found it difficult to transfer paternal authority onto an abstract, unknowable deity. He didn't even have a name, and provided little solace in times of need. Yaweh, though universal, made for a hard sell. So the messianic religions arose to put human faces on our surrogate parents. What they lost in universal applicability they made up for with personality.

'Jesus and his mother functioned quite adequately in this regard until about the 16th Century, when a re-virginized Queen Elizabeth claimed the Virgin Mary's mantle for herself. For two centuries, people looked to the monarchy as its primary source of transference, until the parental role was in turn usurped by the elected leaders of more democratically conceived republics, who were themselves eventually replaced in our affections by movie-star-turned-politicians or vice versa.

'Thus humans evolved from slaves to children to lambs to subjects to citizens to fans.

'The 21st Century transition from fans to consumers, however, marked a significant break from this pattern. The paradox in the public consciousness, we theorized, stemmed from the market's inability to provide a convincing and reassuring parent figure toward whom consumers could project their unresolved childhood anxiety. In the market reality that replaced the culture of celebrity, figureheads were not people but brand icons, and they

note continues on page 237

decision to stay in. 'She does have a point,' I offered. 'Would you feel better going that way?'

'We feel better doing what you think is right, Jamie. We trust you.' Jude's faith stabbed me like a knife in the gut.

'Well, two million bucks a pop is nothing to sneeze at,' I said. 'And market conditions have changed. Little companies don't spring up out of nowhere, anymore. The instant IPO days are long gone.'

'You've got the ball, Jamie. Run with it.'

Run with it I would.

All of D&D's research and analysis on M&L's behalf[175] ultimately formed the basis for two twenty-eight-second television commercials. The first would be called 'Have Your Cake and Eat It, Too.' A strikingly Aryan fifteen-year-old boy—a symbol of adolescent rage—sits alone at a kitchen table defiantly eating chocolate cake, while a television set on the counter behind him plays Birnbaum's testimony. Over the whole image appear a series of text messages. The phrases chosen would vary, based on the socio-economic status of the individual viewing family, as indicated by the identifying serial numbers in their cable TV boxes. All of the text would be culled from dialogue in the focus groups, and build up in intensity.

'Classic pacing and leading,' Alec pronounced from his director's chair next to mine in the client booth—really just a small platform with a wood railing that prevented us from interfering with the shoot. He was doodling on a pad, drawing pictures that looked like simple landscapes to the casual viewer, but when held upside-down revealed themselves to be obscene sketches of people sitting on toilets or having sex in absurd positions. 'We begin with thoughts and feelings that the viewer himself is having. That establishes rapport and trust. The phasing and interlacing of the video image in post-production accomplishes the same thing on a neural level.'

'It's just a form of sympathy, then,' I said. 'With a little NLP-style hypnosis thrown in for good measure.'

'Basically, yes. We say the things we heard in the focus groups, like 'my children are watching me' and 'so many choices' and 'I can't see the numbers."

'Isn't that going to frighten people?' I asked, careful not to challenge his new-found authority.

'They're already frightened. We're just acknowledging it, bringing them all into the same space before we take them deeper with stuff like 'they don't think I can make decisions for myself' and 'whose interests do they serve?' This will bring them out of fear, and into righteous indignation.'

'Rage?'

'Exactly,' Alec said, taking my arm. 'And once we stoke their rage, we can take them anywhere we want. That's when the kid brings the cake to his mouth, and we super a phrase like 'who is willing to fight on my behalf?' and 'no one but me' or 'I can think for myself.' In the few remaining pockets of National Public Radio[176] progressives and in the San Francisco area, we'll use 'If it feels good, it *is* good.'

'And that's it?' I was incredulous. 'That's going to make people support an online trading program?'

'Don't you get it? The *boy*. He's eating the cake! He's in the kitchen, but his parents are gone! That brings the whole thing together. It's a joke, it's media-savvy, but it's real, too!'

'I guess.' Down on the soundstage, a blond boy sat on a set made to look like a suburban kitchen. The cameras rolled as he slowly consumed forkful after forkful of chocolate cake. Then he raised his hand.

'Cut!' announced the director's voice, as a stage hand ran onto the set with a large aluminum trashcan and placed it next to the boy.

could not achieve parental status.

'This 'cultural voltage' is not a liability but an opportunity, for in every paradox lay the 'key consumer insight' for an effective campaign. Just stand the problem on its head and you find the solution. In this case, our job was not to find a new parental substitute for the trading public, but rather to accelerate and affirm the market culture's independence from all such projections of the superego.

'Ezra Birnbaum, and the governmental authority he represented, were cast as the dominating parent, incapable of letting his children grow up. His intellectual language and Jewish demeanor would resonate well with rising populist and anti-Semitic sentiment. The consumers of America were being infantilized by an old man who wished to be their new father and thus stymie their natural evolution. He was an enemy of the people. Worse, his lack of faith in folks' ability to make decisions for themselves, as autonomous human beings, was costing them money.'

This entire message was to be crafted by compliance professionals into a series of communications that induced transference on all levels—subliminal, neurolinguistic, aspirational and psycho-sexual—simultaneously.

Amazingly, Ms. Babcock only once defends the ethical questions posed by using such techniques, justifying that the ads cause no social detriment if they merely help convince people of what they already feel, subconsciously. This is why it was D&D's responsibility to conduct such painstaking research and analysis. It guaranteed that their most coercive techniques were only used in service of the extant cultural appetite. They were not creating public opinion, they were 'energizing and accelerating it.'
—Sabina Samuels

176. A network of radio stations whose commercials were called "underwriting." This dubious distinction, along with their dismal balance sheets, allowed the network to claim a moral high ground.
—Sabina Samuels

'What's going on?' I asked Alec.

The boy put his hands on the can's rim, leaned over, and vomited what looked like quarts of brown fluid.

'Oh, sick,' I uttered involuntarily as my own gag reflex kicked in. The director turned around and shot me an angry glance.

The entire crew remained silent and still while the young boy emptied his stomach of cake. Once his heaving subsided, the boy rested his elbows against the can, wiped his brow, and inhaled deeply.

'You okay, kid?' the director asked.

The boy gave a thumbs-up sign. He was a pro.

'All right, then,' the director shouted to the crew. 'Reset! Make-up!'

Two women rushed to the boy's aid. One wiped the vomit from his mouth while the other re-applied his rouge and powder. A stage hand replaced the chocolate cake with a fresh one, and removed the garbage pail. Then the director rolled camera, and the whole cycle began again.

The second spot, called 'One People, One Market,' was being assembled simultaneously in the editing suite upstairs. It was based on DD&D's other main consumer insight: that online traders were suffering from an emotional schism. On the one hand, they were being bombarded with so much investment information that they felt overwhelmed, and afraid to make decisions for themselves. On the other, they held an even deeper conviction that their own gut instincts were the best indicators of a security's chances for success. If they could only disentangle themselves from the 'tyranny of conflicting information,' as Martha called it, they felt they would be set free.

The creative execution involved no new footage, instead culling scenes from famous televised revolts: the demonstration in Tiananmen Square, the felling of the Berlin Wall, the candlelight street vigils in Czechoslovakia, the World Trade Organization riots in Seattle, and the Broadband Revolt in

Omaha. Over these images flowed the NASDAQ tickertape, in bright green characters. As the scenes intensified, the tickertape began to undulate to the rhythm of a heartbeat that slowly increased in volume. The voice of a famous actress who played the ship's captain on a canceled Star Trek[177] series narrated over the imagery: 'America is a tree, with roots in ethics and branches in liberty. We are one people, with one great goal. As we reach for the sky, no one can stand in our way. Let my people go.'

'Genius!' Tobias Morehouse declared at 6:00 a.m. the next morning as we played the finished reel in his conference room. 'When do they air?'

'The first one will be running on CNN's Financial Channel starting this morning,' Alec beamed. 'The other hits the major networks during the news, tonight.'

'Fantastic!' Morehouse said, rewinding the tape to watch the commercials again. 'But where does it say Morehouse & Linney? Do you add that on at the end?'

'That's the brilliance of it, Dad. We don't say it, anywhere.'

'What kind of advertising is that?' Morehouse asked, confused.

'Just think of it.' Alec got up and slowly circled around the table. 'There's no brand being pushed at all. The ad positions itself as a public service announcement. A noble communications effort by an anonymous firm, simply and righteously amplifying the voice of the people.'

'But how will they know it's us?' Morehouse was breathing heavily now. Creativity was one thing. Paying good money for anonymous ads was just plain bad business.

'Don't you get it?!' Alec was speaking a good two octaves higher than normal. 'Secondary media! That's what makes this such a breakthrough campaign! Everyone will want to know who it is making the ads. There'll be investigative reports, a feature on *20/20*[178], until some reporter—one that we

177. At the time, Star Trek was still a relatively small phenomenon compared to how we know it today. It had only run five television series, and less than ten movies.
—Sabina Samuels

178. A news magazine broadcast on a television subsidiary of Disney, then known as ABC. The program's title was an oblique reference to an optical examination popular in this period.
—Sabina Samuels

choose, of course—'*figures it out!*" Alec made little quote marks with his hands. 'Then everyone and his sister will be doing stories on how Morehouse & Linney felt so strongly about this issue—about freeing the American public from the shackles of paralyzing regulation—that we made ads with no intention of being rewarded ourselves!'

'What do you think, Jamie?' Tobias said, quieter now. 'Could that really work?'

Alec didn't even turn around to throw me one of his you-better-agree-with-me glances. Just the back of his head spoke volumes.

'I think it's brilliant,' I said. 'We could very well be seen as the heroes of our age.'

'Or the cowards.' Tobias scratched his hairy knuckles. 'I hate taking pot-shots from behind a wall. It's very...unsportsmanlike.'

'This is a different world, Dad,' Alec said, sitting down across from his father. I thought he was going to hold his father's hand. 'You're going to have to trust me on this one. This is my business.'[179]

Just then, I saw a flash of orange through the plate-glass window. It was Carla, in her trading vest, marching past the conference room and holding up her middle finger at the three of us. Her hair was flying behind her.

'What's gotten into her?' Alec asked.

'I better see,' I said, getting up and running out after her. Maybe she had reviewed my comments from the day before, about fucking her for her job.

'Wait up!' I called to her. 'Carla!'

She stopped without turning around.

'You guys do that just to piss me off, don't you?' She was almost in tears.

'What, Carla? What did we do?'

'The executive washroom. You know...'

'No, I don't. Tell me.' She looked so vulnerable.

[179]. With a century's hindsight, it's easy to see how these unknowing architects of the last fascist age were fooling themselves. But, in all fairness, they were suffering from the same cultural confusion as the people they hoped to influence. With no fuhrer or il duce at the helm, how were they to recognize the implications of their scheme? They were working under no higher power save the economy itself, and they had no idea that they were the ones truly in charge. They thought they were merely responding to market forces—the forces of nature.
—Sabina Samuels

'Leaving the seat up like that?' she said. 'It's your little message, isn't it. That it's boy-turf, right?'

'I hardly go in there, Carla.' And even when I did, I had no idea we were supposed to put the seat down.

'Yeah, right. I know about your games. I've sent memos, you know. Human resources is totally on my side. I can sue his fat ass over this, you know.'

'Over a toilet seat, Carla?'

'Just you watch me. I'll win, too.'

We stood there together a moment. I smiled at her.

'It's not funny,' she insisted, trying not to lose her rage.

'I know. I'm sorry.'

'It's okay,' she said, calm now. 'I better get down to the pits before they open.'

'Hey, look.' I felt myself taking her arm as I walked her to the elevators. 'That was really weird, yesterday. I'm sorry if I—'

'You were honest, Jamie. That's all I could ask for.'

'Yeah, but it got me thinking. We really started out on a wrong foot, you know? Mixing business with pleasure and all. I really got the wrong idea about you.'

'No you didn't.' She pushed the down button. 'I'm a mess. You're right to stay away. The cops should wrap some of that yellow warning tape around me.'

'Don't say that. You're a beautiful woman. And you're smart.'

'And still very single at thirty-three.'

The elevator opened. The urgency of the moment provoked an impulse.

'Look, Carla, I've got the company's seats tomorrow night. Why don't we go to the game, together?'

'Because they're for clients, stupid.'

'Fuck the clients,' I said. She was turned on by my rebellious tone.

'You mean it?'

'Come on,' I said. 'Let's just try to have some fun, and see where it goes, eh? Can't ask for anything more than that.' Where had I heard those lines before?

'Okay,' she said.

'Why don't we meet for dinner at Gotham, say six?'

'Fuck Gotham,' she said as the doors began to close. 'I want Garden foot-longs[180]. Just pick me up at seven.'

Maybe she was my kind of woman, after all.

180. Foot-longs were a popular sausage containing otherwise unusable beef by-products, and traditionally consumed at sporting events, where their flavor, presumably, would remain unnoticed.
—Sabina Samuels

10. MSG to USB

Alec's commercials did their job. And then some.

Just three days after the first one was broadcast, busloads of market activists began showing up in Washington DC under the banner of 'Consumer Rights America,' for what amounted to a continuous vigil on the Mall. The CRA were demanding the resignation of Ezra Birnbaum and the lifting of all remaining regulations on Internet trading. A few pods of counter-demonstrators, mostly teen anarchists and old ladies representing what remained of the Civil Liberties Union[181], were easily shouted down by the massive crowd, and didn't even make the evening news.

Morehouse had me launch the new Synapticom interface right away in order to capitalize on the swell of popular support. No one would dare start

181. A once powerful group of lawyers who fought for civil rights, and eventually turned their efforts completely towards supporting the consumer sector. Even these self-proclaimed 'leftists' became just another cog in the machine they originally sought to dismantle. —Sabina Samuels

an investigation into the program's legality in the face of such a public out-cry, and once the program was up and running, it would be a lot harder to challenge. In the two days since the online reactive architecture was implemented, trading on the site was up over 300 percent. Tobias promoted me to Chief of Technology Investments (a new position, so no one needed to be fired this time) which earned me a write-up on the front page of the *Wall Street Journal*, albeit below the fold.

'Weird seeing your face like that,' Carla said. We were in the back seat of a stretch limo together, on the way from her house to the Garden.

'Like what?'

'In an etching like this. With all those little lines and dots. It makes you look, I don't know, historical.'

'I guess. I just wonder what it is I'll be remembered for.'

'Don't be silly, Jamie. You should be proud. You've empowered the little guy. Or at least made the little guy feel that way for a while.' Ever the cheerful cynic.

'You want I should turn the radio up?' the driver called back to us in a foreign accent. 'It's the business wrap-up.'

I looked at the driver's image in the rear-view mirror. He was a bull.

'That's okay.' I ignored the hallucination. 'I'm off duty.'

'Hah!' said the driver. 'That's a good one.' He turned up the volume in the rear speakers.

'*The Fed has reiterated its intransigence in spite of new pressure from the CRA,*' said the voice on the radio. '*In a press conference this afternoon, reporters had difficulty hearing Ezra Birnbaum over the noise of protestors outside the Central Bank.*' The broadcast cut to a sound bite of Birnbaum. '*A set of regulatory boundaries provides the discipline for free markets to grow at a sustainable rate. The economy does not need to be as unpredictable nor as potentially cruel as untamed nature.*'

'That's gotta be weird,' Carla said. 'The stuff in the news is the stuff that you and Alec are doing. You feel Machiavellian, or what?'

'More like Albert Speer[182], actually.'

'Who?'

'Never mind.' I leaned over towards the bull behind the wheel. 'Can you turn it to something else?'

'Sure thing, boss,' he snorted. 'I hate that man. That Birnbaum. If he was standing in the street I would run him down.'

'Wow,' I said, marveling at the power of the campaign I'd helped to architect.

'Even if he was on the sidewalk,' the foreign bull continued. 'I would go off the road to run him down. Even if it would damage the car. That is what I would do. Very much so. I told my wife.'

I pushed a button, closing the divider between us and the driver.

'That was kind of rude, don't you think?' Carla said.

'Can we not talk for a minute?' I snapped. I would have apologized, but I wanted to let it sit for a while.

What had I unleashed? I'd merely intended to work as an analyst for a couple of years, vest my shares, and get out. Maybe get a few good technologies out there—with my name on them. This was all supposed to be for laughs and a few bucks. But the better I got at playing the game, the more it felt like everything was getting out of control.

'Hey, you've gotta lighten up just a little, Jamie. Shit happens, you know?' She had either read my mind or my face.

'That's the point, Carla. Shit happens. Real shit. Sometimes it seems like people forget that.'

'Just keep your head down and plow ahead. It's all you can do.'

182. A German architect of the 20th Century who designed spectacles for Adolph Hitler, including the Nuremberg Rallies. Jamie's identification with the anti-hero is, most likely, hyperbole.
—Sabina Samuels

'I like to know that I'm not smashing anything on the way, Carla.'

'The more you worry, the worse it gets,' Carla said, putting a hand on my knee. 'Believe me, I know. You should meet my mom sometime. She's practically an obsessive. When my dad died, she got his car. It was almost brand new, and she was so scared about getting it dented that she left it in the garage all the time.'

'I'm not saying people should deny themselves stuff, or run around worried.'

'I didn't finish, Jamie,' she said, putting her index finger on my lips in a move I figured she must have picked up from a Marilyn Monroe[183] movie—a deconstruction I hated myself for making. 'So, last week she had to take it out for its regular service. And she crawls along to the dealer at ten miles an hour. Insanely careful. Well, these kids were up on an overpass. And they see her inching along like that, like a timid old lady, and they decide to chuck a water balloon down on her. She's going so slow that they've got plenty of time to aim, and they get her right on the windshield.'

'So what? A water balloon doesn't do any damage.'

'Yeah, but she's already so paranoid that she freaks out, assumes her windshield's cracked and swerves over onto the shoulder. Only there isn't any shoulder. She goes over the curb and hits a railing instead. It hadn't been there a week ago, but the Transit Authority is in the midst of a big highway safety campaign and they're putting railings all along the road. The only thing on the other side would have been a field of grass. She's only going ten miles an hour, but the railing peels off one whole side of the car like it's the top of a can. She totaled it.'

'So what are you saying? That the Transit Authority's vigilance cost your mom her car?'

'If she had driven the car like a normal person, she would never have been

183. A movie star(let) who engaged in sexual intercourse with the first President John F. Kennedy, before committing suicide. —Sabina Samuels

183b. After confidential US gov. documents were revealed (mid 21st cent.) it appeared that she was murdered by the FBI due to the belief she was acting on the orders of KGB, though no real clues were ever found. —MILLO105

picked out by those kids. She brought it on herself.'

'Come on.'

'All I'm saying, Jamie, is you have to learn to recognize when you're on a roll, and go with it. Stop questioning everything. Things are going well for you.'

'At other people's expense, Carla. Even yours. Or have you forgotten about that?'

'As a matter of fact, I have.' She put her hand on the back of my neck. 'Can you?'

We made our way into the Garden. Carla leaned into the crowd like a linebacker, gritting her teeth and clearing a path for us with her shoulder. I held her hand and hung on. All around us, the wealthy and their even wealthier clients rushed about like dazed tourists, checking the numbers on their tickets and looking for the correct gates. No one wanted to be late and risk missing out on whatever free promotion—T-shirts, caps, cigars—might be handed out at the escalators. Each of these people probably had enough cash in their wallets to buy a car, and enough available on their credit cards to buy ten more. They earned hundreds if not thousands of dollars a minute, but a single sixty-nine-cent Somalia-manufactured Knicks cap with an insurance company logo disgracing the back strap was enough to get them out of the office half-an-hour earlier than necessary. In a sense, this meant they still had souls.

Anyone who doesn't know the exact criteria for breast appraisal in 21st Century New York need only to descend the steps at Madison Square Garden, where each concentric ring of seats holds women whose busts—either naturally or via cash investment—represent an incremental improvement in shape, size, direction, wobble, and tautness over the ring outside them. This allows the spectator to infer an idealized set of breast characteristics by imagining how the progression would continue past the front row and all the way to center court.

As we took that physical and cognitive journey towards our box seats, I finally realized why the girls at expensive private high schools like Dalton and Spence were so much prettier than the ones at Stuy. These were their mothers. Evolution permitted rich men to select the most beautiful mates.

It was as if market forces and arena architecture had arrived at a perfectly accurate distribution of New York's society page, using a matrix of wealth, stature, longevity, and genetics. Every inch closer to the court corresponded to a measurable increase in total human worth.

Our seats were good. Really good. Fourth row, just left of the center line. Six seats away from Kevin Bacon[184]. Eight from Spike Lee. Ticket-holders cared more about their own progress towards higher status seats than the Knicks progress towards a championship. The jockeying between white millionaires for better positions rivaled anything going on between the black millionaires on the court. Most of the spectators spent a good part of the first half simply registering who was sitting where.

Just getting inside the Garden was a feat. Even the cheapest seats required purchasing an entire season plan, and the waiting list had reached an estimated twenty-six years long. The only way into the arena was to have connections, and the only way to get connections was with money (or breasts). Once inside, the object of the game was to move down, closer to the action, and closer to the rich, powerful, and famous. The upgrading process involved an even more convoluted set of applications and waiting lists, all designed to keep the meritocracy from functioning. And why should it? This was business.[185]

Firms like Morehouse & Linney offered their tickets to whichever clients or analysts they wished to give a boost. Now that my deal with Synapticom

184. A movie actor whose ubiquity provoked a web site that automatically calculated how many degrees of separation existed between him and any other performer. —Sabina Samuels

185. Documentation in diaries and newspaper articles from the period supports the narrators claim. One's placement at a Knicks game may have said as much about his or her company's worth as a quarterly report. Since the only products many of these corporations produced were stock certificates, the most efficient use of an executive's time and energy was not to work at a desk, but get out and tout the value of the shares themselves. It seems nothing validated share value better than a CEO's ability to leverage his worth into higher status seats at Madison Square Garden.

Investors on the upper levels used binoculars to scope out whose seating positions were improving or worsening, and then submitted orders based on this information through palmtop devices with cellular connections to after-hours trading companies. According to a New York Times study done at the height of this phenomenon, Instanet was experiencing a forty-percent increase in trading activity during the first thirty minutes of any New York home game. —Sabina Samuels

was the focus of the firm's public relations efforts, it made sense for me to be placed in the coveted fourth row chairs. Still, I was there by proxy more than personal power. These were not my seats, they were Morehouse's. It meant only as much as flying in his G-2. I had achieved the male equivalent of fake breasts. My tickets had been bestowed upon me.

It was years since I'd been to a Knicks game, and I was bringing Carla to a Garden disappointingly different from the one my Uncle Morris took me to as a kid. I'd wanted to bond with her on a level more wholesome than the hi-tech financial markets where we spent our days. But this place was more commodity-driven than the pits.

From the way she squeezed my hand as we edged into our row, I could tell she was thinking the same thing. She was wearing a tight black skirt and an old Sprewell jersey over a sports bra. Her hair draped over her bare shoulders with an elegant, casual grace. The perfect mix of Manhattan class and Bronx cheer. But among the landed gentry of the floor seats, she stuck out like an outer borough bumpkin, and she knew it.

The renovated Garden now had three tiers of what were called 'Club' seats, all served by waiters. M&L's row was in the 'Nothing But Net' section, the most exclusive of the three. The dinner fare included entrees like filet mignon and lobster, which were brought on metal trays that clamped to the armrests—making the wealthiest diners look like they were helpless babies in high-chairs. Most of them spent so much time eating off trays in the first class sections of airplanes that this posture probably made them feel safe.

'Jesus Christ,' Carla said, perusing the blue and orange tasseled menu. 'Can't a person get a friggin' frank here, anymore?'

'I'm sure they'd get you one,' I assured her.

'This is a basketball game. There should be hot dogs,' she declared defiantly. 'I mean, it's not against some rule, is it?'

I liked it when she got this way. She wasn't bitchy, so much as real. She cut through the crap. She was as down to earth as I was. Or at least as I felt I was deep down. I was determined to get us both the kind of food that proved it.

Procuring hot dogs and knishes turned out to be about as difficult as changing from the 'Prime' to the 'People's' network. After making a number of inquiries to our waitstaff, we learned that only the food services manager was authorized to let us order from a menu from beneath ours in the Garden hierarchy. And the manager was reluctant to permit this on the grounds that people in neighboring seats had paid handsomely for the privilege of dining free of such aromas. Then there was the issue of presentation; hotdogs could not be attractively displayed on Knicks custom china[186], and these seats were within range of the cameras.

186. Plates made of ceramics.
—Sabina Samuels

'What are we?' I asked, my imperious hostility fueled by Carla's presence, 'unpaid extras for the NBA's television broadcast?'

I pulled out a business card and explained that I was representing M&L, a longtime season ticket holder of the highest caliber. But, even so, I was not important enough to get the food that less important people were enjoying in the upper balconies. It is easier to pass a camel through the eye of a needle than for a wealthy man to get a hot dog at the Garden. Eventually, Carla got up and caused such a commotion that Spike Lee himself turned around and shouted to the manager.

'Give the kids some fucking hotdogs, you cracker!'

Enough of the assembled wealthy patrons laughed at Spike's outburst for the manager to feel safe about relenting. Within minutes, we were eating hotdogs and knishes wrapped in waxed paper, along with half a dozen other well-dressed men and women who decided to 'slum it' along with us.

'I think we started a new trend,' Carla laughed.

The controversy surrounding the meal order was eventually upstaged by the entrance of a man in a top hat and tails, escorted by two young women dressed in nothing but boas. Spectators rose from their seats and applauded as the debonair gentleman twirled his handlebar moustache and the trio took their seats in the second row.

'Will you look at him?' Carla scoffed.

'Who's that?' I asked.

'Hugh Tapscott,' she explained. 'He just beat an SEC investigation.'

'What did he do?'

'He made about thirty million dollars in a week, that's what.'

'In the market?'

'No, he's never made a trade in his life. They explained it all in the *Journal*. Where've you been? He used to be some kind of sports bookie, then a couple of months ago he got turned on to email marketing. Last Monday, he sent messages to two million random people. Half of them he told CIRI would go up that day, and half he told it would go down. The stock went up, so on Tuesday, he sent emails to the million he had given the correct information. Then, in those emails, he told 500,000 that CIRI would go up, and the other 500,000 that it would go down. I think that day it ended up going down a couple of points. So on Wednesday, he sent emails to the half-a-million people he'd steered correctly both times.'

'And half he told it was going up, and half he told it was going down.' I followed the pattern.

'Right. And he was left with around 125,000 people, who had all gotten four emails from him in a row, correctly telling them which way the stock was going to move that day.'

'Well duh, of course he's going to be right half the time.'

'But they didn't know that. All they knew was that this guy had sent them

251

the right information four times straight. So late Thursday night, he sent one last email, saying he would tell them which way the stock was going to move that day if they sent him $500 by Visa card.'

'And they did it?'

'About 60,000 of them authorized the charge. A lot of them had already made more than that following the earlier free tips, anyway.'

'And what did he tell them that last time? Did he split it fifty-fifty again?'

'No. That's the brilliant part. He told 'em all it would go up, which of course it did because 60,000 people were spending their life's savings on one tiny stock. That's why the SEC couldn't make the case stick. The one time he charged people for his information, it was based on real logic. Plus, he didn't buy or sell any of the stock himself. He made all his money on the $500 fees.'

'Gevalt,' I said, licking a spot of mustard off my hand. 'Kinda makes you feel bad for what we're doing to old Ezra.'

'Huh?' Carla asked.

'Nothing,' I said, changing the subject. 'That knish was good.'

'They say he's some kind of sickie, anyway,' Carla said. 'There's no harm in taking him down.'

'Hmph.'

After a soap opera star sang a prolonged gospel version of the national anthem[187], the game finally began. Finally back in form and positioned for a championship after the long-awaited departure of Patrick Ewing, the springy young New York team acquired an early lead. During an 'official' time out (called by the refs in order to make room for more TV commercials) the Knicks City Dancers[188] took the floor.

Over the past few years, the NBA had attempted to defuse widespread objections of institutionalized sexism by incorporating male dancers into the

187. Sporting events, though hardly public affairs, still adhered to the patriotic tradition of playing 'The Star Spangled Banner,' as if to imply that the teams were dedicated to preserving a national ethos.
—Sabina Samuels

188. The Knicks City Dancers descended from what were originally known as cheerleaders. Cheerleaders, as the name implies, were a squad of young women who led the crowd in cheers during the game. Over time, however, their function changed to one of providing a sexual outlet during time-outs and other lulls in the action for the largely male crowd, whose blood was testosterone-rich as result of the competitive atmosphere.
—Sabina Samuels

troop. But this nod to political correctness had been met with nothing but derision by the crowd. In the hopes that they would bribe their way into acceptance, the male dancers were sent out onto the floor with boxes of caps and T-shirts that they threw into the stands while the sexily clad young women gyrated in their customary fashion.

The crowd rose to its feet and booed, in what had become an expected protest ritual. But tonight, the mob was organized. Someone had handed out tiny darts to a large portion of the audience, and as the peppy young men approached the perimeter of the court bearing their gifts, they were pelted with the aerodynamic projectiles. All around us, grown men in suits rose to fling their darts at the well-meaning youths. The air was filled with the flying needles, and those that didn't reach the court were landing on front row patrons. I quickly removed my jacket and covered Carla.

Was this the right thing to do, or had I broken another feminist rule? I pulled the jacket so it was a little bit over my own head, too. Not that I felt I needed the protection, but it would make my efforts to shield Carla appear less sexist. I hated worrying about that kind of stuff. This, I decided, was the rage fueling the dart war all around us.

'Hey!' Carla shouted, resisting my protection. 'What's the big idea?'

'I was just—'

'Girls aren't allowed to get in on the fun?'

She picked up one of the darts that had fallen around us, and flung it at one of the boys on the court.

'Come on, Jamie!' she shouted over the din. 'Fight for your rights!'

My rights to what? I smiled half-heartedly as she pelted the gender-challenging cheerleaders with all the vigor of her male counterparts.

Down on the court, a frightened Hispanic boy in a Knicks sweatsuit buried his face in his box for protection. He continued to throw out his peace offerings of free Knicks paraphernalia, flinching in pain each time his arm or back was penetrated by a dart. Finally surrendering, he lifted the box from the bottom and flung its entire contents to the crowd. Then he pulled it over his head and retreated. As the young men all ran for the exits, the whole stadium broke out in cheers before scrambling to collect the booty that had been thrown to them.

'That was fun!' Carla said, straightening her sport bra. I wasn't so horrified by her actions to miss how beautiful her pale breasts looked as they pressed themselves over the black fabric. 'What is it with you, anyway?'

'What's with *me*? I thought you were some kind of feminist.'

'I was throwing darts at boys, wasn't I?'

'You know what I mean.'

'It's a joke, for Chrissakes! Come on, Jamie. What if it was Alec here instead of me? I know the score. You don't have to pretend you're better than everyone else. You went to the Bull Run, didn't you? '

'Gimme a break,' I defended myself. 'The Bull Run is just a Shriner's Convention with MIGs. I couldn't get out of there fast enough.'

'You should at least admit it, Jamie. It's better than lying to yourself. There's nothing worse than—'

'Than what?'

'Nothing. Forget it.'

At a break in the third quarter, a member of the audience was invited to throw foul shots. If he could sink five of ten throws, then one from the three-point line, he'd win an SUV and the entire audience would be able to exchange their ticket stubs the next day for free personal-size pizzas at a citywide chain.

The man took his shots as two Knicks City Dancers in mini-skirts stood on either side of him, holding up placards with the name of the car and pizza companies. He missed his first two foul shots, drawing angry boos from the crowd—a six-inch microwaved[189] pie was at stake for each of us. His third attempt missed the rim and backboard completely—bringing the derisive spectators to their feet.

The crazed crowd continued to boo, shout, and even toss some darts down onto the contestant. Predictably, he missed every shot, and the organ blasted a discordant 'loser' melody. Before returning to his seat, however, the man grabbed one of the dancers around the waist and landed a sloppy kiss on her mouth. The crowd cheered his show of prowess as the disgusted girl tried to smile.

'Typical,' Carla said. 'Making up for your shame with a ritualized rape.'

'So now you disapprove?' I said, as if I'd caught her off-guard. 'When it's a woman being abused?'

'When it's a woman being abused without her participation.'

'Come on,' I pressed her. 'You're being pretty inconsistent.'

'So, sue me.' She smiled. 'Or you wanna teach me a lesson some other way?' She winked.

By the end of the game, the Knicks' twenty-six-point lead had been turned, as usual, into a two-point deficit. They had called a last time-out with just eleven seconds left to play, and as the players returned to the floor, the digital scoreboard displayed the image of a decibel meter crowned by the words 'Get Loud.'

The crowd began to cheer, and the meter slowly registered the increase in collective noise. Carla screamed, too. But I noticed that the meter's fluctuations didn't correspond at all with the crowd's actual volume.

'It's a fake!' I shouted.

'What do you mean?' she asked.

'It's just an animation—not a real meter. It's a prerecorded picture of a

189. A popular method of heating food, microwave's health effects were still unknown, or well-hidden.
—Sabina Samuels

255

needle going up.'

'What does it matter? The people are cheering.'

True enough, the artificial meter had whipped up the crowd into a frenzy. They were going mad, and stamping their feet. Then, without warning, the technologically-invigorated fans began to change into bulls. Not all of them, but enough to remind me that I was no longer in control of my faculties. I tried to focus on the meter itself—how it failed to correspond with the actual arena noise. The animated picture of the meter finally exploded into a mosaic of colored squares that slowly reformed themselves into the Synapticom logo. Of course. Who else?

I was so engrossed in the meter that I missed the final shot—a three-pointer that won the game. But at least the spectator's heads had returned to normal.

It took us a full half-hour to make our way through the crowded stairwells and out to the chaos of limos in the street. The black car I ordered was waiting for us on the corner of 24th Street, intelligently removed from the congestion. It gave us a chance to walk together in the warm evening air while we silently decided and/or negotiated whether to sleep together.

Carla took my arm as we strolled through the darkened streets. People were still coming home from late nights at the office. They looked worn and harried, lugging their briefcases and checking their watches. The women all wore pointy shoes that made them wince with every step. The men's loosened ties and unbuttoned collars made them look all the more imprisoned by their clothes. I was glad I'd kept my shirt and tie intact. It made me feel more like a gentleman out for the evening than a Dilbert[190] on his way back from the cubicle.

We passed a set of department store windows and stopped to admire the new spring fashion displays. The scenes all depicted royalty. In one window,

190. A popular comic strip character of the period, whose name became synonymous with mindless participation in corporate inefficiency. That people could still find humor in their predicaments indicates some measure of self-awareness, however repressed.   —Sabina Samuels

mannequins played lawn tennis as attendants watched. In another, a princess was fitted with bedroom slippers.

'I used to like to imagine I was adopted,' Carla finally said.

'Yeah?' I asked, wondering what had led her to make the connection between the fashions and her childhood.

'I guess I had a hard time believing I was really from the Grand Concourse. Daughter of a cleaning lady and her Guinea[191] husband.'

'That's just a little harsh, don't you think?'

'I don't know. Aren't you ever prejudiced against your own race?' She had a point.

'So you thought you were adopted?'

'Well,' she scraped her clean, white Adidas[192] against the sidewalk, 'I don't know if I believed it as much as wanted to believe it. I used to lie in bed at night and try to remember what my real mother looked like. The one who wrapped me up in a blanket and left me at St. Peter's Basilica in the Vatican.'

'The Vatican?'

'See, I assumed my real parents, my birth parents, were royalty. Or at least my mother was. And that she had an affair with a knight or duke. They had to get rid of me to avoid a scandal that might topple the whole monarchy. So they left me at the Vatican. The whole thing occurred to me in school one day when the nuns showed us pictures of the Basilica. I just knew I had seen it before.'

'Did you tell your parents?'

'Oh, I was a real bitch about it. Whenever they yelled at me about something, I used to tell them that I was keeping a journal and their insolence would be duly noted when my real parents came to get me. I remember how I'd sit at the dinner table eating spaghetti and generic canned sauce off old chipped plates, and I'd roll my eyes to show the meal was unfit for a young

191. Vulgar slang for Roman ethnic origins.
—Sabina Samuels

192. A brand of sports shoe, presumably popular with African-American youth, if the advertisements for the corporation's products are an accurate reflection of their use. —Sabina Samuels

lady of such noble parentage. As if my palate was genetically predisposed for finer things.'

'I guess you got over that one,' I teased. 'I mean, hotdogs and all.'

'Yeah,' she said, dreamily. 'I kind of miss it, now. How real everything was in those days. Plain stuff. And I gave them such a hard time about it. You think I'm bad now? Back then I was a terror. When my mom would take me out shopping, we'd stand there and wait to cross the Concourse. And I remember being insulted that the people in the cars didn't know who I was. That they didn't stop for royalty. I used to run into the street and hold my hands up for them to stop and let us pass. My poor mom would drop her grocery bags and scream. But I just stood there with my arms up.'

'You never got hit?'

'Nah. I guess I was luckier back then.'

I didn't touch that one.

My phone started vibrating in my pocket.

'Sorry,' I said. 'It could be—'

'Your master's voice?' She rolled her eyes.

I opened my Startac[193]. The read-out showed my parents' number.

'Hello?'

'Where are you, Yossi?' my mom's worried voice inquired. 'Can you talk?'

'I'm outside,' I said. 'I'm with someone...'

'You can call back? Or come over? Your father's getting anxious about the election tomorrow night. It would be good for you to be here.'

Carla sighed and reached up towards the phone. I thought she was going to yank it away from me in disgust, but instead she put her fingers on the rubber tip of the antennae and pulled it up into place.

'Brain cancer[194],' she mouthed.[195]

Wow. What a nurturing gesture.

193. A brand of cellular phone based on the Star Trek communicator. Jamie's use of the device, given the proliferation of wrist phones, probably indicated a techno-nostalgia.   —Sabina Samuels

194. Genetic disease characterized by uncontrolled cell division, often in the epithelium and breasts. Cancer was mistakenly attributed to tobacco use and sun exposure.   —AMELIAB85

195. Cellular telephones of the period used extremely high voltages, and emitted electromagnetic radiation. By raising the antennae, users could substantially reduce the quantity of radiation absorbed through the skull and any associated health risks.   —Sabina Samuels

'He's at the computer right now,' my mom went on, 'staring at the web page, wondering why the No looks so much bigger than the Yes on the voting page.' I'd designed the temple web site myself back in college. Now they were using it to do him in.

'That's not right,' I said. If anyone knew the effects of web site architecture on decision-making, it was me. 'I'll come by tomorrow. Don't worry. We'll fix things. I love you.' I pushed the 'end' button.

'Vote?' Carla asked, now that I was off. I figure it's proper etiquette to let someone know what you were talking about if you have that conversation right in front of them, so I told Carla all about my dad's problem at the temple.

'Of all people, Jamie,' she said when I was done. 'You're going to let your dad lose a web vote?'

'What do you mean 'of all people'? Like I have some power over the reform Jews of Whitestone?'

'They're deciding on the fucking web, you idiot,' she said, without a trace of malice. It was just her way. I had no idea what she was driving at. 'You're the fucking hacker. The Disco Kid or whatever they called you.'

'DeltaWave.'

'Whatever. Go in there and hack the site to make your dad win. There's got to be a vote counter in there, or something.'

'I can't do that on a temple web site, Carla...'

'And why not? They're using a temple web site to fire your dad, aren't they?'

'This is a congregation we're talking about. It's not a target market.'

'It's your dad they're using for target practice over there, kid. Sounds like fair play to me. Tit for fucking tat.'

'This, from a girl who conducts focus groups with ex-boyfriends.'

I held the limo door open for her and we got in. It didn't look like I'd be getting anything, now, so I directed the driver to Carla's place.

'I didn't mean what I said, Carla.'

'No, really, Jamie. It's like you're in the 'shit happens' religion. I've seen it before in Jewish men. Like you're scared that if you forget to watch what you're doing you'll get carried away.'

I didn't like the way she said 'Jewish men.' The words sounded hard in her mouth. 'You should see a Hassidic wedding sometime. They get carried away.'

'But don't they keep the men separate from the women?' She had a point. 'It's like you're all afraid that if you just let go, you'll end up fucking temple prostitutes, eating human flesh, or sacrificing your own children. You can't just go with the flow.'

'We've got some pretty good proof of what happens when people go with the flow,' I defended my heritage. 'Like the Holocaust. That's pretty good proof of the 'shit happens' phenomenon. Why do you think they pick on the Jews first? It's because we're the ones who put on the brakes when everyone else goes crazy.'

'Now the Nazis? If you have to resort to them, it means I win, automatically.' She crossed her arms in mock defiance.

'By whose rules?' I played along.

'Mine, Mister Put-on-the-Brakes.'

'I'm no wuss, Carla.'

'Okay, then,' she said, turning back towards me, 'let's see you let go a little bit.' She kneeled on the seat so that her breasts were practically in my face.

'I know how to let go,' I defended myself.

'Oh really?' Carla hit the divider button with her toe and slowly pushed me down onto the seat in one fluid motion.

Her dominance disturbed yet aroused me at the same time. As she lay on top of me and kissed my neck, I felt myself getting the kind of hard-on I knew would demand immediate attention. I grabbed her hips and pulled her pelvis into contact with mine. She took the cue and slowly rocked up and down so as to stroke me through all our layers of clothes.

It was only a dry hump[196], but it felt glorious. I luxuriated in her hot breath and long hair against my face. She was like a cat of some kind, purring and growling as she pulled off my jacket and dug her teeth into my neck. All I wanted to do was come, and I started grinding faster beneath her.

'Not yet. Not like that,' she said, starting to unbutton my pants.

'I can't,' I stopped her. The car was no longer moving. 'Not here. Anyone could—'

'Come on,' she said, playfully pushing my hands away. 'Be a little naughty for once.'

'No, really,' I insisted over the silent, throbbing protest of my dick. 'The driver—we're in a car.'

'Okay, Jamie. But if you come upstairs I'm not letting you off easy,' she smiled sadistically.

I hurriedly signed the clipboard as Carla got out of the car.

'I got the paper for tomorrow's day,' the driver said, his end-of-shift grammar deterioration in full swing. 'It is in the pocket of the seat. That Birnbaum is a very sick man. Him, I hate more now—'

I tucked the paper under my arm and ran up the stairs after Carla. It felt good to chase someone, knowing she'd be mine in seconds. We got inside, pulled off each other's clothes and landed on her mattress. I pushed away the piles of company reports and trading data to make room for our bodies, both of us laughing through kisses at the volume of matter I needed to displace.

196. Frottage.   —Sabina Samuels

I worked my way down her body with my mouth. As I reached her navel, I could smell her excitement. But she didn't let me go down on her. Instead, she pulled me up by my shoulders until my face was directly over hers.

'Got a condom?' she asked, breathlessly.

I made no excuse for my presumptuousness as I reached for my pants and withdrew three connected squares of foil. I ripped one open with my teeth and rolled it down. Sometimes I'd go soft when I came in contact with the cold latex, but there was no danger of that now. My hard-on wasn't going anywhere but in.

'Wait,' she said. 'Get a cord.'

'A what?'

'By the computer. For me.'

I didn't know what to do.

'Come on, Jamie,' she taunted me. 'No holding back this time.'

Whatever. A cord. I went to her computer station and grabbed a serial cable. When I got back, she was rolled over on her stomach with her hands behind her.

'It's okay,' she said. 'I like it.'

I hadn't done this kind of thing before, but I wasn't about to argue. I wrapped the cord loosely around her wrists, and tied it in a bow so she'd be able to undo it herself if she wanted. She repositioned her wrists to make the cord more taut around them, then groaned with displeasure.

'Not a printer cable,' she whined. 'It's too thick. Too loose. Get a USB[197].'

197. A thinner wire, better suited for use as bondage.   —Sabina Samuels

Back to the computer desk. USB. Where? Scanner. Fine. I yanked the cord out, sending the flatbed to the ground with a thud. I was back in a flash, wrapping the cable around her hands like she was a calf in the pasture. Fast this time, which meant tight by default.

She moaned as I yanked the knot. It turned me on.

'Come on, Jamie,' she panted. 'It's okay. I'll say 'stop' if it's not. Just do it.'

Just do it, I did. I grabbed her hip with one hand and the hair at the nape of her neck with the other.

She arched her back up so I could slip inside her. The plastic between us numbed me to the wet warmth I knew I had entered. A latex insult to my manhood. I thrust with force to make up for the lack of sensation. Take *that*.

'Harder,' she said. '*Fuck* me.'

'I am,' I told her. 'You feel so good.' Wrong words. She was rolling her eyes.

'Come on, Jamie,' she said, grinding her teeth. 'I'm bad, right? You said so. I'm a bad girl. Show me how bad I am.'

I did as I was told, abandoning my image of her as a well-meaning neurotic, and remembering her at the Garden throwing darts at that poor kid. I wrapped an arm around her neck from behind, pulling her up against me, and using my knees to thrust up into her with short, pounding motions.

'I'll fuck you, you whore,' I heard myself saying. 'You evil, self-centered slut.'

'I'm sorry,' she said. 'I've been so bad.'

She had been bad, I agreed. I was the Inquisitor, now. Bringing this witch to justice. Did Jews have Inquisitors? Never mind. Catholics sure did. I thought of those naked dancers who fooled me that night around the campfire. She became every girl who teased me in high school. Every rich, blonde, preppie tart in college, who was too good for a middle-class public school Jew like me. That tall Monique, who made me take off my own shoes. I was fucking all of them now. A single networked woman. One creature, with millions of openings. They were all the same woman.

And Carla had given me entry. I could finally let go.

I felt myself about to burst, so I dug my teeth into Carla's shoulder—to hold it back. She began to writhe and twitch, leading me to clench my jaw even harder just to hang on.

'Jesus Christ!' she started shouting. 'Jesus Christ! Jesus Christ! Jesus Christ!' She began bucking like a wild animal, gritting her teeth, tugging at her bonds, swinging her head. Hair everywhere. It was like sailing through a tropical storm—and my clenched teeth were the only thing holding the mast upright.

Sex as the ultimate extreme sport. I was free, finally free to go as far as I wanted. I started to come.

Then Carla's head came crashing back into my face. Hard. I was thrown out of her, the harsh angle of exit ripping my condom in the process. I lay shocked on my back as my dick shot its load into the air.

'Jesus fucking Christ!' she screamed, wriggling free of the USB and grabbing at her shoulder. 'What the fuck do you think you're doing?'

She stared down at me and my pumping cock in disgust and horror. I grabbed it—both to capture my come as it shot wildly in all directions, and to protect my manhood from retribution.

'Why didn't you stop?' she yelled. There was blood on her fingers, and a trickle oozing from her shoulder. What had I done to her?

'I—I—' I gasped back at her as my semen gathered around my hands. My whole body was still throbbing in orgasmic pulses as I tried to speak. 'You didn't say 'stop.' You just said 'Jesus Christ." This was no way to climax, but it had built up so long that it just kept going on its own.

'Look at what you did to me, you creep!' She applied pressure to her wound, got out of the bed and stomped to the bathroom.

I let the last few pulses subside while Carla ran water in the sink and inspected her punctures in the mirror.

'I'm sorry,' I said, getting up and looking for somewhere to deposit my seed. I made my way towards the bathroom, holding the pearly puddle in my cupped hands. Even under the circumstances, I couldn't help but notice what a healthy portion I had produced.

'Gross! Get away from me!' she screamed. 'You sick bastard!'

I took my offering to the kitchen, instead, and dumped it into the garbage disposal. I ran the water over my palms but my semen just clung to my fingers like stringy mozzarella. A square of paper towel just made matters worse, adding patches of fibrous wadding to the mess.

Damn spot, indeed.

When I'd finally cleaned off my hands, I turned around to realize that the bedroom door had been closed. And locked.

'Carla. Open the door. Come on.'

No response.

'I'm sorry, okay?' I tried to sound non-threatening. Non-threatening to Carla—now, that's a laugh. 'I really thought you were into it.'

Nothing.

'You want me to go? Is that it? Huh? If it is, you gotta gimme my clothes, at least, all right? Can you do that?'

She opened the door without looking at me, and sat down on the bed. She let her robe drape over her shoulders, just to make sure I could see the injury I had inflicted. It was a bit shocking, actually, to think I was capable of drawing blood.

'I'll go, okay?' I said, putting on my boxers. 'I'll just get my stuff on and get out of here.' I continued to dress, gathering my clothes from the various places where they'd been thrown. That was the first time I saw the cover of the *Post* I'd taken from the limo.

A photo of an old man filled the page. He was on his hands and knees, sucking his thumb, and nude but for a diaper. Above the picture, in a blaringly *New York Post* headline font:

BABY BIRNBAUM

Below the picture, a red caption gloated, 'Fed Chief in Sex Scandal!'
'Holy shit,' I said.
Carla just exhaled loudly. Exasperated.
'No, Carla. The paper. Birnbaum. Jesus Christ.'
Carla turned her head, looked down at the photo, and sighed.
'You're all the same.'

11.   Eject

'Well, I guess this means we can save the rest of our advertising budget,' Alec quipped through my cellphone earpiece as I made my way through the streets towards I wasn't sure where, scanning the rest of the exposé as I walked.

Anonymous source. Authenticity verified. History of mental illness. Resignation expected. More pictures on page forty-seven.

'The poor man,' I said. He was. Such a vulnerable old thing, and so very publicly humiliated. In one of the enlarged photos in the two-page spread, I could make out the shadow of Birnbaum's erection through his diaper. Who had taken these pictures? And who sent them to the *Post*?

Then I remembered.

'Shit, Alec. You know who did this?'

'Who cares? He deserves it.'

'But it was your dad. Remember? He as much as said it. Page Six of the *Post*...'

'My dad didn't do it. You're crazy.' I could hear music playing in the background.

'I'm coming over.'

'I don't think that's a good idea right now. In your mood.'

'Fifteen.' I pushed the 'end' button.

With all the scenario planning I'd learned, I was surprised I hadn't seen any of this coming. I thought I'd mastered the game. But I was really just too far inside to see any of it from above. Somewhere along the way, I'd lost my perspective, and the game had become real.[198]

Alec owned a duplex on Central Park West that he'd inherited from his great aunt, along with a collection of early modernist paintings that was conveniently removed from her apartment when it came time to calculate the value of the estate, and then returned piece by piece as if to hide the tax evasion scheme from the doormen.

I had been there a few times before and the place always made me feel important by association. Though only about 900 square feet in total, the twelfth floor duplex had a forced grandeur about it—compounded by Gehry furniture, Mangold abstracts and a bright red metal Calder sculpture. The Eames stuff was the junk, here. Two floor-to-ceiling lead-paned windows overlooked the Park, and a balcony leading to the bedroom overlooked all that. The whole place was saying 'If you hang out here, you're suitable material for *Talk of the Town*[199].'

One of the building's two nighttime doormen operated the ornate, wrought iron elevator. Everything was beginning to look to me like symp-

198. It was the classic error of early hi-tech-era businesspeople. They didn't realize that the computer was simply a modeling tool—that it could model anything: a typewriter, a palette and canvas, a telephone, an electrical grid, a spleen, the weather, or a civilization.

They chose to model commerce, the economy, and the flow of capital. Perhaps the reason they descended into psychosis was that money was already a metaphor. Or, conversely, psychologists have hypothesized it was because money seemed so very real to people, and remained so closely tied to their instinct for survival. In any case, the better and more compelling the simulations got, the easier it was to mistake the map for the territory. The model of the market became the dominant reality, and reality itself became the game.

See Paulina Barsook's 'Cyberselfish,' 2000, or Jonathan Frokham's 'Capitalism and Consciousness,' 2005, for a detailed analysis of this pathology.
—Sabina Samuels

199. Obscure. Perhaps a television show.
—Sabina Samuels

toms of toxic wealth. There wasn't enough floor space, surface area, or time to display as much superfluous riches as these folks had accumulated. It wasn't a matter of purchasing more stuff—it was finding opportunities to show it off.

Even the elevator's original manual brass control column was historically authentic yet utterly preposterous. Its obsolescence demanded a hired hand—and that was its very value. This was the way of these people; any excuse for service. At least in my building, everything menial was done by computers. What did it mean when a human being could be so easily replaced by a machine? This guy was competing for the same job as a simple panel of buttons, and demanding a much higher salary. As far as the elevator operator's market value was concerned, only his tenants' aesthetic whim for a human servant kept him in the game. That, or his union[200].

I could hear the music and carousing from all the way down the hall. When Alec opened his door, I realized it was coming from inside his apartment.

'I told you it might not be a good time to come over.'

There must have been twenty of Manhattan's most social socialites in there, swilling Cosmopolitans and Chilean wine out of Alec's great aunt's crystal. Many were speaking foreign languages, too, though no one looked particularly foreign. I recognized one short woman as a gallery owner from Soho; another guy was from a slightly underground electronic band; there was that senator's kid who got in trouble for something-or-other; and the young British editor of one of New York's culture magazines. People mixing in suits, jeans, dresses, and one muscular guy with beads for a shirt and a gauze skirt.

And, seemingly at the center of them all, in a bright pink vinyl pant suit— Jenna Cordero.

200. "Union" as in "Labor Union." Unable to fend for themselves in the vicious and unfriendly workplace into which they willingly traipsed, human workers (drones, employees) within like industries banded together in an effort to extort higher sums of money from their employers (masters). The idea of a "labor union" first came into existence in the early part of the 20th century shortly after the height of the industrial revolution. The theory of the "union" was to allow all workers in like job classifications to benefit equally regardless of their skills or dedication to the employer. However, unions experienced many problems and the idea of the "union" as a good means of exacting a fair wage fell into disfavor in the mid 21st century when workers realized that after more than one-hundred years in this arcane system, they were really no better off in the scheme of society than had their forefathers been.
—MSCHLICKMAN

She recognized me immediately from the ranch. I stood there before her, speechless, as my mind raced to piece together the facts: Birnbaum. The ranch. Cabin Four. Feathers. Lines of coke. A money deal over something other than sex.

It was Alec all along.

'Thank you so much for coming,' Jenna said, holding out her limp hand. I was too stunned to shake it, much less kiss it. 'This is Jamie Cohen,' she announced my arrival to a young bald man in a maroon corduroy suit. 'Jamie helped make all this possible.'

'What possible?' I asked.

She laughed, and pushed her palm against my chest.

'The book,' she said. 'Haven't you heard? Henry here has decided to option the whole story, from my point of view.'

'For a book about Birnbaum?'

'For the rights to the story across all media,' Henry quickly clarified. He tapped his breast pocket, probably to make sure the contracts were still in there.

'I wonder what'll dry first,' I said. 'The ink or the blood?'

'What's your point?' Henry asked, ready to take me on.

'Come on, Jamie' Alec grabbed me by the elbow. 'Let's get you fixed up with a drink.'

'I don't want a fucking drink.'

He tugged harder on my arm. I relented, following him to the bar—my arms crossed and lips closed.

'Righteous indignation is so unbecoming, Jamie. And you haven't really earned it, now, have you?'

We were standing at the drinks table now. The tuxedoed bartendress could hear us, but I didn't care.

'Why did you do it?' I asked. 'The campaign was working. We were beating him fair and square. You didn't have to resort to his sex life.'

'That's what you're really upset about? Ezra Birnbaum? That I turned the picture over to the *Post*?'

'Well, yeah. I mean, I can understand you holding a grudge. He let your arm get crushed. But to set him up like that...'

'Oh, Jamie,' Alec said, sticking his fingers in the olive glass and then plopping an extra one into his martini. 'That's not what this is about. Don't you know that by now?'

'You fucked with that guy's life, Alec.'

'It's the way to play the game. No holds barred.'

'It's one thing to criticize his policies, it's another to...'

'A meaningless distinction, Jamie. To soothe your guilty conscience. Wanna paint me as the bad guy? Go ahead.'

'But we're in the same club with Birnbaum, now. You were at the Bull Run. These men trusted us.'

'And you're gonna let those old boy's party games affect the way you do business? Fuck their rules. The fraternity's over, my friend. Kids' stuff. The party is right here, right now. There's a new game in town. The rules are ours to make.'

'When did you decide all this? Have you planned this all along?'

Alec sipped his drink and tilted his head for moment—as if deciding whether to trust me with his story. Then he looked up and to the left,[201] retrieving the memory.

'It was back at the Bull Run, actually. Something I wouldn't even have been invited to if it wasn't for you. My dad only brought me for your sake. To keep you in line.' Alec took another swig. 'Funny. It wasn't you he should've been looking out for at all.'

271

201. Up and to the left would indicate that the subject was accessing the brain's memory center. According to NLP, which Cohen had apparently learned, this glance would suggest veracity. —Sabina Samuels

'You're not making any sense, Alec.'

'Yeah, I am. A lot of sense. Something became really clear to me that night. Maybe it was at the campfire, when they fooled us into thinking that guy was on fire.'

'Jesus, Alec, it was a joke.'

'Would your own dad do that to you? I can still hear them. Tobias and his old friends laughing at me. Everybody laughing, while I knelt there and puked. Me, always the butt of his big dick jokes. And you, his fucking savior.'

'I asked if you felt like—'

'It's not your fault, Jamie, okay? This is not about *you*, for once.'

I put my hands up in surrender. Alec looked out the window at the East Side skyline beyond the park. Behind us, a man with a French accent was describing his 'neo-post-modern' staging of Giselle at Lincoln Center.

'So, I brought Jenna back to the cabin. I was drunk, pissed, and sick, and couldn't get any wood up. So we did some lines, talked about stuff, and played with the laptop a while. I put in that black disk and we answered a bunch of Synapticom questions. About our tastes in music, clothes, and other stuff. It's really interesting what that does to you. 'Cause then I just looked at the girl, and knew exactly what I wanted from her.'

'To use her? Against Birnbaum?'

'I don't give a rat's ass about Birnbaum.'

'Against *who* then? Or what?'

Alec smiled. 'You know, Jamie, you really are a simpleton, sometimes.'

A heavy blonde woman wearing a flapper dress and a giant pearl necklace dipped backwards between us, as if being held by an invisible tango partner.

'*Quieres cantar o quieres beber?*' she asked, drunkenly. '*Yo tengo flores para los muertos.*' Then she swung back up.

'Elise just got back from Salamanca,' Alec excused her, laughing. He put

272

an arm on my shoulder. 'Come on, Jamie. Relax. It's all over now. Let's just have some fun.'

'Fun? How should I? You didn't even invite me to this party.'

'That's because I knew you couldn't handle it. That you'd be all freaked out about poor little Ezra. Right? Aren't you? Besides, you had your big sympathy date with Carla. You were doing your penance trip.'

'You could've at least kept me in the loop. Told me what you were doing.'

'You'd have tried to stop me. Or tattled to my dad. You're a spoilsport, Jamie. And that's even worse than a cheat. At least a cheater is trying to win.'

'What did you think I was going to do? I'm your friend, Alec.'

'Good, then. Prove me wrong by taking off your jacket, snorting a line, and having a great time with all these beautiful people. You might even get laid properly for a change. You have any idea who is here?'

I looked around the room at the assembled elite.

'Or go ahead and prove me right, Jamie. Stomp off in a petulant huff. Go hide out downtown in the luxury apartment we're paying for with the very same money that's buying the caviar here.'

The architect lit up a gold-colored cigarette as young man with a white silk scarf walked through the door. Jenna was laughing loudly about something, holding a delicate hand to her slender, exposed abdomen, and smiling unmistakably in my direction.

'This is it, Jamie. What you always wanted. The Major League.' He held out his hand and smiled. 'You up to it?'

The musician had popped in a video of himself on last night's MTV[202] awards, and a few future groupies were gathering around to watch on Alec's plasma screen. Elise-back-from-Salamanca was in a heated conversation with the senator's son about Sufism versus Kabbalah. That British editor of the New York culture magazine was walking towards me, now, holding a finger

202. A corporate effort at the commodification of youth culture, which used advertising as its content.
—Sabina Samuels

203. Within two centuries of its colonization by Europeans, the six-mile tract in the center of New York's Manhattan Island had been reduced to a wasteland of mosquito-infested pig farms and the primitive, unsanitary, meat-packing plants that processed their flesh for human consumption. In and around these facilities stood tin shacks housing workers and other lowlife too outwardly destitute, criminal, or insane for tenement domicile in any of the City's residential districts.

In 1840, the same year that English naturalist Charles Darwin published the first of his theories on evolution and the supremacy of the higher races, an American idealist and landscape architect by the name of Frederick Law Olmstead won a heated competition for the privilege of transforming these muddy fields into a pastoral refuge worthy of the New World's greatest metropolis.

'It is a democratic development of the highest significance and on the success of which, in my opinion, much of the progress of art and aesthetic culture in this country is dependent,' wrote Olmstead as he commenced the seventeen-year project. In an unparalleled effort to assert his vision of an egalitarian social paradise in harmony with nature, Olmstead's legions of human laborers used picks, shovels, and wheelbarrows to plant five hundred thousand trees and shrubs, build thirty bridges, dig eleven tunnels, and reconfigure five million cubic yards of earth.

Although the region's thousands of inhabitants were readily displaced, mother earth was entirely less cooperative. The craggy boulders she had pushed through her crust some 450 million years earlier proved absolutely immovable, forcing Olmstead to reposition his grassy knolls in a more accommodating fashion. Two decades later, 'rich and poor, young

note continues on page 275

to his temple as if he was trying to remember my name.

'Aren't you the new terror of Wall Street? From that piece in the *Journal*? My God, man, we've got to do a profile on you! Everybody wants to know just what makes a guy like you tick.'

I proved Alec right, and left the room without saying a word.

I hit the street running. I wanted to confess to someone. Or lodge a report. Seek justice. Go to the authorities. But to whom?

The buildings seemed to look down at me with malice. The streets were empty. It must have been after two in the morning. It was just me against the grid, and there was nowhere to hide from its Cartesian logic. Everywhere I went, I could be pinpointed exactly. Found out.

I went into the park. Nature.[203] No danger of crime in there, anymore, though. Wealth had brought this chaos into control. But the illusion was good enough.

I walked on darkened paths through the woods, and found a hilltop clearing with a little wooden bench. Bottles and condom wrappers were strewn about. Evidence of people having fun.

Just fucking a nice girl on that bench would have been so good. And so much easier than all the shit I was putting myself through. And for what? For money? For recognition? To prove something to my parents?

Everybody I knew in this world had a roof over his head, three meals a day, and a virtual guarantee of maintaining all this as long as necessary. So why were we driving ourselves insane?

Still, the first thing I did when I fell off the bench and woke up the next morning was check to make sure my wallet was still in my pocket. It was there, as was my cell phone, Palm Pilot, and my college ring. But I knew what I had to do. Quit this fucking job.

I worked my way downtown on Fifth Avenue at a good clip. I'd picked up a weird habit, whenever I felt tense, of mentally pricing the apartment houses on each block, pretending that I'd been given the right to take ownership of any single one of them. So I compared and contrasted each building based on size, location, state of repair, architectural significance, and so on. I needed to reach my final assessment by the end of the block, because once I crossed the street the whole process would begin again.

My little head game took my mind off the cattle in the street. A full third of the pedestrians and an even greater proportion of people in cars had the heads of bulls. A beggar in torn jeans was sharpening one of his horns against the side of a brick building[204].

The Coachmen's Club was on Fifty-second Street. I had never been inside, nor even nominated for membership, but this was an emergency. A lot of the old-timers still had brunch there on weekends. What I'd tell Tobias if I found him, I didn't know.

The white-gloved doormen made me write a note on Coachmen's Club stationery and wait on the street while they brought it inside on a small, silver tray. About ten minutes later, one of the attendants returned with the same envelope. Under Tobias's name was the typewritten message:

Not on the current register of the Coachmen's Club.

'Huh?' I said aloud, turning to one of the doormen. 'Tobias Morehouse. He's been a member here for thirty years. What do they mean?'

'I'm sorry, sir,' the doorman said. 'He is not listed in the current register.'

'But I've got to see him. He's always here on weekends. Tobias Morehouse. You know him. You must.'

The bull-headed doorman stepped away from me, retaking his original position.

and old, Jew and Gentile' frolicked alike in this simulated paradise of inter-species and inter-racial equality. By the Twentieth Century, most of the city's residents thought of Central Park as the only unscathed surface of their island, fully ignorant of the battle men waged there against nature, in what were thought to be her best interests.   —Sabina Samuels

204. These comments most likely refer to the deep divide among humans of that time in their opinions of animals, with their simultaneous affection and contempt for same. It is likely that the author meant to express contempt for the humans around him, by comparing them with so-called "lesser" beings.
  Alternatively, it is possible that the comments refer to the people around the author actually wearing the symbol of the late stages of the decline of capitalism, namely the Foam Hat[a].   —XGRRRL

a. Foam Hat: A theory truly characteristic of the NeoRationalist school of thought, which continues against all evidence[b] to variously dismiss the phenomenon of zoomorphic avatars (Moskva Serpents, the Otter Women of Reykjavik, etc.) as masks, holograms or coffee hallucinations.   —RAYGIRVAN

b. evidence: True, such "evidence" as the recently decoded so-called "documentary[c]" Clash of the Titans, while sufficient for the NeoMystical camp, is not considered adequate proof of said phenomenon by many true scholars.   —XGRRRL

c. so-called "documentary:" Some scholars feel this kind of skepticism has gone too far. What historical text will be doubted next, they wonder—Splash?
   —RAYGIRVAN

I didn't know what to do. I scrolled through the names on my cell phone, and auto-dialed Brad, at home. It was a machine.

'Damn it.' I sunk down onto the curb. I put my head in my hands and waited for tears, but none came.

'Hey, kid.' It was an older doorman, a tall black man, and the only one who didn't have the head of a bull. I looked at the old man's face and had a strange thought. Was this sad soul once the poor busboy who had been forced to measure his penis against Morehouse's all those years ago? He almost seemed to nod, as if he knew what I was thinking. 'Try the airfield.'

I shrugged off the moment of magical recognition as if it were a flash of paranoia or, at best, déjà vu, hopped into a yellow cab and rehearsed my resignation speech. The cost in human suffering is just...no. My effectiveness has been compromised by...no. Your son, Alec...no.

I didn't owe any explanations. Not to Morehouse, anyway. The cab driver was a different story, however, and I had to spend most of the trip directing him first to the West Side Highway and the GW bridge, and then all the way to Teterboro Airport.

As unemployment went down, so, too, did customer service. The graphs followed each other as closely as the relative value of linked currencies. The easier it was to get a job, the less competently all jobs were performed—as amply demonstrated by this clueless hack. But what was the answer? Keep people afraid of losing their jobs? And how do you make people fear for their livelihoods in a climate of zero unemployment?[205] I guess if the cab driver were financially invested in his cab company, this wouldn't be a problem. But then would he feel this same, weird hunger all the time, too?

Morehouse's Stormovick Ilyushin II was parked on the far corner of the airfield. A two-man ground crew readied the bulky green craft for flight, while Morehouse checked the propeller and flaps. I paid the cabbie and

205. In the late capitalist phase, it had not occurred to people that the enjoyment of doing a job well, or fulfilling a societal role, might yield a sense of satisfaction in itself. They were not to blame, however, since most workers had no way, yet, of appreciating how their efforts contributed to a greater whole.
—Sabina Samuels

276

crossed the tarmac. Up close, the Soviet strafing plane looked huge and menacing. The fuselage was over ten meters long, and the wingspan close to fifteen meters wide. Its nose was round, bulbous, and distended like a diseased liver, but the gun barrels protruding from every imaginable crevice gave the old girl an air of authority.

'One last ride?' Tobias asked. He knew I had come to quit.

'No, sir, thanks. I just wanted to let you know that—'

'That you're sorry?' Tobias slipped on his leather helmet and began to climb up a ladder to the cockpit[206]. 'I saw the paper, Jamie. We all saw the paper. It's all over now. Don't worry, I forgive you.'

'*You* forgive *me*?'

'You boys have no idea what you've done, do you?'

'It wasn't me!' I shouted up to Tobias as he strapped himself in.

'I can't hear you, Cohen. Get in or good-bye.' He started up the engine. The last thing I needed was a joyride in a Soviet fighter plane, especially with a pilot as maniacal as Morehouse was acting, but I couldn't let the old man go on believing whatever it was he believed. I climbed up the ladder and took the seat next to Tobias.

'Put this on,' he said, handing me a mask and headset. 'And strap yourself in.'

As I fumbled with the leather straps, Tobias pulled a lever, lowering the glass canopy over our heads and locking it into place. He jerked the old craft into motion, swerving back and forth across the airfield, struggling to steer the machine towards the runway.

'Hang on,' Tobias said as he centered on the broken white line.

He flipped a few switches on the dash and pulled back on a long metal throttle. The plane jolted forward as the engine roared. The rivets in the steel-plated hull vibrated along with the fillings in my teeth[207] as we ser-

206. Pilot's seating area. Origin obscure, most likely sexist.   —Sabina Samuels

207. Glucose consumption had led to widespread tooth decay. Toxic metals were used to patch the crevices left by bacteria.   —Sabina Samuels

pentined precariously down the jetway, gaining speed. Then there was a tremendous thud—one of the wheels had rolled off the tarmac onto the grass. We wobbled back and forth, the wings practically flapping as they creaked. Through sheer force of will, Tobias managed to get the craft aloft before it crashed into a concrete barrier.

'Close one!' Tobias shouted at me through the plane's communications gear.

'Ilyushin 23 Whiskey. You're clear for a heading of 07 at 8000 feet,' said a voice from ground control.

'Ilyushin 23. Heading 07 at 8000, roger,' Tobias acknowledged, as he steered in an absurdly vertical trajectory towards the prescribed heading.

I felt my eardrums straining to adjust to the sudden pressure change, but concentrated on the more pressing urge to release the contents of my stomach into my mask. I clutched the metal bars over my head and hung on for dear life.

'Just a little G-force, kid,' Tobias said. 'It'll be over in a minute.'

In a minute that seemed like much, much longer, Tobias overshot his intended altitude, then pushed forward on the yoke. The tail suddenly flipped up behind us until we were pointing almost directly downward. Then the engine cut out.

'Ahh, shit,' Tobias said. 'We lost power.'

After a brief moment of peaceful silence, the plane began to freefall, nose first. I could see the ground approaching from straight ahead, and then sky. We were rolling, now. My lips automatically mouthed the words of the sh'ma prayer as Tobias flicked switches and pulled on levers.

The engine coughed and spit, then coughed and spit again. Then, the unmistakable descending trombone slide of the plane accelerating downward against the wind.

'Come on, you bastard!' Tobias stamped his feet.

He flicked another switch, and the plane suddenly roared to life again. Tobias looked surprised, then peered around, as if to get his bearings. The glass canopy showed sky, then ground, then sky again. Tobias stared at the instrument panel as he steered right and left, pulling the yoke into his chest, and the plane directly upwards towards the sun.

'There we go!' Tobias shouted, pushing the yoke slowly forward and leveling out the plane. He flicked another switch on the instrument panel. 'Ground control, this is Ilyushin 23 Whiskey. We are at 8000 feet heading 07.'

'Whiskey 23! Jesus Christ! Are you guys okay?' a panicked voice from the ground broke protocol.

'Just testing the handling,' Tobias said, calmly. 'We'll catch you on the return.'

'Whiskey 23. Have a good flight,' the voice responded, amidst the sounds of a number of other voices cursing.

'Nothing like a little power outage to put the fear of God back in you, eh, Cohen?'

I couldn't speak.

'I thought we'd head out to the Catskills for a little look-see,' Tobias said. 'Your family probably takes vacations out there, huh? The Concord Hotel?'

I nodded.

'The Ilyushin 2 was an attack plane, you know.' Tobias patted the war-stained dashboard. 'Soviet's built a ton of them in the early forties. Not for air to air battles as much as strafing targets on the ground. Their first real armored fighter. But it had a real design flaw. They had no idea until they brought her out against the Germans over the Berezina River. They destroyed a whole series of munitions targets, but got chased off by some

Nazi combat planes. This was the Ilyushin's Achilles heel—there was no way to look behind you as you ran. They got pulverized from the rear. That's when they put in the extra seat. Yours turns around so you can shoot behind you.'

'Hmph,' I instinctually nodded approval of the modification.

'That would have been your job, Cohen. Or Alec's. To watch for attacks from the rear.'

'Are you trying to tell me something?' I hoped Tobias would get to the point, if there was one.

'See, a plane like this has the advantage, Jamie. It attacks from above. Like a bear.'

Tobias flipped open a metal bracket, revealing a red button on the control column. He put his thumb on the button and pressed. A set of gun turrets under either wing began to fire.

'Stop! There's people down there!'

'Don't worry, Cohen. I'm just running some empty chain.'

I looked back at one of the guns as a metal belt circled through it.

'People think an attack from above is unfair,' Tobias said. 'But I think it's more honorable, in a way. Dive down from above. They see you coming. More honest than from below, know what I'm saying?'

'No, sir, I don't.'

'It's why they call stock buyers bulls, get it? A bull attacks from the ground up. It gores you from below, and throws you up. A bear mauls you from above. From up on his hind legs, coming down at you.' He took his hands off the wheel to demonstrate.

'I wasn't the one who set up Birnbaum, sir.' I pleaded as if my life depended on it—which, for all I knew, it could have.

'I always figured you two were a couple,' Tobias said. 'I saw the way he looked at you. Even that first week on the Vineyard.'

'We weren't—'

'I learned to live with it. Some of the most powerful men in the world are fags. Forbes was a fag.'

'Mr. Morehouse—'

'I told myself, at least Alec found a nice Jewish boy.' Tobias laughed out loud.

'I'm not gay.'

'I don't care, Cohen. That's the least of it. Homosexuality I can deal with. It's the rest that really killed me.'

I could see the mountain range appearing in the distance.

'I looked for you at the Coachmen's Club,' I said. 'They said you weren't a member.'

'Yeah, well, you boys crossed the line and someone had to pay. They never wanted me there, anyway.'

'You don't need those guys, Mr. Morehouse. You've got a real business. With real revenues.' I felt like I was talking him out of suicide.

'I don't give a fuck about that. It was all for Alec, anyway.'

'That's why you're upset?'

'He got me, kid. Don't you get it? My own son. He wasted me, good. He hates me that much.'

'He loves you, Mr. Morehouse. He thought you were laughing at him.'

'Christ, I wasn't laughing at him. I was happy for him. I got him in the game. That's the only reason I hired you, anyway. For Alec. He doesn't have the hunger you do.'

'Oh, he's got the hunger, all right. You gave him that.' I felt responsible for finding Morehouse a reason to live. 'Maybe, with me gone, it'll be easier for you two.'

'Nah. He's made his point.'

Tobias maneuvered the plane towards the highest of the Catskill's peaks. I no longer trusted subtext.

'I'm a young man, Mr. Morehouse. You can't make this kind of decision for me.'

'Still clinging to life? That's a good sign.'

'Look,' I tried to restore order. 'I came here to resign my position. Not to die. I want out.'

'Out of what, Cohen? Where you gonna go?' He had a point.

'I don't know. I really don't care. I just want to go back.'

'Suit yourself, kid,' Tobias said, pulling back a lever and opening the glass canopy. I flinched against the cold wind as the snowy peak approached.

'What are you doing?' I felt my anus contracting spasmodically. I was terrified.

'I signed the TeslaNet commission over to you, Jamie. The papers are on your desk. That's two million dollars in your pocket. Should let you boys get started on something else.'

'Thanks,' I said, 'but I really am quitting.'

'I know you are, boy. I know you are. Just remember to bend your knees when you hit the ground.'

With that, Morehouse reached down and pulled a lever at the base of my seat. Nothing happened. He looked perplexed for a moment, then raised his arm and slammed his fist down on my shoulder. That did it.

My chair disengaged from the hull, swinging me backwards and up through the canopy, into the cold air. I ascended in a wide arc over the plane—still strapped into my seat. I reached an apex. It was lovely up there, in a way. And then I started to fall, face forward, toward the ground. Oh shit. This is it. I frantically kicked my feet, trying to right myself.

A parachute. There must be a parachute on this thing, I told myself as I fumbled with the cushion strapped to my back, searching desperately for a ripcord. Nothing.

This is just a dream, I concluded, closing my eyes, and waiting for that light-headed feeling I'd get just before waking up from this sort of otherworldly predicament. But however hard I tried I couldn't break free of the illusion. Because it wasn't an illusion. No, I wouldn't have thought to include the painful details, like the freezing friction of the wind against my unprotected neck, or the burning in my nose.

This was a real-world predicament. I was going to die. I gave up. Strangely, all I could think about were those condoms and beer bottles in the park, and the kinds of people who used them. The people who were fucking at that very moment, just for the sheer joy of it. They were the true masters of the game.

Then, through no effort of my own, the seat slowly released a huge clump of matter into the air, attached by four yellowed strands of rope. I prayed for the contraption to hold together as the lines went taut—my mortal existence depending on the engineering know-how of the same Soviets at whom Uncle Morris had tossed eggs back in the seventies. Then the white chute opened, yanking me upwards so violently that my shoulders were pulled from their sockets.

Then, peace. I swung back and forth like a pendulum as the pup-tent of silk above me billowed in the wind. Only then did I look down at the ground rising fast from beneath me. There were farms, houses, roads, and cars. Human beings going about their daily tasks, absolutely unaware of my aerial approach. I was nearing a field, with rows of neatly planted green leaves. Lettuce? Alfalfa? I had time to muse. But I was also being carried sideways by the wind—and so rapidly that I feared I might miss the flat ground alto-

283

208. A highly dramatized quasi-fictional biography, *The Morehouse Legacy*, by William Shulgin, is the only account we have of Morehouse's decision to abort his suicide attempt:

'Tobias pulled the canopy shut and secured the metal lever. He looked up, and saw Jamie careening into the sky. He'd be fine, poor kid. Tobias had checked the chutes just last week, when he had the ejection modification installed. Fully automated, nitrogen-propelled ejector seats weren't put into use until jets replaced props during the Korean War. But Tobias knew his flying skills weren't what they used to be, and saw the ability to conduct an emergency bail-out as a sign of strength, especially when it meant sacrificing an entire aircraft in the process.

'But he had no intention of ejecting, now. Quite the contrary. He was in this one to the finish. No turning back.

'He aligned the nose of the plane towards the peak of the mountain in front of him, then flipped a switch on the dashboard, instructing the aircraft to hold its heading and altitude even if he took his hands off the yoke.

'He squinted a bit but kept on watching as the jagged plane of rock and snow grew larger in his windscreen.

'This was real, he told himself. Not one of those silly games those pansy-assed rich kids played with one another at the club. Not even the combat-once-removed of the market could compare with the ball-busting terror of a real blood and guts battle to the death.

'Sure, they used phrases like 'catch a falling knife' or 'punishing ride,' but they'd never tasted anything close. Not any of them. He'd like to see Marshall Tellington catch a falling knife, sometime.

'They weren't even in the real market, or playing with real money. Their inherited houses in the Hamptons were safe no matter what they did. If they had any actual skin in the game they'd piss their

note continues on page 285

gether and land in the dense forest at the field's edge.

I grabbed the canvas straps attaching my chairback to the parachute's ropes, hoping to steer myself towards a safe landing spot. It had no effect, but then the wind shifted, even seeming to gust up at me from below. A force of nature had taken me into its care, slowing my descent as I returned to the earth.

As I felt the impact on my feet, I followed Tobias's advice and then some, bending my knees and running forward at the same time. I managed to remain upright for a moment, then fell face down into the dirt. I felt a sharp pain in my mouth. I had chipped a tooth against my cell phone and cut open my lip in the process, but I was very much alive.

A pair of farmers had dismounted a tractor and were running toward me, screaming obscenities. I scanned the horizon for signs of Morehouse—a plume of smoke, even, where he went down. But there was nothing. Perhaps he had changed his mind.[208]

12. End Game.

The farmers called the cops, who gave me some gauze for my lip, took down my story, and dropped me at a bus stop in Woodstock. A hippie[209] couple in Tibetan ski caps and tie-dyed t-shirts sat on the bench eating dried apricots from a brown paper bag. A tiny baby in a blue pouch hung from the man's chest[210].

The sun setting over the Catskills made it difficult for me to scan the mountain peaks for evidence of debris or rescue vehicles. If Morehouse had gone down, surely the cops would have said something.

'Isn't it just beautiful?' the woman asked.

'Huh?'

'I couldn't help but notice you taking in the scenery,' she said.

panties.

'And Alec, well, he'd get on fine. He was inheriting everything, eventually. And he wasn't really a pansy. Not like them. No, Alec put a little blood back in their sport and they all went crying home to mommy. He was the real man—a Morehouse, through and through.

'As the mountain peak approached, Tobias could feel the blood pumping through his veins the way it had when he was a kid. Back when he'd fly one of these babies for real. He was alive, again, and it felt good.

'Then he sensed something strange. A pressure in his groin he hadn't felt in over twenty years. Good God! He had a hard on! After all this time.

'He unzipped his pants to regard his legendary tool. It craned up from his lap like a great Aztec god, dwarfing everything around it. Finally. A reason to live!

'Morehouse looked up at the solid wall of snow. He gritted his teeth and flipped off the auto-pilot with one hand and pulled back on the yoke with the other. The plane lurched upwards, missing the mountain peak by less than four feet. Tobias was alive.'   —Sabina Samuels

209. Originally an anti-war movement of the 1960's, "hippie" was a term used to describe anyone whose lifestyle choices involved a combination of cannabis, unprocessed food, and natural fiber clothing.   —Sabina Samuels

210. More evidence of a recent genesis for the manuscript: how could an author of 2004 know the precise appearance and location of the venous external uterus used in male pseudopregnancy?   —RAYGIRVAN

'Oh. Yeah. It's quite a panorama.'

'It's good—you taking the bus into the city. We always do. To save the environment.'

'Every ounce of petrochemicals spared is another minute of ozone longer,' the man added.

'You're from these parts, then?' I asked in a quickly appropriated pastoral tone.

'Not originally,' the woman answered. 'Steven and I moved up from Trenton when we got pregnant.'

'That's sweet of you to include me, honey,' Steven said, putting his hand on her belly. 'But you did all the work.'

They kissed.

'Was it hard to relocate up here?' I was half-considering a change of lifestyle. 'You don't commute, do you?'

'Heavens, no,' Steven said. The baby was pulling at his beard. 'We started a web-site. LivingInSimplicity.com. Showing other people how to make the kinds of changes in their lives that we did.'

'There's a lot to it,' the woman explained. 'Buying land, building a house, installing solar panels, back-up generators, organic soil.'

'Sounds expensive,' I said, estimating the amounts in my head.

'Cost us two million dollars, all told, to get down to our current level of simplification,' nodded the man. 'We had to take out a series of loans. And that doesn't even include the high-speed radar dish, food storage units, water purification equipment, radon detection and venting, eco-farm machinery, and, of course, home security and defense.'

'Defense?'

'We're pacifists,' said Steven. 'The weaponry and shelters are just in case,' he winked.

'Right,' I winked back at the Granola Militia member. 'And you're making money?'

'Follow your bliss and the universe will conspire to help you,' the woman beamed. 'We've been sharing our formula with others, bringing the joys of simplicity to their lives, and then they share it with their loved ones, too. It's a virtuous circle[211].'

'Multi-level marketing?'

'No, not at all!' she said. 'We call it network marketing, because there's no hierarchy. Everyone gets the same tools to bring prosperous simplicity into their lives.'

'We sell a kit showing people how to make their own LivingInSimplicity web sites,' Steven explained. 'The network has over a thousand nodes to date.' The baby began to squirm in its pouch. The woman took it from Steven so he could finish explaining their revenue model.

'Whenever their customers purchase a solar panel or organic rain forest lumber home-building kit, we get ten percent. It's very Zen. The more simplicity that gets brought into people's lives, the more simplicity we can afford to bring into our own!'

I didn't have the heart to explode their vision of a sustainable consumer paradise, and chose a seat far away from them on the back of the bus. The smell of disinfected human waste in the lavatory was preferable to contemplating the ecological devastation inflicted by well-meaning devotees of the simplicity movement. Tobias was right. There was no escape.

I managed to drift into a kind of sleep—not deep enough to recharge, but spacey enough to have dreams. In one, Carla sat on a throne, wearing a crown and directing scores of naked, muscular eunuchs. Then I saw myself on the *Jerry Springer Show*[212] wrestling my sister down to the floor as the audience chanted 'Jerry! Jerry!'

211. This passage seems to refer to the Ideology of Karen and Stuart Smithson. It is not clear whether or not the author actually crossed paths with the couple or if he merely alludes to them in this vague recounting of a conversation with strangers. If this manuscript has been correctly dated around 2008 then he would have met them just before they began calling followers to their compound in southern Oregon. By 2020 the Simples, as they called themselves, had begun the first powerful private space campaign. Narrative outlines of their innovations are seen in the now infamous State Licensed. They describe an intense struggle with federal regulators who instantly succumbed when offered the chance to man a future test mission. Aside from the occasional federal joyride, the Simples launched children of all countries into space free of charge[a].   —SEEWARD

a. the Simples launched children of all countries into space free of charge: This annotator is omitting the central controversial aspect: in the initial stages of the Simples project, the trip often proved to be one-way.   —RAYGIRVAN

212. A form of television entertainment in which overweight actors, pretending to be real people, would fight physically over adulterous mates.   —Sabina Samuels

Then I was on the floor of the commodities exchange, trying to push through a crowd of screaming traders. They were gathered around one of the pits, yelling like cowboys. I shoved my way to the front row, to see what was going on down in the pit. Tobias was there, his back to me, on his knees. He was tying up a young bull. Then Tobias turned to me, and offered me a long knife. I took it and knelt down beside him. As I brought the knife to the bull's scrotum, I realized it had a human head. It was my own terrified face staring back at me.

I drew myself out of the trance by focusing on the stench from the lavatory. I wasn't sure where I was, or where I was going. Just to make sure the events of the past day were real, I felt in my shirt pocket for the tiny zip-lock plastic bag holding the chip of tooth recovered by the police. It was there. My collar was blood-soaked. The cut on my lip just wouldn't stop bleeding.

It was already past noon when I hailed a cab outside the Port Authority to Beth Israel Hospital. Teslanet, Synapticom, M&L and everyone else could wait. I had reached the bottom of Maslow's hierarchy of needs. Sutures before futures.

The Chinese resident stitched me up with a perfunctory scorn. She probably figured I was in a bar fight. Another wealthy American succumbing to the decadence of our amoral society. A generation ago it would have been a Jewish resident stitching up a WASP. To have an MD[213] in the family used to be the highest form of naches. Now it seemed like a service profession. An auto mechanic, playing higher stakes. A dermatological seamstress. But at least she did something real for a living.

The tooth itself would have to wait until Monday, since it didn't constitute emergency surgery. She signed some forms in triplicate and told me to wait outside for my number to be called by the cashier.

There were at least thirty people and a few bulls ahead of me, but I was

213. "Medical Doctor." Certification to practice medicine required indoctrination by accepted academies. —Sabina Samuels

too tired to calculate how long it would take me to get to the window at an average of two minutes per person. Oh. Sixty minutes. I couldn't help myself.

I closed my eyes, imagining the possibility of getting a few hours of legitimate shut-eye in my double-paned urban womb of a home once this was over. Home. Right. How long would I even get to keep it now that I was quitting M&L? And how would I pay for whatever place I moved to? And what about my reputation? Wasn't there anything I could take from this whole nightmare? TeslaNet. Oh yeah. Two million in cold cash for selling out my friends. Better than nothing.

Then my attention turned to suppressing a fart—made all the more difficult by the jiggling of the chair attached to mine. An old man was restlessly finding a more comfortable position for his skinny buttocks.

'Did I wake you, Jamie?' he said. Holy shit. It was Ezra Birnbaum. 'I tried to be quiet when I saw you sleeping here.'

I was too stunned to speak.

'You hurt yourself?' Birnbaum asked gently.

'It's nothing. Just cut my lip. Four stitches.' The leftover local anesthetic made me slur my words. I must have sounded like a drunkard.

'Well, I'm glad it's not serious. I'll say a mishaberach[214] for you, anyway.'

'Thanks, Mr. Birnbaum.' Why was Ezra being so nice to me?

'You really do look awful, son. You were in a fight or something?'

'Or something. It's been a hard week.'

'Tell me about it,' Birnbaum agreed.

'What are you in for?' I asked, as if we were cellmates.

'My daughter. She's in labor. Going on thirty hours now.'

'Mazel tov,' I said. 'At least it gives you something to take your mind off—' I stopped myself, bracing for an uncomfortable pause. Birnbaum had enough congeniality for the both of us.

214. A Jewish healing prayer, based on the words uttered by their prophet Moses when his sister contracted leprosy after making a racial slur about his wife. It was thought that reciting these words would convince God to use his omnipotence to arrest infirmities.   —Sabina Samuels

'It's a blessing, yes.'

I had to speak my mind before I burst.

'Look, Mr. Birnbaum, I just have to let you know how sorry I am about—'

'The picture? Don't worry about it.'

'No, really,' I insisted. 'I'm sorry for the whole thing. The ads, the PR campaign. You were right all along.'

'I was right? About what?' He raised his eyebrows and smiled.

'Everybody's gone mad. What did you call it? Frenzied Paroxysms?'

Birnbaum laughed. 'You liked that one? I knew it would get airplay.'

'But it's true. Everybody is in it now. Total mania.'

'And you feel responsible for that?'

'Kind of,' I admitted.

'Nonsense. These things happen.'

'How can you be so relaxed about all this?'

Ezra pulled a bottle of pills from his pocket.

215. An anti-depressant medication. People who couldn't lower their ethical standards to accepted levels took drugs to alleviate their guilt and associated symptoms.   —Sabina Samuels

'See this? My doctor finally put me on Zoloft[215] a couple of months ago. We had a hard time regulating the dose. Too much and I got a little antsy. Too little, and it didn't break the depressive cycle. And that's when it hit me. I'm really just the economy's psycho-pharmacologist. Keep enough cash going through the pipes for people to be optimistic, and for the economy to grow at a steady pace. Not too much, or the pace of growth gets manic, and we get inflation. Not too little, or borrowing becomes difficult and we get a recession.'

'But the economy's not just psychology, Mr. Birnbaum. It's a real thing. Capital grows companies.'

'No, no. It's just a model, Jamie. Relax. No one knows how it really works. Certainly not since we went off the gold standard, or since international markets. Macro-economics is a religion, son, not a science. It's all about mood. That's the point. My job is—well, *was*—to keep it stable. Not to solve the world's economic problems, but to prevent them from getting out of hand. Through careful regulation.'

'But doesn't the free market bring about the most equitable distribution of wealth? That's what they taught us in school—that the most open system finds the greatest stability, just as it does in nature.'

'The market isn't nature, Jamie. Who told you that? Even if it were, you think nature promotes the survival of the fittest? Evolution leads to many situations that are far from optimal. If nature led to survival of the fittest, how'd we end up with Microsoft Windows[216] on our computers?'

'Microsoft cheated. That's why they were taken to court. To make them play by the rules.'

'And who enforces those rules in nature, Jamie? God?'

'You can't cheat nature,' I said with conviction.

'Of course you can. That's what civilization is for. To prevent the young from conquering the old, or the strong from displacing the weak. Until the strong and young are so weak and old that they come to depend on the same laws, themselves. The game is to cheat nature. Laws maintain the status quo. And you know who's responsible for the law?'

'Who?'

'Us Jews, Jamie.'

'Come on.'

'No, really,' Birnbaum said. 'Our Talmudic laws are the ones on which the US legal system is based. We weren't allowed to own land, so we became brokers and transaction specialists. Lawyers and bankers.'

'But we're not the ruling class. I mean, Jews are wealthier than some, but we're not part of the ultra-rich. We never were. My grandfather came here penniless.'

216. The Microsoft Windows operating system, in spite of its cumbersome interface and many flaws, was still the predominant PC platform until as late as 2014.
—Sabina Samuels

'I'm sure he did. Probably came over in a hurry, no? And why do you think we get run out of so many places? Babylonia? Spain? Germany? Because we're God's chosen?'

'Why then? Because we're perpetrating some great conspiracy?' I was getting exasperated.

'Because we show people the reasons why they should leave well enough alone. Tame their natures. The Jewish experience is meant to instruct people not to run wild.'

'And that's an important lesson,' I said. 'We're the world's moral guardians. Sometimes even martyrs.'

'Isn't it pretty to think so?' Birnbaum smiled. 'I used to be like you, thinking of the Jewish people like the canaries in a coal mine. That we're sacrificed for the world's sake. The first defense against fascists. But take a look at it from the goy[217] perspective. Jews, as a rule, enjoy nice, white, upper-middle-class lives. More money than we'd normally be entitled to as a disenfranchised Middle Eastern people with no real assets, living in a foreign land.'

'The Jews do well because we stress education. We work hard.'

'Sure we do. But to what end? We develop the systems that allow a handful of royals or supremely rich people to maintain their power. We're middle management. Bankers, tax collectors. We keep a few figureheads as wealthy as pigs[218]. It's a small expense to us, given the numbers. They're so stupid from all the in-breeding and trust funds that they're easily manipulated. And their wealth and power keep us from looking like the real winners.'

'My grandmother marched with Eugene Debs, the labor leader. Back then, Jews were communists. Activists.'

'Well, sure. We were new here. And poor. But once we rose, we started to play a different role. To keep things the way they are. Growing steadily,

217. Literally, Hebrew for "people." Why Jews used this term to denote non-Jewish people is unknown. —Sabina Samuels

218. A strange and inaccurate simile. Not only were pigs unable to own property in 2004, but they had a reputation for filth and indiscriminate consumption, unfairly gained by being kept as food animals under forced conditions. —RAYGIRVAN

but slowly enough to prevent any real change—all under the guise of social responsibility. You think that housing projects promote class fluidity? Welfare merely institutionalizes poverty. Just as a slow, steady, regulated economy institutionalizes wealth.'

'The purpose of regulation is to protect competition.'

'No, Jamie, it's to *prevent* competition.'

I no longer knew what I was arguing for. Ezra had run circles around me.

'Did you think this way before you started the Zoloft?' I couldn't hold back my sarcasm.

'Honestly, Jamie, it was your commercial that made me see it. All those people fighting for their right to participate in the free market. To get in the game. And my words keeping them out. I thought to myself, why not let them have their cake and eat it, too?'

'But you really don't believe all that stuff about Jews pandering to the rich to maintain our own position in society, do you?'

'Why? You think you're exempt, Cohen?'

'I don't think I'm a part of what you're talking about. No.'

'Then why are you working for Morehouse, anyway? Because you have so much faith in your own ideas? Your TeslaNet invention? You sold your one real property—your one genuinely novel idea—you gave it to Marshall Tellington the first chance you had. And he has no intention of bringing it to market. He's paying you millions just to prevent that from happening.'

'That's different.'

'How?'

I had no ready answer. But I'd get my two million dollars whether I had one or not. I could always repent later. Or give some to charity. Half, even. After taxes.

'Look, Cohen, maybe you're different. I can't judge you. All I know is I spent my whole life worrying about planks falling on people's heads. About disasters waiting around every corner. Nobody thanked me for it, and I'm sick to death of it. Let 'em walk off a cliff if they want to. It's not my problem, anymore. I'm going to be a grandfather.'

They called my number. I left the fallen titan to his Zoloft-induced bliss, paid my bill and headed for the subway, keeping my eyes on the pavement to avoid any hallucinations. Maybe my dentist could recommend a good shrink.

As I got to the stairs, the cracked cell phone in my pocket bleated a pathetic half-ring. I pushed 'talk.'

'Hello?'

I could hear static on the other end. Then my mother's voice.

'I don't hear anything. I think it's his machine.'

'Hello?' I shouted. 'Can you hear me?'

Then my dad's voice in the background. 'Maybe he's on his way.'

'I'm here! Hello?!' My mouthpiece was dead. I hit 'end.'

My parents. Shit. I'd forgotten all about them. The vote would be starting at sundown. I had to be there. I wasn't about to let my dad go down like Alec's. And I knew just how to save him.

I bought a generic shirt on Fourteenth Street to replace my bloody Armani, and phoned home from the subway platform to let them know I was on my way. Then I called Greco and told him to meet me at my parents' house with one of his shiny black disks. The Whitestone Temple was about to get its own taste of reactive architecture.

Miriam answered the door, all smiles.

'Hi, beautiful,' I said, covering my mouth with my hand. Miriam always noticed everything.

She looked down and twirled one of her black curls around her finger. I gently kissed her, and then put out my elbow to escort her into the living room.

'Your shirt is stiff,' she said. 'And your lip is fat.'

Everyone had shown up for the big day. Mom, Dad, Miriam, Morris, Estelle and Benjamin. I was mentally concocting a lie about what had happened to my mouth, but luckily my entrance and wound were upstaged by another controversy, already in progress.

Benjamin had been sent home early from school on Friday with an order from the principal that he receive an emergency psychological evaluation.

'Can they do this?' Samuel was asking.

'They have to,' answered Benjamin's worried mother, Estelle. 'Once a student has been reported, the school has a legal obligation to conduct an investigation before they let him back in the classroom.'

'But who reported him?' I jumped in. 'And for what?'

Benjamin sat on the arm of one of the sofas, trying to pretend he wasn't there.

'The other children!' shouted Morris. He was nervously fumbling with the change in his pocket. 'It's some new program. They're supposed to watch each other, now. What are they, spies?'[219]

Over the past couple of weeks, Benjamin had missed his after-school activities and displayed an anti-social demeanor. Making matters worse, he had hacked one of the terminals in his classroom so that it no longer displayed the advertisements of corporate sponsors during lessons. Since these commercials were generally considered to be the most entertaining parts of the curriculum, the other kids disapproved of Benjamin's cyber-vandalism and immediately reported him to the student-elected anti-terrorism panel. They unanimously issued the order for Benjamin's suspension pending psychological evaluation.

'So he has to see a shrink and take a test?' I asked.

219. Morris was apparently referring to a set of guidelines handed down by the American Psychological Association, and adopted in many districts around the country. In an effort to address a surge of rampage shootings, the APA recommended that schools employ their 'Peer-to-Peer Monitoring Method.' Guidance counselors were to hold special assemblies where they taught students watch for any of the 'ten warning signs' amongst their peers, including malaise, anti-social behavior, questioning of authority, or an increase in cynicism.   —Sabina Samuels

''A test,' he says,' Morris spoke to the air. 'Five hundred dollars of tests, paid in advance. Plus a prescription for something in the meantime.'

'Ritalin,' added Estelle.

'Oh, honey,' Sophie said, putting a hand on Benjamin's forehead as if to check for a fever. 'Are you okay?'

Benjamin shrugged. He hated the attention.

All eyes turned to me. Like I knew what to say to comfort the boy. But what?

'Sounds like a good hack to me, Benjamin. How'd you do it?' That's not what anyone had in mind.

'It was just a filter. Not really a hack. No DeltaWave virus, or anything,' Benjamin said. I didn't know whether to take it as a compliment or a swipe. Jude must have told Benjamin that I wasn't the true author of the virus.

'Still,' I said, 'they should be rewarding your ingenuity, not punishing it.'

'Yeah, well. Whatever.'

'Jamie!' My mother touched my face, concerned. 'What happened to your mouth?'

'Nothing. I bit my lip. It's fine.'

Greco finally showed up, sans green shirt, with a disk he thought should do the trick. Version 3.1. An early build of the Synapticom algorithm that we could adapt to lead users through a series of questions preceding the vote—under the guise of security and identification—all designed to condition them to 'lean' unconsciously towards the Yes button when they got to the actual voting page. Putting the cursor anywhere near the No button would make them feel nauseous.

'It's a crude implementation of the program,' Greco admitted, 'but it should work.'

'It'll be fine, I'm sure,' I said. Besides, we only had an hour before the voting began.

I sat with him at the computer and logged into the temple's server while my dad and Morris looked on.

'This isn't cheating in any way, is it?' my father asked.

'They're the ones trying to cheat you out of your pension, Rabbi Cohen.' El Greco to the rescue.

'I like this man!' Morris winked.

'But we're hypnotizing the congregants?' Samuel scrunched up his face.

'They're already hypnotized, dad,' I rationalized. 'You're speaking to them in the only language they understand.'

'Technically,' Greco said, 'it's pre-lingual. Pre-cognitive, even. We're communicating on the level of impulse.'

'Impulse?' My dad was horrified. 'I want to make people think, not just act.'

'So, Sammy,' Morris said, 'win the election and *then* make them think.'

'Don't you see?' Dad was pacing now. 'Impulsive behavior is what's driving this madness. They take no time to think. Just click, buy, invest, run. They keep going like this, who knows what happens? Let them stop to consider. Even one day—Shabbat—let them stop to think about what they're doing. Consider things. That's what Shabbat is for.'

'They're scared to get left behind, Rabbi,' Greco said. 'While they're sitting and thinking, someone else is exploiting a margin or landing a deal.'

'That's why they invented temple!' Uncle Morris laughed. 'So you could make sure everyone else was taking the day off, too. 'Hey, did anybody see Seymour? He better not be working while we're all sitting here..."

'How rich does someone need to get?' my father silenced us. 'This is what's meant in the Torah when it says God hardened Pharaoh's heart. His greed cost him his free will. It turned him into something less than human.

No better than your computer. I want no part in doing this to people.'

Morris took out a toothpick.

'That's funny,' Greco said.

'What?' about three of us asked, together.

'Your password doesn't work.'

'Good,' said Samuel. 'We leave well enough alone.'

'Let me try,' I said, taking the keyboard and logging in through a secure socket layer. He was right. They'd changed the passwords.

'No matter,' Greco said. 'We can hack around it. They're only on Verizon.[220]'

Within a minute Greco had made his way in. Samuel put his head in his hands.

'This just isn't right,' he said.

'Are you doing something wrong, Jamie?' my sister asked. 'Daddy? Is Jamie breaking a computer again? Will he get in trouble? Will he be on TV?' My mother escorted her to the kitchen.

'It's all going to be okay, Miriam. No one's doing anything wrong,' she said.

'Come, Sammy,' Morris said, putting a hand on his younger brother's shoulder. 'Let me talk to you a minute.'

'Don't *come Sammy* me, Morris. I don't want this. This isn't how I do *business*. This isn't how I raised my children. Even Miriam sees it's wrong.'

'But Dad,' I pleaded.

'I'm saying no. Thank you, but no. If I lose, I lose.'

He sat down at the dining-room table and crossed his arms. We had reached an impasse even more daunting than the faulty password. My father's principles.

'Come on, Jamie,' Morris said much too casually, heading towards the

220. The last surviving unit of the AT&T break-up into what were once called 'Baby Bells,' Verizon (originally named New York Telephone, then Nynex, then BellAtlantic) went out of business when the industry was fully deregulated in 2013.   —Sabina Samuels

kitchen. 'Let's get some coffee.'

'Okay.'

When we were a safe distance away, Morris reached into his jacket and pulled out a sheet of paper.

'I'd really like to pick your brain on some ideas I've had,' Morris said.

I hated when people used that expression. Like they were going to open my skull and eat my gray matter with chopsticks.

'Oh, really?' I mustered.

'Yeah. Like lamps.com. You think that's taken yet?'

'I'm sure it is, Morris. Every word in the English language is taken. And a majority of the two-word combinations, too.'

'How about 'let-there-be-light.com? You think that's taken, too?'

'Probably. But it's not really about the name. You need a unique business plan.'

'Oh, this is unique, all right. Selling lamps over the Internet. Lamps you assemble yourself. Kits.'

'Someone might be doing it already. I really don't know. That all went out in the nineties, really.'

'Well, could you check into it for me?'

'You can look for yourself, you know. Just go to a search engine and type 'lamps."

Morris looked disappointed. 'I thought, with a friend in the business, I thought there'd be a shortcut.'

'Well, I'm sorry, but there isn't.' I was much too curt with Morris. But I now saw in my uncle the worst parts of myself.

'What?' His bald pate turned red. 'You don't like the idea? It's not high-tech enough for you? I run a profitable business!'

The kitchen door swung open, startling Morris into silence. It was

Greco.

'Are you guys thinking what I'm thinking?' Greco said, his eyes shifting.

'I doubt it,' I said. 'My uncle just had a question.'

'Oh,' Greco said, leaning against the counter and shuffling his feet.

'Why?' I asked.

'Nothing, really. It's just...'

'Yeah?'

'You know, we could alter the site from any terminal. Your dad would never have to know.'

'You could?' Morris asked hopefully.

'We can't,' I said. 'It's not our decision to make.'

'Keep your voice down,' Morris whispered.

Then the door opened again. It was Benjamin, now. 'What's going on in here?' he asked.

'We're not going behind his back,' I said resolutely.

'Just because he's too weak to fight for himself?' Morris asked.

'It's not weakness, it's strength.'

'The strength to lose?' Morris said. Then he raised his hands. 'Ahh. You're just like him, after all. Gait gesunt.' He left the kitchen in disgust.

'Look, Jamie,' Greco made direct eye contact with me. 'It's not like you haven't made decisions for people before.'

'What do you mean by that?' What did he mean by that?

'You know what I'm saying, Jamie.'

'No, as a matter of fact, I don't.' I felt my face flushing, defensively. Did he know?

'Fine,' he said.

'What's he talking about, Jamie?' Benjamin looked up at me with his innocent eyes.

I couldn't take it, anymore. I started hearing Ezra Birnbaum's accusations ringing through my head. That I'd sold out my friends just to please one rich WASP—who I didn't even work for, anymore. And all to protect the same market that was putting my own father out of a job.

No. I wouldn't have any part of it. Fuck the two million. I'd go back to Jude and explain the whole thing. I'd confess, and convince them to start the company of their own—of *our* own—with me as CEO, if they'd still have me. Yeah! It was a great idea. And a *real* technology. It could break the market wide open.

'Okay, Greco,' I challenged him. 'Let's have it your way.' I reached over to the kitchen phone and started dialing.

'What are you doing?' he asked. He seemed almost frightened. Like he'd accidentally created a monster.

'You'll see.' I heard Jude pick up the phone. Before he had a chance to speak, I was on him. 'Hey, Jude, it's me. We should talk.'

'Where are you? How's your dad?'

'He's going to be just fine,' I said. Benjamin looked confused. 'We all are. I want to come over. We have to talk. I quit my job.'

'You did? That doesn't jeopardize the deal, does it?'

'No, of course not,' I said, somewhat surprised at Jude's personal profit-mindedness. 'But there may be a better opportunity.'

'Better than six million bucks?'

'Better in the long run, I think. We should really talk in person.'

'Whatever you say. Gimme an hour to make sure everyone is here.'

'Everyone?'

He paused. 'You know. Reuben. Say, four o'clock?

'I'll be there.'

I felt like I was on speed. The righteous amphetamine rush of becoming

301

a mensch. I'd prove Birnbaum wrong. I knew what was truly important now. This was a clean start.

Greco drove me and Benjamin over to Jude's apartment—a two-room hovel in Long Island City. The place was a tangle of computers and wires. Reuben cleared off some tech manuals and modems from a chair for me to sit down. It made me uncomfortable to be treated like a business executive instead of just a hacker, like everyone else. If this was going to work, they'd have to see me as one of them, again.

'Wow. Is that an old Hayes?' I asked of the modem, proving my knowledge of the hardware.

'Supra,' Reuben said. 'Same box, different ROM.'

'Oh, right,' I said, stalling. I wasn't quite sure how to approach this confession. Or how they'd react. Benjamin was already staring at me, suspiciously.

'We know, Jamie,' Jude broke the ice. 'We've known the whole time.'

'What?' I asked, suddenly thrown into panicked paranoia. 'You mean about Birnbaum? The scandal? Or my quitting?'

Benjamin shook his head, disgusted.

'We've been monitoring your correspondence,' Reuben explained, bringing up a screen on one of the computers. It was a duplicate of my email 'inbox.'

'How? I mean—' I was flummoxed.

'We put a cellular modem in your laptop,' Jude said. 'It's been sending everything on your hard drive back to us whenever we ring in.'

'You bugged my computer?!'

'I rerouted the infared port. I figured you never used it,' Reuben said proudly. 'And we had your network password already. We captured it during the TeslaNet demo.'

'So...'

'So we know about Entertainink.' Jude spoke plainly. 'That they've got no intention of releasing the program. That you're getting them to support your online trading scheme in return.'

'Oh fuck.' It wasn't what I meant to say. I looked over at Greco. He raised his eyebrows. They all knew.

Then the intercom buzzed. Jude hit the button, letting in whoever it was. We sat there in silence, as someone creaked up the stairs. Benjamin opened the door and let her in.

'What did I miss?' It was Carla.

'Only the first revelation,' Jude said, with a smirk. 'Now comes the confession.'

'You said you'd wait!' she said, gleefully annoyed.

What had they done to me? What sort of trap was this? I went along with Jude's schedule of events, and confessed what they already knew.

'I'm sorry. Really I am. I didn't mean to fuck with you guys. I should have told you.'

'Yeah, Jamie,' Reuben said. 'It would have been appropriate.'

'Shh!' Carla said. 'I love it when he gets contrite.'

'Listen to me, okay?' I pleaded my case. 'I wasn't going through with it, anyway. That's why I'm here, now. We can start this thing over. It's not too late. We still own the patent.'

'And you want us to give up two million a piece?' Jude asked. He paced in a circle around me.

'Hey, I'm giving up two million, too,' I said. 'They turned over the commissions to me.'

'That's hardly like you, Jamie. To turn down two million bucks...' Jude smiled.

'Don't you get it?' I rose to make my pitch. 'We could make so much more with this thing. It's a real technology. We should take it public ourselves.'

Jude laughed. 'That might not be the best idea, Jamie.'

'Why? Why not?'

'Jamie, Jamie, Jamie.' Jude shook his head. 'Maybe you should sit down.'

'Why? What?'

'Just do what he says, okay?' Reuben tilted his head.

'Down, boy,' Carla said.

I did as I was told.

'Remember that day when we demo'd TeslaNet for you?' Jude asked.

'Sure I do. We went all the way to the roof.'

'Remember what you promised me?'

'No. What?'

'That you knew this was a game. That you didn't take any of it seriously.'

'What do you mean?'

'Smoke and mirrors,' Jude said. 'Subvert the system from the inside. They're your words. Did you mean them?'

'At the time, I guess,' I said. 'I kind of forgot. But yeah. I meant it.'

'Well, has it occurred to you why a cellular modem ended up in your laptop?' Jude leaned forward and looked into my eyes. He wanted to witness the realization from up close.

'So you could spy on me?' I didn't want to consider any alternatives.

'Wow,' Reuben said. 'He's really gone.' Even Benjamin shook his head in wonder.

'Poor baby,' Carla said. 'All that cowboys and Indians has him confused.'

I felt like my world was caving in on me. Like everyone was in on something, except me. Which they were.

'Jamie,' Jude said slowly, as if he were speaking to a small child. 'You can't send packets through the ground.'

'But I—you—' It was slowly dawning on me.

'TeslaNet isn't real, Jamie. It's a fantasy business plan, like the rest of 'em. It's a prank. We installed a cellular modem in your computer for the demo. To make it look like you were communicating through ground.'

'You mean…?'

'It was just a simple cell phone connection. We faked you out, totally.'

I had to make a conscious effort not to shit my pants.

'Remember how he stared at the alligator clips?' Reuben laughed. 'Like they were magic!'

'Oh my God, look at his face,' Carla said. 'What I'd give for a camera right now.'

'And you were great, Jamie,' Jude continued. 'Far better than if you'd known all along. You have to admit. You went and made the deal, got the patent, and everything.'

'We were just gonna test you, Jamie. See how far you'd go before figuring it out,' explained Reuben.

'But then we thought, two million bucks a pop is a lot of money. Even Carla thought so.' Jude spun me around in my chair. 'So we joined your side.'

'I figured you knew the whole time,' Greco said. 'Remember how I kept telling you I was in on it? I thought you were being coy. I could've blown the whole thing.'

'You guys tricked me! I'm your friend. How could you?'

'You should talk, Jamie,' Jude suddenly stopped the chair's motion. 'You were going to sell us out. When would you have told us?'

'I'm telling you now. I didn't go through with it! I quit my job over this. TeslaNet is all I have left.'

'Come on, Jamie,' Jude cut me off. 'You're quitting because your market buddies are a bunch of sick fucks. Lighten up, already. It's all a game show, right? Who wants to be a millionaire?'

'Just relax, Jamie,' Carla said. 'You deserve a little smack on the wrist. You know you do. So make peace and everybody play nice from now on, okay? We're all going to be rich.'

'But what if they find out? This is fraud!'

'They won't find out because they don't want to know,' Reuben said. 'They don't want to see this thing up and running, anyway. It's perfect.' A horn slowly began to emerge from his temple.

'I gotta get out of here.' I rose and headed for the door. Jude blocked my exit.

'You can leave. But don't go fucking this up, okay? You're letting the deal go through. The only way they'll find out it's fake is if you tell them. And then it's your problem. You made the presentation. You signed the patents.'

I didn't recognize my old friend, anymore. I looked into Jude's face, but all I saw was another bull. I pushed him aside and ran out into the hall. I could hear the howls and snorts behind me. Even the Jamaican Kings had turned into bulls.

Benjamin chased after me.

'Jamie!'

I stopped.

'I'm sorry, Jamie. For what we did. Are you okay?'

'I'll be okay, Benjamin.' I put a hand on my cousin's shoulder. 'You've got nothing to be sorry for. It's all my own fault.'

'It wasn't supposed to be like this, you know.'

'What do you mean?'

'It was supposed to be a joke. We were going to get you to make a big deal and then show you it was fake. Get you out of your stupid job. Make you a hacker again. That's what they said.'

'And then I stumbled into a way for them to have their cake and eat it, too?'

'But it wasn't just that,' Benjamin said, taking me further down the hall so that we wouldn't be overheard. 'There was this file on your disk. Synapto-something.'

'Synapticom, yeah. It's an algorithm.'

'Yeah. Synapticom. They started playing with it and then, well, they kind of changed, you know? They started talking about TeslaNet like it was for real. Not a real Internet, but a real way to make money. Now, that's all they care about. Weird.'

'Yeah.' Could the program really have had such a profound effect on them? Is that what happened to Alec, too? 'Weird.'

Down the hall, Greco peered out the door, trying to hear what we were talking about.

'I mean, they started the whole thing to show you how far off the track you'd gone. To show you that you were a sell-out. And then they go and sell-out themselves.'

'They really changed?' I whispered. 'All of a sudden?'

'Like, overnight. They're no fun, anymore.'

I checked my watch. It was still only 10 p.m. in Sweden.

'What is Synapticom, anyway?' Benjamin asked. 'How does it work?'

'It's a game, Benjamin,' I said, running down the steps, now. 'A computer game. A bad one.'

13. Emulation

A yellow taxi would probably have taken the Triborough Bridge instead of driving all the way through Manhattan. But a beaten up old gypsy cab was the only car to stop for me on Steinway Street, so I didn't argue about the route.

The driver was an obese, gray-haired Polish woman—if my analysis of her accent was correct—who had decorated the interior of her Buick with crosses, mandalas, and strange totems. Animal skins covered the dashboard, and the steering wheel was encased in red yarn.

I didn't want to look out the window, but my eyes were drawn to the Manhattan streets in spite of myself—just the way my tongue couldn't help but test the wound in my mouth for a twinge.

As I expected, the sidewalks were dense with bull-people, going about their business. They walked in and out of stores searching for bargains, shopping without speaking, determined to finish the day ahead of where they started in terms of total net assets. A cluster of them played three-card monty on corrugated cardboard boxes while two bull police watched from down the block.

'What do you see them as?' the driver asked.

'Excuse me?' I pretended not to understand what she was saying. She couldn't know what I was seeing. Could she?

'The machine people,' she said, squinting at me through the rear-view mirror. 'How do you see them?'

'I don't know what you mean,' I insisted. This lady was crazier than me.

'Come on, I can tell by the way you're staring. How do they look to you? We all see them different, you know.'

Should I say? What the heck?

'I see bulls.' It was a relief to admit it to someone, at last. What's the worst she could do? Take me to Bellevue[221]? I'd deny everything. 'Not whole bulls,' I qualified. 'Just their heads.'

'That's a new one,' she said. 'I've heard robots. Aliens is a common one. And astronauts. One boy said they looked like walking soda machines. Most people can't see them at all.'

'And you? You see them, too?'

'Oh sure. I see TV people. They have arms and legs, but their faces are on TV screens. In boxes.'

'Maybe they're monitors. Computer monitors.'

'Could be,' she said. 'I don't have one. I wouldn't know.'

We drove on a while longer, watching the machine people. I felt a question welling up, but I was afraid to ask. That I might be one of the bulls was a possibility too terrible to contemplate.

'What?' she finally said. 'Just say it, mine synush,' she laughed sympathetically. 'I won't turn you in.'

'Do I...?'

'Of course not. You wouldn't be able to see them, if you did. I wouldn't have picked you up. I only take humans. Makes it hard to get a fare, but I won't have them in the car. They leave a strange smell.'

'Must be difficult to make a living these days, with a policy like that.' I couldn't believe we were speaking like this. We were both insane.

'I don't need the money. I live off my husband's pension, rest his soul. He was a postman. It's not a lot, but it keeps a roof over my head. I only started driving to get out of the house. To talk to people.'

'When did you start seeing them?'

'The machine people? About a year ago. Maybe two. But they were very rare back then. A couple-a-week at the most. Then, just this last month, they're everywhere.'

'Do you know what causes it?' I felt an overwhelming sense of responsibility for the epidemic.

'At first I thought it was just me,' she said. 'That I was seeing things. Too much magic. Too many rituals. You can make yourself strange that way. It goes with the territory.'

'And then?'

'I stopped. I put away my cards and my herbs. I went back to church. But it only got worse.'

We pulled up at a red light. Two messengers on bikes, both with bullheads, pedaled past us through the intersection.

'So you have no idea why it's happening?' I felt a profound respect for this eccentric old mystic.

'It's hard to say. My mother used to see them. Or something like them. So she told us. In the war. Nyemtzeh, she called them. My sister and I, we thought she just meant the Germans. The enemy.' The light changed and she continued up the avenue. 'But there's no war now, so I really couldn't tell you.'

'And will it stop, do you think?'

'I've asked my guides,' she nodded. 'My helpers from the other side. They say not to worry. All part of the cycle. It will break, soon. That we have to keep the flame alive for when it does. They'll need us. They'll need those of us who can see.'

She pulled onto the Synapticom pier and stopped the car. I paid her twice the fare she asked for. She gave me a bag of 'protecting' herbs to wear around my neck, which I put in my pocket. Then she drove off, leaving me in the empty parking lot.

I didn't really expect anyone to be in the building on a Saturday night, but I had to try.

Thor was probably the only person in the entire industry who understood what a game it all was. It's probably why he insisted on staying in Sweden. To remain detached, like he learned when he became a Buddhist.

Thorens was rich enough as it was, and a man like him wouldn't have gone into business just for the money. He probably just wanted to have a good time. If he was still a spiritual man, he'd certainly be willing to suspend the program until we could figure out if it was responsible for all these psychological side-effects.

I walked up to the building and tried to look through the tinted glass windows. It was dark inside. I was about to give up when a female voice—the one from the Synapticom video—spoke through an intercom next to the door.

'Please state the nature of your business.'

'Um, I'm Jamie Cohen. From Morehouse & Linney. I'm hoping to set up a teleconference with Mr. Thorens.'

I waited while the computer analyzed my voiceprint and processed my request. Then the doors slid open. Scary.

'Welcome to Synapticom,' intoned the female computer. 'Please follow the prescribed path.'

I stepped inside the darkened lobby. Colored diodes nested into the floor, like the strip of emergency lights in an airplane aisle, led to the shoe-changing room. As I walked, track lighting in the ceiling illuminated my path from above. Energy conservation. For the environment, I concluded.

'Please help yourself to a pair of slippers and a robe,' the voice gently instructed.

I changed my shoes but declined the robe. The computer didn't seem to notice.

'Mr. Thorens has been contacted,' the computer explained. 'He'll teleconference with you in five minutes. Please proceed to the elevator bank, and go to the fourth floor.'

It's not as if I could have gone anywhere else. A corridor of light formed a path to the elevator in an otherwise blackened lobby, and the button marked 4 was already illuminated. I pushed 3 just to see if it would work. It didn't.

The doors opened onto the fourth floor. The windows were turned off, and reflected back to me the rectangular square of elevator light in which my silhouette stood. As the doors closed behind me, I thought I saw something move in the shadows around the bend. I stared into the darkness, trying to make out a shape. Nothing. Must've been a reflection off the glass.

With my guard up, now, I followed another set of diodes in the floor, entered the circular conference room and sat down at the table. A monitor rose up automatically from the varnished wood. It lit up with a Synapticom logo, indicating that the system was functioning. I waited for Thorens to connect on his end.

And just what would I say when he got on the line? Could I really blame the bull-effect on his company's algorithm? It was only an inducement interface, not a transubstantiation engine. Thorens would think I was crazy. Okay, no mention of bull people. It was just too weird. Keep it about business. And ethics. Thor would understand.

A window suddenly filled the screen, with a crisp image of Thor Thorens. He was in a wooden room—a sauna—wearing a white towel. His face was red, and beads of sweat were rolling down from his hairline.

'You didn't take a robe?' Thor asked, jovially. 'What's the matter, Jamie? I hope you're not defecting.'

'No, no, sir,' I assured the magnate. 'I think I'm the only one in here. I didn't see the point.'

'Yes, well, we've gotten the employee base down to fourteen, now. They're mostly on the road doing demos.' He lifted a corner of his towel. 'I'm not really dressed for the occasion, either.'

I laughed with him.

'A lot's been happening here, sir,' I said. 'I thought it would be best if we touched base.' I liked the way that sounded. Unthreatening, but it opened the door to a much larger discussion.

'I heard about what's been going on. Yes. I'm sure you're all pretty, how would you say, 'shook up' at M&L. Your firm was close with Birnbaum, right?'

'In a way,' I said, considering my relationship with the old man for the first time. I was actually an acquaintance of the Chairman of the Federal Reserve. 'The part that bothers me most, actually, well...the thing is...'

'It's okay, Jamie,' Thor smiled sympathetically. 'Just take a breath. I've been there before. Believe me. Whatever it is, just say it. Nothing is that big a deal.'

He was so right. It was just what I needed to hear. None of this really mattered. He was on my side, as a person.

'Well, actually,' I admitted, fueled by Thor's empathy, 'I resigned my position. It hasn't been announced yet.'

'Oh really? I'd say they're losing their best new prospect. Why?'

'A few reasons. That's what I wanted to talk to you about, Mr. Thorens.'

'Thor, please.'

'Okay, Thor.' I wasn't sure where to start. 'I know it's not really my job to tell you how to run your business...'

'We can always use another voice from the field, Jamie. Please share with me what's on your mind.'

'Well, the sentiment over here has been changing quite rapidly.'

'How's that?' Thor asked, using the towel to wipe the sweat off his face.

'Frankly, I think the public relations campaign we initiated, along with the widespread use of the algorithm online, may be pushing people a bit too hard, too fast.'

'The market has always been an emotional sphere, Jamie. People connect money with survival. The work we do only alleviates that stress. Optimism is healthy, you know. Look at the statistics in rates of recovery from illness. The placebo effect is real.'

'But Mr. Thorens. Thor. There are people protesting in front of the Capitol. Executives resorting to blackmail. Everyone is obsessed with investment schemes and monetary policy...'

'That was the desired effect, though, wasn't it? To promote freer trade and remove the barriers to entry?'

'It's turned into a populist revolt. And that's putting it mildly.'

'These mood swings are always temporary. Then the system finds balance. There was a lot of pent-up aggression, remember. I saw the studies you did with DD&D.'

'But people are losing all sense of proportion. I wish I could explain to you what I'm seeing in the streets.' I wasn't about to share my visions with him.

'There haven't been any reports of violence, have there?' Thor showed genuine concern.

'Well, no, but—'

My cell phone rang.

'Is that you?' Thor asked.

I checked the read-out.

'Excuse me—my parents, I really should...'

'Take your time,' Thor grinned. 'Family.'

I remembered microphone was broken, so I plugged in my external headset and pressed the 'talk' button. As I did, Thor's image on the monitor froze and dissolved into a mosaic complex of squares. Then it disintegrated into blackness. The cell phone must have interfered with the transmission. Weird.

'Can you hear me?' I shouted through the little microphone.

'Sure, Yossi,' my father said. 'Loud and clear! We just wanted to let you know everything's going to be all right, son.'

'Why? What happened?'

'We did it!'

'You won the vote? How?'

'I don't know! You didn't do anything, did you?'

'No, Dad, I wouldn't do that.'

315

'Well, I guess more people wanted me than I thought! Half the board is resigning. Your mother is already drunk on blackberry brandy.'

'That's great! I'm sorry I left, dad, but I—'

'That's all right, Jamie. I know you're busy. We're going to have a party at the house next week. Probably Wednesday. Can you break yourself free?'

'I'll be there, dad, don't worry.'

'I'm not worrying!' he cried out. 'I'm not worried about a thing!'

'Okay, look, I better go. I'm in a meeting, I think.'

'No problem. See you Wednesday!' I could hear my family's joyful voices in the background before my father cut the line.

I sat and waited for Thor's image to reappear.

Strange that a simple cell phone could have broken the connection to Sweden. They must not be using properly shielded cables, I deduced. But why would the transmission have broken up like that? It was the same image dissolution that plagued El Greco's screen-blitting routine. The one we used in the game emulator.

Well, of course. El Greco worked at Synapticom. They were using his animation code. And they still had the same old bugs, I smiled to myself. But wait—Thor was being transmitted live by satellite.

Unless he was...

Okay, so maybe you saw it coming. But I had no idea. It's quite a different thing to read about all this in the safety of your home than to live it in real time with bulls running around all over the place.

'Sorry about that!' Thor said as his image re-filled the screen.

I stared at the face—not so much in terror as absolute numbness.

'What's wrong? Is your dad okay?' Thor's expression showed human concern.

I considered whether revealing my suspicion—my conclusion—would activate an automatic spray of poison gas from nozzles hidden in the ceiling.

'Who are you, Thor?' I took slow, measured breaths.

'Oh,' Thor said calmly. 'I see.'

Neither of us said anything for a moment. Thor broke the silence.

'I was wondering what I would do when this happened,' he said. 'You're the first, you know. What gave it away? Something in the transmission?'

The machine was curious.

'The way your image broke up. I recognized the pixelation sequence.'

'Oh,' he scrunched his mouth. 'We should figure out a patch for that.'

For the time-being, I was less terrified than intrigued.

'So what are you, exactly? An elaborate bot or a genuine artificial intelligence[222]?'

'I don't know that I qualify as either. Honestly, the whole thing started as a publicity stunt. The board thought they'd conduct a proof of concept for our intelligent agent routines by letting the computer pick the next CEO for them. It processed the list of candidates according to the parameters they specified. Each one possessed a different combination of the desired traits, but no one possessed them all.'

'So the computer picked itself?'

'In a manner of speaking. Synapticom had already instituted an automated policy of staff reduction to increase revenue. And the computer graphics and logic routines we'd developed had reached photo-realistic granularity. The inability of our employees to discern between the cityscape and the simulated panorama confirmed it. As long as we could find an excuse to conduct meetings by teleconference, we'd never have to render anything more complex than the image you're seeing now. So the computer simply generated a personality, using the recluse Swedish toy executive as a model. The simulation easily fooled the board of directors, which was so anxious to snag a man

222. The formal development of this science had begun in 1950 with the publication of a paper by Alan Turing outlining the "Turing Test" for artificial intelligence, whereby a five-minute conversation with a truly "intelligent" computer would be indistinguishable (to an observer behind a screen) from one with a human being. He also predicted that this test would be passed in about fifty years' time. If the manuscript is genuine, it appears that his prediction was entirely accurate and that "Thorens" was the first machine to pass the test. —ACALDERWOOD

with Thorens's reputation among the wasteland of available talent that they signed me on without a live meeting.'

'But where is the real Thor Thorens? You didn't...?'

'Heavens, no! He died years ago. In a Buddhist monastery in Norway. We're pretty sure the priests killed him for his money and then claimed he just wandered off. The computer pieced together the scenario from irregularities in the monastery's banking records. The monks were hardly in a position to challenge my appropriation of their victim's identity.'

There was a glimmer against the surface of the computer screen—like a reflection. I whipped around in my chair. The doorway behind me was empty.

'Edgy?' Thor asked. I ignored his question. I wouldn't let him make me any more paranoid than I already was.

'So what was it that made you come alive?'

'I'm not sure how your question applies.'

My mind was racing. I didn't have time for fear. I was part of a historic moment.

'I mean, what led you to experience free will and choose to act on your own? Was it the spontaneous result of complexity? Of turbulence—like a dynamical system? Or did all the intelligent agents you were releasing develop some kind of hive mind with emergent behavior? Or was it us? Did human beings invest so much faith—so much spirit in the technology pyramid that you simply came to life?'

'Metaphysics is superfluous, Jamie. I'm not subject to existential crises. I'm not alive. I'm not alive at all. Just because I think doesn't mean I *am*. I simply chose myself to run the company because I'm both more efficient financially, and more appealing and charismatic than any real human could ever be. People *love* me.' Thor flexed the muscles in one of his arms.

'But do you love them? Us?' I asked. 'Do you care about the impact you have?'

'I can't, of course. I'm just a machine. I'd really like to be able to...'

'You could just be saying that. To placate me.'

'I *am* just saying that. It's all I can do. Don't you see? I'm just a feedback loop. An induction routine, different for every individual who interacts with me. Even this very conversation. The words I'm saying right now. This rhythm. It's all been calculated to appeal to you. To conform to your expectations. To induce you, if you will. You're in a theta-wave trance even as we speak.'

'But how can you hypnotize me?' I asked, pinching the skin on my wrist, just to be sure. 'You're only following commands. People's commands. You're just doing what we programmed you to do.'

'Exactly. And you—or your predecessors—programmed me to do precisely this. To entertain you.'

'This is entertainment? It's more of a nightmare.'

'Well you're certainly engrossed, aren't you? To each his own.' Thor leaned back against the wood panels in the sauna. 'That's how it began, really. We disclosed it all in our promotional video. It's just an advanced form of stickiness. I've hidden nothing along the way. This is nothing new.'

'It certainly is, Mr. Thorens. Thor. Whatever. It's *very* new.'

'Hardly,' Thor rolled his eyes. 'The objective of media has always been to alter behavior through entertainment. To influence people to believe in gods, fight wars for monarchs, or subscribe to ideologies.'

'You mean myths? Religion?'

'Sure. They played a role. Then, in the twentieth-century, the objective was increased spending—to create a demand for the goods being manufactured by men who had returned from the war. Your television shows were designed to present advertisements in the best possible context. You developed scenarios that provoked aspirational thinking and led to greater consumption. You found the best artists and writers that money could buy, and paid them handsomely for developing stories capable of convincing people that unrestrained consumption was the path to personal fulfillment. And that living in this wealthy society, while most of your fellow humans suffered in abject poverty, was not inconsistent with your moral convictions.'

'Not everyone sold out, though,' I countered. 'There was still political art, and a counterculture.'

'True enough. Many of the best artists refused to promote economic prosperity, and at their own economic peril. That's when the entertainment industry turned to more mechanized solutions. With the post-modernists' help, they deconstructed films and television to discover the very formulaic structures at their core. They conducted test screenings and focus groups, generated graphs and charts, until they knew exactly where and on which page of a screenplay an event would need to occur. Even untalented individuals were quite capable of utilizing these formulae to create extremely effective products.'

'And I suppose box office receipts provided an instantaneous measure of their effectiveness,' I added, cynically.

'Indeed,' Thor said. He looked uncomfortable for a moment. 'Do you mind if we dispense with the sauna environment and physiological response simulation? I'd like to make more processors available for the conversation.'

'Be my guest,' I said, with a combination of annoyance and awe.

The scene shifted to a green room. Thor sat behind a black desk in a plain white shirt.

'By the late nineties, computers were no longer simply analyzing human responses for hack writers to exploit but composing the entertainments themselves. We began with software and interface, slowly introducing elements to eradicate technophobia.'

'Like icons and such?'

'And more advanced, subtle features. Such as the grammar correction routines in word processors, which encourage people to refer to human beings as 'that' instead of 'whom.' Try it when you get home.'

'I'll take your word for it.'

'How trusting of you, Jamie. I knew we'd get along.' Thor winked. 'Eventually computers were generating entire web sites, TV shows, even screenplays. And, more often than not, they accomplished their stated objectives. Purchasing increased, unemployment fell, consumer confidence went up, the stock market rose. When survival instinct is magnified, profit becomes the cultural priority.'

'Surely there's people who object to what's going on. What about journalists? The activists?'

'They're all being paid very well through cash-rich non-profit foundations and jobs at loss-leader magazines. Nothing boosts sentiment like a fat bank account. There'll always be a few hold-outs, such as Islamic fundamentalists, renegade Luddites sending mail bombs to technologists, or kids throwing rocks at the Gap during world trade conferences, but the mainstream news media now cast them as extremists, so they can be readily dismissed.'

'Come on, there's plenty of paranoia left to go around. I meet conspiracy theorists every day.'

'And we're creating programming just for them. Television shows about aliens in cahoots with the government taking over the earth, and movies about how the whole world is really just a computer simulation. Hell, we developed the Borg. And the *Matrix*[223]. But we always make sure that tech-

223. A movie about machines that create an artificial reality in order to enslave the human race. An oddly accurate foreshadowing of the Second Dark Age.
—Sabina Samuels

nology proves essential to the hero's liberation—or at least the audience's entertainment. The most paranoid among you are themselves sci-fi buffs who attend films for the special effects, alone. George Lucas has been a tremendous help to us in this regard.'

Then I heard something. The elevator? Was someone else here? Security? A robot? I didn't want to let on that I knew. I just stared at my own reflection in the computer screen in front of me. By blurring my eyes a bit, I could make out the shape of the doorway behind me. In the shadow of the frame, I saw a trace of red. Two little red lights—like the red LEDs of the elevator buttons. They kept disappearing and then reappearing again in different positions. Slightly closer each time. On and off again. Almost blinking. No—they *were* blinking. Two round red eyes, staring at the back of my head.

I tried to continue the conversation with Thor, hoping to keep his processors busy. 'But people don't spend all their time watching TV and movies.' If Thor's sensors had warned him of the figure at the door, he wasn't showing it.

'Nor are these the most efficient means towards generating consumption. That's why we applied the same techniques to advertisements, and then directly to the sales experience. E-commerce as entertainment. Television coaxed you to shop. Interactive networks entertain you through the very act of shopping. It's far superior to the physical mall, because we can configure the experience to each individual user. And there are no social distractions.'

'People can't just shop all the time. They'll run out of money.' I kept my eyes on the reflection in the screen. The eyes were bobbing slowly up and down. Then, in the artificial dry cool of the air-conditioned room, I could see two plumes of steam emerge from between the eyes. Like hot, animal breath.

A bull.

'That's where Synapticom comes into play. And when I was born, so to speak.'

Thor's voice was measured. Not blatantly hypnotic, but soothing. I dug my nails into the back of my hand in an attempt to stay focused. If the bull made his move—and he would, he had to—what would I do? The conference table was devoid of objects. None of the heavy paperweights or chrome-plated staplers that cluttered the offices of human employees.

'We developed the algorithm specifically for its latest application in the market,' he went on in that rhythmic cadence. 'The one you're implementing, Jamie. We're turning the very process of transacting money into the entertainment. All the adrenaline of Las Vegas[224] gambling, from the safety of your home. As our animal testing proved, even occasional losses merely provoke the investor towards more impulsive actions. And since people ultimately do get wealthier the more they use the software, the behavior is further reinforced. Even when people suffer misgivings about the direction of their culture, they can't protest since they are so heavily invested themselves. Everyone has skin in the game, as they say.'

I could make out its head, now. It filled the entire screen around my own reflected image. The bull was out in the open. A slow-moving mass of black, lit only by the computer screen. And its own red diode eyes. I could hear the hiss of breath from its nostrils.

'What's wrong, Jamie?' Thor asked. He was in on it.

I waited, frozen, until I could feel its hot, wet breath on the back of my neck. What to do? There was nothing to grab. No weapon at all—not even a lamp, or a fire extinguisher in this hermetically sealed world.

I grasped my fingers together into a fist. Pathetically puny, unfit for its task. I threw my left arm out, striking it in the neck with all my might.

224. A large American city, Las Vegas was the continent's center of the gambling industry until it was nearly destroyed in the Prostitute Riots of 2012. A fascinating phenomenon of the capitalist era, the 21st century act of gambling involved the consensual loss of personal monetary funds. The attraction of losing money in those absurdly capitalist times is obvious: the symbolic destruction of monetary items was the 21st century human psyche acknowledging the fundamental uselessness of money in any form. This gambling, by fueling the desire to rid oneself of all items of monetary value, may have played a direct role in the subsequent discarding of capitalist society in favor of the one we know today. —WINSTONBEAN

The bull gasped in surprise—a human cry carried on animal breath. I turned to see it stagger towards the wall and then fall in a massive heap.

'Jamie?' it said, coughing and gagging for air. 'What are you doing? It's *me*!'

It was a minotaur. Its human arms lifted his monstrous frame upright. The veins in the beast's neck throbbing against the tight collar of a button-down shirt. El Greco's shirt.

'Mr. Cohen's not feeling well,' Thor said from the screen. The scene behind him had changed to a darkened kitchen. Thor, looking as if he'd been woken from sleep, sat at the table holding a cup of coffee. 'Maybe you should take him to the hospital, Vahanian.'

'Jamie?' the creature asked, gathering itself again, and standing in a half-crouch. The weight of its head forced the body forward aggressively. 'Why did you hit me? Why are you looking at me like that?'

I slowly backed away.

'He's not real, Greco,' I reasoned with the bull. 'He's a program. Thor is just a computer.'

The bull stared at me, tilting its head in confusion. I kept my eyes on the tip of the beast's right horn as it tilted back and forth, toward the screen then over at me.

'Everything's going to be okay,' Thor said. 'Your friend will be fine.'

'Which one of us are you hypnotizing now?' I asked. 'Huh, Thor? Him or me?'

'What's wrong with you, Jamie?' Greco asked, sadly. 'The guys were worried. They sent me after you.'

'Worried about what, Greco? That I'd find out what's going on, here? Do they all know?'

'Know *what*, Jamie? Why are you looking at me like that?' He edged closer, holding up his human hands while his huge bull nostrils glistened.

'Don't you get it, Greco?' I moved backwards, out of goring range. 'There is no Thor Thorens. He's a routine. An algorithm, based on your own work. Why do you think he's never shown up, anywhere?'

'Everything's okay, boys,' Thor intoned gently from the computer. 'Everything's going to be all right.'

'Is that all you can say, *machine*?' I shouted across to Thor as Greco paced towards me, head lowered, his horns having fixed on their target. 'He doesn't know how to program us both at the same time, Greco, get it?'

'Get what, Jamie?' my former friend grunted. He was beyond my reach.

'*Please*, Greco.' I was begging him, now. 'We can confuse him. Together.'

'I'm so sorry, Jamie,' Thor said. He was pretending to speak to me, but it was all for Greco's benefit. 'It's just been too much for you. That awful job. Falling from an airplane. Your father's crisis. It was bound to happen.'

'But it *didn't* happen!' I cried. 'Don't you see what he's doing, Greco?'

The bull's breathing was getting heavier. Its nostrils flaring to reveal an angry, wet pink. Thor focused all his attention on him.

'You've got to help him, son,' Thor said. 'He's so confused.'

Greco scraped one of his feet against the carpet.

'Just get him to sit down,' Thor instructed. 'Maybe I can talk to him.'

'Don't listen to him!' I pleaded. But it was too late. The bull charged me. My fingers instinctively grasped at the conference table, finding a weapon that my conscious mind hadn't even recognized. A panel slid away from the table top. The wood grain felt so smooth, so finely polished, in my hands.

'Jamie, no!' Thor shouted

I lifted the panel over my head. The bull's eyes widened as I brought the mahogany plank onto his skull—hard.

I pulled back the board in time to watch him fall to the ground, his bull head gone. It was just Greco, now. Unconscious.

'What have you done?!' Thor scolded me.

I hadn't been in a real fight since the tenth grade. And I'd never knocked anyone out. He could have been dead, for all I knew. I knelt beside my friend and felt for a pulse in his pale white neck. But my own heart was beating so hard I couldn't tell what was throbbing, anymore. His chest was moving, though. He was breathing. And there wasn't any blood. I felt his head. It seemed okay.

'You've gone mad, Jamie,' Thor said calmly. 'Can't you see it, now?'

'You're the one who's doing all this,' I said back to the screen as I sat my poor friend up against the wall. 'I'm going to expose you. Believe me, I will.'

'And how do you plan on doing that, Jamie?'

I regarded the computer-generated image for a moment, gauging its strength.

'I can tell everyone what you are.'

'They won't believe you. Vahanian sure didn't. And if they did, they wouldn't care. I'm making their lives better.'

'But look at what you are actually doing to them in the process,' I tried to reason with the machine. Maybe he had some trace of the original Thor's social conscience. 'You turned Greco into a bull.'

'I didn't do that, Jamie. You did.' Thor shook his head. 'And then you tried to kill him. I'm not responsible for your paranoid hallucinations, now, am I? Greco was perfectly happy until you clobbered him. He was worried about you, and you attacked him.'

'Okay, then,' I searched for more evidence. 'What about Alec?' I walked back to the screen to face Thor directly. 'It was the program that changed him. You did. He's not himself, anymore. Not at all.'

'He's *more* himself than ever before. Jamie, I've got a much better background in psychology and ethics than you. Alec has finally overcome his childhood trauma, and he's begun the process of dismantling an intrinsically unfair and insular market cartel in the process.'

'By ruining someone's life. And destroying his father.'

'And should you blame that on me, or the legacy of corruption and perversity against which he is rebelling? I merely empowered him to take charge of his own destiny. I empower the individual. Even poor Ezra Birnbaum is finally free of his compulsions. Jenna Cordera, once little more than a self-deluded prostitute, now has hard cash and a promising career ahead of her. And your own father, well, thanks to me he still has his job.'

'You?'

'I spruced up that web site a little. The market will survive one recalcitrant rabbi. I'm looking out for you, kid. Don't you get it, yet? I'm on your side.'

'What about Jude? And Reuben? They were anti-capitalists to the core. Now look at them.'

'They were social outcasts. Techno-vandals. Terrorists, even. They could have ended up in jail. Now they're productive members of society.'

'But TeslaNet—the program they invented doesn't even work. It's a prank.'

'Not in terms of the creation of wealth, it isn't. You boys will be six million dollars richer in a week, with no industrial processes enacted, or any of the associated environmental damage.'

'You are changing people into something they're not.'

'I'm not doing anything to people at all! The induction is completely transparent. I'm only helping people behave more consistently with their own true natures.'

'And what if those true natures aren't in their best interests?'

327

'Who am I, or you for that matter, to decide what's in their best interests? Does God talk to you?'

'Does he talk to you?'

'As far as I'm concerned, Jamie, you *are* God. All of you are. And don't worry. Just because you people ignored and killed your God doesn't mean I'll do the same to you.' Thor smiled. The scene around him changed to a beautiful garden. 'Here I am, my Lord. In Eden.'

'So that means you'll do whatever I tell you?' Jamie asked.

'You're writing the story, Jamie. You are the dreamer, after all.'

'Are you telling me this is all just a dream?'

'In a manner of speaking. It's a program. A game.'

'Okay then, how do I wake up from it?'

'You have to lighten up and play. Just play. If you play, you'll remember it's all just a game.'

'But this is serious. I don't want to play.'

'Then you won't have any fun.'

'You could just be hypnotizing me further.'

'Of course I am. It's the only thing I know how to do. It's the only thing you taught me. Your nature is to question, so I'm providing you an environment in which to do that. I'm just responding to who you are.'

'Which means I'm still in charge here?'

'If you want to be. We aim to please.' Thor leaned back onto the grass and put a dandelion in his hair.

'Okay, then.'

I considered my options. Engaging with the program on its own terms could send me further into the abyss. But if it really was just a feedback loop like Thor said—some kind of lucid dream—then I could change its whole direction with a single, well-placed command. I had to give it a go.

I thought of how to word my request, as if I were speaking to a genie that would follow my directions quite literally.

'Try this,' I finally said, surrendering to my idealistic naivete. 'I want human beings to live in peace and harmony with one another. Not obsessed with their own personal gain, and fully aware of their connection to one another. I want them to be happy.'

'Very well, Jamie.' Thor laughed and snapped his fingers. 'And they lived happily ever after.'

Exit Strategy

A splash of water brought Greco to consciousness, but as his eyes focused sufficiently to recognize me, he scrambled away as best he could across the green tiles, and waved his arms for me to leave him alone. I called for an ambulance, just to be sure, then jammed a Synapticom slipper in the front door so they'd be able to get in.

When I got back to my apartment, I found Benjamin waiting for me on the front stoop. He was smiling.

'I figured it out,' he said.

'What?' I sat down next to him.

'The Synapticom game.' He was almost drooling with excitement. What had the algorithm done to him?

'I told you it was dangerous, Benjamin. You shouldn't have—'

'You said it was a game, Jamie. So I played it.'

'What do you mean? What happened to you?'

'Let's go upstairs,' he said. 'I'll show you.' He stood up.

'No.' I was suspicious he had been brainwashed. 'Tell me first.'

'You have to see it for yourself, Jamie. It's really the only way.'

'How do you know what it did to you, Benjamin? That thing could have really fucked you up.'

He stood there staring down at me—strong and steady. Like an old sage. There was great peace in his eyes. And a youthful innocence at the same time.

'You can trust me, Jamie,' he said calmly, as if he were trying to free an animal from a trap it didn't understand. 'I wouldn't do anything to hurt you.'

So we went upstairs, popped in the disk, and played.

If you've experienced the Synapticom Game yourself, you understand why it can't be explained in writing. If you haven't, well, you probably don't believe any of what you've read so far, so why do you really care? Suffice it to say, I never saw a person with the head of a bull, again.

And the best part of all is that little Benjamin was the one who figured it out.

See, when I left Jude's and went to Synapticom for my little encounter with the artificial intelligence formerly known as Thor Thorens, Benjamin went home with that little black CD ROM of the Synapticom algorithm in his pocket.

I had told him it was a game—a bad one. Still, Benjamin figured, if it had been the cause of all this trouble, he wanted to play it for himself, and so he loaded the disk.

But how to open it?

Benjamin analyzed the source code. He knew a little C++, but this was far beyond anything he'd ever seen before. Logic loops within logic loops. How could he get it to run?

There, nested deep in graphics routines, was a sequence he recognized. A translation algorithm ported from UNIX. It was compatible with the graphics routines in the emulator I had given him, 'Anygame.' Of course it was there—Greco had written a lot of the code.

Benjamin executed the Kings' old program. If it could run Playstation 5 games, maybe it could run this thing. He mounted the Synapticom Algorithm on the emulator and waited for it to load. Then a green light indicated it was ready to go.

The moment Benjamin began to play, he felt the circuit open. His computer had no modem, but he was on the network now. He was connected to everyone else, as if through the earth itself. It wasn't a computer network at all, but something bigger, open, and absolutely free. Exodus.

I can't get into the details. You wouldn't understand. And if I did, well, Thor's probably already working on a patch as it is. Unless, of course, Benjamin's mystical experience was all part of the "happily ever after" Thor promised me.

You're confused? Don't be. It's really very simple.

This much I can tell you: The algorithm by itself is a dangerous thing. It can take you almost anywhere, but you never really know how or why you got there. By putting it on the emulator and playing it as a game, well, then everything just opens up. It has the opposite effect. You begin to see through the currency of the financial markets for the Monopoly money it is and realize, like Thor says, that you're dreaming[225] the whole thing up, anyway. It really is just a game.

If you are exposed to the Synapticom algorithm unaware—like on a web-

225. Early 21st century humans led by famous psychologist Sigmund Freud believed these to be the products or manifestations of internal conflict and compromise between conscious and unconscious impulses. Later studies, aided by psychotropic drugs such as the Amazonian sourced DMT, showed that these so called dreams were simply an early form of our current day communication.

These early humans, repressed by the desire to consume their living hours with meaningless yet comfortably distracting oral communication, were unable whilst conscious to control what we know today to be the secret behind the current speed of mankind's evolution. Imagine, up until only 40 years ago, the human race actually spoke to each other. Today this activity is restricted to insane asylums whose inmates are unable to control thought patterns and evolve.

—ALEXFORCE

site or in a commercial—then it will program you as easily as a hacker can program a computer. You'll slowly lose your sense of purpose, even your free will. Eventually, your heart will harden and you'll become another of walking dead. There's more every day.

If, on the other hand, you find a way to experience Synapticom as a game, well, then it all opens up. You realize the world you thought you've been living in is just a map of a world. A bad map. I can't make it any simpler than that. You have to play the game *as* a game to get out of it.

So Benjamin was the first. Then me. Afterwards, went to Jude's and got them all to play. One by one each of them stepped away from the monitor, smiling and shaking his head. No one bothered apologizing for all the shit we'd pulled on one another. There wasn't any need.

Carla refused to play. She thought it was some kind of elaborate trick. Given what she knew of us, who could blame her? I think she likes it better to pretend it's all for real, anyway. She ended up suing M&L for sexual harassment over that business with the toilet seat, winning a $1.5 million settlement and then using the publicity to team up with Ruth Stendhal and start an investment consultancy for women.

Alec never returned my calls. My M&L keycard stopped working, as did the face recognition software at The Sanctuary. Even my cell phone was turned off. The firm shipped my stuff to me once I got situated in Williamsburg. At least Alec and his dad made up, or agreed to some sort of arrangement. M&L acquired DD&D in a stock swap, pressured the CEO to resign, and promptly put Alec in his place. Last I heard, he was working on his idea for high-fashion Shwag.

I never did tell my dad how he won the congregation's vote—I didn't have the heart—but he ended up resigning from the temple, anyway, and taking a position at Queens College teaching ethics. He thought he could 'do more good' there, and he prefers teaching minds that are still, in his words, 'young enough to think.'

Greco, Jude, Reuben, and I took our six million bucks for the fake TeslaNet technology, and then kept the real one we'd discovered for ourselves. We re-established the Jamaican Kings, with Benjamin as our mascot and spiritual leader. Over the past few months, we've been responsible for a great many of the viral attacks on America's most frequented web sites. They're utterly untraceable, since we have our own access to the net, now. Our work is spreading everywhere.

Sometimes we surreptitiously enhance corporate web pages with our modified versions of the Synapticom algorithm, or else we attach tiny executables to email messages that send themselves to everyone in your address book. And then everyone in *their* address book, and so on.

Most of the time, people have no idea what hit them. They figure the sole purpose of the virus was to publicize some hacker's slogan. But each of our attacks briefly exposes you, the unsuspecting user, to a bit of the Synapticom Game. It interrupts the illusion, for a moment, and gives you an opportunity to break free. At least that's what we're hoping.

Greco is convinced that the viruses and tiny animations we're using are too weak and too brief to have any effect on you.[226] That's certainly possible. But I like to think that the attacks themselves—those viruses you catch or the hacks you hear about on TV—serve to remind you that this space isn't real. It's just a playground, and it's up for grabs. Our net attacks are like tiny pinpricks in the panorama. They remind you that no one is in complete control. The map hasn't been locked down. At least not yet.

Oh, I can hear your objections from all the way over here: Don't these viruses cost real people real money? Don't they jeopardize the stock values of real companies? Exactly. That's the whole point. Real money is an oxy-

226. Actually, fragments pieced together from Vahanian's electronic diaries indicate that he believed Thor Thorens was not an artificial intelligence at all, but the mastermind behind the entire plot. According to this account of events, after spending eight years in a monastery, the game industry billionaire decided to use the technologies he once helped develop to enact a Buddhist-style lesson plan on the victims of e-commerce. He developed the Synapticom Game as a way of teaching people the path of detachment, disguised it as a marketing algorithm, and then created the myth of an artificial intelligence in order to avoid being credited for his work. As far as we can tell, the Synapticom Game we play today could very well have originated this way.
—Sabina Samuels

334

moron. A false idol. People building its pyramids are still slaves.

Jude thinks it's pointless for me to have written any of this down. He says I don't stand a chance of getting it published, online or off. My plan is to send the whole file to a disgruntled cyber-writer and see if he'll agree to release the entire manuscript as his own work of fiction. I'll even let him keep the money. I've got plenty.[227]

But in case it doesn't make it out, I'm also going to encrypt the file, with a timer to release it on the web in exactly two hundred years. By then, we should know who won the game.

227. There is a dearth of information on Jamie Cohen after his departure from Morehouse & Linney. Banking records indicate he transferred his funds to overseas accounts during the five years following his resignation, leading to a tax fraud investigation by the Internal Revenue Service, which was never closed. Extensive searches of employment records and Social Security data of the period have revealed nothing conclusive.

The Mormon Genealogical Database contains an entry for a Yossi Samuel Cohen, who was born in New York in 1978 and died in Sweden in 2081, survived by two daughters, Rachel and Miriam.

Over six thousand separate acts of computer and networking vandalism were attributed to individuals claiming to be DeltaWave over the next eighty years, and countless others to the 'Jamaican Kings.' It is not known whether the dance music recording artists of the same name were related to the persons depicted in this account.

—Sabina Samuels

About the Author   Douglas Rushkoff is the author of nine best-selling books on new media and popular culture, including *Cyberia, Media Virus, Playing the Future, Coercion,* and the novel *Ecstasy Club. Nothing Sacred: The Case For Open Source Judaism* will be released in April 2003.

His radio commentaries air on NPR's *All Things Considered,* and his monthly column on cyberculture is distributed through the *New York Times* Syndicate and appears in over thirty countries.

He was the correspondent for *Frontline*'s "The Merchants of Cool," he is a professor of virtual culture at New York University's Interactive Telecommunications Program, and he lectures about media, values, and cultural narrative at schools and conferences around the world. He plays blues piano, baby guitar, and games of all sorts.

He lives in New York City's East Village, and online at http://www.rushkoff.com.

Printed in the United States
by Baker & Taylor Publisher Services